Duets

**Two brand-new stories in every volume...
twice a month!**

Duets Vol. #101

Popular Darlene Gardner serves up not one,
but *two* quirky stories this month in a very special
Double Duets volume. Join the fun as she focuses
on past loves—the One Who Got Away and the
One Who Never Left. Would *you* ever look for these
people? Darlene always spins "a delightful tale with
an engaging set-up and lovable characters," says
Romantic Times magazine.

Duets Vol. #102

Boxers or briefs? That's what every woman
wants to know about the sexy hunk in her life.
Talented Delores Fossen tells us the answer and
more in the hilarious *Truly, Madly, Briefly.* Joining
Delores this month is newcomer Katie Gallagher,
who hails from North Carolina, but has set her very
first story in *Tried and True*, Kansas. Enjoy this tale of
a runaway fiancée and the sexy sheriff who
nearly arrests her on the way!

Be sure to pick up both Duets volumes today!

"The Full Monty," Bobbie declared.

She tapped the toe of her meringue-colored heel on the tile floor. "Catalog number 233A. See-through-front bikini brief for the man with nothing to hide. Contour-hugging, barely-there backside for a rakish and yet daring display of your manly assets. Available in Exposed Ebony and In-the-Buff Buff."

Jasper gasped. "But you said no man could ever look good in The Full Monty."

She gave her hand an indignant little wave. "I said that before I met Aidan."

Touché. One for the lady in pink. Flattered, taken aback and slightly confused, Aidan went and held the door open for Jasper to leave.

"This isn't over, Bobbie," Jasper insisted. "We'll talk about it when I pick you up on Sunday afternoon for the picnic and watermelon thump."

"Bobbie's going to the picnic with me," Aidan stated.

"I am?" she questioned.

"You are." He nodded. After all, he'd already agreed to go. So what if it meant he had to play the Twango-Drifter game a little longer? He'd, *ahem,* suffer through it, especially since his cohort was none other than one Bobbie Fay Callahan!

For more, turn to page 9

"I have a proposition."

Clementine just stared at him.

"Stay," Callum said. "In two weeks, leave as planned. And in the meantime…we pretend to date." He walked toward her and stopped so he stood very close to her.

"Don't get me wrong, this is a selfish proposition. When you leave, everyone will blame me. They've been on my back for a while to settle down and, frankly, it's getting on my nerves, even though they mean well. Hopefully, after you leave, they'll concentrate on other poor bachelors in town."

"Pretend to date you."

"What are you afraid of?" He smiled. "Are you attracted to me? Is that it?"

She rolled her eyes. "Arrogance is such a turn-on." Pressed against him, she had to admit, she'd never felt as sexual as she did right now. Clementine had thought she was bad at sex because of one bad encounter in college and because Reg was so platonic. Whatever Callum had must be rubbing off on her.

Rubbing off…

Now, there was an image she wanted to ponder.

For more, turn to page 197

HARLEQUIN DUETS

ISBN 0-373-44168-1

Copyright in the collection:
Copyright © 2003 by Harlequin Books S.A.

The publisher acknowledges the copyright holders
of the individual works as follows:

TRULY, MADLY, BRIEFLY
Copyright © 2003 by Delores Fossen

TRIED AND TRUE
Copyright © 2003 by Sarah Addison Allen

Truly, Madly, Briefly

Delores Fossen

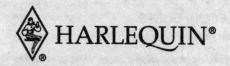

HARLEQUIN®

TORONTO • NEW YORK • LONDON
AMSTERDAM • PARIS • SYDNEY • HAMBURG
STOCKHOLM • ATHENS • TOKYO • MILAN • MADRID
PRAGUE • WARSAW • BUDAPEST • AUCKLAND

Dear Reader,

I love a fish-out-of-water story, and I think it's a great premise for not only comedy but a sizzling romance. For example, in *Truly, Madly, Briefly* I take Aidan O'Shea, a cute Boston cop who has sworn off women, and plop him in a small Texas town where the females significantly outnumber the males. Estrogen is heavy in the air, and it doesn't get any lighter when Aidan meets Bobbie Fay Callahan, the manager of Boxers or Briefs, a factory that makes risqué men's underwear. Bobbie's immediately attracted to Aidan, but after being jilted twice, she's decided she needs another man about as much as a longhorn needs panty hose.

So Aidan's sworn off women. Bobbie's sworn off men. That means they should have no trouble pulling off a pretend relationship meant to rid them of unwanted suitors—right? Well, this is romance, so there is a problem or two. Aidan fights the attraction between them. Bobbie fights it even harder. Neither win, but they certainly have fun losing and manage to steam up Texas along the way.

Let me know what you think of *Truly, Madly, Briefly*. You can e-mail me at fossent@earthlink.net. I'd love to hear from you.

Delores Fossen

Books by Delores Fossen

HARLEQUIN DUETS
94—THE DEPUTY GETS HER MAN

To SARA, the San Antonio Romance Authors—
sisters, goddesses, friends

1

The Twango: Catalog Item 231B. Comfort, style and illusion—all rolled into one bottom-shaping, stomach-minimizing brief. Available in Foxtrot Red, Cha Cha Gold and Midnight Mambo.

IF IT HADN'T BEEN for the missing case of size triple-X Magic Magenta thong underwear, Bobbie would have kept her distance from Deputy Aidan O'Shea.

Yes, indeed.

As it was, she had to put aside thoughts of lotteries, love and lust so she could report a possible crime. A really weird crime but a crime nonetheless.

She peered through the window to make sure the deputy was in his office. He was. And he was alone. He had his back to her, the phone squished between his shoulder and neck. It gave Bobbie an unrestricted view of the bottom-snuggling khakis that some had dubbed the item of clothing most eligible for removal. Not that anyone had personal knowledge of such removal, but it'd given the town fuel for fantasies.

When the bell on the door jangled, Deputy O'Shea glanced over his shoulder, and Bobbie eased inside the office. She motioned for him to continue with his conversation.

"Yes, I have that," he assured the person on the other end of the line.

Ah, the Boston accent. It was pure music to her ears, which were accustomed to Texas drawls. It made her thankful that Boston had actually agreed to the six-week law-enforcement exchange program. Liffey, Texas, however, had gotten the better part of the deal since Bobbie's cousin, Wes, was already on his way to his exchange station. That put Aidan, eye candy extraordinaire, right in front of her.

"But you'll actually have to come to the office to press charges, Miss Determyer," Aidan went on. He paused. "No, you'll have to come here to do that. With Sheriff Cooper still out with the flu, I can't leave the office unless there's a crime in progress." Another pause. "No. A funny feeling in the pit of your stomach doesn't constitute a crime."

Bobbie sank down in the chair in front of his desk and just listened. She couldn't stop the little trickle of heat that made its way through her. It was stupid, really stupid, but just hearing his voice made her go all warm and gooey. Too bad warm and gooey were the very things she had to avoid— hot fudge sundaes excluded. Deputy Aidan O'Shea was a temporary fixture in town, and she didn't want to mess with anything temporary.

"How can I help you?" he asked.

Pulling herself out of her daydreams, she got to her feet. "You probably don't remember me—"

"You're Bobbie Callahan, manager of Boxers or Briefs, the men's underwear factory at 225 Everton Road. You've had four parking tickets in the past six months. One citation for jaywalking. Yesterday, you were a no-show for your dental appointment. And you have an overdue library book titled *The Joys of Swamp Tours through the Everglades.*"

So he did know a few things about her after all. Rather embarrassing things. Sheez. What a town of tattletales.

It probably wouldn't do any good to mention that her cousin had issued each and every one of those parking and walking citations and that he'd done it just to aggravate her.

"I paid the tickets," she explained. "And I'll reschedule the dental exam and take care of that library book first thing in the morning."

But apparently he wasn't finished. "You're also the winner of the Aidan-o-rama lottery."

Oh. That.

Bobbie should have realized that he'd catch wind of something as ridiculous as the ill-contrived lottery put together by a bunch of women with obviously too much time on their hands.

Heck, Aidan had probably known the winner within seconds after Henrietta Beekins plucked Bobbie's name from the hat. Or rather the gallon-size Crock-Pot that Henrietta's lottery committee had used to hold the 137 slivers of paper.

Aidan glanced down at the Hank's Feed and Bait desk calendar. "I didn't think the lottery thing was supposed to start until tomorrow morning."

"It isn't. I mean, I guess it is. I'm really not sure. Look, I didn't even enter that stupid lottery."

Mercy, it sounded like a bona fide fish story. But the truth was she *hadn't* entered the lottery that would have given her a whole week of sole pursuing rights for the hottest guy in town—Aidan O'Shea.

Nope.

Bobbie hadn't even considered entering it. After tangling twice with Jasper Kershaw, she needed another man about as much as a longhorn needed ultra-sheer panty hose.

"My uncles thought they were doing me a favor," Bobbie explained. "They were wrong, as they usually are when it comes to meddling in my personal life. I have no intentions of pursuing you tomorrow or any other day. Not that you're not worthy of pursuit. But I'm just not in the market for a man. *Any* man. I'm sort of taking a hiatus from romance and, um, all that other stuff.''

From the deputy's crisp nod, it seemed he was pleased with her babbling. ''Is this because of the travel agent who jilted you twice?''

She hadn't dared to hope that he hadn't heard about Jasper's jiltings either. Despite Aidan's arrival merely a week earlier, he'd probably heard the fiasco discussed in complete fiasco detail. Jasper and she were still one of the town's hottest topics. ''Let's just say it's jaded my outlook about any and all future relationships.''

Jaded, jinxed and junked them.

Again, he nodded in approval. ''Your uncles,'' he commented. ''I met them.''

From the way he pulled his rather well-shaped mouth together, it hadn't been a pleasant meeting either. Since Bobbie didn't want to speculate about what such an encounter would entail, she settled for an inquisitive sounding ''Oh?''

''They were in here this morning.'' Aidan unwrapped a small candy-striped mint and popped it into his mouth. ''They tried to talk me into modeling for the Boxers or Briefs Internet catalog.'' He paused. ''I declined their *generous* offer.''

"Oh."

Well, that was to be expected. Still, she couldn't fault her uncles for trying. Aidan O'Shea appeared to have a first-class rump, and there was a shortage of those around Liffey. Actually, there was a shortage of fully functioning males under the age of fifty. With those cool sea-green eyes, rich chocolate-colored hair and lanky six-foot-tall build, Aidan more than qualified as both male and functioning. He was the stuff that dreams were made of.

Or in her case, nightmares.

For some reason he kept reminding her that she was indeed a functioning female. Not good. Not good at all. Her hormones, and other female parts, would just have to find some other way to amuse themselves.

"How's Sheriff Cooper?" she asked, hoping to get her mind off *functioning* things.

"As sick as a small hospital."

"Oh. That sounds pretty sick."

Aidan nodded. "Let me guess. You're here to file a complaint about—" He held up one finger. "A Beeping Tom. And you want me to come immediately to your house so I can check it out."

"Uh, don't you mean *Peeping?*"

"No. I mean someone who drives slowly past your house and beeps his horn in a suggestive manner."

Bobbie frowned. "No. I'm not here to report anything like that. Call me naive but I didn't even know a horn could sound suggestive. Guess I've lead a sheltered life, huh?"

He didn't seem amused by her comment. A second finger went up. "You've had a possible UFO sighting, and you want me to stand guard inside your house tonight."

She shook her head.

He lifted a third finger. "Your cat's stuck in a very big tree, and you want me to go to your house to see if I can coax it into coming down."

Bobbie wrinkled up her nose. "You get a lot of complaints like that?"

"Loads."

Sheez. And she thought she'd had a rough day, what with the vanishing underwear. "No, actually I'm here because a case of merchandise is missing from the warehouse."

Aidan blinked, probably stunned at the possibility of a real crime. "And you want to report it?"

That didn't seem to be a trick question. "Sure."

None of the skepticism left his eyes. "What kind of merchandise?"

"Thong briefs." She felt the blush make its way from her cheeks to her daffodil-gold toenail polish. After five years of managing Boxers or Briefs, she probably should have been more accustomed to discussing risqué Magic Magenta underwear with a man, but Bobbie had never quite gotten the hang of it.

His eyebrow rose.

It didn't help because she figured that minor facial adjustment was a request for more information. When his other eyebrow slid up, Bobbie knew she was right.

She nodded. Shrugged. And shuffled her feet. "The design is called the, uh, Gigolo. It has a loose silk front with a nearly invisible, um, understring thingamajig."

She had to give it to Aidan. Other than those raised eyebrows, he didn't have a reaction. No smirking. No cough to cover up a snicker. He just sat there with his shoulders squared and a cop's demeanor plastered all over his incredibly cute face.

"Any other identifying details regarding this merchandise?" he asked.

Bobbie gave him the stock number. What she wouldn't mention was that the sales pitch for the Gigolo was *a garment to insure easy access to your family jewels*. Nope. She'd keep that little gem of advertising wisdom to herself.

"The case contains three dozen," she added. "All in magenta. And, uh, all in size triple-X."

Still no smirk. As if it were the most mundane crime of his entire career, Aidan extracted a form from the letter tray on his temporary desk, and grabbed a pen. He'd hardly gotten past the first line when the door flew open. The knob and the bell smacked against the wall, and the sudden rush of wind sent papers scattering.

"You have to come right away!" Maxine Varadore announced. She wriggled herself between Bobbie and Aidan but not before giving Bobbie a what-the-devil-are-you-doing-here? glare.

Bobbie glared back, but then she'd had a lot of practice glaring at Maxine, especially since she'd recently fired the woman from her seamstress job at the factory. Maxine had an uncanny knack for squeezing her size-fourteen butt into a pair of size-six jeans, but she'd been an absolute disaster at decorative stitching and boxer fly assembly.

"He's busy doing a report," Bobbie informed her.

Maxine flicked her off with an icy glance and a piqued lift of her makeup-slathered nose. "You're not my boss anymore, so I don't have to listen to you." When she turned her attention back to Aidan, she tossed in a whimper and batted her mascara-gummed eyelashes for good measure. "My poor little kitty, Sue-Sue, is stuck in that big hackberry tree in my backyard. You need to get her to come down. I'll warn you though, it might take a while."

Aidan gathered up the scattered papers and

dumped them onto the center of the desk. His gaze eased to Maxine. Then to Bobbie. There was a you-didn't-believe-me-huh? look in his eyes. Bobbie conceded his point with a shrug. So, this is what he had to deal with on an hourly, perhaps minute-to-minute basis. She actually felt sorry for him.

"Miss Varadore," Aidan said at the end of a sigh. He picked up his pen and got back to work on the report. "I don't do kitty rescues. And at the moment, I'm attending to Miss Callahan's situation."

Maxine huffed. It was enough to extinguish candles on a birthday cake at the senior citizens' home. "You might have won the lottery, Bobbie Fay Callahan, but you weren't supposed to start hanging around him until tomorrow morning. That was the deal."

"I didn't agree to the *deal*," Bobbie let her know. She tipped her head toward Aidan. "And neither did he. I'm here on official business."

"Yeah, like I believe that. You don't even own a cat."

Aidan stood and dropped the pen onto the desk. "But she does have a situation that requires my official attention. So, if you'll please excuse us…"

Bobbie would have seconded that, but her pager went off. While Aidan continued his explanation, and while Maxine continued to plead her case for a full-scale kitty rescue, Bobbie rifled through her purse, pushing aside the fist-full of travel brochures, to locate the vibrating flamingo-colored device. One look at the tiny screen, however, and she pressed the green button to stop the noise. She snapped her purse shut again.

"Jasper," she mumbled under her breath. But she obviously didn't mumble it softly enough because both Aidan and Maxine looked at her.

"Jasper Kershaw's back in town?" Maxine asked, her voice filled with hope.

Bobbie nodded. "He got back a couple of hours ago."

To be specific, it was two hours and fourteen minutes. Six people, excluding Jasper himself, had already phoned to tell her about the jilting fiancé's return. Bobbie vowed to quit answering her phone. Too bad she couldn't turn off her pager, but she was hoping for a call from the warehouse to say they had managed to locate the case of missing thongs.

"And you're getting back together with Jasper?" Even more hope abounded in Maxine's voice.

"No!" Bobbie answered so fast that she risked having her teeth fly out of her mouth. And her assertion was one-hundred-percent true. Too bad Jasper hadn't quite figured that out yet. In the past two hours and fourteen minutes, he'd called or paged her seven times.

Maxine tsk-tsked. "You'll get back with him. You always do. Of course, that'll cancel out the lottery so we'll just have to have another one to figure out who gets first dibs on Aidan. But this time you can bet your britches that I'll be the one drawing that name from the Crock-Pot."

"This is just a guess, but I don't think the deputy wants a lottery," Bobbie pointed out.

Bobbie's pager went off again. She glanced into her purse and saw Jasper's number highlighted on the screen. She smashed the button to stop it and shut her purse in a hurry.

Darn it.

The man was obviously aiming for a round three, which wouldn't happen. After being left at the altar not once but twice, she'd learned her lesson regarding Jasper Kershaw.

"The report?" Aidan reminded Bobbie. It was no doubt also a reminder for Maxine to vamoose because he ignored her and got to work. He studied the form a moment. "Estimated value of the missing merchandise."

"Four hundred and thirty-two dollars," Bobbie gladly answered.

Maxine leaned over the desk, examined the form and rolled her eyes. "Gimme a break. You're saying someone stole a case of triple-X

Gigolos? Yeah, right. Nobody, but nobody in this town wears a size triple-X.''

Apparently realizing that she'd just given away a rather intimate detail of her not-so-private love life, Maxine hiked up her chin again. ''I'll be back,'' she warned, casting another glare in Bobbie's direction.

Bobbie would have breathed a lot easier if her pager hadn't gone off again. She didn't even look. It was Jasper. It had to be. No one else could possibly be that annoying.

''Would you care to use the phone?'' Aidan inquired.

''No, thanks. I have a phone in my purse.'' Bobbie reset her pager again and sank back down in the chair across from him.

He gave her a considering glance. ''Does this mean Jasper Kershaw will be coming in here to file a missing person's report because he can't get in touch with you?''

She shook her head. No missing person's report. But it did likely mean that Jasper would pester the heck out of her. Why couldn't he have just stayed on the run, and away from a telephone? The man certainly knew how to use speed dial.

Aidan turned the form around so that it was facing her. ''Check to make sure I have all the facts right and then sign at the bottom—''

The phone rang, and he snatched it up while he handed her a pen.

"A Peeping Tom who drove slowly past your house and beeped his horn, you say?" Aidan asked the caller a moment later. "And you'd like me to come to your house to check out things?"

Bobbie would have tried to convey some sympathy if her pager hadn't gone off again. This time she did look. And it was Jasper.

"Great day in the blooming morning!" she grumbled. This was past pestering and into a whole new realm of aggravation. She took the pager from her purse, stabbed the off button and tossed it in the trash can next to the desk.

"You believe I'll have to spend the night at your house in order to catch this beeping Peeping Tom?" Aidan continued, obviously repeating what the caller had suggested. He squeezed his eyes shut and grimaced.

Bobbie did the same when her pager went off again. She'd obviously not turned it off after all. The metal trash can rattled and echoed the series of annoying, pulsing beeps. It was the proverbial back-breaking straw, and she didn't have to be a camel for it to be majorly effective. She ripped her phone from her purse and punched in the numbers. Jasper answered on the first ring, but the only thing he managed to get out was the hel-part of hello.

"Don't call or page me again," Bobbie warned. "As far as I'm concerned, Jasper Kershaw, you're no better than highly contagious foot fungus, and I'll do whatever's necessary to avoid you."

Obviously engulfed in his own battle of wills, she heard Aidan continue with his call. "No, I'm afraid I can't come out, Miss Martindale, since this person only beeped and didn't come onto the premises. My advice is not to undress while standing in front of an open window."

"Bobbie," Jasper crooned as if she hadn't just issued a really disgusting insult. "It's good to hear your voice. We need to talk. Where are you? I'll be right over."

"No, you won't," Bobbie said at the very moment that Aidan concluded, "No, I can't."

Their gazes met. In the swirl of all those shades of tropical green, Bobbie saw the same frustration, the same aggravation, the same why-the-heck-me? look that she was sure she had in her baby-browns. Without taking her gaze from his, Bobbie clicked off the phone. Without taking his gaze from hers, Aidan placed his phone back onto the desk.

"Are you thinking what I'm thinking?" she asked.

He squinted one eye. "I don't know. Why don't you tell me what you're thinking?"

It seemed a reasonable request, but it could lead to a thoroughly embarrassing moment if they weren't on the same frequency here. After all, Bobbie had been thinking something totally ridiculous.

But perhaps necessary.

"You first," she insisted.

Their phones rang again. Her pager rattled and beeped from the trash can. They didn't answer any of the annoying communication devices. Bobbie and Aidan just stood there with their gazes locked.

"Look, we hardly know each other. Heck, we're practically strangers, but maybe we can help each other out," Bobbie suggested.

"Maybe."

It wasn't the most enthusiastic response she'd ever received, but it was a start. A start that just might buy them both some time to regain their sanity.

"I'm not looking for anything remotely romantic," Bobbie added. Since the rattling and beeping were driving her to the brink of madness, she reached into the trash can, calmly removed the pager and smacked it with her foot. It took three good stomps before it shattered into a dozen flamingo-pink chunks. "I've had enough romance to last me a couple of lifetimes. And this is more than just a guess, but it appears you'd like to avoid any more kitty rescues and Beeping Tom reports."

He nodded. "Go on."

Bobbie took a deep breath, hoping a good analogy would come to mind.

It didn't.

Unfortunately, a bad one popped right into her head and found its way straight to her suddenly chatty mouth. "It's sort of like the Twango, one of Boxers or Briefs' best-selling products."

From the look on his face, she'd dumbfounded him. "The Twango?"

The bad analogy just kept coming. "It's a satin-lined, control-top foundation garment for men."

He just stared at her.

Bobbie probably should have shut up, but the non-stop ringing of phones gave her enough courage, and perhaps the insanity, to continue.

"The Twango," she explained, the slogan slipping right off her tongue. "Comfort, style and illusion—all rolled into one bottom-shaping, stomach-minimizing brief."

All right. So, that wasn't her best attempt at explaining things.

But then, sadly, it wasn't her worst either.

Rather than keep digging a hole that was getting awfully deep, Bobbie took a step back and waited to see if Aidan O'Shea was desperate enough to snap up her offer.

2

The Drifter: Catalog Item 421. A machine-washable cotton-spandex brief for the man on the move who wants to keep things in place. Available in Stop Sign Red, Alert Amber and Go-get-'em Green. Comes with complimentary Boxers or Briefs travel toothbrush.

"THE TWANGO," Aidan said under his breath.

Heaven help him.

So that he wouldn't have the urge to demolish his phone the way Bobbie had her pager, he turned off the ringer. Besides, he needed a moment of quiet so he could think straight. He was almost positive this was one of those situations where he needed a clear head.

"Comfort, looks and illusion," she repeated as if that would help.

Well, it wasn't exactly what he'd hoped Bobbie Fay Callahan would offer. Aidan had thought maybe she could put an end to this lottery business by canceling it. He'd further hoped that she would tell the ladies of Liffey to stop calling him about everything from faucet drips to flat tires. He just couldn't understand why the female population had taken such an interest in him.

Or why they had such a distorted view of the duties of a law-enforcement officer.

However, at this point, he was open to suggestions—any suggestions—that would make his life easier and quieter. He hadn't had more than fifteen minutes of peace since he'd arrived a week earlier in what was supposed to be a sleepy little town where peace and quiet were plentiful.

"It's not often a man finds himself compared to an item of underwear," he commented.

A lobster-red blush covered her cheeks. It matched the color of her skirt and silky top. "You think I'm a candidate for the loony bin, don't you?"

Absolutely. Her, her uncles and, seemingly, three-quarters of the town.

While Aidan was trying to figure out how to put that observation into kinder, gentler terms, Bobbie just kept right on talking. "Okay. So using the Twango probably wasn't the best comparison, but stay with me here, and I think I can explain this better."

Good. She had a hundred-percent chance of doing that, because so far she hadn't made an eye-lash of sense.

Bobbie turned off her phone before she continued. "I want the illusion that my love life is good. *Very* good. That way, it won't give anyone, including my uncles and Jasper Kershaw, the right to feel they can monkey with it. And maybe, just maybe, the same could happen for you."

Aidan certainly hoped this sounded better when he said it aloud, but he wasn't counting on it. "What exactly would we have to do to stop people from…monkeying with us?"

She shrugged as if the answer were obvious. "We'd have to pretend to go through with the lottery, of course. We'd do the Twango, so to speak. And remember, the Twango is a garment of illusion. I've seen before and after pictures. Trust me, it flattens even the worst beer guts, and I mean the worst. It's even better than the Drifter, and the Drifter's twice the price."

"The Twango and the Drifter," he managed. Heaven knows why he repeated the names of the comparative items, but Aidan had no idea what else to say.

Bobbie stuck out her hands like balancing scales. "The Drifter is for men who don't want a lot of wiggling around when they're on the go. Like you. You don't want people pulling and tugging at you." She slightly lifted her right hand.

"Now, couple that with the Twango, and you'll see what I'm getting at here."

Part of him—the part controlled by logic and sound reason—wanted to issue Bobbie a polite good-bye and send her on her delusional way. But he heard a little voice in his head. That little voice, along with the vivid memories of what the past seven days had entailed, made him want to learn more about what she was proposing.

And it had nothing, absolutely nothing, to do with the fact that she was reasonably attractive.

No way.

He absolutely, emphatically, would not allow himself to be set up in a relationship, and that lottery business smacked of a set-up in its purest form. If he hadn't known better, he'd have thought it originated with members of his own family.

Still, Aidan clung to the notion of peace and quiet. His notion of paradise had been lowered significantly. He'd settle for simply getting through a shower or a meal without the phone ringing.

"What would I have to do for this Twango-Drifter Plan?" he asked.

She hesitated. Tipped her amber-brown eyes to the ceiling. Fidgeted. And started to nibble on her glossy bottom lip. So, this had likely been an impromptu idea on her part, or else he'd have to do something so thoroughly ridiculous that she could hardly get out the words.

"Well..." And Bobbie hesitated again. She twirled a strand of her shoulder-length, ginger-colored hair around her finger. "To make it believable, I suppose we'd have to spend time together."

"I don't have a lot of time as it is."

He wasn't counting on that to change much either after the sheriff returned to work. Of all the calls Aidan received since Sheriff Cooper had gotten sick, not one of them had actually been for the sheriff. And no calls had come in to the night deputy, Sam Teton. That likely had something to do with the fact that Sam was seventy-one, had only three strands of hair and could, and did, spit watermelon seeds through the gap in his front teeth.

Her eyebrows flexed. "Hey, I got it. Maybe you could just come to my house after work and watch TV for a couple of hours. Actually, you wouldn't have to do much of anything other than let people think something's going on between us. I could even turn off the phone if you'd like."

It sounded like, well, paradise. Or maybe it sounded like something too good to be true.

"What about your uncles? They live with you." And that would likely mean he'd have to spend time with them as well. If his first impression of them was correct, having them around wouldn't give him much of a reprieve from the lunacy. Instead, it would put him shoulder-deep in it.

"It's a big house with two wings and separate entrances. I live on one side, and they live on the other. You wouldn't necessarily run into them."

Aidan looked for flaws in her proposal and soon found one the size of the Himalayas. After all, Bobbie was the winner of the lottery. A lottery he'd sworn to ignore. Maybe this was just her way of making sure as the winner that she got her shot at him after all.

He shook his head. "As good as the offer sounds, I'd better pass. Thanks anyway."

"Oh."

But it wasn't a plain, ordinary *oh.* Nor was it a question to ask why he'd come to that decision. It was a hurt, embarrassed *oh.*

Heck.

One look into her eyes and he confirmed that. He'd lived with his six sisters, a mother and a grandmother long enough to know when he'd stepped in something he should have stepped around.

"It's not that," Aidan assured her.

But it was hard to put into words exactly what *that* was. He couldn't very well tell her that he was tired of women, could he? No. That'd make him sound like a wuss.

Which he wasn't.

He just wanted a little vacation from the fairer sex and the constant matchmaking of seemingly every woman in the entire city of Boston. Just because he was thirty-three, why did everyone think he was ready to settle down?

He. Wasn't.

And he wouldn't let others dictate that for him. Monkeying indeed. If anyone monkeyed with anything, he'd do it himself, and he damn sure wouldn't use the word *monkeying* when he did it.

"This arrangement wouldn't be, uh, right," Aidan continued. He could almost taste his own foot in his mouth, and it wasn't very appetizing. "I mean, I like my privacy."

"I see. Of course. I hadn't thought of it that way." She moistened her lips in a nervous gesture that made him want to find a large rock and hit himself on the head. He hadn't intended to hurt her feelings.

"It's not you," he reiterated. He resisted the urge to reach out and touch her. For comfort naturally. It had nothing to do with her warm brown eyes and sensuous mouth. Nope. Absolutely nothing. Even if he had a thing for warm brown eyes just like hers.

And he really had a thing for sensuous mouths.

She nodded and tipped her head to the missing merchandise report. "You'll look into that, please?"

"Of course." He might even frame a copy of it when he was done. It was the first true job-related assignment he'd had since his arrival in Liffey.

"I just want to make sure I don't have an employee with sticky fingers," she added. "The floor manager, Rudy Tate, will answer any questions you might have. I've listed his number there at the bottom of the form."

And with that, she turned to leave. Aidan had a three-second debate with himself. *Stop her. Don't stop her. Tell her why her plan made me squirm. Don't tell her. Apologize for hurting her feelings. Don't apologize. Touch her. Don't touch her.*

Especially don't touch her!

He was still adding more issues to that mental debate when he saw Maxine Varadore making her way across Main Street. She was headed straight for the office, probably to press him again to come and rescue her kitty.

Among other things.

"Have a nice day, Deputy O'Shea," Bobbie said over her shoulder. "And don't worry about this lottery stuff. I have no intention of pursuing it." She would have made it out the door if Aidan hadn't stopped her.

"It isn't you," Aidan let her know—again. He swore under his breath and shoved his hands deep into the pockets of his khakis. "It's just—I have

these six older sisters, and they're always...
monkeying with my life."

Heaven's bells, why couldn't he stop using that
frickin' word?

He regrouped and tried again. "It's a knee-jerk
reaction for me to back off when someone sug-
gests anything to do with romance."

Slowly, Bobbie turned back around to face him.
"I understand. Believe me."

She probably did. After all, he'd met her uncles.
God knows what kind of torments they'd put her
through, all under the guise of insuring her lifelong happiness.

She eked out a smile. "It's all right, really."

The mental debate started again in earnest. And
Aidan was losing big-time. The losing went up a
considerable notch when Maxine stepped inside.

She glanced at Bobbie and huffed noisily. "Are
you still here?"

Maxine didn't wait for Bobbie to confirm the
blatantly obvious. She whipped her attention to
Aidan. "Can you pretty-please come and rescue
my poor little Sue-Sue now? She's been up in that
tree a long, long time. I'm sure she's getting awfully hungry."

Gone was the snippy tone that she'd used to
address Bobbie. In its place was a silky purr that
had scalding steam rising from it. It was enough

to make Aidan take a step back and inform her that he didn't wear size triple-X underwear either.

"I can't leave the office unless there's a crime in progress," Aidan insisted.

It was a line he'd found himself repeating often, and he was glad he could use it as an excuse right now. However, Sheriff Cooper was due back in a couple of days, and Aidan's excuse wouldn't be worth the sudsy scum left inside an empty beer mug.

What then?

There were four weeks, six days and a couple of hours left on this particular exchange tour. Four weeks, six days and a couple of hours that would no doubt make it seem as if he'd lived in monastic seclusion in Boston.

He hadn't.

But it seemed the women of Liffey could outdo even his own family when it came to forcing romance on a man, and his family had had thirty-three years of practice. Just how proficient would these Texas women be after another week or two of lottery-like shenanigans?

And when the heck had he started using words like *shenanigans?*

"My little bitty kitty?" Maxine coaxed. She crooked her finger. Smiled. And winked, revealing an eyelid caked with about a kilo of turquoise eye shadow. "Come on. I'll even make you a big tall glass of iced tea. Or something."

That wasn't all she was offering. No way. Aidan recognized that lustful gleam in her eye. A year or two ago, he'd have done his level best to fan that gleam into a scorching blaze. But not now. Like Bobbie, his fanning activities were on hiatus.

"Uh…" And that was all he managed to get out. He didn't want to hurt Maxine's feelings, but then he didn't think he could survive another kitty rescue.

Aidan looked at Maxine. Then at Bobbie. This was probably a case of the lesser of two evils. Still, if Bobbie could pull off a Twango-Drifter relationship, then she would have his undying gratitude.

"Well?" Maxine again. She gave her finger one more seductive crook.

"I need to rest up for tomorrow," Aidan heard himself say. "For the start of the lottery. I'll be spending every waking hour of the next week with Bobbie."

Maxine snapped her shoulders so straight that he heard joints crack. "You're actually going through with that stupid nonsense?"

Aidan nodded. He glanced at Bobbie again. Her mouth had dropped open, but beneath all that dumbfoundedness, he saw a glimmer in her eyes as well. Not lust. No. Not this. This was something more akin to hope.

"You bet," he answered.

"But, but, but—" It took Maxine a couple of seconds of sputtering to remember how to say more than just that one objection. She fluttered her fingers in Bobbie's direction. "But she already has a boyfriend."

"No, I don't," Bobbie insisted.

Maxine turned her still-hopeful and somewhat pathetic gaze to Aidan.

"She doesn't," he piped in, hoping it'd give Maxine motive to leave. "Besides, a deal is a deal. Bobbie won the lottery, and therefore she has my undivided personal attention for an entire week."

He thought he saw flames dance across Maxine's mud-brown eyes. "Then you're in for a very dull week. Ask Jasper Kershaw if you don't believe me. He's jilted her twice."

And with that totally irrelevant comment, she turned on her heels and headed out the door.

Aidan figured Bobbie would lose her composure over such a tacky confrontation. But she didn't. She didn't even spare Maxine a parting glance.

"Hope her little bitty kitty will come down from the hackberry before the week is up," Bobbie commented, a touch of humor in her voice. She checked her watch. "Oh, I gotta go. I'm meet-

ing a client over in Dalton City. Listen, why don't
you drop by my house after work so we can iron
out the details of our plan?''

Heaven help him. Now it was called *our plan*.
Just like the term *blind date,* it made him itch.

''I'll put out the word that you're officially off
limits to the women of Liffey,'' she assured him.
''It'll go faster if you do the same.''

Aidan managed a nod before Bobbie all but
sprinted out of the office. It took him a second
before he realized what he'd done.

Well, heaven's bells!

Hadn't this been exactly what he'd tried to
avoid? He'd actually been talked into monkeying
with his own life.

3

The Naughty Guy: Catalog Item 451A. A cheeky but classy traditional-cut faux silk brief in nontraditional colors. A subtle way to make a not-so-subtle impression. Available in Brazen Brass, Rowdy Raspberry and, for a limited time only, Scandalous Scarlet Stripes.

GREAT. Now, there were three dogs, two cats and an ornery raccoon following her. As if she hadn't already had an eventful day, now she had to put up with this.

While Bobbie turned down the narrow road that led to her house, she continued to fan herself with the latest copy of *Travel-or-Bust Monthly.* Maybe, just maybe, the icky scent of the massage oil would fade before Aidan came over to discuss the details of the Twango-Drifter Plan. A plan that had plagued, tormented and needled her the entire afternoon.

Geez Louise, what the devil had she been thinking when she suggested that *brilliant* idea?

It was one of the worst ideas she'd ever had. Well, not counting the time she'd let her best friend, Crystal, talk her into getting her navel pierced. But this was definitely the second worst.

"Yes, I'm sure," she repeated to Mr. Eidelson, the client she'd met with only an hour earlier. "I believe I made that clear before I left. I'm sorry, but Boxers or Briefs will not be marketing your Sensuous Musk Massage Oil."

She rolled her eyes when the man had the nerve to ask why. Bobbie gave her phone headset an adjustment so he'd clearly hear her every word. "Well, for one thing, your product stains like crazy. And I'm not just talking about the big splotch it left on my skirt either. My thighs, palms and kneecaps are purple as well. I stopped at the gas station and tried to scrub it off, but it seems to have embedded into my skin."

"I'm sorry about that," Mr. Eidelson said. "The bottle slipped right out of my hand."

Yes, and that slip had sent a pint of the industrial-strength massage oil right into her lap. In addition to the goop causing her an uncomfortable drive home, it now appeared the musky scent was attracting critters.

And speaking of critters, she saw Jasper's devil-red sports car when she turned into the driveway. Even in the already dusky light, it didn't take her long to spot him. There he was, leaning against her mailbox as if he had every right to be there.

She issued a mumbled goodbye to Mr. Eidelson and tossed the headset phone onto the passenger seat.

"Bobbie," Jasper greeted when she stepped from her car. "I'm glad you're finally home. I've been waiting for you." He lifted his nose in the air and sniffed. "Say, what's that smell? A new perfume, huh? Guess the animals like it. It's a little strong, but I could get used to it."

She ignored his idiotic observation and turned to see if the other critters were still there. They were, and they were gaining now that she'd stopped. Bobbie rolled up the travel magazine in case she had to ward them off. Not that she planned to hit them, but waving the glossy pages around and shouting might work.

Jasper walked down the flagstone steps to join her. "Say, that really *is* a great perfume. You oughta wear that more often." He sniffed her again. "By the way, something must be wrong with your phone. I've been trying to call you for a couple of hours."

"I had your number blocked." Bobbie kept her attention on the animals. One of the cats and the raccoon didn't look especially pleased when they realized she wasn't a potential girlfriend.

"I know you're angry about what happened,"

Jasper said as if his latest jilting were only a mild inconvenience instead of the life-altering, humiliating experience that it had been. "But I can explain everything."

"I don't want an explanation."

She grabbed her purse and headed for the house, taking the steps two at a time. The critters didn't come any closer, but Bobbie didn't plan to take any chances. Besides, she wanted to get away from Jasper more than she did the animals.

Unfortunately, Jasper followed her. Bobbie barely managed to get inside the house and slam the glass storm door between them.

"I got scared," Jasper prattled on. He pressed his face right against the glass, making himself look a little like a severely mashed Mr. Potato Head. "I guess I wasn't ready to settle down."

"Too bad you didn't let me in on that little revelation before I showed up at the church."

He shrugged. "Hey, what can I say—I'm human. I make mistakes."

She wanted to throttle him. Eight months earlier, the man had left her high and dry to face 179 guests, a food-laden reception and an unpaid limo driver. Worse, Bobbie had learned later that he'd actually gone on their honeymoon trip to London—a place she desperately wanted to visit. Then, rather than return to Liffey and try to grovel his way back into her good graces, Jasper had been working in his father's travel agency in San Antonio.

"You're leaving," she insisted. "And I don't want you to come back. Our relationship is over, and we'll never get back together again, understand?"

Jasper nodded but then reached inside the pocket of his perfectly tailored jacket and brought out a thick envelope. "It's an itinerary," he announced. "For our trip to Paris. I've already paid for everything, including a stay at a five-star hotel. Dad says I can have as much time off from the agency as I need so we can leave as early as next week. All you have to do is say yes."

He flashed that dimple-enhanced smile that had once done a fairly decent job of melting her toenail polish. Today, her nail polish frosted over.

Bobbie was on the verge of telling Jasper exactly what he could do with that blasted travel itinerary when she heard the voices. Male voices.

She peered over Jasper's shoulder and saw something that sent her stomach plummeting to her purple kneecaps. Her uncles and Aidan were leaving the other side of the house, the uncles' side, and they were headed for hers. Fortunately, they had their attention focused on the four-legged critters, so it gave Bobbie a couple of seconds to try to compose herself.

"Good-bye, Jasper," she snarled.

His moronic grin slipped a considerable notch. "You don't mean that."

"I do mean it." To prove her point, she aimed her index finger at Aidan. "That's my boyfriend, and he's here to pick me up for a...uh...date."

The grin vanished. Jasper propped his hands on his hips. "Is this about that dumb lottery?"

"No." And it was the truth. This was about the preservation of what was left of her sanity.

In the nick of time, Uncle Winston saved her from having to add some lies to that truth. "Hey, what's that weasel doing here?" Winston called out.

"He's leaving," Bobbie announced. "He thought he could show up here and talk me into going to Paris with him. I'd rather have my tonsils removed by a toddler with a rusty spoon."

"No, Winston meant the other weasel," Uncle Quincy corrected.

"Huh?" Another glance over Jasper's shoulder, and Bobbie saw that her uncle was right. There were two weasels. Jasper and a furry one that had joined the other critters. Bobbie thought the furry one might actually be Henrietta Beekins' missing ferret, Sugarfoot.

As if they'd rehearsed it, her uncles walked forward, each of them latching onto one of Jasper's arms. Winston and Quincy were in their late sixties, but both men were still in remarkable shape.

Together, they lifted the wirily-built Jasper right off the flagstones.

"You're not welcome here," Winston informed Jasper. "We don't take kindly to you breaking Bobbie's heart. Leave now, or Quincy here just might put an uncomfortable knot in that Gigolo underwear that you're so fond of."

Quincy agreed with a gravelly, snarling growl. He was by far the smaller of the two, but since he'd been the state mud-wrestling champion in his prime, and since he had hands the size of SUV hubcaps, few people cared to argue with Quincy Callahan.

In no time flat, and with seemingly no exertion, the uncles had her former fiancé and reigning cow-dung champion headed toward his car.

"This isn't over," Jasper called out. "I'll win you back, Bobbie. You'll see."

Ferrets would fly first.

When Jasper finally drove away, Bobbie stepped out on the porch again. From the dooms-day look on Aidan's face, he wasn't so sure of this lottery stuff either. He'd probably come over to call the whole thing off.

"I'll take a stab at what happened to you," Winston said coming back up the steps. He tow-ered a good twelve inches over his fraternal twin, Quincy, and even had a few inches on Aidan. Her uncle gave his ornate feather-banded Stetson an adjustment. "That purple blotch on your skirt is from Eidelson's Sensuous Musk Massage Oil, right?"

Flabbergasted, Bobbie just stared at him a moment. "How'd you know that?"

Winston cast an uneasy glance down at Quincy. Both shook their heads. Both mumbled. Quincy finally motioned for his brother to continue. "We had a meeting with Mr. Eidelson a couple of years ago, before you took over the business."

"And you didn't warn me?"

They shrugged in unison. "We figured he'd have a new product by now," Quincy offered. He didn't wait for her to verify that there was no product other than the staining, stinky oil. He hitched a thumb in Aidan's direction. "The deputy was looking for you."

Since the cheerless look was still on his face, Aidan had probably been with her uncles longer than he wanted. Of course, there were times when five seconds was too long to spend with Quincy and Winston.

Bobbie caught onto Aidan's arm and pulled him inside. "Thank you for bringing him over," she let her uncles know. She glanced around the yard. It was dark, but she figured it wasn't so dark that she'd missed his vehicle. "Aidan, where'd you park?"

"By the pond. I took the back way."

So that he wouldn't be seen. Oh, yeah. He was definitely ready to put an end to this.

Bobbie gave a farewell wave to her uncles, but they just stood there grinning at her. When a second wave didn't get them moving, she issued a good-bye and shut the door. Later, she'd have to inform them that this visit from the deputy wasn't the start of the glorious romance that they obviously thought it was.

The full impact of the Twango-Drifter Plan hit Bobbie the moment she turned around to face Aidan.

Oh, my. Oh, my, my, my.

He was certainly an eyeful in those snuggy jeans and crisp white shirt. And here he was. Right in the middle of her entryway—the last place an attractive man should be, since she'd sworn off men for all of eternity.

"I'll save you some time here," she started. "My second thoughts are having second thoughts. I figure you're feeling pretty much the same."

"I am." The corner of his mouth lifted. Not a toenail-dissolving grin like Jasper's. This one made her smile and feel warm and tingly inside.

"It sure seemed like a good idea at the time," Bobbie continued. "Well, maybe it did. But I caught us both at a weak moment. Now that the phones aren't ringing and people aren't pestering us, well, the Twango-Drifter Plan doesn't seem, um, necessary, does it?"

Aidan no doubt would have agreed, but before he could even get out a word, one of the cats scurried across the windowsill. It clawed its way up the screen and onto the eaves.

Bobbie shook her head. "Just for the record—I don't expect you to do a kitty rescue."

He smiled again. And just stood there. Bobbie tried not to look at him. She really tried. But her eyes seemed to have a whole different notion.

She took in everything about him that she didn't want to notice. The way his dark hair languished against his tanned neck. The little flecks of blue and gray in his luscious green eyes. She probably would have started drooling if the rattling sound hadn't pulled her out of her Aidan-induced trance.

She glanced behind her. A second cat was making his way up the screen.

Aidan motioned toward the plate-size stain on her skirt. "You might want to take care of that before you attract a bear or something."

"Of course." Strange, but she'd almost forgotten about the massage oil. "I'll just grab a quick shower and change. I won't be long. Then, we can talk about...well, about our situations."

Naturally, that would mean coming up with a different plan, or maybe no plan at all. Aidan was a grown man, incredibly grown, and he certainly didn't need her to fix his problems. Besides, she absolutely, emphatically, positively didn't want another relationship.

Really.

Once she was safely in the bathroom and had the door closed, she placed her fingertips over the pulse on her neck to verify what she already knew. It was racing. And not just racing either. It was in a full gallop.

So, she did what any other female who had sworn off men would do. Bobbie blamed it on Eidelson's Sensuous Musk Massage Oil.

AIDAN BLAMED his visit on basic stupidity. And, of course, politeness.

The bane of his existence.

Why he hadn't ended this fiasco with just a phone call, he didn't know. But he did know that he had to put this Twango-Drifter Plan to bed in such a way that it didn't hurt Bobbie's feelings. Of course, after her comment just moments earlier, it was clear she wasn't very comfortable with things either. After all, her second thoughts were having second thoughts. You couldn't get any more unsure than that.

While he waited for Bobbie to finish her shower, he ambled around the living room, glancing at the cheery yellow and lilac décor. There were posters of Big Ben, Mount Rushmore, Limerick Castle and the Grand Canyon. A huge stack of travel magazines lay on the coffee table. Apparently, Bobbie had a bad case of wanderlust.

"It's an obsession," he heard her say.

Aidan turned to see her in the doorway. She was barefooted and wore jeans with a cropped T-shirt. There was nothing especially attractive about the outfit, but it seemed to garner his attention. He cleared his throat and forced his attention to garner something else.

"What's an obsession?" he asked.

"Traveling." She walked closer, and he caught the scent of her soap. She'd washed her hair as well, and it fell in damp strands against her neck. Like the outfit, it wasn't especially attractive, but for some reason it was appealing. Appealing in a make-me-squirm sort of way.

He cleared his throat again. "You travel often?"

"No." She gave a heavy sigh. "I rarely go anywhere because I work six days a week. That's why it's an obsession—I only get to dream about it. I guess you've been a lot of places, huh?"

"Some. I joined the law-enforcement exchange two years ago. The first place they sent me was London to work at Scotland Yard."

A wistful, longing look glazed her eyes. "Ohh. London. I suppose you've been to Hawaii, too?"

He nodded. And nodded again when she asked about Italy and France.

"You are *so* lucky," she concluded. "The closest I get to places like that are my travel magazines. A pitiful substitute, I can tell you."

She stuffed her hands into the back pockets of her jeans. Not the best maneuver. Of course, she probably didn't know that it hiked up her top so he could now see her stomach. Not just her stomach though. Her navel.

And it was pierced.

Hmmm. For some strange reason, he found that intriguing. And sexy. It reminded him of things best forgotten. Things that involved slow, wet, lingering kisses in the general region of her navel.

Aidan was forced to clear his throat once again. If he did much more of that, Bobbie would think he was coming down with a cold.

He was about to tell her the Twango-Drifter Plan was a no-go and get the heck out of there, but the lights suddenly went off, plunging them into total darkness.

"Sorry. This happens all the time," she assured him. "There's a flashlight in the kitchen. I'll get it."

He heard fumbling around when Bobbie walked into the adjoining room. Aidan also heard when she bumped into something.

"Darn it," she mumbled.

She repeated that when she bumped into something else, adding some "shoot's" and "blast's." Apparently, Bobbie didn't have good night vision. Of course, it was so dark that he couldn't see his hand in front of his face.

Another bumping sound sent him in search of her. "Need any help?"

Aidan stuck out his hands like Frankenstein to feel his way around.

"I know I have a flashlight in the drawer somewhere. Now, if I could just find the drawer," he heard her say—right before he bumped into her. As bumps went, it was probably the best one he'd ever had. His Frankenstein hands were suddenly filled with her breasts.

"Oh!" she gasped.

Aidan said an entirely different kind of *oh*. It sounded more like a beached whale's groan. Her cute little breasts fit perfectly in the palms of his hands. Touching them, however, was a big no-no.

He snatched his hands away and stepped to the side. "Sorry about that."

She probably was sorry too, but unfortunately Bobbie stepped in the same direction he did. This time, his lowering hands skimmed over her waist. And the skimming didn't stop there either. Their middles swished against each other. Man, did they swish. As swishes went, it was a prizewinner.

"Don't move," she demanded.

Aidan was sure he'd misunderstood her. They were touching from waist to kneecaps. Surely, she didn't approve of that. His body did though. In fact, his body was rather pleased with the fact that it had Bobbie plastered against it. It was obvious he'd have to have a man-to-man talk with his body.

"My earring," she explained. "You're caught on it. Don't move. It'll hurt."

He was nowhere in the vicinity of her earlobes. "Excuse me?"

"The earring in my navel—it's caught on your shirt or something. Please don't move." He didn't have to see her face to know there was a frown on it. Aidan could hear it in her voice. "It's something my friend, Crystal, talked me into last month for my twenty-eighth birthday. Needless to say, it was a stupid idea. Then, the skin closed around the earring, and I can't get the darn thing out."

Aidan eased his hand between them and encountered the snagged earring. And some female flesh. Bobbie's stomach was soft and firm at the same time. Best not to dwell on it though. Best not to dwell on anything that made his body feel like an overly productive furnace.

"It's caught on my belt," he let her know.

"Can you untangle it?"

Probably, but not without feeling around a lot. His body was about to volunteer him for the job, but Aidan vetoed it. His body had no vote here. It was already making some pretty bad suggestions.

"Your hands are smaller," he answered. Which probably didn't have a thing to do with anything, but it was the only semi-plausible reason he could come up with. "Why don't you try?"

She did. With a vengeance. Bobbie stuck her hand between them as if she had no plans whatsoever to encounter him along the way. And she encountered him all right. Her agile fingers slid against his chest, stomach and even slightly lower—to the fly on his jeans.

All that encountering would have been okay— maybe—if he hadn't been stirring like crazy beneath that fly.

"Flashlight," he managed. "It'll make this easier."

Or at least it might get his eyes uncrossed.

Bobbie made a sound of agreement and reached around behind him to get to the drawer. Not the best position for them to be in. Now, all of her was plastered against all of him. Breasts. Stomach.

And most especially, other things.

The torment didn't stop there either. Aidan could feel her warm breath on his neck. He could smell the scent of soap on her skin. That wasn't usually a turn-on for him, but it apparently was now. Soon, he'd have to beg for mercy.

Or beg to have sex with her.

Aidan remembered who he was with—Bobbie. Nope, it'd have to be begging for mercy. There was no way he could become involved with her. She was one tempting morsel that he intended to leave on the proverbial plate of life.

She fumbled for several moments. Wiggled. And otherwise nudged and rocked. ''Got it,'' she announced.

Aidan was so worked up that it took him a while to realize she meant the flashlight. She clicked it on, and golden light sprayed between them. He could hope that she wouldn't notice that their little bump-and-grind session had caused some changes in his body. Of course, she was definitely close enough to feel it if she moved just slightly to his right.

Part of him—a disgusting vile part—very much wanted her to move to his right.

And wiggle back and forth a little.

''Darn it,'' Bobbie mumbled.

Heck! Had he said that wiggle part out loud? He hoped not. He didn't stand a chance of coming up with a plausible explanation for it.

''What?'' Aidan asked, his voice cracking.

''My navel ring's not tangled on your belt but on some loose threads on the loop of your jeans. I don't think I can get us apart. I'll have to use the scissors.''

She might as well have said she was about to boil him in rancid snake oil. There was no way he wanted Bobbie near a certain part of his temporarily enlarged anatomy with a pair of scissors.

"Let me try," he insisted.

The lights flared on. It wasn't exactly the best time for that to happen. Now, he'd actually have to look at her while he tried to disjoin them.

She chuckled softly. "Weird things like this always happen to me."

That wasn't hard to believe. Bobbie definitely had a Calamity Jane, I Love Lucy thing going on. Still, this had to be a first. "You've caught your navel ring on a man's jeans before?"

"No, but once when I was a teenager, I got my braces caught on some deep-pile carpeting. Don't ask for details." She put the flashlight aside and flattened her hand on his chest. "Lean back just a little, and let me see if I can do something about this. Hmmm."

Bobbie stared down at the bodily connection.

Aidan was still aroused and hoped like the devil she wouldn't notice. Of course, only blindness, paralysis or virginal naiveté could have prevented her from noticing something like that.

"It's the Austrian crystal on the earring that's actually caught," she continued. "I think I can—"

When she didn't finish her sentence, Aidan

glanced at her. Except it didn't stay a glance. Their gazes connected—and turned into a full-fledged stare.

"You wear boxers," she mumbled. But then her eyes widened to the size of turkey platters. "Ohmigosh. I didn't mean to look. Or to say that out loud."

He knew the feeling.

"I mean, it's no big deal," she babbled. "It's just there's a poll making the rounds. Most people in town thought you were into briefs."

"There's a poll about my choice of underwear?" Aidan asked.

She nodded and swallowed rather noisily. "Last I heard, most people figured you for a Naughty Guy."

"Excuse me?"

"Oh." She blushed. "That's one of Boxers or Briefs' products. Item 451A. A classy traditional-cut faux silk brief in nontraditional colors. It has an ad slogan that I'd rather not mention if you don't mind."

Aidan couldn't help it. He had to smile. So did Bobbie, eventually.

Man, did she ever smile.

This was not good. Bobbie looked centerfold-sexy with that smile and her hair tumbling around her face. Her mouth was slightly damp, too.

Mercy, he couldn't be thinking about kissing

her. He just couldn't be. This Twango-whatever idea, the one he didn't want, was all for show. A faux relationship with faux kisses and faux feelings.

Too bad the heat stirring in his body didn't feel so frickin' faux.

It felt like a blazing inferno.

Aidan shook his head, hoping to clear it. It didn't work. Nothing cleared, especially the sudden, urgent ache he had brewing below the waist.

Ah, heck.

He didn't want that part of his body to get in on this. His mouth was already thinking things that were way out of line, but those thoughts were G-rated compared to all the stupid ideas that brainless part of him could suggest.

"Uh, Bobbie." He'd just tell her to slap him, to make it a good hard one so it'd knock some sense into him.

"Yes?"

But she didn't ask it like a question. It sounded more like an invitation. Of course, that was the opinion of that brainless part of him below the waist. Aidan could pretty much discount any interpretation it came up with.

He felt his head lower. Tried like the devil to stop it. Couldn't. His eyes were already trained on her mouth. On her sweet, warm mouth.

Aidan couldn't remember ever wanting a mouth

this much. It was stupid to want it. Wrong. And reckless. Heck, after his earlier experience with her, it might even be hazardous to his health.

His head still dipped lower.

He decided to hope for a miracle because that was the only thing that stood a chance of stopping him now.

Apparently, he was about to kiss Bobbie Fay Callahan. And he was about a hundred percent certain that there'd be nothing faux about it.

4

_____

The Ace: Catalog Item 522. For the man who loves to soar into action. Fly high with this sturdy thong with patent-pending "ejection-seat" breakaway sides. Guaranteed no sagging. Available in Stealth Black, Fighter Jet Silver and Ruby Rocket Red.

SHE WAS ABOUT to kiss Aidan O'Shea. Bobbie was too fuzzy-headed to think of why she shouldn't be doing that. At the moment, it seemed right. It felt right, too. Of course, with him this close, making love with him on the kitchen table suddenly seemed right.

"Uh," she got out.

She should stop this. This would complicate things that were already too complicated. However, with his mouth only a fraction of an inch away, all Bobbie could manage was another "Uh."

"Uh," he repeated.

So, they were both past the point of even simple

coherent speech. It didn't matter. She didn't want to talk anyway. She wanted him to kiss her until her eyelashes curled to tight little coils.

His eyelids lowered. Bobbie's automatically did the same. She angled her head. Mercy. This would be good. She just knew it. A man who looked like Aidan could certainly send a woman jetting straight to the stars.

"Say, what's going on here?" someone asked.

The soaring and jetting came to an abrupt halt, and instead Bobbie did a crash-and-burn. Mainly because it wasn't soaring-inducer, Aidan, who was doing the asking. Even in her passion-induced stupor, Bobbie figured that out.

Their visitor was her best friend, Crystal, and her presence was both a blessing and a curse. Bobbie apparently wouldn't get that eyelash-curling kiss after all, but freedom from a navel-ring attachment was only moments away.

The other downside to this situation was that unless Bobbie could convince her friend that absolutely nothing carnal was going on, then for the next six years or so, Crystal would torment her with questions about this incident.

Aidan tried to step back from her, but Bobbie caught onto his shoulders before he could do that. No sense injuring herself at this point.

"Crystal," Bobbie said as calmly as she could. "What are you doing here?"

"I closed the salon early and thought I'd drop by and snag some leftovers for dinner. The front door was unlocked so I let myself in."

As usual. Crystal's self-invitations didn't normally bother Bobbie. In fact, she usually welcomed them. But then, she'd never been caught in a near lip-lock with a cute deputy either. "You scared the life out of us."

Crystal shook her head. "Mmmm. You sure that's all I did? Because I think I might have interrupted something here."

But Crystal dismissed it with the flippant wave of her hand. "Hey, what am I saying? This is you—Bobbie Callahan. Senior citizens without access to Viagra see more action than you do." She picked an apple out of a wicker basket, levered herself onto the counter and started to munch. "So, what's really going on?"

"Nothing, really. My navel ring got caught on his jeans," Bobbie explained. "We're having a little trouble untangling ourselves."

Crystal stopped in mid-bite. "How'd that happen?"

"You don't want to know," Aidan mumbled.

Bobbie quietly agreed. "Crystal, could you just get us loose and stop asking all these questions?"

Crystal shook her head again, sending the heap of tiny tangerine-colored curls bouncing. "The idea of putting my hand on the front of his pants doesn't appeal to me. Well, maybe it does a little, because he is on the hot side.'' And with a chunk of apple still in her mouth, she winked and grinned at him. ''But I wouldn't feel right doing that since he's sorta yours. I mean, you did win him in the lottery and all. That'd be like cheating if—''

''Crystal!'' Bobbie said through clenched teeth. ''Get us loose now.''

''All right. All right. Don't go all crazy on me. I'll get your big sharp chef's knife from the drawer—''

''No!'' Aidan yelled. ''No scissors or knives. It's time to put an end to this.'' He reached between them and used his thumbnail to saw the threads off the navel ring. After a few seconds, he had them free.

Bobbie stepped back and pushed her hair out of her face. She didn't look at Aidan. Couldn't. And he no doubt felt the same. What in the name of heaven had she almost done? She wasn't the kind of woman ruled by lust glands.

She wasn't even sure she had lust glands.

Crystal stuck out her hand for Aidan to shake. ''Crystal Pudney. You probably don't remember me, but I own the Curl Up and Dye Beauty Palace over by the Piggly Wiggly on Main. We met the first day you got to Liffey.''

Bobbie waited for Aidan to rattle off a plethora of unsavory details about Crystal the way he'd done to her in his office. But he merely nodded. No comment on the fact that Crystal had missed gobs of appointments and had scores of moving traffic violations. Just the briefest handshake in the history of that particular form of salutation.

"I have to go," Aidan announced.

"Oh. I'll see you to the door," Bobbie offered when he took off like a fighter jet in that general direction. She had to sprint after him.

Unfortunately, Crystal followed right on their heels. Shoot! Bobbie couldn't very well ask for a moment alone with Aidan, or Crystal would think something was going on between them.

Which there wasn't.

That almost-kiss had been a mere minor setback in her not-so-minor plan to swear off men forever and ever. It was also a hindrance to them dissolving their plan to rid themselves of romance and other assorted aggravations. But it wouldn't happen again.

Nope.

Now, that she knew the potent effect of Aidan's mouth, she'd just distance herself from those luscious lips. While she was at it, she'd subscribe to a couple more travel magazines. It would give her mind something else to do other than dwell on dwellings it shouldn't be dwelling on.

"You'll call if you find out anything about the

missing Gigolos. I mean, the underwear?'' Bobbie asked.

"Oh. Sure. Will do. Good evening, ladies.'' At that same supersonic speed, Aidan turned on his afterburners and jetted out the door.

"And don't worry about that, uh, other thing,'' Bobbie called out to him. "We'll discuss it some other time. Not tomorrow though. I've got a meeting in Austin. But soon.''

He didn't even spare her a glance. "Okay.''

"Well, well,'' Crystal said coming up behind her. They both watched as Aidan flew away. "I thought the Aidan-o-rama didn't interest you.''

"It doesn't.'' And it was the truth. The lottery didn't interest her.

Too bad the lottery prize did.

Crystal crunched into the apple again. "Hmmm. I figure one of two things could be happening here. You want to spend some time with Deputy Hot-Bod to get Jasper off your back. Or you just want to spend some time with Deputy Hot-Bod because he's, well, a hot-bod. So, which is it?''

Bobbie wanted to be mortified by that question. She wanted to flat-out deny it. She wanted to gasp and look outraged. Too bad she couldn't. Crystal would detect the lie right away. It was a knack of hers. A kind of heightened sensory awareness in the region of her brain that sorted out malarkey from truth.

Bobbie attributed it to Crystal's overuse of hair dye.

"Aidan is interesting. And not just because of his good looks but because he's traveled all over the world," Bobbie explained. "And it did occur to me that Jasper might leave me alone if—"

"You were about to kiss Aidan when I walked in, and Jasper wasn't around." Crystal paused a heartbeat. "Guess you were practicing your pucker, huh? Or maybe you were just testing the durability of your lip gloss?"

Bobbie huffed. "I thought you were here to get some leftovers for dinner."

Crystal giggled. "I rest my case. You're side-stepping the questions, so that means you're interested in Aidan. Can't say I blame you, though, even if you're too scared to risk getting another broken heart. After all, Jasper did pretty much turn you into an empty, broken shell incapable of future emotional entanglements and things like that."

And with that hurled gauntlet, Crystal headed for the fridge.

It was a trick to get her to 'fess up, and Bobbie wasn't about to fall for it. But she couldn't just let it lie either. So, she lied. "I'm *not* interested in Aidan."

"Whatever." Crystal hauled out some lasagna and a hefty slab of mocha cheesecake from the fridge, and with her dinner in hand, she headed for the door.

"Don't you 'whatever' me. I'm not interested in him. I'm really not. What do you think I am—stupid? I'm done with men."

Crystal shrugged, pinched off a smushy dollop of cheesecake and popped it into her mouth. "Too bad. Aidan's really something." Crystal mixed her musings with some "mmm's" as she savored the cheesecake. "That lean hard body. That strong angled face. That voice. Holy Moly, Aidan O'Shea sure has a way with words."

Yes. He did have all those assets. Along with solid, muscular shoulders and great abs. Bobbie knew a little about his abs since she'd been plastered against them during that navel-ring debacle. Just thinking of him and his abs made her mouth water, so she helped herself to a dollop of the cheesecake as well.

"And those eyes," Crystal went on. "Mmm. Make-me-sigh green."

They could do that, yes. Too bad he was male, the very species that she needed to avoid.

"Mmm. Mmm. Mmm. Mmmm," Crystal concluded as she licked the cheesecake off her finger. "And I just bet Aidan looks darn good when he's stripped down to his Naughty Guy briefs, too."

Bobbie reached for more cheesecake. "He wears boxers," she mumbled.

The realization that she'd just blown it came at the exact second that Crystal flashed a victorious grin.

"Gotta go," Crystal insisted. She barreled out the door.

"Wait—"

"Don't worry. I won't tell a soul."

No, but she'd tell people. Lots and lots of people. Liffey didn't need standard communication devices with Crystal around. Her mouth could travel faster than the speed of light.

"What have I done?" Bobbie asked herself.

Talk about the ultimate crash-and-burn faux pas.

Within an hour, maybe less, everyone in town would know that she had intimate knowledge of Aidan O'Shea's underpants.

5

The Paddy Wrangler: Catalog Item 216B. A bottom-shaping, poly-padded enhanced boxer for the man who likes to sit tall in the saddle. Fringed, leather-look front pouch! Guaranteed to give you a shapelier, manlier posterior or your money back. Available in Bodacious Bay and Pert Palomino.

AIDAN CHECKED the phone again. It was working just fine. Ditto for his pager, the fax machine, his e-mail account and the bell on the door. They were all silent. Completely, utterly silent.

It was nothing short of a blessed miracle.

Here it was ten o'clock on a Wednesday morning, and there'd been only one kitty rescue request and only one plea for a flat-tire repair. The only other call had come from the mayor, who merely wanted to invite him to the town picnic, wranglers' barbecue and watermelon thump.

Whatever the heck that was.

But even with the picnic invitation, claims on his time were down by more than ninety percent.

Aidan nearly shuddered at the thought, but was it possible that the Twango-Drifter Plan was a success after only forty-eight hours?

He sank down into his chair to contemplate that and read over the background reports he'd requested on his main suspects for the underwear theft. The fact that he was actually able to contemplate it in silence said loads about his situation. It was working, and that was both a blessing and a curse.

The plan had worked. Thank heaven—as, in halleluiah.

The plan had worked. Oh, mercy—as in, he was in deep trouble. The kind of trouble that could only create more trouble.

That near-kiss a couple of nights ago in Bobbie's kitchen had clanged bells the size of boulders in his head. Bells that warned him to put some serious miles between him and her. Still, there was immense pleasure in finally having some peace and quiet.

If he stuck with the plan, however, it'd no doubt call for even more kitchen encounters. Even more navel-ring sightings. And yep, even more near French kisses. Which couldn't happen if he hoped to keep his life uncomplicated. But maybe, just maybe, he could have his cake and eat it too if he could stay away from Bobbie's mouth.

And take a lot of cold showers.

The door flew open, and Aidan braced himself for a kitty-rescue request. But this was no kitty owner. He got to his feet and came face-to-face with jilting Jasper Kershaw. From the surly expression on the man's face, it was pretty obvious that he wasn't pleased about something. Aidan didn't have to guess about that displeasure either. After all, Jasper had seen him at Bobbie's house.

Jasper aimed an indignant, wagging finger in Aidan's direction. "It's all over town about your boxer shorts," he accused.

Okay, of all the things that Aidan thought Jasper might say, that wasn't one of them. Not even close. "Is there some sort of weird city ordinance that prevents me from wearing boxers?"

Jasper's Adam's apple began to bob at the same zealous speed as that wagging finger. "Quit playing Mr. Innocent with me. You know what I mean."

"Uh, not really." And even more, Aidan wasn't sure he wanted to know.

"I heard it from Maxine who heard it from Henrietta who heard it straight from Crystal that Bobbie knew you wore boxers. I don't want to know how Bobbie came about that little tidbit, but I'm here to tell you that she's hands off to you and anybody else."

Contemplating that chain of communication, Aidan scratched his chin. He didn't have to contemplate long. "I'm not exactly comfortable with you mentioning my boxers in the same breath that you mention 'little tidbit.' And I doubt Bobbie's comfortable with you declaring her to be hands off."

"Bobbie doesn't know what she wants, and I won't have you and your boxers confusing the situation, you got that? That means you back off so I can mend some fences with my future wife."

That idiotic-sounding ultimatum didn't set well with Aidan, and he'd already geared up to send this dense chowderhead on his finger-wagging way when he spotted Bobbie crossing Main Street. Her eyes widened, then narrowed to slits when she looked in the window of the office.

"Jasper," she snarled, throwing open the door. She stepped inside and propped her hands on her hips.

Man, she looked good.

Aidan wanted to concentrate just on the riled expression on her face, but that was hard to do with her wearing that well-above-the-knee pink-lemonade-colored jacket and skirt. It gloved and hugged her trim body and made her legs seem to go on forever. To his suddenly parched mouth, she truly looked like a long, tall drink...of something.

Whoa.

Not good.

Aidan gave his head a hard shake and threatened it with a good wall-pounding if it kept up thoughts like those. It wasn't a smart idea to think of Bobbie and satisfaction of thirst, any kind of thirst, in the same sentence.

"What's going on here, Jasper?" Bobbie demanded.

He hitched a thumb in Aidan's direction. "I'm here to tell Mr. Paddy Wrangler boxers that you're off limits, hands off and otherwise engaged—to me!"

Aidan almost intervened. Almost. But that fiery look that shot through Bobbie's eyes made him realize she wanted to fight this battle herself.

"Aidan has no need for the Paddy Wrangler," she said, her voice low and edgy. Bobbie took a slow, calculated step toward Jasper. "His posterior is fine without enhancements. More than fine. It's so fine that he could be a poster model for the Full Monty."

Jasper gasped.

"Say what?" Aidan questioned. He wasn't sure this particular comparison was one he wanted to have applied to his gluteus maximus.

"The Full Monty," Bobbie repeated without moving her venomous gaze from Jasper. She tapped the toe of her meringue-colored high heels on the tile floor. "'Catalogue number 233A. See-through-front bikini brief for the man with nothing to hide. Contour-hugging, barely-there backside

for a rakish and yet daring display of your manly
assets. Available in Exposed Ebony and In-the-
Buff Buff.''"

Jasper gasped again. "But you said no man
could ever look good in the Full Monty."

She gave her head an indignant little wobble.
"I said that before I met Aidan."

Touché. One for the lady in pink. Flattered,
taken aback and slightly confused, Aidan went to
the door and held it open for Jasper to leave.

"This isn't over, Bobbie," Jasper insisted.
"We'll talk about it when I pick you up on Sunday afternoon for the picnic and watermelon
thump. Maxine will be there, and she'll keep Deputy Full Monty here occupied while we spend
some quality time together."

Bobbie suddenly looked ready to trim Jasper's
sails. Maybe because he was feeling particular
generous—and ornery—Aidan slipped his arm
around Bobbie's waist. "Actually, Bobbie's going
to the town picnic with me."

"I am?" she questioned.

Aidan nodded. "You are. It's Sunday afternoon
around three."

After all, he'd already agreed to the picnic, and
he didn't want to have to face Maxine and the
other Liffey women alone. He figured Bobbie felt
the same about Jasper. So what if it meant they
had to play the Twango-Drifter game a little

longer? What were a few more days in the grand scheme of things?

And so what if he'd apparently lost his mind?

To add a tad more insult to Jasper's obvious injury, Aidan leaned in and planted a quick kiss on Bobbie's glossy mouth.

Hmmm.

Strawberry-flavored lip gloss. It tasted as good as she looked.

"Oh, come on. You don't fool me," Jasper concluded. "You're doing this to make me jealous."

Bobbie dismissed him with a wave of her hand. Apparently wanting to add some insult of her own, she came up on her toes and gave Aidan an affectionate peck right on the lips.

She pulled back almost immediately, but not before Aidan felt the zap. It was like a mini jolt of saturated electricity from her mouth to his.

Aidan just stared at her. She just stared at him. Had she felt that zap as well?

His heartbeat started to drum in his ears, but even over the drumming, Aidan could hear Jasper drone on about Bobbie doing this only to get back at him.

Bobbie made a little sound of surprise, but it wasn't surprise that Aidan saw in her eyes. Or even surprise that shaped her mouth when she blew out a strawberry-scented breath.

Nope.

This was something...hot.

Something smoldering.

Something fruity.

Something Aidan suddenly had an overwhelming urge to sample.

"I know you're just trying to make me jealous," Jasper repeated.

Without taking his hot gaze from Bobbie, Aidan latched onto Jasper's shoulder and *helped* the man outside. He elbowed the door shut.

Aidan watched Bobbie's eyelids flutter down. At first he didn't know why she'd done that, but Aidan soon figured it out. He was making a move on her, closing the already miniscule distance between them.

Their lips touched. Breath met breath. He skimmed his hands down her back and edged her closer until their mouths met in full force. She didn't resist. Bobbie slipped into his arms as if she'd done it a thousand times. And she kissed him. Really kissed him.

Uh-oh.

This was more than zaps. More than jolts. And even more than a bare-all Full Monty. It was a fruity-flavored blast of pure pleasure.

And Aidan felt what was left of his resolve fly straight back to Boston.

"Mmm," Bobbie moaned.

Aidan deepened the kiss, angling his mouth to hers. Bobbie did her own share of deepening and angling. Their tongues met. Fooled around a little. They just continued to fool around until she forgot she needed air to live. Gasping, she pulled away from him.

That's when reality hit her like a three-hundred-and-fifty-pound Dallas Cowboys' linebacker.

She'd kissed Aidan! And not just any old ordinary kiss either. A French kiss. Nothing short. Nothing sweet. It'd been lengthy and incredibly, deliciously satisfying. The kiss of a real pro.

Oh boy, she was in trouble.

Aidan didn't appear to have fared much better. He looked poleaxed, out of breath and a little dizzy.

"Wow. Guess we showed Jasper, huh?" Bobbie commented as casually as she could. Which wasn't very casual considering she was breathing heavily and trying to lick the taste of Aidan off her lips.

"Yeah, guess we did." Aidan was doing his own share of heavy breathing.

"Maybe he'll finally get the message that I'm through with him."

He nodded. "Maybe. And if this didn't work, the picnic on Sunday will do the trick for sure."

She nodded. "It should help you with your kitty

rescue woes too since just about everybody in town will be there to see us together."

Aidan nodded again. "This will help both of us in the long run."

Bobbie didn't dare return the nod. She was starting to feel a little like one of those bobblehead dolls. Besides, all the nodding, breathing and bobbling in the world wouldn't ease the awkwardness—or the startling reality—of the situation. With that kiss, they'd moved well past the faux-pas stage and had done a Full Monty-ish blunder. The only way she could save face was to brush it off as part of their plan to make their lives romance-free.

But she didn't have time to brush off anything. By the time she managed to gather some of her breath, Aidan had already gathered his.

"Uh. How'd you ever get hooked up with Jasper anyway?" Aidan asked. "He doesn't really seem your type."

Small talk. It was a good start while she tried to get her heart rate back under control. Bobbie stepped away from him, hoping a little distance would clear the pea soup in her head. "I blame it on Pavlov's dog."

Aidan quit looking uncomfortable long enough to look thoroughly confused. "Beg your pardon?"

"In hindsight, I think Jasper was just a conditioned response like Pavlov's dog. I used to spend hours staring at all those posters in the window of his dad's travel agency. Jasper was always there, sandwiched between the Parthenon and the Pyramids. I guess I just started to associate him with all those other feelings of wanderlust.''

"Wanderlust, huh?'' Aidan commented. He put some distance between them as well. He went to the other side of the room and gave the visitors' chairs an unnecessary adjustment. "That's certainly a powerful stimulus.''

"Oh, yeah. Well, for me it is. And obviously for you too since you spend your life traveling around.'' She checked her watch. Why, she didn't know. Her vision was still too blurred to see the tiny numbers. "Where has the time gone? I really need to get back to the factory.''

"You didn't say why you dropped by.''

She stopped midway to the door. "Didn't I? Must have slipped my mind when I saw Jasper here.'' And it was continuing to slip her mind.

Bobbie finally snapped her fingers. "The missing Gigolos? That's what I wanted to talk to you about. My assistant said you stopped by the factory this morning when I was in a conference call with our suppliers.''

"I was just asking a few questions. No one seems to know anything about the merchandise, but I'll keep digging.'' He picked a manila folder from his desk and handed it to her. "I requested background checks on several of your employees. It's routine procedure.''

Bobbie thumbed through the papers in the file to find the names of all the supervisors and several newly hired warehouse workers. ''You think one of these might be our thief?''

He shrugged. ''Maybe. But I want to add Jasper to that list. After all, the underwear vanished the very day he returned to Liffey.''

Bobbie nodded and handed the file back to Aidan. ''Good job. Maybe you'll catch this person before they strike again.'' She opened the door. ''Don't worry about picking me up for the picnic. I'll ride over with my uncles and just meet you at the park.''

''Sure.''

Since there was no way she could hold onto her faux composure a moment longer, she issued an overly perky goodbye and went on her way.

This was the last time she'd play kissy kissy with the studly Aidan. The absolute last. She had to be smart about this. No more Pavlovian conditioned responses. No letting wanderlust get in the way of common sense.

But that left Bobbie with one burning question.

Wanderlust aside, how was she supposed to get rid of this sudden bout of regular lust that she felt for Aidan?

"AIDAN, we're sure glad to have you with us here in Liffey," Sheriff Cooper commented. He downed another half cup of coffee and tackled the remainder of his Blue Plate Special—a hamburger just slightly smaller than Aidan's head and a platter full of thick chili fries.

"I'm glad to be here. And I'm glad you're feeling better." Of course, with the volume of food the sheriff had just consumed, that *feeling better* status might not last much longer. After all, the man had only been out of his sickbed two days.

Both Sheriff Cooper and Aidan sat in the window booth at the Chew and Chow, the tiny but bustling diner on Main Street. Since the sheriff's return to work, he'd insisted that Aidan join him for the cholesterol-laden lunches that were the diner's trademark.

"You probably miss all the noise of the city," the sheriff continued. "I guess you're used to a little more activity than this, huh?"

Aidan shrugged and sipped his coffee. "It depends. Each assignment is different. Some are quiet like Liffey. Others are nonstop."

And therein was the lure of his job in a nutshell. For him, different was good. Variety was even better. And in just four short weeks, he'd be gone from Liffey, and the Twango-Drifter Plan—and Bobbie—would be a dimming memory.

Well, probably.

She'd be as much of a dimming memory as he could manage to dim. Too bad he hadn't had much success in dimming anything when it came to her.

Even now, if he closed his eyes, he could see her. Bobbie, in one of those snug little business suits. Bobbie, smiling at him. Bobbie, her mouth poised for him to kiss. And Bobbie, as she made those sounds of pleasure as he did all sorts of things with her.

Of course, that last part was pure imagination sprinkled with some fantasies, but he hadn't been able to dim those raunchy musings either.

"I've been giving all this stolen underwear business some thought," the sheriff went on, pulling Aidan out of his sprinkles and fantasies. He waved at a couple of elderly ladies who strolled past the window. One of them winked at him, and then at Aidan. "My thoughts have been straying in the direction of Rudy Tate, the floor manager at Boxers or Briefs. Call me old-fashioned, but there's just something a little unnatural about a man who likes being surrounded by butt-enhancing underwear."

Aidan nodded. It certainly wasn't one of his top ten job choices. "Nothing came up on his background check, but I'm looking into his past employment records."

The sheriff grinned and stuffed some more fries in his mouth. "I figured you'd be right on it. My detective skills are a little rusty since we hadn't exactly had a real crime here in a dozen years or so, but I'm hoping you'll put this to bed before your time with us is up.''

Aidan hoped the same thing. And that time was practically ticking away. Four weeks and counting. ''What about Maxine Varadore? You think she could have done something like this?''

''It's a good possibility,'' the sheriff agreed. ''She's riled because Bobbie fired her, but from what I heard the woman just couldn't sew a fly on straight. A man can overlook plenty of things in his Skivvies, but that's not one of them. Seems Bobbie did us all a service by letting Maxine go.''

Aidan just nodded and moved on to his next suspect. ''And then there's Jasper Kershaw. He's at the top of my list.''

Sheriff Cooper grinned some more. ''Now, you sure that's your badge talking, or does that have something to do with all the personal attention you've been giving Bobbie Fay?''

It seemed a good time to nod again and continue with the business at hand. ''What does concern me about this case is that none of the stolen merchandise has surfaced.''

''Oh, it'll turn up somewhere I'm sure. Hard to keep magenta Gigolos a secret for very long.'' The sheriff finished his last French fry and eased out of his side of the booth. ''I think I'll head over to the counter to chat with Esther Lynn. Wanta come?''

Aidan glanced at the woman in question. She had more facial hair than he did and could probably arm-wrestle him into traction. ''No thanks. I'll just stay here and finish up my chili.''

''Suit yourself. I won't be long.''

With the same easy pace as his drawl, Sheriff Cooper moseyed toward the counter. He'd hardly gotten there when Aidan's cell phone rang. He unclipped it from his belt and answered it.

''Hi, Aidan. It's Mom.''

It was one of those good news–bad news sort of deals. He loved his mother dearly, but she never called in the middle of the day unless she had matchmaking on her mind.

Aidan checked the time—something he usually did when he experienced one of her impromptu calls. Just how long would it take for her to let him know that she'd found him the perfect woman?

His mother started the covert attack with some chitchat about the weather in Boston. Aidan listened and watched as the second hand on the clock ticked on. He was betting she couldn't make it a full minute.

''It's been muggy...''

The sound of her voice faded when he spotted Bobbie coming out of the bank across the street.

Aidan smiled before he could stop himself. Sweet Nantucket, she had on one of those short skirt sets again. Somehow, he had to find a way to make himself immune to her fashion choices.

"By the way," his mother continued. "Did I mention that my new kick-boxing instructor is a woman? Her name is Tracy Hillman…"

Aidan checked the time. Thirty-nine seconds. His mother was obviously in a hurry today.

He just listened to the droning explanation about the toned and perfect Tracy while he watched the rather toned Bobbie make her way up the street. She stopped to say hello to a couple of people and even stooped down to give Mrs. Fortenberry's poodle an affectionate rub behind the ears. The poodle looked ready to start drooling. Since Aidan had been on the receiving end of some of Bobbie's attention, he knew how the pooch felt.

Bobbie was, well, *moving* for lack of a better word. No doubt about it. She was like a trim little package of temptation, and all of a sudden, temptation was something he was having a hard time resisting. In fact, such a hard time that he'd begun to consider the unthinkable. Would it be completely stupid for him to test the temptation to see just how far she could tempt him?

Or something like that.

It couldn't be anything serious, of course. Or

permanent. But suddenly he was giving some thought to—

"So, what'd you say?" his mother asked. "How about I invite Tracy over for dinner the next time you're home?"

That jarred Aidan back to reality. The hot and steamy fantasies about Bobbie faded into the sunset. That call was just the reminder he needed. He'd adopted his no-rings-attached philosophy for a reason.

A good reason.

A reason he had a little trouble recalling when he looked at Bobbie again.

Oh, yeah. He didn't want to be tied down by someone else's game plan for life. No monkeying. No paddy-wrangling. Just living the way he wanted to live.

"I have to go, Mom," Aidan insisted.

He hung up and closed his eyes. He could thank his lucky stars for that much-needed attitude adjustment. Bobbie Callahan was one package of temptation that would just have to stay unopened.

6

The Slap Stick: Catalogue Item 333C. Amuse
your friends and significant other with this
glow-in-the-dark Ruffy the Raccoon cartoon-
print boxer. Wait until you see where we've
put the punch line. Comes with detachable
raccoon tail and is available in most sizes.

AIDAN STOOD in the parking lot and sized up the
place. Davy Crockett Park was a zoo. Not literally.
But there were enough people and activities that
it looked like a huge ant farm gone awry.

Smoke billowed from several open barbecue
pits. There were carnival rides, assorted amusement booths and a couple of people rolling water-
melons down a hill. Others were thumping the
melons to make music that no one could have possibly found enjoyable. And, of course, there were
women. Lots and lots of women.

Estrogen was heavy in the air.

Aidan glanced around and, even with all the
activity and other females, he spotted Bobbie right

away. With a magazine resting against her knees, she sat under a sprawling oak. She seemed engrossed in whatever she was reading, but she was also talking on the tiny phone she had pressed to her ear. He caught a phrase here and there— O-ring thong straps, water-filled wonder pouches and heated bun enhancers. She was probably talking to a supplier.

Well, he hoped she was.

Just as Aidan got closer to Bobbie, Crystal hurled a Frisbee in his direction. He caught it, barely.

Crystal hurried to him, an enormous wad of pink gum cracking in her mouth. "I'll make this quick. During the past week, I've been watching Bobbie and you get closer and closer. I like you, and I think you have a whole lot of potential for making her happy. I also think you two make a hot match. But if you hurt her, I *will* get even, no ifs, ands or buts about it."

"But—"

"It won't be pretty," Crystal continued as if he hadn't tried to speak. "I'm talking about a bikini wax that starts at your head and goes to the bottom of your feet. It'll get particularly nasty and painful in areas that are most sensitive to you. Got that, O'Shea?"

"Yes, I do. And I can promise you that I don't want to hurt Bobbie," he simply answered. In fact, he didn't plan to get involved with Bobbie in such a way that hurting was even an option.

"Good intentions don't count here. Hurt her like that larvae-headed Jasper did, and I start heating the wax. A huge vat of it."

And with that bizarre threat, Crystal snatched the Frisbee from him and walked away.

"A problem with Crystal?" Bobbie asked when Aidan joined her. She clicked off the phone and tossed it aside on the blanket.

"No." But then Aidan caught sight of her outfit. *There* was the problem. Man, he might have to classify her clothes as deadly weapons. She wore denim shorts. The operative word being *short*. And a tiny little knit flowered top that not only accented her breasts but also showed a couple of inches of her midriff.

She smiled, caught onto his hand and had him sit next to her. "It looks like rain, but it's still a nice day for a picnic, don't you think?"

Aidan nodded. It was an even nicer day for planting some wet kisses on her stomach.

He mentally kicked himself. No sexy thoughts today, especially after that waxing threat from Crystal. Besides, with their luck, he'd get his tongue caught on Bobbie's navel ring, and it'd require major surgery to get them untangled. Then everyone in town would know about his sudden, unexplainable navel fetish.

She put her mouth right next to his ear. "Everyone in town is here," she whispered. Her hot, cinnamony breath brushed against his cheek and neck. "After today, I doubt you'll get another Beeping Tom report."

No, but he might have to deal with a permanent state of arousal.

Heck.

Why did he have this reaction to Bobbie? Why couldn't his brain figure out that an entanglement, any entanglement, with her would be too high-maintenance? For better or worse, she had her roots firmly planted, and firmly planted was the very thing Aidan planned to avoid.

"I just got my latest copy of *Travel-or-Bust Monthly*." Bobbie grinned and held up the glossy magazine for him to see. She began to flip through the pages. "There's an article about Boston, and they talk about the swan boats in the Public Gardens. Sounds like a blast."

He smiled at her enthusiasm. "They are."

"Listen to this," she continued. She wiggled closer until their heads, shoulders and hips were pressed together. "'Glide through an urban oasis and feel your troubles slip away. Although a short ride, this trip through a sun-dappled lagoon will carry you to another time. Another place. All you have to do is relax and let the sun and city caress you.'"

"Caress, huh?" Aidan repeated.

Not the best choice of words when his mind was on other types of caresses.

"Afternoon, Bobbie and Aidan," Winston called out. He was dressed in an Old West getup and was carrying an enormous mackerel-shaped watermelon on his shoulder. Five women of varying ages were following him, apparently vying for his attention. One of the females was using a walker and was doing her best to keep up.

"The seed-spitting contest is about to start," Winston added. "Don't miss it."

Bobbie gave her uncle a distracted wave and got back to the article. "It talks about the museums and the shops. You are so lucky to have been born there."

"I guess. But a lot of people would think you were lucky to be born here in Liffey."

Her gaze met his. She blinked. And paused. "Do you really think I'm lucky?"

"Well, Liffey's not a big city, but it's thriving. And it's, uh, quaint in a non-touristy sort of way." At that exact moment, her Uncle Quincy hurried past them. He had a ferret on a leash. A ferret wearing a pair of tiny raccoon-print boxers complete with a fake bushy tail. "Well, it's quaint, or something."

What was left of Bobbie's smile evaporated. "Yeah. *Or something.*"

So, she had a point. Liffey wasn't exactly a normal place with normal residents. He'd seen a lot of weird things, but never a leashed ferret wearing raccoon-print boxer shorts.

"Have you ever thought about taking a break from the factory so you can travel?" he asked.

She shrugged and turned her gaze back to the magazine. "My uncles have owned Boxers or Briefs for nearly thirty-five years. It's a family business, and since my folks died, I'm the only family left around to run it. My cousin, Wes, isn't a good candidate because he'll eventually have to take over for Sheriff Cooper. And I can't very well ask my uncles to come out of retirement just because I want to travel."

Family duty. Yep, he understood that. It was what brought him home for holidays and an assortment of births, weddings and funerals—or as he liked to call them: hatch, match and dispatch events. But Aidan also understood that wistful, longing look in Bobbie's eyes.

Definite wanderlust.

He hated to tell her that it was an itch that was awfully hard to satisfy by staying in one place. Especially a place like Liffey.

Because he had an overwhelming urge to touch her, Aidan picked a piece of grass off her knee. What he didn't do was move his hand even after he'd tossed the grass aside. He just sat there, touching her bare knee while she turned the page to a glossy picture of Beacon Street.

"I talked with Sheriff Cooper about the missing underwear," Aidan informed her. Maybe if he discussed business, his brain wouldn't dwell on Bobbie's body. "He thought maybe we should take a harder look at Rudy Tate, your floor manager."

She paused and pursed her lips. "I guess it's possible he was involved, but I can't imagine why he'd do it."

"Maybe he's selling it?" Even though Aidan didn't want to speculate about how someone would go about finding an illegal market for thongs.

"Miss Callahan?" a man called out.

Aidan braced himself for one of the uncles, but their visitor wasn't a local Liffey-ite.

"Oh, God." Bobbie put the magazine in front of her face and tried to hide. "That's Mr. Eidelson, the maker of that awful Sensuous Musk Massage Oil that attracted the critters. I hope he doesn't see me."

"Too late. He's headed right for you."

She groaned and yanked down the magazine. "I'm not working today, Mr.—"

"This won't take long," Eidelson interrupted. With a toothy grin on his too-thin face, he set a bright orange gift bag next to her. "It's a sample of my new and improved Sensuous Massage Oil. Let me know what you think of it.''

And the man practically sprinted away. Bobbie groaned again, but that was the only protest she had time to make. Before the dust had settled from Eidelson's departure, more visitors sauntered their way.

''Well, well,'' the woman purred.

It was the queen of kitty-rescue requests and excessively tight jeans—Maxine Varadore. And to make matters worse, she had Jasper with her. However, despite her accompanied status, she had a come-hither look in her eye. Aidan had no intention of taking her up on that hithering, though.

''Bobbie,'' Jasper said crisply. But his voice got a whole lot crisper when he spoke to Aidan. ''Good afternoon, Deputy O'Shea. I see you didn't take my advice about staying away from my fiancée.''

''Nope. I didn't,'' Aidan informed him.

Realizing this could turn ugly, or just plain stupid, Aidan got to his feet. It was probably a fluke and not some bad omen that it thundered at exactly that same moment.

Jasper slipped his narrowed gaze to Bobbie. ''And I can see you're still playing hard to get.'' He didn't give her time to deny that absurd claim. ''Well, two can play at that game, darling.''

And with that announcement, Jasper hooked his

arm around Maxine and hauled her against him. The lovers' embrace perhaps would have been far more effective if Maxine hadn't winked at Aidan.

Bobbie got to her feet as well. "Is there a point to all of this, Jasper?"

"Yes!" Jasper gave Bobbie a heated look and blew her a kiss. "The point is that one way or another, I intend to win you back, darling. You *will* be mine, and we *will* go on that honeymoon to Paris."

Another wink from Maxine. "Plus, Deputy, the lottery's over tomorrow, and everything will get back to normal. Bobbie won't have dibs on you anymore."

That threat alone was enough to make Aidan want to extend the Twango-Drifter Plan indefinitely.

Bobbie took a step toward the winking, puckering couple. They looked as if they had nervous tic disorders. "You know, I'm a little tired of all this dibs talk."

"Yeah?" Maxine challenged.

"Yeah," Bobbie countered.

Uh-oh. Hoping to stave off disaster, Aidan reached for Bobbie. Too bad that reaching caused him to step the wrong way. His foot landed right on the gift bag that Mr. Eidelson had left on the ground.

Aidan heard the too-familiar sound of breaking

glass mere seconds before he got his first whiff of new and improved Sensuous Massage Oil. Ohmigod. Like a deadly top-secret-weaponized chemical agent, the reeking aroma engulfed them.

"Ewwww." Maxine clothes-pinned her nose. Jasper began to fan his hands around.

Aidan took full advantage of the distraction and turned to Bobbie. "Why don't we skip the seed-spitting contest and get out of here?"

"Agreed."

She latched onto him, and they headed away from the smelly toxic spill. "I don't have my car here. I rode in with my uncles."

The first drops of rain splattered on them as they made their way across the baseball field. If Aidan had been thinking right, he might not have led Bobbie in the direction of his car. But the massage oil had obviously dulled his senses because that's exactly where they ended up when the sky opened and it began to pour.

"I think Jasper and Maxine are following us," Bobbie let him know as he stuffed her into the car. A jolt of lightning zipped across the sky.

Aidan climbed into the car and checked the rearview mirror. She was right. Jasper and Maxine were in hot pursuit.

But they weren't alone.

Raccoons and squirrels scurried out of the trees and adjoining woods. Most went straight for the squished orange bag, but a couple of especially obstinate-looking raccoons made a beeline for Jasper and Maxine.

But that didn't mean Bobbie and he had escaped disaster just yet.

Sugarfoot, the boxer-clad ferret, broke away from the crowd and headed for Aidan's car. Obviously, enough of the scent had permeated their clothes for the critter to take notice and come after them.

It was like a scene from a Hitchcock movie.

So Aidan did the only thing he could do. He gunned the engine and put some distance between them, the amorous ferret and the human couple trying to catch them.

"Whew, we made it," Bobbie said looking back at the chaos they'd left behind. She laughed.

Aidan probably would have laughed too if he hadn't cast his gaze in Bobbie's direction. With that simple innocent glimpse, he glimpsed at a lot more than he'd counted on glimpsing. Pressed against her rain-soaked, nearly transparent shirt, her rose-colored nipples had tightened. They were perfect little buds that his fingers itched to touch.

Oh, man.

He forced his itchy fingers into a death grip on the steering wheel. Talk about icing on the proverbial cake of needy things. Not only was he alone with Bobbie. And not only did she smell like bottled sex. She looked like bottled sex.

No, he didn't need this.

He didn't need her.

And as soon as his body started to soften, Aidan was sure he'd remember that.

BOBBIE STUCK her index finger in her non-listening ear to shut out the storm noise so she could hear what the factory-floor manager had to say. Too bad she hadn't waited until Aidan had gotten her home to take this call, but if Rudy Tate had just said what she thought he said, then this wasn't something she could put off.

"There's a whole case of triple-X Bold-as-Brass Sheikh Yerbootees missing," Rudy repeated. "I've double-checked the inventory, Bobbie, and they just aren't there. I don't think I'm jumping the gun here if I say that someone's taken them."

She wrinkled up her nose. "You looked in the overflow stock room, I suppose?"

"Absolutely. But I only found some glow-in-the-dark Boogie Boxers, some fantasy briefs and a couple of cases of those seatless Casanovas—the ones with the padded red silk lips on the fly-front. But I tell you, there's not a Sheikh Yerbootee in sight."

Thank goodness Aidan couldn't actually hear

the bizarre phone conversation. It was a definite silver lining to an otherwise silverless moment.

Obviously, the thief had struck again, and he or she delighted in stealing underwear with weird, kinky names. Why couldn't this sticky-fingered person steal Gladiator boxers or Happily-Ever-After briefs? At least those were items that she could comfortably discuss in public.

She'd have to make a report to Aidan, of course, but at least she wouldn't have to give him a running commentary of their most bizarre inventory in the overflow stock room.

"A problem?" Aidan asked when she hung up and dropped her phone into her purse.

He stopped the car in front of her house. What he didn't do was look at her. In fact, he hadn't looked at her since they'd left the park. He sat soldier-stiff on the seat and kept his attention focused straight ahead. And he'd cleared his throat at least a dozen times. Maybe that massage oil had caused some kind of strange allergic reaction.

"That was Rudy Tate. He says there's more vanishing underwear." Bobbie glanced up at the sky and huffed. The rain was still coming down in buckets. "Why don't you come in for a while, and I'll give you the details? There's too much water on the road for you to be driving back into town anyway."

He hesitated but finally nodded. And he cleared

his throat again. That time, Bobbie had a pretty good idea what caused that throat clearing and the hesitation. It probably wasn't a good idea for them to be under the same roof alone, but the sudden storm hadn't given them a lot of options. She didn't want him getting into an accident after rescuing them both from Sugarfoot the ferret and her navel-lint ex-fiancé.

She covered her head with the travel magazine, and they made a mad dash into her house.

"This time there's a case of briefs missing," she explained as she tried to shake off some of the rain. Still, Aidan didn't look at her, and he had his hands clenched by his sides. Definitely weird. What was going on? "Hold on and I'll get you a towel."

"Uh, were the briefs size triple-X?" he asked.

Bobbie opened the linen closet and yanked out several thick towels. "Yes, how'd you know?"

"Lucky guess." He took one of the towels she offered and scrubbed it over his water-beaded face. Actually, he covered his entire face with it. "But it might be an important clue. Maybe size matters."

Bobbie fought to stop herself from laughing, but she didn't quite succeed. She playfully nudged his arm with her elbow. "I'll bet that's the only time a man's ever admitted that to a woman."

Aidan slowly lowered the towel. His mouth twitched, but he too lost the battle and grinned.

All that arm-nudging and grinning came to a grinding halt, however, when his gaze dropped. The moment might have been light, but they were right against each other. Arm touching arm. Their bodies only a couple of inches apart, and they were definitely sharing the same air space.

Not good.

Bobbie cleared her throat and stepped away from him. "Anyway, about those Sheikh Yerbootees. I mean, that's the name of the underwear. Rudy checked around the factory, and the case is definitely missing."

"Uh, Bobbie?"

There was a look almost of pain on his face. "What is it, Aidan?"

He motioned in the general direction of her shirt. "You're sort of...well, I mean the rain..."

Bracing herself for the worst, Bobbie glanced down.

Yikes!

Her flowered print top was practically invisible. Ditto for her lacy push-up bra. In fact, the only things that were perfectly visible were her breasts.

She jerked the towel from her face to cover up, swatting herself in the eye during the process. "I'm sorry. I had no idea."

"I know. That's why I decided to tell you."

Bobbie motioned toward her bedroom. "I'd better go change."

She managed to keep her voice calm enough, but on the inside, that was a different story. The intimate apparel gods were obviously having a good belly laugh at her expense. First, she had to discuss Sheikh Yerbootee underwear with Aidan. And then, there was that whole "size matters" thing.

But those were mere appetizers in the whole humbling underwear scenario of life.

Now, he'd seen her breasts in all their glory. Or rather their less-than-ample glory. She might never be able to look him straight in the eye again.

The phone rang the moment that she shucked off her shirt. "Aidan, get that for me, please?" she called out.

With her luck, it'd be Rudy with yet more news of missing underwear. This time, it would likely be a case of those seatless Casanovas with the attached padded lips. Or maybe some of the ultra-classy Cheek-a-boos.

Bobbie hurriedly changed and rushed back into the living room to face her fate. She came to a halt the moment she saw Aidan.

From the look on his bleached face, it was more than fate she'd have to face. Much more. It appeared he'd received some horrifying news. Maybe the entire factory inventory was missing, and she'd have to discuss each item in excruciatingly embarrassing detail.

"That was your Uncle Quincy," Aidan informed her. "He said the rain washed out the road leading back to the highway, and they'll have to stay in town tonight."

Even though on the surface that didn't seem as much of a calamity as missing Cheek-a-boos, Bobbie knew differently. If the road was gone, then that meant Aidan had to stay. At her house. With her.

Alone.

All night.

The Cheek-a-boos would no doubt have proven a lot easier—and much less hot—to handle.

The Buff Buns: Catalogue Item 339A. Ultrasheer, silky-back, high cut briefs with a patented Feels-Like-Mink front pouch. Guaranteed to fool even the most discriminating eye and touch. Available in Simply Sensual Black, Champagne Gold, and for a limited time only, Snazzy Platinum Stripes dotted with rhinestone studs.

"IT'S NO big deal," Bobbie mumbled to herself.

Really. It wasn't.

So what if Aidan was spending the night? It wasn't as if he were *really* spending the night. And if wasn't as if she *really* wanted this to happen either. In fact, nothing about this was anywhere near *really*.

Really.

Besides, they were simply business partners, of sorts. Mere participants in a plan to get members of the opposite sex off their backs.

And so what if they'd kissed a couple of times?

Those kisses were all part of the game plan and meant zip. Nada. Zilch. That was something akin to shaking hands to finalize a business deal, that's all.

With her toothbrush still hanging out of her mouth, Bobbie glanced at herself in the mirror. She shook her head. It was a sad day in a woman's life when she started lying to herself.

Those kisses meant more than zip. More than nada. Much more than zilch. And she knew it. They meant that despite all her precautions, she wasn't immune to the opposite sex.

Or maybe it was just that she wasn't immune to Aidan.

After all, she'd had absolutely no trouble whatsoever resisting Jilting Jasper. Of course, he was lower than impacted hoof grit. Aidan, on the other hand, was a tempting morsel of tasty...

Bobbie pinched herself hard. "Good grief. I can't stop thinking about him for even a whole minute."

With that challenging admonition, she forced her mind to clear. Five seconds went by. She hummed the national anthem and rinsed out her toothbrush. Another five seconds. She was succeeding. She was almost there. And then the image of Aidan wearing a pair of snug Buff Buns briefs popped right into her head.

She was obviously in need of professional help.

There was only one way to handle this—go to sleep and not think about the hunky man staying in the guest room...directly across the hall from hers. Nope. She wouldn't think about him at all.

But she did.

Despite all attempts to stop it, Bobbie wondered what he was doing over there. She hadn't heard a peep since they'd exchanged goodnights nearly a half hour earlier. Maybe he was reading. Or changing his clothes for bed. Except Aidan didn't have any extra clothes to change into.

Oops.

Some hostess she was. Bobbie hurried out of the bathroom and across the hall.

"Uh, Aidan?" She knocked on the door. "I should have asked sooner, but do you need any pajamas or anything? I probably don't have anything that'd fit you, but I'm sure my uncles have a pair if you'd like me to—"

The door flew open. Aidan was naked.

Well, almost.

He'd stripped off his shirt and shoes and wore only his unbelted, unsnapped jeans. Nothing was in the way of her getting a great view of his chest.

As chests went, it was a mouth-waterer. Toned. Tanned. Tight. Nothing over- or understated. Just an absolutely perfect chest sprinkled with dark coils of hair.

Without meaning to, her attention drifted lower.

His stomach was a prize-winner too, but she stopped her gaze from going below that.

Well, she stopped after a quick peek.

"Pajamas," Bobbie repeated after she swallowed hard. No, he might not be naked, but her mind had no trouble whatsoever filling in the blanks. Or in this case, her mind had no trouble mentally stripping him down to bare skin.

He shook his head. "I don't use pajamas. But thanks anyway."

"Oh. Okay. I do have some extra large T-shirts if you'd like that instead."

"I don't need a T-shirt either." He paused. "Unless you object to me sleeping raw in your guest bed."

"Raw." He meant naked. Stark-naked. His nude body on her two-hundred-thread-count percale sheets. "Of course I don't object."

But it'd be a first. And something she wouldn't mind catching a glimpse of.

Bobbie felt her cheeks grow warm. What had gotten into her? These get-Aidan-naked thoughts had to stop. Now. Immediately! This instant!

So, why did that image of Buff Buns and his buff buns keep tormenting her?

He reached over and took a box from the top of the chest of drawers. The simple motion caused a gazillion muscles to flex in his chest. It also did an effective job of sending her breath into the vicinity of her left big toe.

"This was tucked just beneath the bed, and I accidentally stepped on it. I don't think I damaged any of the rhinestones though."

Nestled in the fuchsia gift box were a black-laced chartreuse corset and a tacky tiara. The rhinestones were arranged to spell out Ima Goddess.

"Oh. They're birthday gifts from Crystal," Bobbie mumbled. She quickly took the box from him. "I wondered where I'd left them."

Well, not *wondered* exactly. That implied she had wanted to find them. Actually, Bobbie had stuck them and other assorted Crystal-ish gifts beneath the bed in the guest room in the hopes she wouldn't have to see them again. Crystal had been her best friend since second grade, but the woman had absolutely no taste.

"Not exactly your style, huh?" Aidan asked.

She shook her head. "I would have preferred a subscription to a travel magazine, but Crystal thinks I have too many of those as it is."

He smiled at her. Just smiled. And stood there looking better than any man had a right to look.

Oh, mercy. What he did to her hormone levels.

Bobbie was about to issue another goodnight and get her own buns away from the provocative sight of his chest, but Aidan spoke before she could figure out how to get her mouth working again.

"I've been thinking about your missing underwear problem. Have you thought about installing security cameras in the warehouse?"

Oh. Business talk. Good. It might help keep her head straight. "Umm, not really, but this is the first time anything like this has happened."

"Well, I think you should try them out for the next few weeks anyway. I could order some cameras from a friend in Boston and install them for you. That way, it'd keep the surveillance hush-hush, and we might be able to catch the thief on film. Any objections?"

"No. Of course not. You think even more underwear might go missing?"

He shrugged. "Hard to say. This isn't your usual, run-of-the-mill crime."

No. And Bobbie decided to leave it at that. The discussion about underwear only made her want to speculate about the color, or lack thereof, of Aidan's. With him that close, and with his musky male scent stirring around her, it wasn't a good idea to dwell on "lack thereof's."

It only reminded her of all the things he wasn't lacking.

"Goodnight, Aidan. See you in the morning."

Bobbie forced herself away from him and heard the door close between them. Good thing, too. If he knew the thoughts she had on her mind, he'd have shut it in her face the moment she knocked.

Or maybe he would have invited her to his bed.

Which couldn't happen.

No way.

She was really starting to feel a little desperate. It was obviously time to read some of her travel magazines. Reading of faraway place would certainly…remind her of other things she couldn't have.

But still, they were safe unattainable things.

She'd just gotten into bed when the phone on her nightstand rang. "Hello, Crystal," Bobbie answered without waiting to verify who it was.

"How'd you know it was me?" Crystal asked.

"Because you're the only person who calls this time of night."

"True. But tonight I have a reason for calling. I heard from Etta who heard from Marilee who heard from Quincy about the washed-out road. Then, I heard from Carol who heard from Sissy that your uncles weren't at the house. They're staying in town tonight, meaning that you are out there alone with Mr. Wonderful. I just wanted to make sure he's not giving you any trouble."

"No trouble," Bobbie quickly let her know. Well, not the kind of trouble that Crystal meant. "Why'd you ask?"

"Oh, I don't know. Maybe it has something to

do with the fact that Aidan's practically a stranger, and yet you invited him to spend the night. Alone. While your uncles are miles away, and there's no one around to hear your pitiful cries for help if you do indeed need to make pitiful cries for help.''

Bobbie huffed. ''Aidan's not a stranger. Besides, he didn't have a choice about staying here. It wasn't safe for him to try to drive back into town.''

''You think a washed-out road will put a sick, twisted mind on hiatus? Ever thought of that, huh?'' Crystal didn't wait for Bobbie to answer that vague but ridiculous question. ''Anyway, I want you to lock your bedroom door tonight.''

Another huff. Most of her conversations with Crystal were weird, but this one had taken weirdness to a whole different level. ''Okay, I'll bite. Why would I want to do that?''

''Because when you get right down to it, we don't know a lot about Aidan O'Shea, do we? He could be a closet serial killer. Or an escapee from the loony bin who forged his credentials so he could come to Liffey and pretend to be a deputy. He could even be one of those weirdo perverts who steals women's underwear.''

''Stop this, Crystal. Aidan isn't a criminal, insane or an underwear snatcher.''

''Yeah, right. You think that's what people said about Jack the Ripper?''

Bobbie frowned. "He's not Aidan the Ripper either. I'm hanging up now, and I plan to go to sleep so don't call back until morning."

"I won't if you promise me that you'll lock your door."

Bobbie wasn't in the mood to quibble with Crystal. Unfortunately, Crystal was a champion quibbler and usually won by pestering her opponent into submission. "I'll lock it." Bobbie crossed her fingers and hung up.

She snuggled into her pillows and pulled the quilt up to her chin. Crystal's concerns really were unfounded. Imagine, suggesting that Aidan was a criminal.

Imagine.

So what if she'd only known him a couple of weeks? So what if no one else in town knew him either? And so what if the underwear started to go missing only after Aidan arrived in Liffey?

So what...

And with that so-what question on her mind, Bobbie drifted off to sleep.

AIDAN GLANCED at the little porcelain fairy clock next to his bed. Midnight. And he still hadn't fallen asleep.

Of course, he hadn't expected to sleep well in Bobbie's house. The room smelled like her. Nothing perfumy. Just Bobbie. Like baby powder and summer rain. It was a scent he didn't want to get used to smelling, even for one night.

Did she have a clue just how close he'd come to asking her to join him in bed? Maybe. And maybe in her rose-colored world, she hadn't considered that he had something so lecherous on his mind as hauling her off to the sack. Too bad that wasn't his only lecherous thought. The proof of that was causing a three-ring circus in the nether regions of his body.

Angry about the washed-out road and even angrier with himself, Aidan tossed back the covers and got up. Maybe he could find a beer in her fridge or at least something that was totally unhealthy.

He'd already reached for the doorknob before he remembered he was buck-naked. Probably best not to shock the beer or the refrigerated item, so he stepped into his jeans and went downstairs. There was a small light on above the stove, and he used that to navigate.

Moving as quietly as he could, he opened the fridge. Unlike his, this one didn't contain moldy unidentifiable products. It contained food. Plenty of it. Even his usual brand of beer was on the bottom shelf.

Aidan grabbed a bottle of brew, then kneed the fridge door shut. Turned. And came face-to-face

with a raised, about-to-smack-his-head broom.
Startled, he nearly dropped the darn bottle.

"Great day!" Bobbie gasped and flicked on the
lights. "You scared the heck out of me."

Aidan had to clamp a hand on his chest to make
sure his heart stayed put. "I think we can say that
scaring part was mutual."

She put the broom aside, but Aidan thought he
still saw concern in her eyes. Not concern exactly.
Fear, maybe.

"Is something wrong?" Aidan asked.

"Oh, nothing." She took in a hard breath. "Uh,
there's some, uh, laundry in a hamper underneath
the sink in the bathroom. I was thinking about, uh,
moving it, um, out of your way. So you wouldn't
bump into it or anything."

He was sure he gave her a dumb look. With
reason. It was a dumb remark. "It's not in my
way."

"Well, still I shouldn't have left my, uh, underwear lying around in the hamper."

His dumb look must have intensified consider-
ably. "I thought you said they were under the
sink?"

She nodded. "But if it gets in your way, let me
know. That way, you wouldn't have to, uh, like
touch it or move it or anything."

God knows what she thought he'd be doing beneath her bathroom sink with her underwear. That

corset aside, Bobbie didn't look the sort of woman to have kinky lingerie or sex toys lying around. Still, she'd piqued his interest with those uh-ing, um-ing remarks, and he might have a look if he had to go back in there.

"I'm babbling," she confessed.

"Really?" Aidan tried to leave off the sarcasm but couldn't.

"I guess I'm just not used to having people here in the wee hours of the morning."

So, she didn't sleep around. Not that Aidan ever thought she had. Heck. That and the thought of kinky underwear kicked the lust factor up a notch. Why did he suddenly want to kiss her again?

Because he was obviously one sick puppy, that's why.

Bobbie glanced at the beer. The look of fear and discomfort left her eyes immediately. "Oh, you're thirsty. Let me get you a glass." Before Aidan could tell her no, she took the beer from his hand and headed for the cabinet. "Why don't you sit down at the table?"

"I don't expect you to wait on me."

Bobbie glanced over her shoulder and smiled. "I know, but isn't it nice every now and then to get something you don't expect?"

Not really, but Aidan made his way to the small tile-topped table anyway. He didn't want to feel obligated to this woman. Lusting after her was bad enough. He didn't want to add anything else to the mix.

As she'd promised, she brought him a glass of beer and set it in front of him. She didn't join him though. Bobbie got a glass of water and leaned against the counter that divided the kitchen from the dining room.

He tried not to notice how she was dressed. He really tried. But only blindness would have prevented him from noticing the pajama shorts set that skimmed her trim little body. Just like the outfit at the park, it was short in places best reserved for long things. Too bad she didn't own any extra-large, floor-length caftans.

Knowing he couldn't take much of that shortness, he chugged down the beer.

"Want me to get you another one?" she asked.

"No, thanks." He stood, intending to put the glass in the dishwasher. There was one problem with that. Bobbie stood between him and the dishwasher. Not good. In that little pajama set, she looked edible.

"How about some buns then?" Bobbie asked. But her eyes widened with alarm. "I meant *cinnamon* buns." She motioned toward the oven. "They're homemade with gobs of cream-cheese icing on them. Baking high-fat, high-sugar foods is one of my hobbies. It keeps me occupied while

I'm on the phone haggling with our suppliers and distributors.''

"Thanks anyway, but I'll pass on the baked goods." Best not to deal with anything bun-related while standing this close to her.

She set her glass on the counter. "Is it my imagination or are we both a little uncomfortable tonight?"

Aidan shrugged and tried not to appear amused that she'd stated the obvious. "It's the whole male-female thing. I don't usually spend the night with women that I, well, with women that I—"

Well, heck. He'd gotten right back on the subject of sex, and he hadn't even seen it coming.

"You only spend the night with your girlfriends," Bobbie provided. "I understand."

Girlfriends was a good word. But it wasn't exactly true. It implied some kind of relationship instead of just mindless, raw sex. He hadn't had a real relationship in nearly three years, not since Maggie Riley got tired of waiting for him to commit and ditched him for an accountant with a timeshare and a great dental plan.

"I'll admit I'm uncomfortable too," Bobbie continued. She motioned toward the phone. "Crystal called earlier. She was a little worried about you staying here."

"And she should be. You're a nice woman, and plenty of people would take advantage of that."

Like him, for instance.

"You think I'm nice," she repeated, the last word forming a smile. "Thank you."

Enough of this. Between her sexy outfit and that suddenly sexy smile, his brain was getting ready to crank up production of gallons of male hormones. With those stirring around inside him, his body could make all kinds of suggestions for a situation like this. Really ridiculous suggestions.

Like, he should kiss her so she'd quit smiling.

Aidan started to step around her. He didn't quite make it. The step around her turned into a brush against her. There was heat, and he could have sworn he felt another jolt of lightning pass between them.

Bobbie opened her mouth. But quickly closed it. What she'd been about to say, he didn't know, but she'd obviously changed her mind.

Aidan lowered his head. He *did* know why he did that. His body was no longer listening to the fact that this idea totally sucked.

He brushed his lips across hers. It was no more than a borderline peck. Well, maybe it had some punch to it, probably because her mouth had still been slightly open. Her breath was warm. Her lips, soft. And maybe it had a punch because she made that tiny noise that sounded like a sigh.

He waited for her to push him away. She didn't.

Not good. Aidan had counted on her to put a quick stop to this.

"Mercy," she whispered. "You're sooo good at that. I mean, *sooo* very good. You've got moves, Aidan. Real honest-to-goodness moves that make me crazy."

That wasn't the best thing a woman could say to a man trying to put a leash on his libido.

Especially when he knew he could do so much better.

"Moves, huh?" he questioned.

Aidan skimmed his hand down her back and edged her closer. Bobbie tightened her arms around him and pressed her body against his. And just kept on pressing. Even through her top, he could feel her breasts and her hardened nipples against his chest.

"Uh," she mumbled. Bobbie pulled in several deep breaths. Her hands trembled on his shoulders. "Uh."

That's about all Aidan could manage for several moments. He forced himself to take a step back so he wouldn't go for her mouth again.

"You should go to bed. Alone," he quickly added.

"Yes." She looked like a woman who'd just been whirled around in a high-heat wind tunnel. Aidan didn't have a mirror but figured he looked pretty much the same. "That kiss shouldn't have felt that way, should it?"

He could lie. But Aidan tried to avoid unnecessary, blatantly obvious lies whenever possible. "No."

"And we won't be doing it again, will we?" Bobbie asked cautiously.

"No. I'm leaving in less than a month. We don't have time to finish anything we start here."

And there was so much they could start.

She nodded. "I see what you mean. This was all like the Paddy Wrangler, but it's sort of turning into a bare-everything Full Monty."

Aidan nodded. Just nodded. Because frankly there was no good comeback for that. His life and this strange non-relationship he had with Bobbie had somehow turned into one big underwear analogy.

Bobbie paused a moment longer before she turned toward her room. The little swirling motion caused her shorts to swirl as well.

Great.

Now, he'd gotten an especially good view of her right bun. It was a winner, and it let him know that she did indeed have skimpy taste in underwear. Yep, he just might have to lower himself to having a look in her laundry basket.

"Good night, Aidan," she added over her shoulder.

Good night? Not a chance. Not after that kiss. Not after that peek at her buns.

Forget that the kiss they'd just shared was utterly insane.

Forget that he could still taste her.

What Aidan couldn't forget was that he, his mouth and just about every other pertinent part of him wanted her—bad.

8

The Secret Agent: Catalogue Item 007. This sleek and slinky daring brief has a concealed pocket next to the lightly padded pouch. For the man with more than a touch of class and adventure. Available in Cloak-and-Dagger Crimson, Secret Sapphire and Khaki Camouflage.

Caution: concealed pocket is *not* for sharp or flammable objects.

"TA-DA," Uncle Quincy proclaimed as he made his way into Bobbie's office. He extracted a ragged swatch of nutmeg-colored leather from a bag and plopped it onto her desk. "What do you think?"

Bobbie finished up a call with one of their iridescent fabric suppliers and then studied the item that was no doubt responsible for the gleeful look on her uncle's face. Over the years, she'd learned to choose her words wisely in situations like these.

"Hmm," she commented. Bobbie stood and

walked around her desk, observing the swatch from different angles.

It didn't help.

The only thing she could ascertain with any certainty was that it was brown and that it was slightly smaller than a breadbox.

"So?" Quincy inquired, anticipation all over his still-gleeful face.

"Hmm."

"It's for that new Heroes-a-Plenty line I told you about," Quincy added several moments later.

So, it was underwear and not a dust cloth or some preschooler's art project.

"Heroes-a-Plenty," she repeated. "Yes, I remember you talking about that."

That, and about a dozen other proposed lines with equally weird monikers. In fact, her uncles never proposed anything with normal names.

"Okay, you give up?" Quincy asked.

Bobbie gave it one last perusal but finally had to concede defeat. "Tell me."

"It's a lion-colored loin cloth. You know, as in what Tarzan wears? What better hero figure to use to launch the line?" Quincy used his fingers to make quotes in the air. "'The Jungle King. A wild, loose, free-form brief for times when you don't want to swing around with something tame.'"

Bobbie sincerely hoped that she was keeping a straight face. "Oh, that's, uh, nice."

Quincy beamed. "It's just the start." He yanked a pair of ruby-red boxers from his bag and laid them on her desk as well. "The Secret Agent. It's got a concealed pocket near the front pouch. And finally—the Law Enforcer."

He tossed a shimmering pair of silver briefs next to the Secret Agent. There was an equally shimmering cloth extension right in front that resembled the barrel of a gun. Bobbie didn't want to ask, but she assumed the wearer was meant to insert...something into the elongated projection. And she didn't have to guess what the wearer was supposed to insert. The shape left that embarrassingly clear.

"Obviously that one's for the man who's looking for a little something extra," Quincy explained.

Bobbie had already geared up for another "hmm" when she saw Jasper in the doorway. Despite the scowl that she immediately offered him, he invited himself in anyway.

Dressed in his best business suit, Jasper waltzed across her office and dropped a fat manila envelope among the underwear. "A travel itinerary," he announced without so much as a hello.

Bobbie folded her arms over her chest and tapped her foot on the floor. "Jasper, the only itinerary that would interest me would be one that sends you to a faraway land so you'll stop hounding me.''

That obviously didn't sink in, because Jasper continued his sales pitch.

''Just hear me out. Now that the lottery is officially over and you've had a couple of days to rid your system of Aidan O'Shea, I thought it was time for us to start making wedding plans. That itinerary is for a flight to Vegas. We'll get married tonight and leave for our honeymoon in Hawaii. Two weeks on the number-one rated beach in all the world. All the details are in that envelope.''

''Good grief,'' Bobbie mumbled.

This was past presumption. Past arrogance. Past low-level intelligence.

Bobbie snatched up the itinerary and shoved it back into Jasper's hands. It would have been a much more effective gesture of refusal if she hadn't snagged the Law Enforcer brief along with the bulky envelope. When Jasper grabbed hold of it, the shimmering elongated projection was, well, in a projected *up* position.

He frowned and handed her back the garment. ''This is your absolute last chance,'' he informed her, somehow ignoring the weird piece of underwear that had just passed between them. ''Bobbie, either you accept my proposal right here, right now, or you'll never be Mrs. Jasper Kershaw.''

"Is there a problem, Bobbie?" she heard someone ask.

Gripping a cardboard box, Aidan was in the doorway with a charming but irked expression on his face. It was obvious he'd heard Jasper's now-or-never ultimatum.

"Nope, there's no problem," Bobbie assured Aidan. "I was just about to tell Jasper what he could do with his wedding plans."

Quincy laughed. "And I was about to help her."

"Thanks, but I can handle this on my own." Bobbie turned her gaze to Jasper and gave him a look that could have easily chilled molten lava. "Have a good life, Jasper, but for heaven's sake, leave me out of it, please. I'd rather have an hourly dousing in Mr. Eidelson's Sensuous Massage Oil followed by multiple root canals than accept any proposal that you're offering. Goodbye."

Jasper's jaw twitched. "You'll regret this, Bobbie Fay Callahan. You'll see. One day you'll want me back in your life, and I won't be there."

And with that totally inaccurate observation, Jasper spun around and headed out, but not before giving Aidan the evil eye. Aidan's only response was a so-what, who-cares shrug.

She smiled at Aidan. "I didn't know you'd be coming by today."

"Is it a bad time?"

Bobbie shook her head. Funny, it never felt like a bad time to have Aidan around. Of course, that likely had something to do with his appearance. He looked yummy in his jeans and navy shirt.

Had it only been three days since he'd spent the night at her house? In some ways, it seemed as if it'd been years, and yet with him always on her mind, it was as if he was by her side every moment of every day. Life before Aidan was merely a dim memory.

"I'll just be going too," Quincy quickly let them know. "Get back to me on this new Heroes-a-Plenty line, will you, Bobbie?"

"Sure."

Bobbie added a mumbled good-bye to her uncle as he hurried out the door, but she couldn't seem to take her eyes off Aidan. But then, Aidan didn't take his eyes off her either. It was one magical moment. Until she noticed the slight arch of his right eyebrow and the puzzled line on his brow. Not only that, his attention wasn't exactly on her face. It was lower. In the general area of her hands.

Afraid of what she might see, Bobbie looked down and saw the shimmering Law Enforcer underpants. The projection thingy was still projecting onward and upward in the worst possible sort of way. And to add even more to an already embarrassing situation, she had her right hand clasped around *it* in a chokehold.

"Oh!"

She chucked the briefs onto her desk. However, the projection didn't waver. It was like some swamp thing that kept coming back to life. It reared its shimmering head even when she tried to push it down. Evidently, Uncle Quincy had used some sturdy padding. Bobbie finally gave up and gave it a good whack to flatten it like a fritter.

"Ouch," Aidan mumbled. He winced. "Let me guess—it's a new Boxers or Briefs' product?"

"More like an experiment gone awry. Uncle Quincy is the design brains of the business, but sometimes he gets a little carried away."

"I can see that." Aidan walked closer and held up the box. "These are the security cameras I ordered from a friend in Boston." He deposited the box on her desk and opened it so she could see the three golf-ball-sized devices. "After everyone's gone home for the night, I figured we could sneak into the warehouse and install them. That way, no one will be alerted about what we're doing."

"Good thinking." She checked her watch. "I guess I can meet you at the warehouse around eight then? Everyone should have gone home by then."

He nodded. "But don't park nearby. We don't want anyone to see us here."

"Clandestine stuff, huh?" She almost made reference to the Secret Agent, but there'd been enough underwear incidents for one day.

Aidan pushed some of the packing paper aside and extracted two thick glossy magazines from the box. "I ordered these for you."

"For me?" Bobbie took the publications as if they were fine precious crystal. "*Autumn Tours in New England*," she read aloud. "And *Weekends in New Orleans*."

Aidan moved closer and looked over her shoulder. "There are some articles about Boston that I thought you might like to read. And the New Orleans one has some great pictures of the French Quarter."

"Oh, Aidan. Thank you. No one's ever given me travel magazines before."

And that was all she managed to say before she whirled around to add more thanks to that and maybe even a hug. Too bad she caught him in the stomach with her elbow. At least, it only knocked the breath out of him for a couple of seconds. "I'm so sorry."

He waved off her apology. "I guess you like the magazines, huh?"

"Like them? No. I *love* them."

Aidan chuckled. "You're an easy woman to please, you know that?"

"There are hundreds of people who'd disagree." Bobbie flipped through the pages of the New Orleans guide and immediately landed on a moody black-and-white photo taken on Royal Street.

"Oh, Aidan, listen to this. 'Evenings in the Big Easy are a time for the slow, easy rhythm of a sax whining out the blues. For lazy strolls beneath the dim streetlights. For long, lingering dinners in the Vieux Carre. For dancing under the stars along the Moonwalk.'"

Bobbie pressed her hand over her heart. "Oh, doesn't that sound like a vacation to paradise?"

Aidan mumbled an agreement.

"'New Orleans,'" she continued to read. She had to fan herself. Was it her imagination that it was getting warmer in the room? "'Bask in the hottest, wettest…wildest city on earth. They don't call us the Big Easy for nothing.'"

Okay. So she hadn't expected to become aroused by reading a travel article. But then, Aidan and she were standing so close to each other.

Bobbie felt the air change between them. Electrons started to snap and crackle.

Uh-oh.

It was happening—again. She was thinking about kissing him. But then, she was always thinking about kissing Aidan. Not a peck either. A hot, wet, wild, mind-altering kiss. It would be pure kissing finesse with enough power to coax her straight to the bedroom.

Or even the desk.

She felt her body soften, and she struggled to keep a grip on the magazine. *Wow,* was all she could think, and it was a poor expletive for what was happening. That look in Aidan's eyes and that manly scent emanating from his body managed to alert every gland in her body.

Bobbie wanted to give in to the moment. Mercy, did she. And she might have if she hadn't heard an eerie little noise. It was like a muffled squeak, and it came from her desk. More specifically, it came from one of the underpants.

She slowly turned in that direction.

Ohmigosh!

There it was on the center of the desk. A shimmering Law Enforcer stiffy. The cloth projection obviously had some very stubborn fibers.

Under normal circumstances, Bobbie might have been able to laugh it off, but since Aidan was close to her and since he had some rather obvious needy fibers of his own, she thought it best to drop the subject.

Apparently, so did Aidan.

"So, I'll see you at the factory later tonight," he mumbled.

And Aidan walked away, their travel excerpts leaving her dizzy, breathless and with no solution about how to stifle certain shimmering feelings that were projecting all over the place.

"ALL DONE," Aidan let Bobbie know. He gave the monitor an adjustment to a split screen so it'd pick up all three camera angles at once.

She walked across the narrow stock room toward him. "Wow, we can see the whole warehouse. I should have done this weeks ago."

"It's motion activated," Aidan explained. "And the monitor's small enough that we can hide it on one of these shelves. But you won't have to come up here just to check the monitor. I can rig the video feed to go straight to your computer."

"Sounds great. Thanks."

He picked out a spot on the top shelf and tried to work quickly. It didn't take a brilliant mind to figure out that he shouldn't be huddled in a glorified closet with Bobbie. The physical attraction between them was like a lean, mean eating machine. The longer he stayed near her, the harder she was to resist. Of course, it was getting harder to resist her even when she wasn't around.

Heck, everything was getting harder in every sense of the word.

Aidan pulled down a box from the shelf to

make room but didn't see the smaller box stacked on top of it.

"Careful," Bobbie warned, a little too late.

The bulky cardboard box whacked him in the head and dumped soft, silky things all over the place. Underwear, of course. He hadn't expected anything else in the Boxers or Briefs' storage room.

"They're from our defunct private-order fantasy line," Bobbie explained as she quickly plucked the garments off him. "Uncle Winston wanted to save them for gifts for bachelor parties and such."

Aidan held up a nearly transparent pair of boxers. It had a beach on it with two scantily clad lovers being sloshed by waves.

"Do they all have the same design?" he asked, rubbing the whacked spot on his forehead.

"No." Bobbie didn't look at him. She stooped down and began to snatch the garments from the floor. "They're supposed to be various fantasies. You know—the perfect place, the perfect time, the perfect person sort of thing?"

What a way to pique his interest.

Before she could gather up all of them, Aidan grabbed another pair. Oh, man. It was one of those Roman fanning scenes, and a lot of things were getting fanned.

He made a sound of amusement.

"What—did you find one that was your particular fantasy?" Bobbie asked, her voice teasing.

He tossed the briefs into the box. "Sorry to disappoint you, but guys don't really have fantasies. Sex in itself is the fantasy."

Bobbie laughed. "In other words, there is no wrong place, wrong time, wrong woman."

Just like that, Aidan's grin faded. A couple of weeks ago he would have totally agreed with her. But not now. Timing and place were sure up for grabs, but if he were honest with himself, Bobbie was the only woman he wanted.

The *only* woman.

Heck. That was a sobering thought, and it came at time when he wished no such sobriety.

She stood, the box still in her hand, and she proceeded to shove it back on the shelf. When he saw her struggling with it, Aidan stepped closer to help her. Instead of helping though, Bobbie looked at him, and her mouth dropped open.

"Oh no." She dropped the box and sent the underwear sprawling again. "You're bleeding, Aidan."

It wasn't what he thought he'd hear after discussing fantasies. "Where?"

She grabbed a pair of the silky fantasy briefs and pressed them to his forehead. "It must have happened when the box hit you. I'm so sorry."

Florence Nightingale couldn't have sprung into

action any better. She gently dabbed and wiped, all the while right in his face examining him.

"Are you dizzy or anything?" she asked.

"I'm fine." And because she looked slightly frantic, Aidan gently caught onto her wrist. "It's just a paper cut. Odds are I'll live."

Her mouth quivered a little. "Good. Because you look a little ridiculous with this hologram belly dancer brief pressed to your head."

Aidan glanced at the scene on the underpants. Yep. It was indeed a hologram belly dancer, and when the angle of the fabric changed, the dancer undulated her stomach. "Who thought up these fantasies anyway?"

"The uncles." Bobbie sighed heavily. "I thought once they officially retired, they'd leave this sort of thing to the design folks, but as you witnessed earlier today, they still like to dabble."

Yes. Dabbling indeed. Hard to forget an aroused Law Enforcer brief. Aidan pitied the poor model they'd have to talk into wearing that one.

"The bleeding stopped," she let him know. Bobbie moved closer to examine his forehead again.

Too bad that examination took on a whole new meaning when her breasts swished across his chest.

And it was really too bad that she lost her footing on the silky underthings on the floor and landed right in his arms. Her leg between his. She came within a fraction of kneeing him in the groin.

It might have been better in the long run if she had.

Without the excruciating pain that would have resulted from a good kneeing, Aidan had nothing to concentrate on but the fact that he had Bobbie smashed against him. The smashing proved too much to handle. He lowered his head and did what he'd been wanting to do for days.

There was one word for how she made him feel. *Pleasurable.* When their mouths came together, it was like a holiday cruise and a round-the-world trip all rolled into one. She kissed him as if it would be the last kiss she'd ever experience. He kissed Bobbie as if she were the love of his life.

Uh, whoa.

Aidan ran that idea through his head again. Had he really thought of Bobbie and love in the same sentence? Yeah, he had. Not his brightest idea, even if it hadn't felt as repulsive and foreign as it should have.

But he didn't love her.

No.

He respected her. Admired her. Lusted after her in the worst kind of way. What he didn't do was love her.

The kiss continued. Bobbie slid her hand around the back of his neck and started to play with his hair. Aidan took that as a challenge and started to play with hers. Hers, however, lay practically on her breasts. Well, it was close enough to her breasts that he didn't have to lower his fingers more than an inch or two.

She was perfect. Small but firm. He hadn't remembered small necessarily being so darn erotic, but mercy, it was just that. Aidan cupped his hand around her and enjoyed the little shiver of pleasure she made.

Normally, playing with Bobbie's breasts would have occupied him completely, but he kept going back to that ridiculous notion of love. And it *was* ridiculous. Even if he wanted to fall in love with Bobbie—and he absolutely, emphatically didn't—it would turn her life upside down and inside out. He couldn't do that to her. After all, he was leaving town soon.

So, there it was. No love. Just a mutual kind of respect for each other, some serious making out, and perhaps even full-blown lovemaking once or twice before they went their separate ways.

Aidan felt himself floating downward, downward, downward and realized he was easing them to the floor. Not necessarily a good thing since they were in a cramped storage room. But since Bobbie was doing as much floating downward as he was, it didn't seem preventable.

Hands and bodies adjusted when they landed in

an embrace amid the fantasy briefs. Aidan's right hand lucked out and ended up on the buttons of her snug peach-colored business jacket. While still kissing her, he undid them only to find a nearly naked woman beneath. She wore only a bra. A tiny one at that. All lace. It was the best fantasy Aidan could have imagined.

He sampled, of course. Both the lace and the woman beneath it. And he sampled more when she urged him on by latching onto his ears and hauling him closer.

"You are one amazing woman," he let her know.

"You're not so bad yourself, Deputy O'Shea."

Oh, man. She didn't just whisper it. She said it a sultry, sexy way that had him grinning from ear to ear.

Aidan suddenly wanted more. A lot more. And he slid his hand along her panty hose. It didn't take him long to figure out that they weren't panty hose after all but thigh-high stockings. They gave him a couple of inches of bare skin for his fingers to explore. Bobbie moaned and arched into his touch.

Talk about the ultimate fantasy.

And speaking of fantasies, Aidan remembered something that had given him lots of lusty thoughts. He unzipped her skirt, slid it down a bit and located that tasty little navel ring. He eased himself lower. Pressed his mouth to her stomach. And circled her navel with his tongue.

He kissed.

Tasted.

Lingered.

Until Bobbie gasped.

He lifted his head, worried that he'd snagged the navel ring with his tongue. "What's wrong?"

She pointed to the monitor on the table just above them. "That's Rudy Tate. What the heck is he doing here this time of night? And look, he's on his way up the stairs."

Aidan glanced at the screen, and sure enough, the man was headed right their way. Somehow, he managed to untangle himself from Bobbie, but it wasn't easy. He could hardly move, much less untangle.

Bobbie redid buttons as fast as her fingers could manage. He gave his jeans an adjustment. They both tried to get rid of the I-nearly-got-lucky gleams in their eyes. In fact, they were still ridding themselves of various gleams, discomforts and disarrays when the door flew open.

The floor manager looked. Blinked. And looked some more. "Uh, Bobbie?" Rudy questioned.

"Hi, Rudy." She'd obviously aimed for a light tone. She failed.

The floor manager stared at them a moment, and it was hard to say who looked more uncomfortable. "I, uh, was driving past the factory and saw somebody skulking around the place. The person ran off, but they managed to spray-paint some ugly, misspelled words on the side of the building. Something about Naughty Guys. At least, I think that's what it says. The person didn't have very good penmanship. Oh, and your name's on there, too, Bobbie."

"Good grief," she mumbled.

Aidan mumbled something much worse. While he'd been playing underwear-navel games with Bobbie, someone had been committing a crime right under his nose. Not the best testament to his law-enforcement skills.

"I was about to go after this spray painter," Rudy continued. "But then I saw the light on and thought I'd better check things out. Is there more underwear missing? Is that why y'all are up here?"

"No," Aidan and Bobbie said in unison.

They glanced at each other. Bobbie's lipstick was smeared to a blotchy peachy blur, and her hair was sticking out in various places where it normally wouldn't be sticking out. But neither of those things was as telling as the pair of silky fantasy boxers snagged on the buttons of her jacket.

Aidan didn't dare hope that his appearance was any better, especially since he really needed to give his jeans another adjustment.

Fortunately, like most people in town, Rudy wasn't an idiot. Or a person who wanted to see them squirm unnecessarily. After a quick perusal of their clothes, he tipped his fingers to his eyebrow in a mock salute. "I'll just be saying goodnight then. You two can go back to, uh, whatever you were doing before I interrupted you."

"We were just leaving," Bobbie informed him. And to prove her little-white-lie point, she grabbed her glossy travel magazines and her purse.

The hasty exit was obviously a maneuver to make it seem as if Bobbie and Aidan were casual acquaintances instead of almost lovers. It didn't fool Rudy, and it probably wouldn't have fooled anyone else with partial eyesight and limited reasoning abilities either.

Even more, Bobbie and Aidan couldn't very well claim that this was all part of the Twango-Drifter plan because there hadn't been a soul around to witness the romantic tangle. Ditto for blaming it on the lottery. It'd ended days earlier.

So, for better or worse, his relationship with Bobbie had just gone public in a very public sort of way. By morning, just about everyone would know that he was one naughty guy.

9

The Hot Shot Fireman: Catalogue Item 259. This racy minibrief with see-through back could be just the thing to add a spark to your love life. Patent pending, water-filled front pouch for a natural-looking enhancement. Can you stand the heat that you'll start with the Hot-Shot Fireman? Available in Fiery Red, Smoky Gray and Daring Dalmatian.

BOBBIE CHECKED her watch and drummed her fingers on the armrest of the styling chair. She should have just cancelled her weekly appointment and fixed her hair herself. "Could you hurry it a little, Crystal?"

Crystal met her gaze in the enormous mirror and clamped the curling iron over another chunk of Bobbie's hair. "Hey, beauty can't be rushed."

"Well, in this case it has to be. I don't want to be late."

"Yeah, you've said something along that same vein two times already." Crystal gave her gum a crack. "And two times I've put off asking you exactly what has you in a lather. I've also avoided asking you why you're wearing your best-fitting black jeans, silk shirt and an ample splashing of your most expensive perfume."

Yes, Crystal hadn't asked, but she moved closer in such a way that Bobbie knew she was waiting for her to tell all.

Bobbie glanced around the salon. There were two women with enormous pink rollers on their heads perched under mauve bubble-head hair dryers. The dryers were off, and they were gossiping about a possible romance between Jasper and Maxine. Two more customers were waiting, gossiping about her Uncle Quincy and Thelmalita Hopkins. And Mary Feldman, one of Bobbie's employees, was having her chin waxed by Crystal's assistant, Buffy Leigh. They were going on about Uncle Winston keeping company with three different women, including one of the ladies under the hair dryers.

Telling a secret in the Curl Up and Dye Beauty Palace would be similar to broadcasting it on an international satellite link.

And boy, did Bobbie have a secret.

Aidan and she were doing a stakeout. At least that was the way Bobbie had proposed the idea to Aidan. Since it'd take at least two days for the additional outside security cameras to arrive, a

stakeout was the best way to catch the graffiti artist. And since Aidan wasn't familiar with the
woods surrounding the parking lot, she felt com-
pelled to show him a way to sneak onto the property. That meant she had to sneak on as well, and
since she was doing that, she'd just stay with him
and become his second pair of eyes.

Of course, that idea had sounded a lot better
before she gave it some thought.

And then it just sounded truly stupid.

That second-eyes part aside, it meant that she'd
be alone with Aidan in a delivery van. A-l-o-n-e.
As in, the last possible thing she should be when
it came to Aidan.

Of course, it was only for an hour or two. And
she had no ulterior motives. Really. But for that
hour or two, she'd no doubt be tempted beyond
belief. This time though, there might not be an
interruption from Rudy Tate, and then where
would they be?

Bobbie pushed that question aside.

Best not to dwell on things that created a warm
glow in her body.

Crystal's eyebrow lifted a fraction, and she
leaned closer so she could whisper in Bobbie's
ear. "Is this about that stakeout Aidan and you are
doing tonight over at the factory?"

Bobbie gasped and looked around to make sure
no one had heard. Thankfully, she noted that they

all still seemed to be engrossed with their gossip sessions. "How the devil did you know that?" Bobbie demanded in an angry whisper.

Crystal shrugged. "I heard you talking about it on the phone last night when I dropped by to get some leftovers. Don't worry, I won't tell a soul. But a stakeout sure seems a little, well, drastic, doesn't it?"

"Not really. It was bad enough when I had someone stealing underwear, but now there's a spray painter out there. And I want this person caught, immediately. A stakeout is a valid law-enforcement course of action to help identify the culprit."

Crystal just stared at Bobbie and hot-curled another hank of her hair. "I'll just bet this has something to do with that hickey on your neck."

Bobbie sighed. So, she hadn't hidden it as well as she'd hoped. So much for the industrial-strength cover-all concealer she'd slathered on.

Crystal leaned closer and examined the evidence of Bobbie's encounter with Aidan. "That's a real beaut. Nice form. No zazzedy edges. Shows he's got good suction. I give it high marks."

"You actually have a rating scale for hickeys?"

"You bet. That's at least, umm, a nine on a scale of one to ten. Possibly a nine-point-five. The only reason I'm counting off a half point is because he put another one so close to it. Aidan could of spaced them a little farther apart for better balance.''

Bobbie begged to differ. Each one of those hickeys was dead center on an erogenous zone. You couldn't get better balance than that.

"By the way," Crystal continued, "I heard from Donette who heard from Agnes Masterson who heard from Sissy that last night Aidan and you were in the storage room trying on belly dancing underwear.''

"What!" Since her outburst had obviously drawn the attention of the other customers, Bobbie waited until their eyes and ears were off her before she continued. "We were not trying on underwear. That's preposterous. We were in that storage room, uh, looking for the thief.''

Crystal grinned and winked at her. "And those hickeys are Aidan's special search-and-seizure attempts, huh? Boy, I wouldn't mind a full-body search if I could get that kind of treatment.''

Bobbie scowled. "Could you please just finish my hair? I have to go.''

Crystal put the curling iron aside and started combing her out. Finally. "You're going to sleep with Deputy Hot-Bod tonight?''

"No!" Bobbie was almost certain that she managed to look indignant. And she had to wait again until the other ladies looked away. This time, however, she was sure a couple of them were still listening so she lowered her voice to a whisper. "Where do you get these absurd ideas? I swear, Crystal, you have a wild imagination. And you're an incurable romantic, in a weird degenerate sort of way. Added to that, you also have a bad memory. I've sworn off men for all eternity, remember?"

Bobbie had already geared up to point out other aspects of Crystal's silly assertions, but she suddenly heard her own words ringing in her head. The lady was definitely protesting too much, and the protest was somewhat diminished by the fact she was sporting hickeys from the very man she was protesting about. Plus, she'd put that emergency condom in her purse.

"Okay, you got me," Bobbie admitted on a loud huff. "Despite all my efforts to stop it from happening, I like Aidan."

"You like him," Crystal repeated. She grinned in victory. The grin, however, quickly faded. "Then, why don't you look happy? It's not because Aidan's pulling a Jasper routine, is it?"

Bobbie shook her head. "Other than the fact that they're both male, Aidan and Jasper have nothing in common. And I'm not completely sure about that male parallel. I have a sneaking suspicion that Jasper is really of the fungal family."

"No argument here." Crystal put the comb aside and spritzed Bobbie's hair with some floral-scented spray. "So, why aren't you happy if you've discovered that Aidan's the best thing to come along since the creation of the hot fudge sundae?"

Bobbie shrugged. "I think that's obvious. Because there can never be anything between us other than hickeys and travel discussions, that's why."

"Who says?"

"Common sense and logic say. Aidan's in the law-enforcement exchange program. Have you forgotten that he's leaving town soon?"

Crystal tossed that indignant look right back at her. "Have you forgotten that you could follow him if you really wanted to?"

Bobbie stared at her as if she'd sprouted a third eye. "I can't. I've got to run the factory—"

"Enough of those tired old excuses, Bobbie Fay Callahan." Crystal did a blah-blah-blah motion with her hand. "You can't travel because of the factory. You can't fall in love because of Jasper's jilting. Well, let me tell you something—that factory can't cuddle with you on a cold, stormy night. It can't take you to Paris. And Jasper's jilting can't give you a nine-point-five hickey."

"Who said I wanted hickeys?" Bobbie yanked off the chartreuse vinyl styling cape and handed it to Crystal. "I spent the last two hours just trying to cover these up."

But that didn't stop Crystal. Oh, no. She was on a roll, so it didn't matter if the premise was plain stupid. She just kept on. "You're probably well on your merry way to falling in love with him. The way I see it, that means you should at least try to figure out if there's a possibility for all that happily-ever-after stuff."

Bobbie got out of the chair, grabbed her purse and headed to the door. She still kept her voice low but had no doubts that she was providing future fodder for the gossips of Liffey. "Happily ever after is the last thing I'm looking for, Crystal. And I'm not in love with Aidan O'Shea. It's just lust. Plain old-fashioned—"

"Okay, I get it. Lust. Yeah. Yeah. Nothing more." Crystal followed Bobbie outside and shut the door behind them. "Well, except for that *really like him* part that you admitted to a couple of seconds ago. Sounds like more than lust if you ask me."

Bobbie waved her off. "I don't have time for this." Besides, she was losing the argument. She reached for her car door but not before noticing that every single customer in the beauty palace was at the window staring at them. Mary even waved, despite the fact the lower half of her face was covered with gunky yellow wax.

"So let me get this straight," Crystal said softly. "Even though you *really like* Aidan, you'll just let him leave without trying to figure out if there's something possible beyond the hickey stage of this relationship?''

Bobbie got into her car so she wouldn't have to answer. The truth was—they were already well beyond that particular stage of intimacy. After all, Aidan had tongued her navel.

That sort of thing just created a special bond between people.

She almost managed a getaway, but Uncle Winston's frantic waving and shouts stopped her. He barreled out of Piggly Wiggly and hurried to her, the jingle bobs on his cowboy boots jangling.

Bobbie gave her collar an adjustment so she could cover up her neck. Fortunately, it was practically dark, so her uncle wouldn't get a good look at the hickeys. Such an observation would only result in more questions and loftily raised hopes that love was in the air. Hopes that would get dashed when Aidan rode out of town.

Of course, her uncles knew Aidan was leaving as well as she did. Still, she'd seen those matchmaking glimmers in their eyes and the way they grinned uncontrollably when they saw Aidan and her together. Heaven knows why they would encourage something that was so temporary, but maybe they felt Aidan would change his mind and stay in Liffey. Bobbie knew without a doubt that wouldn't happen.

Aidan wasn't a put-down-roots sort of guy.

And she was.

Well, she was because of the factory. Even though it seemed harder and harder to keep those roots from easing right out of the ground.

Winston handed her a dollar-bill-sized gift bag through the window. "It's from Mr. Eidelson. It's his new Fire Starter Massage Oil. He dropped it off earlier."

"And you actually took it?" Bobbie tried to hand it back to him, but Winston pressed it into her hands. "The man's a lunatic, Uncle Winston. You should have run in the other direction when you saw him."

"But this is a new product. It's colorless, only lightly scented and chocolate-flavored at that. None of that smelly concoction he's been trying to sell. This stuff's even edible. I thought maybe we could include it as a promotion when we premiere the Hot-Shot Fireman." He yanked the fire-hydrant-shaped vial from the bag. "See? It'd be perfect for our Dalmatian-print briefs."

"Cute," Bobbie mumbled as she glanced at the little silver object. "But I have no intentions of opening that. I have horrible recent memories of being chased by critters because of Mr. Eidelson's mixtures. Personally, I think we should get a restraining order against the man. Or else buy a case of gas masks."

"All right, I'll figure out what to do with it tomorrow." Winston gave her a maternal pat on the cheek and slipped the vial into the bag. He reached over and crammed both into her purse. "Just put it on my desk when you're at the factory doing the stakeout with Aidan, will you?"

Bobbie's jaw almost hit her ribbed leather steering wheel cover. "Who says I'm doing a stakeout with Aidan?"

He shrugged as if it were the most obvious answer in the world. "I overheard you talking about it yesterday when he dropped by."

"Oh, for Pete's sake."

If Winston knew, then dozens of others likely did as well. So much for anything covert. Half the town had probably gotten wind of the stakeout, and they were no doubt telling the other half. By the time she made it to the parking lot, there probably wasn't a soul who wouldn't know.

So why didn't that stop her from going?

Bobbie almost pondered that question, but she knew the pondering would just frustrate her even more.

With a huff, she pressed the accelerator. She wasn't fast enough, however. She still managed to hear Sheriff Cooper calling out to her. Bobbie pulled over. Sweet heaven, at this rate she wouldn't make it to the stakeout in this century.

"I guess you're on your way to join Aidan?"

the sheriff said. "Well, I won't keep you. I just wanted to let you know that we found some of the missing underwear a little while ago."

That captured her attention. "Really, where?"

"They turned up in the donation box over at the Shady Days Senior Citizens' Home. Gotta tell you though, Bobbie, that not all of them were recovered. A couple of folks refused to give back the Bold-as-Brass Sheik Yerbootees. Said those racy underpants really put sparks in their love lives, and they'd settle up with you next time they saw you. I thought about confiscating them, but since the fellas had already worn them, I thought it best not to."

Bobbie eagerly nodded. "I agree. Thanks for letting me know." She started to drive away.

Again, she didn't get far.

"By the way," the sheriff casually called out. "Tell Aidan I said hello. Oh, and you did a really good job covering up those hickeys. I can hardly see them."

Bobbie gave her head a good bop on the steering wheel and started driving.

AIDAN TOOK the mini binoculars from his jacket pocket and surveyed the grounds. Bobbie had picked a good spot. The delivery van was at the far end of the parking lot, but it gave them a good view of both the back and side entrances—the two most logical places for the graffiti artist to make a repeat performance.

Of course, it wasn't a given that this particular culprit would react in a logical manner. After all, they were likely dealing with a certifiable nut who had trouble spelling. Two to one it was someone he knew. He'd met a lot of certifiable nuts since his stay in Liffey.

"See anything?" Bobbie whispered.

"Nope. All clear." Aidan settled deeper into the seat to get more comfortable.

"I hope, this won't be a waste of time." She paused. "Sheriff Cooper told me about the underwear showing up at the senior citizens' home. I guess that rules out theft for profit, huh?"

Aidan shrugged. "Not necessarily. The thief could have gotten antsy and decided to ditch the stolen goods. In other words, this might not be over." He put the binoculars aside and took the cup of coffee that she poured him from the thermos. It had a nice chocolaty smell, and the aroma filled the cab of the van. "Thanks."

"I've got some extra packets of sugar in my purse if you need it," she offered. "Oh, shoot." A look of horror crossed her face. "I forgot about Mr. Eidelson's massage oil."

Aidan fully understood that horrified look when Bobbie extracted the tiny silver fire hydrant and held it up for him to see. "Please tell me that doesn't contain what I think it contains."

"It does," she admitted. "I don't know about you, but I don't want it near me."

He agreed. Aidan didn't waste any time. Treating it like the dangerous potion that it was, he snatched the container from her hand, opened the van door and tossed it into a nearby grassy area. Later, he'd call the fire department and request a biohazard clean-up.

"Whew." Bobbie added a sound of relief. "Close call. Uncle Winston handed it to me right as I was leaving, and somehow I forgot about it."

Aidan wasn't sure he wanted to know what was so enthralling that it would make her forget something like the unforgettable massage oil, but he thought it might have something to do with those love bites he'd left on her neck. As hard as it was to broach a subject like that, he did owe her a whopper of an apology.

Aidan motioned to the general area of his indiscretions. "I'm really sorry about, uh, all of that. I don't know what got into me. I mean, I haven't done anything like that since junior high."

She dismissed it with a flippant wave of her hand and an oh-that sound. "Don't worry about it. I think we both lost our heads. A temporary lapse in judgment, that's all. I haven't given it a moment's thought."

Good.

So, they were in complete, total agreement.

Well, except for that *moment's thought* part.

Aidan had certainly thought about it—and for far more than a moment. In fact, it was all he could think about while he had tossed and turned the night before. And the morning after. And through lunch. He'd still had it on his mind while he ate dinner.

And even now.

He just hadn't been able to get the taste of Bobbie out of his mouth. Or the sound of her responding to him when he kissed her. Or the way she'd whispered his name. For that matter, the memory of her breasts had haunted him, too, but that no doubt would have happened even if he hadn't felt guilty about the love bites.

In short, he wanted her more than his next law-enforcement exchange assignment.

It was a truly terrifying thought. Even now, with her this close, it felt as if someone had super-honed his senses. Every fiber of his body was completely aware of every fiber of hers. Too bad all that fiber awareness made him remember the letter he had in his pocket.

The letter that contained his next law-enforcement exchange assignment.

The letter that would send him on his way.

Away from Bobbie.

Aidan hadn't opened it yet. There was no particular reason for that. Really. He was just looking for the right moment, and that right moment hadn't surfaced yet. That likely had something to do with all that tossing and turning he'd done while trying to forget that Bobbie Callahan was the most unforgettable woman he'd ever met.

"What happened between us was really no big deal," Bobbie continued, her voice a little strained. She made another of those oh-that gestures with her hand. "It was just a case of lust. Temporary lust," she added, sounding even more strained and not the least oh-that.

Aidan mumbled an agreement. But this didn't feel quite as temporary as temporary should feel.

"And besides, it was practically meaningless," she went on. "You're leaving town soon. I'm staying here, of course. Like I always do. Basically, we have no chance of a future together. And so what if we indulged in a little kissing? And touching. And all that other stuff."

It was the thought of some of that other stuff that started to fan fires that in no such way needed fanning. Big fires. Hot ones. Big blazes. Fires that throbbed and raged through his body. Fires that only Bobbie could extinguish—

"Ohmigosh, what the heck is that big thing, Aidan?"

Sweet Nantucket! He hadn't meant for her to

notice *that!* Except she wasn't looking anywhere near his jeans.

Aidan followed the direction of her suddenly wide gaze and saw the bulky dark object lumbering through the grassy patch near the van. The blob stopped where he'd tossed Mr. Eidelson's massage oil.

"It's a bear," he informed her.

She gasped. Even though it wasn't a very manly reaction, Aidan nearly did the same when the creature latched onto the bag and began ripping it to shreds. He gobbled down the vial of oil in one gulp.

Aidan had never actually seen a bear outside the confines of a zoo, and this sucker was huge. There was no way he wanted to tangle with something that size. Thank heaven the animal seemed only interested in the massage oil and not in the two wide-eyed humans in the van.

The bear turned.

Looked right at him.

And began to climb onto the hood.

Bobbie shrieked and crawled into Aidan's lap. "Ohmigosh. Ohmigosh. Ohmigosh. What do we do?"

It took Aidan a moment to find the soothing words that Bobbie obviously needed. Heck, he needed them, too. "We wait. He'll go away eventually."

At least he hoped he would.

Because they had a thick slab of glass between them, Aidan didn't panic. But it was a definite challenge to stay calm under this sort of pressure. The bear looked determined to locate more of that massage oil, and he probably wouldn't mind chomping on a few humans if they got in his way.

Bobbie buried her face against his shoulder. "Is it gone yet?"

"Uh, not exactly." He wouldn't dare tell her that it was licking and pawing the windshield. "Maybe it'll help if he can't see us. You know— out of sight, out of mind?"

With Bobbie still tangled like a vine around him, Aidan eased out of the seat and stepped into the narrow corridor that led into the body of the van. He positioned them behind some stacked boxes of underwear.

And waited.

Unfortunately, they waited with Bobbie snuggled in his arms. To be more specific, on his lap. Even with the threat of the bear, it was hard not to dwell on contact like that.

"I should have known this would happen," Bobbie whispered. Her breath was hot and fast, and it brushed like delicate lips against his neck. "That massage oil's been nothing but trouble from day one."

"I have to agree with you there. Must be potent

stuff to attract a bear, and yet, it doesn't seem to have any effect on humans.''

She paused, stiffened slightly and lifted her head from his shoulder. In the darkness, their gazes met. ''No. No effect whatsoever.''

Too bad her voice wavered on that last word. And too bad he knew that look in her eye meant she'd realized they were squished against each other. But Aidan couldn't blame this reaction on the oil. Or the moment.

Or anything else.

She gulped. ''And with that bear just outside, there's no way that either of us could be feeling any...''

''Lust?'' Aidan finished.

''Yes. There's no way we could be feeling anything like that.''

It was the right thing to say, even if it was a pitiful lie. The lie was only seconds old when Aidan brushed his mouth over hers. She brushed her mouth over his. And they just kept brushing until it turned into a full-fledged kiss.

''Why do we do this kind of stuff?'' Bobbie mumbled against his lips.

Aidan shook his head. ''To heck if I know. Maybe it *is* the massage oil after all. Or maybe there's a full moon or something. Tell you what. Let's save ourselves some time here. We can't talk ourselves out of kissing. We're moronic and weak-minded when it comes to each other. So, I say let's just enjoy the kisses, maybe some necking, a little fondling, and it'll keep our minds off the bear.''

It was a stupid premise. Really dumb. The bear posed far less danger than making out with Bobbie. He knew it. She knew it.

The bear probably did, too.

''So, we'll just kiss a little bit?'' she asked, sounding way too breathy and aroused.

Heck, no. Their kisses never stayed anywhere in the realm of *a little bit*. That wasn't, however, what Aidan heard himself say. ''We'll keep it like a PG movie. The way it was back in junior high.''

And that was apparently the only assurance Bobbie needed. She pressed her mouth to his again and gave him a kiss that nearly took off the top of his head. Aidan was absolutely certain no girl in junior high had put her tongue in his mouth that way.

He slid his hand over her breast and cupped her. Her clingy shirt wasn't really a barrier to his touch, but it was still too much between them. He was in a bare-skin kind of mood, especially when that bare skin was Bobbie's breasts.

Aidan pushed up her shirt and pulled down her bra. Oh, yeah. Definitely bare now. Soft yet firm. He ran his fingertips over her nipples. She rewarded him with an *ohyesyes* and another great kiss.

His other hand didn't behave either. It inched its way down her body. Off her hip. And lower. Bobbie wore a pair of loose jeans. He located the waist and unsnapped it.

Sweet Nantucket.

He slid his hand down her stomach. And lower, into the jeans. She had on panties, flimsy things that were practically nonexistent. Lace and silk. Something meant to make a man drool. His hand slipped into those, too. And then the slipping took on a whole new meaning.

Sweet, sweet Nantucket.

"Yes," she whispered. She somehow managed to inch closer so he had no trouble locating the exact spot that caused her to declare him a god with magic fingers. "But this is more than a PG rating, isn't it?"

Yeah, it was, but Aidan still managed some creative reasoning. "We're practically in the dark, and I can't even see where I'm touching you so that still makes it PG."

Okay. So, it didn't make much sense. Of course, passion had a way of making even the dumbest remarks sound like post-graduate discussions.

"It feels like more than PG," Bobbie added. It didn't, however, stop her from wiggling closer. And closer. And closer. "But what do I know?

It's been so long since I've done anything like this.''

That piqued his interest right away. ''How long?''

''Too long.''

Not the best thing to say to a man who had his hands in her underpants, but he couldn't tell her that. That's because he was too busy sucking in his breath. Bobbie was wiggling right against his *exact spot*. Of course, his exact spot was a lot bigger than hers so it probably hadn't been difficult for her to locate. She shoved his hand away and pressed her lower body to his.

Sweet, sweet, sweet Nantucket.

The fit was out of this world. Sure, there were clothes between them, but Aidan had no trouble imagining what it would feel like if they were naked and doing exactly what men and women had been doing since time began.

Her mouth was everywhere. On his jaw. His neck. His chest. Her hands didn't behave, either. She fondled his ear. His lips. But not for long. She slid her hand down his stomach. Lower. Lower. Lower. She wrapped her fingers over a part of him that made his eyes permanently cross.

That PG rating went south in a hurry.

Aidan lunged for her zipper.

She lunged for his.

They fumbled, cursed and begged. She bopped

him on the nose with her breasts when she took the condom from her purse. Distracting, but it didn't deter him. Aidan finally shoved her jeans over her hips and down her legs. She did the same for him.

"I'm on fire," she let him know.

"Me, too." He gave her a full, hot, raging kiss. "And I've got an extinguisher that'll help both of us."

"Then use it now."

That was exactly what he had in mind.

Underwear didn't pose obstacles for them. Of course, nothing would have stopped them at this point, probably not even the bear. Aidan rid Bobbie of the panties, repositioned her and eased right into her fiery feminine furnace. He didn't have much of a mind left to boggle, and that pretty much eliminated the rest of it.

Bobbie arched against him and took every last inch of his fire extinguisher. "Oh, yes. Definitely yes," she let him know. "Yes. Yes. Yes. Yes. Yes."

But before he extinguished anything, Aidan fanned those flames higher and hotter. Until Bobbie and he did the only thing they could do.

They combusted.

10

The Roman Gladiator: Catalogue Item 314C. In the race for style and adventure, you'll emerge the victor wearing this lace-up-front, reinforced-side mini brief. Spartan styling for the man who enjoys heart-pumping action and nonstop excitement. Available in Flaming-Chariot Cerise, Breastplate Brass and Pompeii Plum.

BOBBIE STIRRED a little to make sure she wasn't paralyzed or otherwise permanently impaired. She had a tingly feeling in her toes so that probably meant she'd survived. Even if she hadn't, it would be a heck of a way to go.

"If they gave out awards for lovemaking," Bobbie mumbled. "You'd win hands down."

"We'd tie," Aidan corrected.

He rolled to the side but kept her snuggled in his arms. Bobbie didn't break the embrace either. She just lay there—as limp as a school-cafeteria noodle—and savored what had just happened.

Despite the not-so-right location and the not-so-right timing, it'd been perfect. Absolutely perfect. Aidan had made love to her the way she'd always dreamed her partner would make love. Talk about a mind-blowing, life-altering experience.

She grinned.

Then frowned.

Of course, it would ruin her for any other man, but this wasn't the time for regrets.

There'd be plenty of time for that later.

During those old-maid years. Yup, those years that would likely constitute the rest of her thoroughly boring life.

"You're not saying anything," Aidan pointed out. "Are you sorry about what just happened?"

Best to play it light, so Bobbie flashed him a perky smile. "No. Of course not. Are you kidding? It was amazing. Incredible."

There were dozens of other adjectives, but each one suddenly became a stark reminder that she wouldn't be experiencing such adjectives as them again.

Aidan pushed her hair away from her eyes. "Whew. For a moment there, I thought something might be wrong."

"What could possibly be wrong? You did everything right. *Everything.* I'll think fondly of you in my old age."

When Bobbie heard that come out of her mouth,

she nearly groaned. It was practically a goodbye handshake and a see-you-around nod. It was light-hearted all right, but it didn't match the glumness that started to glum around her heart. Aidan would be leaving soon, and there was absolutely nothing she could do to stop him.

Crystal's advice came back to her. *Have you forgotten that you could follow him if you really wanted to?*

What Crystal hadn't considered when she doled out that nonsensical suggestion was that Aidan had never asked her to follow him.

Nor would he.

He'd made it clear that he wasn't in the market for a serious relationship or double occupancy in his future itineraries. That included having a former lover follow him around the globe.

So, that meant this incredible, wonderful experience was temporary.

The shrill screeching and screaming put a halt to that depressing thought. Aidan and Bobbie came off the floor of the van, both of them peering out the front windows.

It didn't take Bobbie long to spot the screamer and screecher—Maxine. She was in the parking lot, a huge cardboard box in her hands. A box with Size-XXX Gladiators in bold letters on the side. And it didn't take Bobbie long to figure out the reason Maxine was yelling. Like a big furry sentry, the bear was on all fours between Maxine and her car.

Aidan cursed and grabbed his clothes. Bobbie did the same, but he managed to get his jeans on a lot faster than she did. He climbed into the front seat and threw open the door.

''Maxine!'' he yelled.

Still wailing at a deafening frequency, the woman snapped her head in their direction. That glimpse was apparently all it took for Maxine to realize she had been rescued. She hurled the box at the bear and sprinted toward the van. Even in four-inch heels and shrink-wrap capris, she broke a couple of Olympic speed records. When she reached Aidan, he latched onto her arm and hauled her inside.

''OhGodohGodohGodohGod! You saved my life.'' Maxine slung her arms around Aidan's neck.

Even though she knew Maxine's impromptu hug was brought on by fear, it did funny things to Bobbie's stomach to see a woman wrapped around Aidan. The funny things didn't get any funnier when Maxine proceeded to press a flurry of kisses all over Aidan's face.

''You are so incredible,'' Maxine spouted while she tightened her grip around Aidan. He tried to loosen her hands, but Maxine had a death grip.

She also had her foam-padding-enhanced boobs pressed right against Aidan's chest.

"You're safe. The bear can't get to you in here," Aidan assured Maxine.

"And that's because you rescued me. I owe you my life and my undying devotion." Maxine didn't seem so hysterical anymore. In fact, her voice had a tinge of sultriness to it.

Bobbie could take no more of the hysteria-induced sultriness. She grabbed Maxine's arms and peeled the woman and her foam padding away from Aidan.

"I'm glad you're safe," Bobbie let Maxine know. "But I'd like an explanation as to why you were here at the factory tonight and why you were hauling a box of size triple-X Gladiators to your car."

Maxine blinked.

Bobbie plucked Maxine's key ring from her hand, searched through the assortment and found what she was looking for. She dangled something for Maxine and Aidan to see. "This is a key to the factory. A key that should have been turned in when I fired you. This doesn't take much of a guess, but I'll bet you used this key to break in and steal the underwear."

Just as she'd done before, Maxine blinked. Opened her mouth. And blinked again. What she didn't do was offer a reasonable explanation about anything. Probably because there wasn't one, other than the fact she was the thief.

"Maybe I should read you your rights first," Aidan suggested.

"Rights?" Maxine gasped. "You don't think I was trying to steal anything, do you, Aidan?"

He pointed to the box of Gladiators. The bear was eating them, but one was stuck on his furry ear. "I think that says it all, Maxine. I'm afraid I'll have to take you to the office and book you."

Bobbie gave him a satisfied nod, and while she was doling out gestures, she gave Maxine a smug nannie-nannie-boo-boo wobble of her head. Maxine howled about foul play and alleged misunderstandings, but Aidan didn't listen to her. He started the van and drove away.

Bobbie's feeling of smugness only lasted another second or two. When Aidan pulled out of the parking lot, his jacket skittered across the back of the van. With that skittering, an envelope slipped out of his pocket and skittered, too. It was probably freaky kismet or something, but that was also the exact moment that Aidan drove past a street light. And with that light, Bobbie saw the return address.

The Law-Enforcement Exchange Program.

Oh, no.

Her heart sank. It certainly put a damper on her

mood. On her breathing. And on pretty much the outlook for the rest of her life.

That letter no doubt contained Aidan's next assignment. An assignment that would soon cause him to drive out of town and leave her behind.

Well, shoot!

Bobbie carefully examined all the emotions that the sight of that letter caused, but there was one particular emotion that stood out far above the rest. An emotion that nearly caused her to run for cover. It was the créme de la créme of all emotions. The dreaded L-word.

Love.

Somewhere this Twango-Drifter Plan had gone awry, and she'd fallen face-first in love with Aidan O'Shea.

Talk about a wrinkle in their plan.

And it was a wrinkle that Bobbie feared she couldn't just iron out.

AIDAN WATCHED as Jasper Kershaw led a still-sobbing Maxine out the door. Jilting Jasper had posted bond for her—finally—but it hadn't been a pretty scene.

Literally.

Aidan had no idea how much mascara Maxine had once had on her eyelashes, but after that four-hour crying spell, there were two three-inch-wide midnight-blue streaks down her cheeks. Add to that her blotchy nose and red eyes, and she was a sight to be reckoned with. He hoped she didn't scare any children or old people on her way home.

In the end, however, Maxine had saved him some paperwork and made a full confession. She was indeed Liffeys' infamous underwear bandit and misspelling graffiti artist. Her motive? To make Bobbie look incompetent because Maxine was angry that Bobbie had fired her for all those ill-fitting flies. Maxine had added the graffiti part, she said, to throw Aidan off her scent, since everyone in town knew that she could spell.

Aidan intended to recommend probation and hours of serious counseling. The woman definitely needed to learn how to redirect her anger to something other than swiping men's undergarments.

That might solve Maxine's problems, but it didn't do baked beans for his.

Aidan picked up the envelope from his desk and stared at it as if it contained the answers to the mysteries of the universe. "The Law-Enforcement Exchange Program," he mumbled as his gaze skimmed over the return address.

It was his ticket to his next assignment and to the life he'd always wanted. It was freedom. Adventure. Excitement. And most importantly, no rings attached.

So, why didn't that make him feel as good as it should have?

The answer was simple, and he didn't even have to think about it. Bobbie Callahan was the cause of morose mood and second thoughts.

Somewhere between the time she'd reported those missing Gigolos and now, Bobbie had gone from merely being his Twango partner to his non-Twango lover. There was definitely nothing faux about them making love, even if there was something enhancing about it.

And that left Aidan wondering—just what else did Bobbie have the potential to be?

He might have come up with the answer to that burning question if the door hadn't opened. Like gunfighters at the OK Corral, Quincy and Winston stepped inside. They both wore their reenactment cowboy gear that they'd had on at the wrangler's picnic. Appropriate, since this was a showdown of sorts.

"We're here to discuss those hickeys you put on Bobbie's neck," Quincy announced.

Not the best greeting he'd ever had, but it was one Aidan had expected sooner or later. After all, they were Bobbie's uncles, and they probably felt some old-fashioned need to avenge her honor.

He pulled in a weary breath and slipped the letter into his pocket. He hoped like the devil that this didn't turn ugly. Of course, with Quincy and Winston, there was a one-hundred-percent chance of that happening one way or another.

"I've already apologized to Bobbie about those hickeys," Aidan let them know.

It was paltry. Yes, he had apologized, but part of him—a rather huge part—still savored the way it'd made Bobbie and him feel when he applied those overly suctioned kisses to her silky neck.

Quincy's eyes narrowed slightly, and he bracketed his ham-sized hands on Aidan's desk. "We're not exactly interested in an apology. Are we, Winston?"

Winston snarled an agreement.

The uncles loomed over him, and Aidan stood so he could take his punishment like a man. The truth was he deserved to be punished. Here, Bobbie had just recovered from the Jasper mess, and the last thing she'd needed was a man dealing out unsavory things to her.

So, what had he done?

He'd given her hickeys. Lots of hickeys.

And other stuff.

If another man had done those sort of things to her, Aidan would have wanted to beat him senseless. For several reasons. The main reason being that it riled him to the core to think of another man hickeying Bobbie's silky neck. He felt very territorial when it came to her neck. And her mouth.

And pretty much the rest of her.

"You know where this is leading, right?" Winston questioned.

Aidan nodded. "You're here to beat me senseless for what I did."

The uncles frowned in unison. "Uh. Not exactly," Quincy informed him.

He didn't believe them. Not with that gunslinging look in their eyes.

"Oh, just get on with it," Aidan insisted. "I deserve whatever you dish out. I should never have kissed her or made love to her, but I swear I couldn't help it. She's just so...well, she's just so..."

"Well?" Winston prompted after Aidan just kept *so*-ing. "She's so what?"

Aidan had nothing to lose, except maybe a pint or two of blood, so he went for it. "She's hot, sexy, alluring, sensual and delicious. But she's also considerate, interesting and funny. Oh, and smart. Bobbie's definitely smart. And sensitive. And sensual."

"You've already mentioned that sensual part," Winston pointed out.

"Well, it's worth repeating—all right? And you know what else? If it weren't for the factory and her commitment to her family, she'd be a perfect...traveling partner.... Among other things."

Aidan smiled just thinking about that. Scenes started to play out in his head. Scenes of Bobbie in Paris. In Rome. In Venice. Scenes of them in bed. And not in bed. Of them strolling along the Left Bank. Images of them hand-in-hand as they experienced all the places they both longed to see. And all the places that Aidan longed to show her.

"I'd love to be the man who gives Bobbie the whole world," Aidan mumbled.

But he mumbled it a little louder than he'd planned, and the room went deadly silent. His gaze came to the uncles who were both just staring at him.

Winston latched onto two chairs and dragged them in front of Aidan's desk. "Sit down, Deputy O'Shea. It appears we have some serious wrangling to do. Don't worry though. This won't hurt…much."

11

Happily-Ever-After: Catalogue Item 02. A sturdy but sensual custom-fit boxer for those extraordinary occasions when ordinary just won't do. Lifetime guarantee. Available in dozens of custom colors and sizes. Our aim at Boxers or Briefs is to fit you with a fit that fits you.

BOBBIE DABBED some cotton-candy-colored polish on her middle toenail. At least, she thought it was her middle one. It was hard to tell.

This wasn't the best idea she'd ever had—painting her toenails while she was crying her eyes out. Still, she had to do something to stop fidgeting. There was an alley-cat war going on inside her body, and she needed to wear the little suckers out before she exploded.

She couldn't clean the house to burn off some of that excess tension. She'd already done that. She'd also sorted through clothes. Straightened out her closet. And tried on some weird yet-to-be-worn presents that Crystal had given her for her last six birthdays. She still had on a combination of three of those presents while she sat on the floor and polished her toenails.

Her eating binge was over, too. There was no more ice cream in the freezer. She'd gone through all the peanut butter as well and the chocolate truffles she'd been saving. They hadn't tasted that bad with the three bottles of beer she'd used to chase them with. She would have had the champagne but couldn't get it open. Sugarfoot, the ferret, was probably still in the kitchen, trying to nibble off the cork for her.

There was nothing left for her to cook. A huge stockpot of beef stew was simmering on the stove. There were two apple pies cooling on racks and enough bread dough to stuff a king-size mattress.

She'd done her part to fill the fridge, too. Inside was an array of gelatin molds, puddings and a triple-layer chocolate cake.

In short, she'd run out of things to do and cook. Besides, she didn't have any more groceries or fun things to eat. Pigging out on broccoli and mineral water didn't seem very self-indulgent.

Bobbie globbed on more toenail polish while she relived the phone call that had started this whole trek down misery lane. The stupid phone call she'd made to Aidan at his office. Sheriff Cooper had answered and simply told her that Aidan was packing to leave. Obviously, his assignment had ended early. Nothing about Aidan saying goodbye to her. No message. No *if Bobbie calls, tell her I'll get in touch with her soon to explain everything.*

Nothing!

How could Aidan possibly do this to her? After all, they'd kissed. They'd given each other hickeys. He'd shared his fire extinguisher with her.

Yet, after doing all of that, Aidan hadn't felt as if he needed to let her know that he was leaving town. This seemed more like a stunt that Jasper would pull, but Bobbie had expected so much more from Aidan. And therein was the reason she'd left work, come home and proceeded to cry her eyes out.

She swiped away some tears, smearing the side of her hair with the toenail polish. A second swipe merely transferred some of the smear to her arm, so Bobbie gave up and continued the mental Aidan-bashing.

If he did come over to say good-bye, she'd just pretend she wasn't there. No sense enduring what would be a gut-wrenching situation. Besides, she was starting to go past the annoyed stage and into an area of being thoroughly riled. Why hadn't Aidan told her about the letter from the Law-Enforcement Exchange Program? And the even bigger question—had he really planned on leaving town without saying so much as a goodbye?

"If that's what you had in mind, Deputy Aidan O'Shea," Bobbie grumbled, "then you're more moldy than stagnant stump water."

Bobbie wiped away a trickle of tears and smeared more polish on her cheek. Even though she couldn't see more than an inch in front of her face, she tackled the next toe.

If only Crystal were home from work so she could cry on her shoulder—and help her remove the stray polish—but Bobbie hadn't even called her. Crystal was working the hair salon alone today and wouldn't get off for hours. No sense alarming her friend when there was really nothing she could do about it anyway.

After all, what could be done about a man who couldn't take two minutes of his precious time to say good-bye to a woman he'd combusted in the back of a van?

Not one simple good-bye. Nothing.

Maybe his next assignment would be to the Artic Circle. Or maybe a town where kitty rescues and pushy, needy women were in massive abundance.

The doorbell rang as Bobbie was reaching a pinnacle of her hissy fit. She shot a narrowed glance at the door and continued with the polishing. No way would she answer it. *No way.* Suddenly, she didn't want to see Aidan or anyone else.

Another ring.

Then another.

Moments later, there was a heavy-handed knock on the door. "Come on, Bobbie. I know you're in there. Your car's out front, and I called your office and they said you'd gone home early. So, open up."

"Go away!" she yelled. "I'm not here."

"We have to talk—"

"No!"

"Bobbie—"

"No! No! No! You are absolutely the last person in the entire Milky Way galaxy that I'll let walk in here."

The door opened, and Aidan walked in. "Before you give another ultimatum like that, you probably want to make sure your door's locked first."

Bobbie sprang to her feet and braced herself to tell him off. Too bad she didn't *look* braced for much of anything. There were fluffy green cotton balls squished between her toes, and she had to stand on her heels to make sure she didn't get even more polish on the carpet. Her face was no doubt splotchy and red from crying.

But that wasn't the worst of it.

She was wearing the three presents from Crystal.

Bobbie took inventory. Glittery purple panties with ruffles on the butt. Then, there was the Gothic chartreuse-and-black strapless lace-up corset that had her breasts squeezed and pressed to new heights. Since there hadn't been anyone to help her, she'd laced it in front—and not very well either. The laces had knots and gaps that were a lot more revealing than they should have been.

Her final accessory was the gaudy rhinestone Ima Goddess tiara nestled in her tangled, toenail-polish-smeared hair. She was sure she looked like a stripper.

Or a very desperate drag queen.

She watched a series of expressions cross Aidan's face. Concern. Followed by surprise. Then, shock.

All right, and maybe some lust flickered through his eyes, but she wasn't positive. It could have been simple pity.

He didn't come any closer. He just stood there and stared at her. "Are you, uh, all right?"

"Do I look all right?" That probably was not the correct question to ask, but Bobbie didn't give him a chance even to attempt an answer. "I know about the letter from the Law-Enforcement Exchange

Program. I saw it in the van last night. And I also know you're leaving town because I called Sheriff Cooper. He said you were packing. Packing! How could you pack without telling me first?"

"I know. I'm sorry. But the packing didn't mean I wouldn't be coming back to Liffey for the rest of my assignment. I just need to go to New York for the day. My best friend arranged his son's christening for tomorrow afternoon, and I'm the godfather. I need to be there."

"Christening?" she repeated. "But I saw the letter from the Law-Enforcement Exchange Program."

He took out the letter in question from his pocket and dropped it onto the coffee table. "I haven't opened it yet. I couldn't."

She had to give it to him. He looked apologetic. Still, he should have told her that he'd gotten his assignment. "You should go now."

"I will, after I've explained everything."

"I don't need an explanation."

But boy did she *want* one. The tears returned in full force. Her life was going straight down the garbage disposal, and there was nothing she could do but cry.

Aidan made it to her in one step and pulled her into his arms. He scooped her up and sat on the sofa. "There are lots of things we need to discuss, and I'm not leaving until we talk."

Bobbie couldn't gather enough breath to ask him what he meant by that. And a part of her didn't want to know. She just wanted to wallow in her misery and cry until she was dehydrated. Maybe then, she'd just pass out on the sofa. Of course, if that happened, she'd risk gluing herself to the sofa fabric since the toenail polish was still tacky.

Aidan took off her tiara and laid it on the coffee table. He suddenly looked very uncomfortable, and she even heard him swallow hard.

With reason, she soon figured out.

He was staring at her corset. Or rather the gaps in her corset. Bobbie knew that she should do something to cover herself up, but she simply didn't have the energy or inclination. Let him look. Let him get an eyeful. She no longer cared about such things.

But she did hug a throw pillow to her chest.

"What's this all about?" he asked. He plucked one of the green cotton balls from between her toes.

"Therapy." She sniffed. "Of sorts."

"You didn't finish," Aidan pointed out. "And a couple of them are real blotchy."

Bobbie shrugged. "Hard to see through tears."

"I'll bet." Aidan set her beside him and pulled her foot into his lap. "I'll finish it for you."

That instantly dried up the waterworks. Aidan was going to polish her toenails? "Why?"

"Why not?" He took the bottle of polish and started. "It might be good therapy for both of us."

It still didn't convince her. "And I suppose you do this often—go around and paint women's toenails?"

If so, she didn't like it. Worse, she didn't want to think about why she didn't like it either.

"Never done it before in my life," he let her know. "But I don't think I'll do any worse than you have."

True. Besides, he was gentle, and it felt kind of nice. However, Bobbie kept her attention focused on her toes so she wouldn't have to look at him. Now, that she'd stopped crying and carrying on, she was a little embarrassed about the way she'd reacted.

"I didn't tell you about the letter because I didn't know how," he admitted. "I mean, we've grown close over the past couple of days, and I didn't know how you felt about me leaving."

"I don't like it—that's how I feel about it," she blurted out. But then Bobbie huffed, "Look, I know this is your job. This is what you do. And

I knew sooner or later you'd leave. I just hadn't counted on it hitting me like this."

Aidan blew on her toenails to dry the polish. At least she hoped that's why he was doing it. It felt rather stimulating, and there was something erotic about his mouth puckering that way.

"When I first got to town," he continued, "I'd sworn off women. My six sisters, my mother, my gran, and at least a half-dozen assorted female cousins have made it their life mission to marry me off."

Okay. So, she hadn't expected his life story, but it was definitely something she wanted to hear. "Your family sounds, uh, interesting."

"They're nuts. All of them. Don't get me wrong. I love them, and they love me. But I wish they'd take a little less interest in my love life." He polished her baby toe and started that blowing thing again.

Mercy. His warm breath made it all the way to her purple glittery panties. It brushed way up high against a spot that probably didn't need such activity.

"Telling you about my meddlesome family probably sounds like an excuse," Aidan continued. He blew. And blew. And blew. "But it isn't. I overreacted to what were really good intentions on their parts. Weird intentions, but I know they just want me to be happy.''

Bobbie could hardly concentrate on what he was saying. He blew every third word. It felt good. Delicious. Wicked. Warm. Moist. And it felt like something she wanted to experience more of.

"Um," she managed, in case he was waiting for her to answer.

He dabbed some polish on her big toe. She braced herself for more blowing, and he didn't disappoint her. Oh, the man was good at this. It set every nerve in her body on edge. It heated her blood. It made her want him in the best and worst possible ways.

"So, here's the bottom line," Aidan continued. Another blow. It hit pay dirt and made her eyes roll back in her head. "I spoke to your uncles earlier, and they want to take a more active part in the business. They didn't know how to tell you, so they asked me to do it for them.''

Once those words filtered across the toenail-polish fumes, Bobbie fought her way through the quickly enveloping passionate haze. "Say what?''

"Quincy and Winston want to come out of retirement. They're bored. That's why they keep coming up with all those new underwear lines. They still want you to manage Boxers or Briefs, but they're satisfied you can do that even if you're in Rome, Paris…wherever. They didn't think it'd be much of an adjustment since you handle most of the business over the phone and Internet. So, as long as you return for visits and the occasional holidays, they'll be pleased as punch. Their words, not mine.''

That revelation started to sink in. But then, Aidan started the blowing again. Bobbie tried to push the overwhelmingly erotic sensation aside so she could grasp what he'd just told her.

''I don't have to be in Liffey to manage Boxers or Briefs?'' she summarized. ''And my uncles are actually *pleased as punch* about this?''

Aidan dabbed and blew. Dabbed and blew. ''Yep. They only want you to be happy.''

She sucked in her breath. ''And so that means, uh, I could, like, travel since Uncle Quincy and Uncle Winston want to come out of retirement?''

Aidan nodded. Dabbed. And blew. Dabbed. And blew. Just when Bobbie thought she might have to demand that he combust her just so she could concentrate, he stopped dabbing. He stopped blowing.

He took a travel magazine from the table, tore off a strip from one of the pages, folded it and looped it into a makeshift circle.

''Uh, Aidan, what are you doing?''

He place the paper loop in his palm and held it

out in front of her like an offering. "I'm proposing marriage. And traveling. And other things. Sexy, sultry, smutty things. I say we get married and you accompany me to assignments—and beds—all over the world. How's that for an offer?"

Marriage! Marriage? Ohh, marriage.

Sweet heaven, it hadn't even crossed her mind. Well, maybe it had, but Bobbie had dismissed it because Aidan was a no-rings-attached kind of guy. She hadn't let herself even hope that he'd want to end his days of bachelorhood and tie himself to her.

Aidan tipped his head to the makeshift ring. "By the way, that's temporary. I'll get something better first thing tomorrow."

She glanced at the two-inch ring and then him. "You're serious?"

"Do Gigolos provide easy access to a man's family jewels?"

Bobbie nodded. "That serious, huh?"

"Completely." Aidan circled his arm around her waist and hauled her to him. "I love you, Bobbie. I need you. And I want you. This is definitely a full-package itinerary for a lifelong trip to paradise."

"Oh, me too," she practically shouted. "I mean, I love you, too. And I need you, too. And I definitely want you, too."

He grinned and kissed her. "So, what do you say about marrying me?"

Bobbie could go two ways with this answer. She could do it the right way—which meant giving it days, maybe even weeks of thought. It'd mean sitting down and writing out the advantages and disadvantages of the impact of such an enormous decision. Or she could say to heck with all of that and do what her heart insisted she do.

It took her less than a second to make up her mind. Bobbie answered him first with a kiss that had him breathing pretty hard by the time she was done.

"Yes, Aidan, I'll marry you. Oh, and don't worry about the ring. I think we can have it sized."

He laughed and scooped her up his arms. "Now the celebration begins. I'm taking you to bed, and we're not leaving there until I have to get on that plane tomorrow morning."

There was no way Bobbie could turn down an offer like that.

Aidan had already headed in the direction of the bedroom when Bobbie remembered the envelope. "Wait. Don't you want to know where we're going on your next assignment?"

"You bet." Aidan dropped back down onto the sofa, and with her still snuggled deep in his arms, he tore open the envelope. "This is it, Bobbie. The start of our adventures." He unfolded the single sheet of paper. "This is the beginning of our lives tog—"

His eyes doubled in size.

"What's wrong, Aidan?" Alarmed when he didn't answer, Bobbie took the letter. She skimmed the page, but it didn't take much skimming to see what had caused his drastic ocular reaction. "We're going to Boston."

He turned and stared at her. Slowly, his expression began to change. "Hey, this isn't such a bad deal. Whew. All that conditioned-response stuff stopped my heart for a couple of seconds. I've got a significant other in my life now—you! That means no blind dates, no matchmaking and definitely no monkeying with romance. For the first time since puberty, I can look forward to visiting with my family."

"And I get to meet them."

Aidan grinned. "They'll love you as much as I do."

Awww. Her heart practically melted.

This was it. The life she'd always wanted, always dreamed of. And she got to share it with the hottest, cutest law-enforcement exchange officer in the whole world.

She put her head on his shoulder when he headed

for the bedroom. "Where do you think we'll go after Boston?"

"That's easy. Anywhere. Everywhere. It doesn't matter as long as I'm with you."

"I feel the same way. The world is ours, Aidan."

And it was. Theirs—all theirs.

It'd taken a miracle, but it'd happened. The Twango-Drifter Plan had somehow morphed into a Happily-Ever-After, and Bobbie couldn't have asked for more.

Tried and True

Katie Gallagher

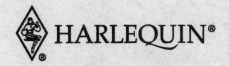

TORONTO • NEW YORK • LONDON
AMSTERDAM • PARIS • SYDNEY • HAMBURG
STOCKHOLM • ATHENS • TOKYO • MILAN • MADRID
PRAGUE • WARSAW • BUDAPEST • AUCKLAND

Dear Reader,

I'm so excited to be writing this to you! This is my first book, and when I think back, it's hard to believe it started with just one word. *Wanderlust*. I love that word. It's alluring, the idea of setting out with no direction and seeing America, like my heroine Clementine does. Think of all that's out there—possibly the love of your life and the adventure of a lifetime! You just need the courage to take that first step.

I hope you enjoy Clementine's adventure, one that leads her to the sleepy paradise of Tried and True, Kansas. That's where she finds Callum. He doesn't know it yet, but his adventure is just about to begin.

Happy reading!

Katie Gallagher

In loving memory of my elegant great-aunt, Charlotte White, who taught me that cordial isn't just a candy with a cherry in the center.

Thank you for your faith in me.
I wish you could have seen this, C.

1

CALLUM MCCUTCHEON took the old stretch of Highway 108 back to Tried and True. There'd been some trouble out at the Moseley farm; just more of the same. The two Moseley brothers, both in their late seventies and sworn bachelors, were at it again. One of the farmhands had called, sure they were going to do each other in for good this time. The farm had been divided in two years ago and if one of the squabbling brothers even set a foot on the other's property, it meant war. The last time Callum had shown up, the elderly brothers had actually been throwing potatoes from their root cellars at each other.

Callum had reached the end of his twelve-hour shift when the call had come in. Luke, one of his deputies, had already arrived and offered to take the call, but Callum knew how to handle the Moseley brothers. He'd known them all his life. He'd even worked on their farm one summer. Despite their ongoing feud, they operated one large farm that stretched across both their properties, and supplied a large part of the local produce in Tried and True. They wouldn't know what to do if they didn't bicker. Callum was convinced that they picked fights with each other now because that's what they'd always done, and one was afraid to hurt the other's feelings by offering a truce.

Callum preferred the old highway route to the Moseley farm instead of the newer interstate that sliced neatly through the farmland that made up most of Truly County in the High Plains of northwestern Kansas. Now he had enough time to stop by his sister's house to have Sunday dinner before finally going home to sleep for the next twelve hours straight. One of his three deputies, Jess, had broken an arm and nearly half his ribs playing some roughhouse football on the first pretty day in April when everyone seemed to come out of hard-winter hibernation. Since then, the others had been pulling some grueling hours to make up for Jess's absence while he recuperated.

The sun was just beginning to set and it cast rays of deep, warm colors across the landscape. The new interstate meant there wasn't much traffic other than the occasional pickup truck on Highway 108 anymore, which was why Callum was surprised to see a flash of light up the highway.

As he got nearer, he saw that it was the reflection off the windshield of a classic dark green Mercedes, a two-seater convertible with Georgia license plates. Earlier, Callum had sped past the driver—a woman—as he'd headed to the Moseley farm. She'd been going just below the speed limit and he'd assumed she was one of the few tourists who had taken the wrong exit off the interstate and then driven around, lost and in awe, in this picture-postcard slice of time gone by.

He noticed that she had pulled over to the side of the road and, for whatever reason, was having a heated argument with her car. She kicked the car door and pounded the hood, then grabbed the door handle and shook it furiously.

Callum made a mental apology to Maggie for missing yet another dinner. He passed her vehicle and made a U-turn farther up the road, coming back to park behind her.

She gave him a momentary glance that was almost

panicked, then turned frantically back to the car door handle as if she was in a cheesy horror flick, trying to get away from the living dead. Getting out of his patrol car, he took in her form. Tall and curved nicely, she had a small waist and *great* hips, hips that made a man think of holding on and getting down to some serious baby-making business. Her hair was a wild tangle of long golden-brown curls that she'd tried unsuccessfully to tie back at the nape of her neck with some flat leather thing that had a small wooden stick through it. She looked at him again as he approached her. She had beautiful eyes that were almost exotic in their almond shape. "It's all right," she said, smiling a little thinly at him. "I'm handling it."

"Car trouble?" he asked. He knew nervousness when he saw it.

"I'm handling it," she grunted, pulling at the car handle some more.

He calmly watched her technique for a moment. "Does intimidation often work with your car?"

She frowned at him.

"Just wondering."

She finally sighed and stopped trying to force the handle. "I locked my keys in my car," she said angrily, slouching against the door. She blew some curls off her forehead. "I think it was the scenery. I was distracted." She pointed across the field to where the sun was setting behind the abandoned barn on the Flannery property, outlining the structure in fire-red.

She was Southern. The license plates told him, the accent confirmed it. He put his hands above his hips, a little confused, a little wary, a little aroused. A little annoyed by that last one. This was certainly an interesting end to his day. "It's beautiful, I agree," he said, looking at her, not the barn.

"I wasn't looking forward to the long trek up this

highway. There's not a house in sight. Then suddenly you appear out of nowhere." She looked as if she wasn't sure if she should consider him a godsend yet. "Is there such a thing as a law enforcement sixth sense?"

"I've sworn never to tell. My solemn oath as a knight in shining armor. We want to keep our mysterious image." He walked over to the driver's side to look in the window and she almost stumbled as she backed away from him. He narrowed his eyes at her. She was skittish. He looked her up and down. It would be hard to hide a weapon in those tight jeans, if you didn't count her hips, which were definitely lethal.

Keeping her in his periphery, he looked away from her for a moment and peered quickly in the window. There were several disposable cameras sitting on the back seat. He saw a map, a travel journal and some scattered postcards from everywhere from South Carolina to Pennsylvania, with Illinois, Michigan and the Dakotas thrown in. There were a few books on the floorboard, the thick books people take on vacation because they think they're going to have time to read *War and Peace* and *The Collected Poems of W. B. Yeats*. And then there was the motherlode of old fast-food wrappers and bags wallpapering the interior. The car was practically a shrine to Burger King.

The keys were in the ignition and the driver's side was indeed locked. He even tried the door for good measure, which earned him an exasperated look from her, as if he believed the car door wasn't cooperating because it was waiting for a *man* to try the handle.

He straightened and looked at her fully for a few seconds. "I know what you're thinking," she said quickly. "You're thinking what kind of fool person gets herself stranded in the middle of nowhere with her doors locked and her purse inside her car. Well, meet Clementine Spencer, fool person.''

''Clementine,'' he repeated.

''Yes. My license and registration are in the car, if you don't believe me.'' She hesitated. ''Okay, the car is locked. But honestly, I am who I say I am,'' she said, almost imploring him to take her word.

''I'm inclined to believe you.''

''Well, good,'' she said, trying to be cocky but sounding more surprised than anything. ''And what is your name?''

''I'm Sheriff Callum McCutcheon.'' He crossed his arms over his chest, irresistibly intrigued by this woman. He had to fight not to smile. She was exotic and unusual and, apart from her obvious youth, definitely held a polish that screamed *city*. She was so far out of her element she could have been on Neptune.

''Tell me, Clementine Spencer, what are you doing out here in the middle of nowhere, as you say? You're a long way from Georgia.''

She apparently mistook his curiosity for suspicion because she gave a grunt of frustration and pushed her hair harshly out of her face. ''I knew it!'' she bellowed as she paced away, which gave him an excellent view of her nicely rounded, heart-shaped behind. ''The moment I saw you do that U-turn, I knew it! She has an A.P.B. out on me, or I'm on some Most Wanted list, aren't I? Honestly, I called her when I was in Virginia and told her I was fine.'' She paced back. ''But that wasn't good enough, was it? No-oo. She has to call the *law* out on me! I mean, I kept telling her I was leaving. It's not as if I didn't give her warning.''

He raised his brows, surprised that he had set her off like this. ''Who are you talking about?''

"My *mother!*"

That didn't clear up much. "And why exactly would your mother call the law on you?"

She paused. "Because she wants me home," she finally said.

"You ran away?" he asked dubiously. "How old are you?"

She looked startled by the question. "I'm twenty-four," she said, rubbing her forehead. "Believe it or not."

She'd be fun and sweet to be with, he thought, surprising himself. This was the first time since Liza that he'd even had a fleeting thought of getting involved with another woman. But it was okay because she was just a tourist, he justified. She wasn't going to be a problem to his love life. He could enjoy her for now. "If it's any consolation, there's no A.P.B. out on you and, believe me, I would remember your face if you were a Wanted woman," he said.

"Oh," she said, giving him a curious look. He watched her give him a once-over, a thoroughly unconscious reaction to his flirting. "That's good to know."

"I'm sure it is."

"Someone up in Noosely, Nebraska...you know Noosely, don't you? Home of the most per capita registered republicans in the country, or so I was told. Someone there told me that this stretch of highway was beautiful, so I came down to see and I noticed that barn and just had to have a photograph." She paused and stuffed her hands into the front pockets of her snug jeans. "Never mind. To make a long story short, I locked my keys in my car and I don't want to need help, but I do."

"So you're just passing through." Yes, he felt safe knowing she wasn't going to be a future fixture in his part of the country. The ladies in town would love her. She'd be snatched up by one of their bachelor projects in seconds. Oddly, that made Callum feel snarly, thinking of someone like Doc Malone with his hands on those hips. *Just a tourist,* he reminded himself. *Don't panic.*

"Sort of. I think I'm more meandering than I am passing. How far is the nearest town, by the way?"

"Tried and True is about eight miles up the highway. But the ramp back to the interstate is only five." He tipped an imaginary hat to her and went back to his patrol car to get his cell phone. When he opened the door, he heard her give a little squeaky sound.

"You're leaving? I thought you guys were supposed to aid people in distress." Her voice rose. "I could not *possibly* be more distressed! I am probably the most distressed woman in the modern world right now, and you're *leaving?*"

He paused. "Actually," he said, "I was going to call AAA for you."

He could see the blush rise from her neck as her look of indignation made a painful transformation into embarrassment. She turned away, but not before he saw the expression on her face. She looked as if she'd bitten into a lemon. Definitely an I-can't-believe-I-said-that look.

He grinned and reached into his car for the phone. "I'll just make that call."

"No!" she said suddenly, putting her arms out as if to stop him. "I mean, I'm not a member. Isn't there another way?" She paused, and he could see her mind working. "Maybe you could just shoot the window out." She backed away from her car as if he would really do it.

He rested his arms on top of his open car door and stared at her. "You want me to shoot your car."

"Just the window."

"That would be sacrilege." He shook his head and looked at the car she wanted him to kill. It was a beaut. "What year is it, anyway?"

"Nineteen sixty-three."

"So no electric locks."

"No."

"Okay," he said with resignation. He reached inside the patrol car and grabbed the slim-jim tool he always carried with him for popping manual locks.

When on duty, he was only supposed to help unlock car doors when there were children or animals locked inside, but he reasoned this was the only way he was going to get her out of his county, taking temptation with her. He walked back to her car and slipped the tool between the window and door, found the lock mechanism and pulled. She had leaned forward to watch, but immediately stepped back when she realized he had turned his head to look at her. She smelled nice, like magnolias, warm and sultry and Southern.

"Thank you," she said sheepishly, and she was just so cute standing there that he was almost sad to see her go. Almost.

He opened the door for her. "You're in Truly County, Miss Spencer. Home of the most per capita knights in shining armor in the country. We specialize in distressed women."

Clementine's lips twitched into a smile. He returned the smile and walked away, climbing into his patrol car. He looked at her in the rearview mirror as he headed back. That was the most enjoyable time he'd spent with a woman in a long time, he thought, and it just further proved his point that temporary dalliances were all a man really needed.

CLEMENTINE TURNED at the sign that said Welcome
To Tried And True, Pop. 1,955. The first thing she
came across was a large, brightly lit grocery store and,
next to it, a small motel bearing the name Gardenia
Inn. She knew she was wasting precious fuel, but she
couldn't resist driving into town. She discovered it
was a quaint place, with several residential neighbor-
hoods branching off Main Street, which was small but
prosperous, with all the storefronts occupied.

Main Street was lit by several arched, old-
fashioned street lamps. Though most stores were
closed for the night, there were several cars and trucks
parked in spaces along the sidewalk and kids were
assembled in what was apparently a ritual gathering
of teenagers standing around their vehicles, talking
and laughing. The girls were in a cluster, and the boys
in cowboy hats were striking James Dean poses
against their trucks, casting glances at the girls to see
if they were looking.

They all stopped to watch her car with blatant teenage curiosity as she made the Main Street loop. Circling back, she passed a bank, a gas station—which
she stared longingly at—and a large Feed and Seed
store before finally coming to the Gardenia Inn again.
She pulled into the strip motel, which was obviously
old but, to its credit, was brightly painted and well-
maintained. She'd become an expert at cheap lodging
and, compared to some places she'd stayed in the past
two weeks, this was the Waldorf-Astoria. She just
hoped the prices weren't inflated, it being the only
obvious lodging in town.

The front office smelled of dinner cooking and it
made Clementine's stomach growl when she entered.
Her lunch at Burger King in Noosely, Nebraska, had
long ago worn off. When she rang the service bell,
an older woman opened a door to what was appar-

ently an apartment behind the office. She smiled, setting off an array of wrinkles that charmed Clementine right off the bat. Wiping her hands on her apron, which read Watch Out! Hot Cook, she introduced herself as Mrs. Elliott, then asked, "What can I do for you, dear?"

"I'm hoping you have a vacancy."

"You're in luck," Mrs. Elliott said. "Three rooms are already taken. Mid-May Festival has brought in some relatives of Clyde and Betty Tula, but Clyde and Betty don't have room to spare at their house. And Charlotte Lovelace's son and his children are staying here because those kids drive poor old Charlotte crazy. They're here for the festival, too. Are you in for Mid-May Festival?"

"Um, no," Clementine answered, a little confused, wondering if she should already know what a Mid-May Festival was.

Though it was dark, Mrs. Elliott called to her husband, a Kriss Kringle/Burl Ives look-alike, and together they insisted on giving her a tour of the small motel, proudly pointing out the gardenias Mr. Elliott had hand-painted on each of the eight bright blue doors.

They led her to room four, bid her good-night, then left her alone, her heart fuller because of their genuine welcome, but her wallet a little emptier than it had been five minutes ago.

She knew she could have asked for, and Mrs. Elliott probably would have happily supplied her with, information about a certain sheriff. That was one handsome man. He damn near took her breath away. But he was the last—the *last* thing she needed. Not only because he was a man, but because he was a law enforcement officer.

It wasn't as if she'd done anything illegal. All she'd

done was go against her mother's wishes, which was sin enough. It had caused gasps, and probably even a faint or two, in the circles her mother traveled in in Savannah. Clementine had *disobeyed* her mother. And if it wasn't bad enough that half of Savannah society thought Clementine was two years old, she had to go and make a fool out of herself in front of one of the sexiest men she'd ever set eyes on. That man sizzled. She'd never met a man who sizzled before. Reg didn't sizzle. Reg was more like raw meat.

That man also wore a badge, she told herself. Focus, Clementine. He had the potential to notify her mother as to where she was with the simplest act. And she had barely avoided the AAA incident as it was.

On her Jack Kerouac adventure, she knew it was best to just hit the road in the morning despite Tried and True's interesting allure. The town might boast a sexy sheriff, but one thing Tried and True didn't have was a pawn shop. Reg's ring was the last thing of value, besides her car, that she had to sell. It had now come down to selling Reg's ring, or going back and wearing the ring forever.

From under her shirt she pulled the string of yellow yarn she wore around her neck. She pensively fingered Reg's ring, which was dangling on the yarn, then set it on the counter in the bathroom. It was too expensive to not have on her, but she couldn't bring herself to wear it on her finger. So now it was an albatross around her neck, constantly reminding her of her predicament. She was an engaged woman. Clementine Spencer, who had never taken a vacation without her mother, who went to college in Savannah so she could still live at home, who'd graduated a year ago next week and had never held a real job, was engaged to be married.

She just knew there had to be *something* in be-

tween. She had to do something on her own before
she settled down. She had tried to explain it to her
mother and Reg. But they'd looked at her as if she
were crazy when she'd said she wanted to get away
by herself for a while before the wedding. They were
probably thinking that the vacation she really needed
was a month of quiet time in a discreet, expensive
clinic hidden in the heart of Atlanta where no one
would ever know. Why else would someone with
such a perfect life want to get away from it, if not
because she was crazy? So she'd stopped talking
about getting away for a while, and just did it. She'd
packed two bags and left.

She took a long, hot shower in the small, pine-
cleaner-scented bathroom. It felt good to wash off the
day of traveling and the warmth of the shower got rid
of some of the kinks. She stepped out and combed
her hair, then donned a long T-shirt with Great Smoky
Mountains National Park on the front. She had bought
it when she'd passed through the beautiful mountains
of western North Carolina. In hindsight, it was a foolish purchase because she hadn't realized then how
tight money would be. She had exactly four hundred
and forty-two dollars and seventeen cents, a pair of
pearl earrings and a Cartier watch when she discovered that her credit had been revoked on her credit
cards and that her bank accounts had been frozen. It
was her mother's subtle way of getting her to come
back to Savannah.

After reluctantly slipping the necklace back on, she
plopped down onto the bed. It was surprisingly comfortable and was covered with a pretty Dutch-girl pat-
terned quilt that Mrs. Elliott said she had made herself.

Clementine smiled and grabbed her travel journal

that, along with the disposable cameras, she'd bought before she'd left Savannah.

Tried and True, Kansas, May 6

Met Callum McCutcheon, Sheriff. Tall. Lean— great body. Devil-dark hair. Have mercy. Squinted his eyes a lot, like Clint Eastwood, so I couldn't see their color. Locked keys in my car in middle of Kansas countryside. Sheriff met the doofus Clementine. Apparently I had a slight relapse, but I'm happy to report the better, independent Clementine is back, in Room #4 of the Gardenia Inn, in Tried and True, Kansas, 1200 miles from my mother and Reg and the end of my life as I know it.

2

THE NEXT MORNING she dressed in jeans, a pink T-shirt and her driving moccasins. She fought to put her curly, unruly hair, the bane of her mother's neat existence when Clementine was little, into a thick braid. No matter how polished she wanted to appear, her hair never fully cooperated. She secretly admired her hair for this. It *never* did as it was told. She then applied some sunscreen and light makeup. A canvas backpack substituted for her purse these days and she stuffed one of her disposable cameras in it before heading out to see what Tried and True had to offer by way of cheap food.

Not wanting to use more fuel, she left her car in the parking lot of the Gardenia Inn and walked half a mile down the road to the heart of Main Street. Her feet felt like lead by the time she reached the shops, which only served to remind her just how many fast-food meals she'd consumed over the past two weeks, especially since Burger King had been running that nationwide special of two Whoppers for two dollars.

As she walked down Main Street, she noticed the names of the stores that had escaped her attention the night before. Among them, there was a restaurant called Cripes, a clothing store called Lovey's Boutique and Fine Apparel, and Howard's Drugstore. Then she noticed a small barbershop with just the word Barber on the window, with several old men sitting in mismatched chairs outside the door. Next to it was Tangles, a beauty parlor with flower boxes filled with bright pansies outside, and lace curtains inside. There were a couple of older ladies walking into the parlor, ignoring the men completely.

Main Street ended in a cul-de-sac with, she noticed with interest, two older deco buildings—one done in old pink tile, the other in gray—that housed the sheriff's department and the courthouse. There was a blond pregnant woman on the sidewalk watering some potted geraniums outside the sheriff's department. She found herself wondering about Sheriff Callum McCutcheon again, not for the first time that morning. She knew that men like him, men who sizzled with sexuality, probably wanted nothing to do with hippy, fleshy, decidedly undirected and unsexual women like herself. That was what Reg said made them so compatible. Neither one of them cared very much about sex.

The sheriff would care about sex. She knew that without a doubt.

Get a grip, Clementine, she told herself harshly. One ticket, one minor infraction, one little call to AAA, and her mother would know exactly where she was. She definitely did not need to associate with the sizzling sheriff, even if he wanted to associate with her.

Which he did not.

So there.

She turned around and walked back to Cripes. The restaurant was about half-full and she attracted some attention as she walked in. There were a lot of men, wearing either denim, flannel or overalls, and a few chatty women at corner tables.

"What can I get for you?" a tall, young woman in blue jeans said when Clementine settled herself in a booth. She handed Clementine a menu. Her name tag said she was Naomi, and she had long, beautiful, auburn hair.

Clementine looked at the menu and ordered the breakfast special, knowing she should just go for toast and coffee, taking advantage of all the free packages of jam at the table. But, damn it, she was hungry, and she wasn't going to make what could be the biggest decision of her life, the one to go back to Savannah and become Mrs. Reginald Remington Richards III, on an empty stomach. She had thirty-nine dollars and a fourth of a tank of fuel left. Her mother had left no stone unturned. Even her gas cards were useless now.

Naomi scribbled something on her pad and took the menu from Clementine after she ordered. "You're new here, aren't you?" she said, pocketing the pad. "In for Mid-May Festival?"

Clementine started to say yes, just so she would look as though she knew what she was doing, but instead she said, "I'm starting to feel out of the loop. That's the second time someone's asked me that. What is Mid-May Festival?"

"An excuse for the ladies in town to make more pies," Naomi said, grinning. "Mid-May ranks right up there with the Fourth of July celebration, the Halloween masquerade and the Christmas pageant as Tried and True's big annual events. It's a street festival right here on Main. The street is closed and booths are set up. There's music and food and a legendary pie contest."

"Legendary?"

Naomi laughed. "Legendary in this part of Kansas, anyway. The contest dates back to the founding of the town. It's quite a to-do. The ladies take it very seriously. My mother is one of the contestants this year and she's determined to win. Pie is very important to this town.''

"Well, I'm all for anything that involves pie," Clementine said.

Naomi chuckled and someone called to her from a table across the room. "Sorry. Be back with your plate. The morning waitress quit last week to elope with the guy who delivers Budweiser to the grocery store, and I'm pulling a double shift until Harlan finds a replacement for her. I don't have a handle on what the regulars want yet, because frankly I'm not used to thinking this early in the morning. I'm plainly about to be reminded."

When Naomi walked away, Clementine sat back and looked around. Her eyes landed on the Help Wanted sign in the window and she felt a tingle run along her skin as she leaned forward thoughtfully. A month. She told her mother she'd be back in a month. That was in two weeks. Wouldn't it be great to be able to say that she'd gotten a job and supported her own trek around the country, despite her mother's efforts at sabotage? Wouldn't a real job be fantastic? In two weeks she could make enough money to go home on her own, an independent success.

And then what? Marry Reg?

She decided not to think that far ahead.

Naomi brought her coffee, then a huge plate of scrambled eggs, pancakes, sausage and biscuits. Clementine ate, enjoying every bite, then lingered over coffee. She finally took her check to the cash register where she waited for Naomi.

"Sorry you had to wait," Naomi said as she came up to the register. "Harlan's wife, Joanne, usually does this, but there was an emergency Ladies Club meeting today."

Clementine smiled. "My mother's clubs regularly

call emergency meetings. She flies, in the middle of dinner, in the bathtub, in her garden gloves, she literally *flies* out the door as if she's going to save the world." Naomi laughed and Clementine paused. She didn't want to go back to that. Not yet.

"Listen, I'm new here, which I know doesn't work in my favor because no one can vouch for me. But I'm a fast learner, a hard worker and I can start at any time. The sooner the better."

"You want the job?" Naomi blinked in surprise.

"Yes."

"Oh, you are an angel from heaven!" Naomi threw her arms in the air. "When you walked in here I should have known. I'll vouch for you. Hold on. Just sit here at the counter and I'll get Harlan. I have a ten-year-old boy at home and these hours are no good for him. I get here at five-thirty in the morning and leave at six in the evening. He's been practically living with my mother for the past week. But I had to help Harlan out. He's been good to me. He gave me this job when I really needed it. I'll make sure he does the same for you." The fact that Clementine had carefully counted the money from her pocket, rubbing the bills between her thumb and index finger to make sure no bills were sticking together, obviously hadn't escaped Naomi's attention.

Naomi disappeared into the kitchen and Clementine felt a twinge of guilt. She hadn't meant to present herself as down on her luck. Naomi thought she really needed this job. The waitress had no way of knowing Clementine was a woman with thirty million dollars to her name, who was running around the country trying to make herself come to terms with marrying a perfect man she had no reason not to marry, except for the one small fact that she didn't love him.

Clementine had expected a burly man with a handlebar mustache, but Harlan turned out to be a small, thin man neatly dressed in chef's whites. "Naomi, here, recommends you, so you're hired. Can you start tomorrow?"

Clementine beamed, thrilled that someone was actually giving her a chance to prove herself. "Absolutely."

"Watch Naomi for a while. Follow her around today and I'll give you lunch on the house for it. Be here at five-thirty sharp tomorrow morning. Naomi will show you the routine. I'm going to need information from you later, social security number, that kind of thing. For now, just watch and learn and be on time."

"Yes, sir," she said, determined to avoid the paperwork. The minute something like a ticket or a credit check got out into public access, some clever detective could trace Clementine on his computer. Okay, so maybe she was being a little paranoid, but her mother was a force to be reckoned with, someone who did her best work when she was underestimated.

Naomi and Clementine had fun that morning, and Clementine was so excited that she asked to take the breakfast menu home so she could study it.

As eleven o'clock approached, Clementine excused herself to call the Gardenia Inn to ask Mr. and Mrs. Elliott to hold her room. When Naomi told her what the normal tips were, Clementine thought she could handle the room fee for the next two weeks, with a little left over to get her back to Savannah. She didn't worry too much about the paycheck itself because Harlan couldn't very well give her one without social security information.

When she got off the pay phone by the rest rooms, Clementine noticed that nearly everyone in the restaurant had turned to look out the sidewalk-front windows. A group of ladies had come out of the Tangles hair salon, and they were walking down the sidewalk carrying big placards attached to long pieces of wood.

"I don't believe it," Naomi mumbled, astonished, as Clementine came to stand beside her. "I didn't think they were serious."

"What's going on?"

"They're going over to Wild Rose Lane to picket the tearing down of one of the houses. It's an old house that's been the meeting place of the Tried and True Ladies Club for years. That," she said, pointing to a tall, blond, sweet-looking lady about sixty years old, "is my mother." Naomi shook her head. "You've definitely picked an interesting time to come to Tried and True."

Naomi handed her a white paper bag containing the lunch Clementine had ordered, a specialty of Harlan's, six-cheese manicotti. One of the churches she passed that morning had a large grassy field area with picnic tables where she planned to eat and go over the menu she borrowed. She was going to work her butt off and be a damn good waitress. Clementine knew she wasn't going to make much money, but it was going to be enough.

"I'll see you tomorrow," she said, taking the bag, which was warm.

"Where are you staying?" Naomi asked her.

"At the Gardenia Inn." Clementine paused, realizing that didn't sound very ambitious for a person looking for employment. "For now, I mean. As I said, I just arrived here. Everything's still pretty new."

Naomi looked thoughtful. "You know, Vera Suttles has a basement apartment that she can let. I'll talk to her."

Clementine was startled by the offer. She wasn't expecting anything so generous as help looking for a place to stay. "I'm going to save up some money first. Give me two weeks."

Naomi nodded, still looking thoughtful. "I'll talk to her."

Shouldering her backpack, Clementine told herself not to get too attached to these people. She was going to have to leave in two weeks. She had to.

She headed outside and down the sidewalk, glancing in windows and enjoying the warm day. There were several streets that turned off Main and, happening upon the first one, she discovered where the ladies had gone to protest. The first house to the right on Wild Rose Lane was just a stone's throw from Main and about twelve women were congregated on the front lawn of an old, two-story house with peeling gray paint and a beautiful columned porch.

Clementine turned the corner to get a better look.

The placards they carried read Save The Talbert House and This Is a Tried And True Monument and Down with Fast-Food Restaurants. Clementine brought out her camera, thinking this definitely needed to be caught on film.

She had taken about three different shots before two of the women broke ranks and walked over to her.

"Are you Ed Harlow's new photographer?" the one with perfectly coifed salt-and-pepper hair asked.

"Ed Harlow?" Clementine repeated, lowering her camera.

"He runs Tried and True's weekly the *Examiner*. I guess you're not, then." She looked disappointed.

"No, sorry. What's going on?"

The other woman, Naomi's mother, sighed. "Robert Talbert is making noises about selling this old place. Says a nice fast-food restaurant chain might want to buy the land, it being so near Main Street.

The house hasn't been lived in for about twenty years, but back then he gave the Ladies Club permission to meet here, and we've kept it fixed up. Ever since he moved over to that fancy place on Crane River Road he's been wanting to get rid of this house, and now we think he's finally going to do it. But he just can't! It's historical!''

"Now calm down, Callie. Watch your nerves." The other woman, who Clementine found out was Vera Suttles, patted Callie's arm.

"If it's historical, he can't tear it down. Do you have a local preservation society?" Clementine offered hopefully, having learned something being the daughter of a member of the reputable Georgia Historical Society in Savannah.

"It's not officially historical," Callie Parrish said. "But old Robert's grandmother was Grace Talbert, one of the founding women of Tried and True. She lived in this house in her later years, then it was passed on to her children. She was known for miles around for her pies. Most of us knew her when we were children, and our mothers and grandmothers baked with her. Meeting in her old home seemed appropriate for our Ladies Club because we share recipes and plan bake sales and our booth at Mid-May. Grace Talbert won the county pie contest every year, even before there was a Mid-May Festival. Oh, what would she think of Robert doing this?"

"She wouldn't like it one bit," Vera grunted.

"Have there been any actual offers on the land?" Clementine asked.

"No! Isn't that awful? That old fart is trying to get fast-food places to look at it. To actually bring them in! It's a disgrace to his grandmother's memory."

The longer Clementine listened, the more involved she became in the Ladies Club's plight. She spent

about a half an hour with them and was introduced
to the dozen or so women, who constituted just a
portion of the Ladies Club's actual membership. The
rest either couldn't make it or their husbands had
caught wind of it and had argued them out of coming.

She was just about to leave when a patrol car pulled
up in front of the house. The ladies huddled together
with steely resolve, staring at the young man who
alighted, looking distinctly nervous. He pulled a bullhorn, of all things, out of the car.

"Ladies," he called, his mouth to the bullhorn
even though he was less than twenty feet away. He
cleared his throat and the sound echoed throughout
the neighborhood, bringing people out onto their front
porches to see what was going on. "Ladies, you were
warned not to do this. I just got a call from Robert
Talbert. You know you're not supposed to be doing
this on his property. I'm going to have to ask you all
to…leave."

Cries rang out.

"That's not fair!"

"We've been meeting here for years!"

The young officer lowered the bullhorn slightly and
Clementine saw him pinch his lips together nervously.
He tried to square his shoulders professionally as he
put the handheld device to his mouth again. "Ladies,
Robert says you're trespassing. If you don't leave, I'll
have to take you in."

"Is that old coot pressing charges?"

"Arrest us then, Mac."

"That'll draw attention!"

"Come on, girls, we're being arrested," someone
shouted. "Let's walk over to the jail."

Mac watched, openmouthed, as the Ladies Club
members marched up to Main and toward the sheriff's

department. Clementine and her bag of manicotti, caught in a death grip between Vera and Callie, were hopelessly towed to the last place in Tried and True that Clementine wanted to be.

3

MONDAY MORNING the phone rang and Callum nearly fell out of bed trying to get to it. "Yes, what is it? I'm here," he barked, trying to unfold his naked self from the sheets. What on earth had he done in his sleep to get his leg wrapped up like this? It wasn't as if he had anyone in bed with him to roll around with, which he was starting to feel acutely. Especially when he first awoke. And especially in one particular place on his body. Light shone sharply through the windows and he scowled, squinting against the sunlight as he pushed his getting-too-long dark hair off his forehead. He needed the sleep, but he always felt this crazy time-warp sensation when he awoke so late in the morning. Still kicking halfheartedly to free his leg, he reached for his bedside clock. Whoa. It was after noon.

"It's me."

"What's wrong, Maggie?" he asked his sister, the department's dispatcher.

"I think you should get down here right now, Callum."

Calls like this had been frequent since Jess had broken his arm and ribs. "I'll be there. What is it? Is Luke in yet?"

"Not yet." There was a lot of noise coming from Maggie's end. "Don't you remember? He's not scheduled until this afternoon. Mac was all alone here this morning."

"Right." Callum rubbed his eyes, recalling the schedules he had made out. "But he's still wet behind the ears."

"You can say that again." More noise. It sounded as if there was some commotion down at the station.

"What's going on, Maggie?"

"Just get down here." Then she hung up. He could have sworn she was laughing. She didn't give him any codes, nothing to alert him to an emergency, so he had no idea what exactly was wrong.

He pulled himself free of the sheets and trudged to the bathroom. He dressed quickly in a pair of jeans and a faded denim shirt, then slid into his boots.

As he walked through the kitchen on his way out, he saw his overweight cat, Mabel, sitting patiently on the countertop, her calico tail swishing. Callum sighed and quickly opened a can of food and left it on the counter beside the perpetually perky cat.

Mabel had been a gift to Callum from his sister when he'd first moved back to town. He could barely tolerate the cat at first because he had always fancied himself a dog man, but the nosy cat had soon grown on him. Not that he would ever tell another living soul. Not even his sister, whom he suspected already knew because Harold at the grocery store told her Callum bought the most expensive canned cat food he had.

He patted the cat on the head, earning his ears the buzz of her broken chainsaw purr. Walking outside into the warm, bone-dry day, he climbed into his dusty, old black Jeep Cherokee. He headed out, yawning most of the way.

One of the reasons he had taken over the sheriff's job after old Ronald Cobb died midterm was because he'd owed Tried and True. He had been a trouble-maker, a real bad seed, when he was a kid, and had had more than his share of run-ins with old Cobb. But Cobb had been a big influence on him and the main reason Callum had gone into law enforcement. When Cobb died and Callum was offered the position, everyone was in agreement and Callum couldn't refuse. And it couldn't have come at a better time. He had wanted to leave Topeka and his ex-wife and the pain of his divorce behind. He had liked his job on the force in Topeka, but he'd found himself longing for the quieter pace and the astounding sense of community of Tried and True.

But since one of his deputies had been laid up, the pace hadn't been very quiet. Though Mac was full of zeal, the presence of a more experienced lawman was missed. And with Jess out, there were inevitable times when Mac was alone on duty. Such as this morning.

What was wrong now?

Instead of getting answers, Callum was even more confused when he finally walked into the station. He stood in the doorway and pushed his hair off his forehead with the palm of his hand. There were women everywhere, talking loudly. Some were arguing with their husbands, who looked none too pleased to be there. Mac was sitting at his desk looking bewildered and Maggie was chattily serving coffee to everyone.

When Mac saw Callum enter, the relief was evident on his face. He sprang from his chair and weeded his way through the people. "Sheriff, boy am I glad to see you."

"What the hell is going on?" The young deputy winced and Callum had to remember to go easy on him, he was still learning. In a calmer voice he said, "Tell me what happened, Mac."

Mac looked warily over his shoulder. "These

ladies seem to think they're under arrest," he said in a hushed voice, as if afraid of what would happen if one of the Ladies Club members heard him.

"And they're not?"

"No. I did *not* place them under arrest. I've tried and tried to tell them, but they still insisted on coming to the station. I told them there wasn't room enough for them all, but then they started hollering about getting their one phone call. That's why some of the husbands are here. They came waving money and demanding to pay their wives' bail. But, Sheriff, none of these ladies is under arrest!"

Callum ran a hand over his chin, remembering he hadn't shaved. "All right, Mac. Tell me why they *think* they're under arrest."

"Because we got a call from Robert Talbert this morning saying some members of the Ladies Club were picketing on his property over on Wild Rose and he wanted them off before they drew too much attention. So I went over there, but they seemed to *want* the attention. And, let me tell you, they got a lot of it as they marched down Main Street. They shouted 'Down with fast food!' all the way over here."

"I'll take care of it, Mac." Callum had to smile. He couldn't help it. "Ladies," he called loudly, just once, pushing his hair off his forehead again. The room went silent. "I'm here to tell you that you aren't under arrest and no one has to pay any money to get out of here. There weren't any charges pressed and you are all free to go home. And by that I mean *home*. Do not go back to the old Talbert place and stir up more trouble."

"But, Callum, Robert means to tear the house down!" Vera Suttles, owner of Tangles, spoke up. Her husband, Vernon, frowned at her.

Callum nodded with understanding. "Vera, you

know as well as I do that Robert likes to talk a lot about big business deals and ways to make money. But how many times has he actually done anything? He's letting you ladies meet there, and will continue to let you meet there until he decides what to do about the house, which might be soon or it might be never. He just doesn't want you picketing on his property.''

There were a few more protests, followed by some scattered mumbles, but finally the room started to clear. Some of the husbands muttered apologies to him as they sheepishly escorted their wives out. They were obviously still in that state of confused disbelief that men often are when it comes to the women they marry. Callum sympathized. The hell if he could understand now why he'd married Liza. And he wasn't likely to make that mistake again.

Maggie came up to him and shoved a cup of coffee into his hands. "You look awful, Callum. Couldn't you have at least shaved?''

He smiled at his very pregnant sister. "I would have, but I was in a hurry to get here. I thought it was an emergency.''

"Well, to the Tried and True Ladies Club it is,'' she pointed out, walking back to her desk.

"You're still mad that I missed Sunday dinner last night, aren't you?''

She pulled a wry face. "Someone needs to take care of you, Callum McCutcheon.''

Callum gulped his coffee, figuring he would just stay the rest of the day now that he was here, even though his sister was half mad at him. First he'd grab a sandwich, then he'd shave, maybe even find time to brush his teeth. Mac looked as though he needed some time off for lunch anyway.

The last group of ladies had just walked out of the building and was strolling by the window. He only caught a glimpse of them, but something caught his eye. Some*one* caught his eye. Someone taller than the rest, with long, curly hair. He turned fully to look out the window.

It was her. He lowered his mug in stunned disbelief.

"Mac?" he said, not taking his eyes off her.

The deputy walked up to him and followed his gaze. "I don't know her name, but she was with the ladies at the protest," he explained. "And she walked with them over here. Or, I guess more accurately, they dragged her with them. She was real quiet. Funny thing is, she was the only one who didn't want to make a phone call. I think she must be new to the area. Or related to one of the ladies. She's a looker, isn't she?"

Callum put his mug down and headed for the door. "I'm going to grab a sandwich at Sandy's. I'll be right back," he said to Mac and Maggie as he jogged out the door and down the sidewalk toward Clementine.

He caught up with her and her five friends. From behind them he said, "May I have a word with you, Miss Spencer?"

All six of them turned simultaneously.

"Well, hello, Sheriff," Clementine said, giving him a what-a-coincidence smile. She adjusted the canvas backpack she had thrown over one shoulder, looking thoroughly uncomfortable. "Fancy meeting you again."

"Yes," he replied, tipping an imaginary hat to the ladies. "Fancy that." The sun angled down and hit her face in such a way as to make her eyes shine. They were a sparkling, crystalline green, an exotic surprise to their almond shape.

The ladies looked reluctant to leave, but, having no

real excuse to stay, turned and continued down the sidewalk, *very* slowly, casting several glances back along the way.

"Before you say a word, I have to tell you I didn't have anything to do with starting that protest," she said, tilting her head to look at him. "I just sort of…happened to be there."

Mad at himself for pondering too long on the color of her eyes, he said too brusquely, "I thought you said you were just passing through, Miss Spencer."

She looked a little startled by his tone. "I decided to stay for a little while. Mid-May," she said, as if suddenly remembering. "I want to see Mid-May."

"You're staying," he said.

"You can get that look off of your face," she said. But he could tell she was absolutely serious. "I'm just staying for a little while."

"Where is your car?" he asked, inadvertently sounding as if he couldn't get rid of her fast enough. He looked down Main Street. It was easy enough to see that there wasn't an expensively restored green vintage sports car parked in any of the spaces.

"I left it at the inn," she said.

"You walked all the way from the Gardenia Inn?"

"Is that so unusual? It's only about a half mile."

"More like a mile and a half."

She suddenly laughed. "Well, that explains it. But it's not like I couldn't use the exercise," she said, patting a hip with one hand.

She had to go and do that. She had to make his eyes go to the one place they shouldn't. He didn't know what it was about this woman. His ex-wife was a stick. And he usually had an appreciation for lithe, more athletic female bodies. But then Clementine had to waltz into town with those hips and that small waist and that heart-shaped behind. Right there on Main, he was practically drooling over a woman he didn't know, didn't want to know and, by God, would never know. He must be more sexually frustrated than he thought. Here he was, living in a town where no God-fearing man could have a casual fling without having his ears boxed by a Ladies Club member. And he had long since determined, a fling was all the relationship he was ever going to have with a woman again.

"I'm going to Sandy's," he announced suddenly, aware of the audience they had attracted, and of the spectacle he was making of himself. The ladies had made very little headway down the sidewalk, and Mac and Maggie were watching them from the station's front window. Mac was at the nearest desk, shuffling papers needlessly, but Maggie was blatantly staring.

"Sandy's?" She called after him as he started walking. The women in front of them picked up speed as if they had been poked with a stick, and with a hop they started trotting toward Tangles.

"Sandy's Soda Shop. Right down there." He pointed to the shop a short distance from the station that had a green-and-white-striped tin awning shading the front windows. She caught up with him and he could, for a moment, smell her perfume. Damn, she smelled good.

"Why don't you go to Cripes?" she said factually, obviously proud of her growing knowledge of the town.

"Because Cripes is all the way at the other end of Main Street. And it's a sit-down restaurant. Sandy's has deli stuff and take-out sandwiches."

They reached the front of Sandy's and he stopped, but she continued walking, which was disappointing. "Enjoy your meal, Sheriff," she said.

Just because he wanted to, definitely not because

he couldn't help it, he watched her walk away. That's when he noticed the large laminated menu sticking out of her backpack.

"Whoa, wait a minute." Taking three long steps over to her, he plucked the menu out of her backpack, causing her to spin around. "Do you want to explain this?"

She tried to grab it from him, but he held it away from her. "What do you mean, explain it?" she demanded.

"Is this a little souvenir you decided to take from Cripes?"

"No," she said, then seemed to realize what he was implying. "No! I did *not* steal that. Harlan said I could take it home tonight and study it."

He had a sinking feeling. "Why would you want to study the breakfast menu from Cripes?" he asked slowly.

"Because I'm going to be working there. For a while."

"Working there?"

"Stop looking at me like I'm some sort of criminal. I'm not doing anything wrong. I'm sorry if I put you out by locking my keys in my car last night, and I'm sorry I gave you the impression that I'm unstable for wanting you to shoot my window out. But that can easily fall under the stress of being lost and tired. I'm sorry for whatever it is I did to rub you the wrong way, but I hardly think I warrant this kind of concern, like I'm some bad influence on your town."

He studied her for a moment before coming to a conclusion. "You're fairly young for twenty-four."

She looked almost appalled, as if he'd just called her a wailing baby. "What?"

"I mean, you're a little naive." He shook his head. "Or maybe that's not the word. Guileless."

She pulled herself up and lifted her chin haughtily. "I'm not about to defend my intelligence to *you*."

"I said you were guileless, not dumb."

She snatched the menu from his hands and turned on her heel to march down the sidewalk. He watched her go, admiring her long-legged gait and the swish of her beautiful hips. But then he saw Randy Maddox walk out of Howard's Drugstore across the street and do the same, and he felt something almost like jealousy.

Randy ambled across the street and started a conversation with him, but Callum kept watching Clementine. Vera came out of Tangles as soon as Clementine marched by. She obviously called her name because Clementine turned, startled, then smiled.

A few words passed and he saw Clementine motion vaguely in his direction. Vera turned and glared at him. She shooed Clementine into Tangles and, Callum could hardly believe it, Vera started toward him.

It took her a minute to get to him even though her short little body was doing overtime. Her perfectly coifed salt-and-pepper hair, immovable with hair spray, didn't stir at all. Callum saw no point in trying to get away. Randy, however, saw her and made a hasty excuse to leave. Everyone in Tried and True knew that look. The look of an indignant Ladies Club member.

Vera finally approached him, out of breath.

"Hello, Vera," he said, being overly cordial. "How are you? Nice day, isn't it? Think we'll get any rain?"

"Don't you try to make nice with me, young man. You upset Clementine," she accused without preamble. The fact that Callum was at least a foot taller than she was didn't seem to temper her a bit.

"She said that?"

"She didn't have to say anything. She looked burning mad when she walked by my shop, and when I came out to ask her what was wrong she would only say she'd just talked to you. As far as I'm concerned, that's enough said. You listen here, Callum McCutcheon, you may be the sheriff, you may even be a pretty good one, but you don't go around offending pretty women. It's just not done." She wagged a finger at him. "How on earth do you hope to land yourself a wife with that attitude?"

I shouldn't have gotten out of bed, he thought. *That's all there is to it.* "I'm not in the market for a wife," he returned wearily. *I could, however, use a good roll in the hay.* Out of concern for his ears, he didn't say that out loud.

"Well, you know how I feel on that subject," she said with a tone of disapproval. "But really, Callum, what kind of impression of our town do you think you gave that poor girl? A pretty pitiful one, if you ask me. Honestly, you would think you could be a little nicer. Clementine is our newest resident and we want her to feel welcome. I'll bet Doc Malone will do a much better job than you."

With that, she turned and made her way back down to Tangles.

Well, damn, he thought. He was pretty sure he had to save Clementine now.

CLEMENTINE NOTICED something about Sheriff Callum: he pushed his hair off his forehead a lot. It was almost too long, and made him look rakish. She still didn't know the color of his eyes because he always seemed to be squinting into the sun when she talked to him. But he thought she was a royal ditz, his feelings lightly veiled by the words, *naive* and *guileless.*

In other words, he thought she was *young* and *stupid*.

She pressed her lips together as she swung her motel room door shut behind her that evening. She fell back onto the bed, hugging her backpack, and stared at the ceiling.

She had taken one look at him as he'd walked in the door of the station that afternoon and felt her stomach clutch. She should *not* be feeling this way about a man when she was still officially engaged. She had tried to hide herself among the ladies and, once she was out the door, thought she had successfully avoided him and a possible criminal record. But he'd spotted her, which she'd discovered was a fairly easy thing to do in this town. Everyone had spotted her, and now most people knew she was the morning waitress at Cripes and was staying at the Gardenia Inn.

Passing by Tangles after her run-in with the sheriff, Vera had pulled her in and had insisted on giving Clementine a welcome-to-town shampoo and style. That had snowballed into we're-sorry-the-sheriff-was-rude-but-we're-sure-you'll-like-our-doctor blond highlights. How it had all happened was still a blur, but now she had a new color for the new her. Her mother had never approved of hair color on Clementine, but Clementine would eat her moccasins if her mother was a natural redhead.

Clementine loved her new color. *Loved* it.

She had eaten her manicotti at Tangles while listening to the ladies regroup after their unsuccessful coup that afternoon. Then talk had turned to the Mid-May Festival and the pie booth the Ladies Club was going to set up there. Clementine had found herself caught up in the hype of Mid-May. She had even watched that afternoon as a huge banner proclaiming the festival's imminent arrival on Saturday was hung high across Main Street.

It was only later, alone in her room, that she realized how nice everyone was being to her, as if they expected her to stay and become one of them. This town thought she was an independent, spunky traveler looking for someplace to settle down. And she liked that image of her. She liked what it said, that she wasn't afraid to go out and find what she wanted.

She didn't like, however, that she seemed to have fit in so comfortably so soon. And then there was the slightly distressing fact that the ladies had mentioned several men they wanted her to meet. This had prompted Clementine to give the ambiguous blanket statement that she had just left a relationship, which was mostly true. She just didn't tell them she had to go back to it. She refused to give the ladies details, but, by not wanting to talk about it, she inadvertently had the ladies cursing this unknown lover who'd done her wrong.

She propped herself up on the bed and set the alarm on the clock radio to wake her up with music from a country station in the neighboring county. She left the curtains open and could see that the sun was low in the beautiful smooth Kansas sky.

She pulled her travel journal and the breakfast menu from Cripes out of her backpack and set them on her stomach. Sighing, she closed her eyes for a moment.

She fell asleep before she could, number one, trash Sheriff Callum in her journal, and, number two, study for her new job.

4

CALLUM'S SUSPICIONS were confirmed the moment he walked in. Cripes was filled to capacity, and people were crowded just inside the door waiting for seats.

He'd never come to Cripes for breakfast before. As soon as the first person said hello, everyone saw that he was there and everyone knew the reason why. It was the reason everyone else in town seemed to have shown up.

Clementine.

"Why, Callum," said Joanne, seated behind the cash register. "What are you doing here?"

"Um," he replied stupidly. Most of the Ladies Club members were there, and all of them were looking at him with knowing smiles. They were sizing him up, planning his wedding, wondering just how many children he was going to have. He fought the urge to run.

"There's a forty-five minute wait, Callum. Clementine is learning the ropes this morning and that, combined with the crowd she's brought in, has made for a busy morning." Joanne smiled at him. "You should have been here when we opened. Doc Malone was."

Callum looked over to where a bleary-eyed Doc Malone was seated with Vera and Mimi Creavy. "Yeah. He makes a point of eating with Vera and

Mimi every chance he gets. You ladies are being a bit obvious, aren't you?''

"Why, Callum, I don't know what you mean," Joanne said, trying but failing to sound innocent.

"Doc Malone isn't looking for a wife any more than I am. If there's one man with worse hours than I have right now, it's him. Don't you have any compassion? Getting him out of bed like this for your own cruel matchmaking purposes. You should be ashamed."

"You're just jealous. Everyone knows how you argued with Clementine on her first day here. You missed your chance."

There was a loud crash and all heads turned to where Clementine was profusely apologizing to Randy Maddox for dropping his plate on the floor in front of him and covering his work boots with his order of sunny-side-up eggs.

Randy was grinning at her, telling her it was all right. Everyone around him was murmuring in agreement, telling her she was doing just fine. Callum almost shook his head. She'd mesmerized everyone.

Okay, so she'd done the same thing to him. But now the whole town was involved and she had no idea what she was in for. The members of the Ladies Club were exasperating sometimes, but Callum understood their underlying motives in relentlessly badgering the single younger locals. It was a small town, and a good chunk of its population was over fifty. With so many kids leaving after high school for college or better jobs, the Ladies Club desperately wanted growth and rejuvenation and assurance that Tried and True and the community they loved so much would go on. Clementine was, whether she knew it or not, now a part of their plan.

Carrying the remnants of one of Harlan's thick

white breakfast plates, Clementine bustled up to the counter. "I'm sorry, Joanne," she said breathlessly.

"Don't worry about it. Look at this crowd you've brought in. That more than makes up for a couple of plates."

Clementine's hair was knotted into a bun at the base of her neck and the curly tendrils fell haphazardly around her face, which was shiny from the obvious exertion of her new job. Her hair was blond, he thought suddenly. It wasn't a bright blond, nor was it a drastic change from the light brown it had been before, but it was definitely different. She was wearing denim Capri pants and a short red button-down shirt. She had a yellow pencil tucked behind her left ear and a white hand towel thrown over her shoulder. She also had a look of absolute concentration on her face, as if determined to listen and remember every word anyone said to her. She looked, in a word, enchanting.

"Hello, Clementine," he said, crossing his arms over his chest.

She turned and he almost saw her breath catch. Hmm. Interesting reaction. Her eyes were beautiful, he found himself thinking again. The almond slant, the bright green. Whether she knew it or not, and he was willing to bet she didn't know, she was one hell of a sexy woman. "Hello."

"You seem to be doing all right."

She looked down at the broken pieces of plate in her hands. "I thought your powers of observation would be a little keener, considering you're the sheriff."

"Don't forget, I'm also something of a politician."

"Ah, that explains the compliment you didn't mean. I've got to get back to work." She looked around at all the people taking great interest in their conversation. "Nice talking to you."

"You, too."

"Are you going to wait for a table?" Joanne asked him, grinning like a monkey.

"No. I've got to get to work, too." And with that he walked out the door.

"HOLD ON, CLEMENTINE," Joanne said as Clementine was about to leave after her shift. Joanne disappeared into the kitchen and Clementine walked up to the counter to wait for her, her feet hurting, trying not to say *Ouch, ouch, ouch,* every time she took a step because she didn't want to look like a pansy. She could do this. What she wasn't sure she could do was walk the mile and a half back to the Gardenia Inn. Maybe with the tips she'd made, which she knew were generous because she was new, she'd be able to buy some fuel for her car so she wouldn't have to walk so far. Or maybe not, she thought, doing some math. She'd have to save all she could to pay the daily rate of the motel. Clementine looked at her feet. Maybe she could at least afford to go to the grocery store and buy some arch supports for her two-hundred dollar Nieman Marcus driving moccasins, which were now smudged with strawberry jam.

"Sorry to make you wait, dear," Joanne said as she came back out of the kitchen with a white paper take-home bag. "I know you're tired, but you did great, just great. Everyone liked you." Joanne grinned at her from behind the register. "Was there anyone you liked, in particular?"

Clementine looked at her, confused. "Everyone was super. I liked them all. No one yelled at me, which I consider a good measure of how patient the people are in this town."

"Uh-huh," Joanne said patiently. "What I meant was, is there any *man* in particular that you liked."

Clementine paused, not knowing what to say. Somehow, *Well, the sheriff does something funny to me,* didn't seem advisable.

"Doc Malone looked pretty smitten with you. He's single, you know. A great doctor. He'd be a good provider. I know he has that ponytail thing—" Joanne made a swiping motion behind her head "—but that's okay, right?"

Clementine opened and closed her mouth. "I didn't get to talk with him much. He fell asleep in his pancakes."

Joanne waved her hand dismissively. "He's just tired. He had a house call last night. He's handsome, isn't he?"

"Very," Clementine agreed, then added, "Not every man can pull off that maple syrup look."

"I think I'll invite him to lunch here tomorrow so you can spend some time with him after your shift." Clementine felt like a deer caught in headlights. Yes, Joanne was trying to set her up on a date. "Don't worry, dear. He's nothing like that cad who left you for his private masseuse."

Clementine smiled. Obviously, without the details about the beau she left behind, the Ladies Club had made up their own. She almost laughed at the sudden, ludicrous image of Reg with a private masseuse. Reg would never consent to a massage. Not unless he was fully clothed. Clementine was pretty sure Reg had been born fully clothed. He wore a suit and tie to pool parties.

"Oh, I almost forgot," Joanne said, holding out the paper bag. "Callum called in a lunch order. We don't usually do deliveries, but with Jess out with his broken arm and ribs, they're busy over at the station, so we try to help out. Could you walk this over to Callum before you go home?''

So much for trying to avoid the sheriff. But what could she do? Refuse? Joanne and Harlan had been so nice about her breaking plates and her utter confusion that morning. "I'll be glad to, Joanne." She took the warm white bag from her. "See you tomorrow."

"You did a good job today, Clementine."

Despite herself, Clementine smiled at the praise. She knew she'd done an awful job, but tomorrow she would do better. And the next day, even better. The important thing was that she was doing it herself. This was money she'd earned, not inherited. She wasn't expecting the rush it gave her. She'd been a child of privilege and had always taken money for granted. She was tired and her feet hurt, but she had a little money in her pocket, money that she'd earned, and it felt so good.

Clementine Spencer, breadwinner. She smiled at the thought.

As she walked down Main, the sunshine warm on her face, some people greeted her by name. She answered, knowing most of their names now, too. There was Randy Maddox, whose shoes she'd spilled egg on. Charlotte Lovelace, into whose bowl of oatmeal Clementine had poured coffee. And Howard Lime, to whom she'd given the wrong order, but he'd eaten it anyway.

When she opened the door to the sheriff's department, she was relieved to see only the cute, blond pregnant woman, the department dispatcher, who was there yesterday. That meant she could give the bag to her and not have to see Callum at all.

"Hi," Clementine said, lifting the bag. "Delivery."

The woman smiled at her. "He's in his office. He said to tell you to bring it in there."

Clementine looked at the door as if it led to a fiery pit.

"He's harmless, I promise. And a nice guy, if you want the truth. I'm his sister, so I *could* tell you that when he was five he liked to run around the house wearing nothing but cowboy boots and a red towel that was supposed to be his Superman cape, held together with a clothespin at his neck. But I choose not to reveal this embarrassing phase of my brother's youth because I am a mature adult."

Clementine laughed. She was really beginning to like this town. She walked to the door and knocked once.

From inside he barked loudly, "Come in."

Clementine looked over her shoulder at Callum's sister, unsure. "I have pictures," she said reassuringly. "Naked as a jaybird."

Callum didn't look up when she opened the door. "Close the door and take a seat."

She paused, frozen. She just wanted to give him the bag and leave. She didn't want to sit in front of that mammoth scarred desk, which looked like something out of a headmaster's office, and she definitely didn't want to close the door.

He looked up briefly. "Close the door and sit down," he repeated.

She closed the door behind her with a timid click and reluctantly took one of the two chairs opposite him. She put her backpack on the floor beside her and set the bag in her lap. The office had dark paneling and an entire wall was taken up by several old-fashioned wooden file cabinets that looked as if they weighed about a ton each. The drawers alone would probably take two hands to pull them open.

There were several framed photographs of a short, portly man wearing a sheriff's uniform and accepting awards from various people. In a prominent place on the wall by the desk there was a photograph of this same man with a teenage Callum who, by the way he was stooping, looked uncomfortable that he was so much taller than this older man. They stood close, their arms around each other, outside a home near some concrete front steps. Something about that photograph touched her, that Callum would want it where he could see the awkward boy he used to be, the one who didn't want to be taller than a man he obviously admired.

The room was awkwardly silent. After a few minutes she cleared her throat and finally said, ''Do you do this to everyone? No wonder Cripes doesn't normally deliver to you.''

He didn't respond. He was busy writing something down and comparing it to something on the computer. He finally scribbled what she assumed to be his signature and put the paper into one of the three wire-mesh stacking baskets on his desk—the basket labeled Fax.

He flicked the pen he was using into an old, handleless earthenware mug full of other pens, and sat back in his creaky wooden office chair. He stared at her thoughtfully.

Blue, she thought suddenly, her heart fluttering nervously. His eyes were blue.

They were light blue, contrasting beautifully with his dark hair. And he had long eyelashes—long, sexy eyelashes. Of course he would have light blue eyes with long, dark, sexy eyelashes. Why did she bother being surprised? Everything about him was sexy, why should his eyes be an exception?

He continued to say nothing, and her heartbeat

went from a flutter to a thud. He was just staring at her. How could a man convey so much sex in just a look?

She stood, trying to smile. She knew she must look a fright with her shiny face, tired clothes and, most probably, food in her hair. In other words, as far from what a sexy man would want as she could possibly get. He overwhelmed her with possibilities that would never come true, like a demented fairy godfather. *You are alone in a room with a sexy man. Do you want him? You can't have him!* "Well, here you go, Sheriff. Delivery from Cripes. No tip, please." She set the bag in front of him on the desk, then bent to get her backpack.

"Sit down, Clementine."

She looked at him. He looked at her very seriously. She slowly sat.

He took a deep breath and shook his head. "No matter what happens, I'm going to end up looking like the bad guy."

"Excuse me?"

"You said you were staying a little while. How long is a little while?"

She screwed up her face, then finally had to admit, "Two weeks."

He had yet to take those eyes off of her. "Have you actually told anyone, other than me, that you're only planning to stay here two weeks?"

She squirmed a little. "Well, no. But I did mention something about a two-week trial at Cripes. Everyone is being so nice. I don't want to hurt any feelings."

"I don't think anyone with even your considerable naiveté could have missed the fact that several ladies in this town are trying to set you up with Doc Malone."

"*Considerable naiveté?*" she repeated.

He leaned forward and put his elbows on the desk, moving the bag to the side so he could see her better. "The ladies are a little...taxing sometimes, but their hearts are in the right places. It's about keeping this town and community alive. They think you're a part of Tried and True now. They think you're staying, therefore they want you to find a nice man to settle down with and have children."

"Oh," she said as she stood automatically, feeling a little chastised and embarrassed, as if she'd been called to the principal's office. There wasn't much else she could do now. This had been a temporary respite, anyway. She was just putting off the inevitable. "I'll leave then."

"Sit down." There was a very long silence until she did.

"I've set myself up just by talking with you. My sister out there is going to tell everyone that I asked to speak with you alone. She's probably on the phone right now."

"You didn't ask," Clementine pointed out. "You told me to close the door and sit down. That's not asking."

"So if you leave now," he continued, unfazed, "everyone is going to think I ran you off."

"I'll tell them you didn't."

"They wouldn't believe you."

Clementine looked at him, thoroughly confused now. "What do you want me to do, then? I didn't mean to disrupt things. I just need to make some money."

"For only two weeks?"

She shrugged. "I need money to get home, and I need to be home in two weeks."

"Correct me if I'm wrong, but isn't that a Mercedes you're driving?"

"Yes."

"Yet you need money."

"Yes." She cast him a sideways glance. "You're very nosy, even for a sheriff. It's personal. A family problem, if you will."

"A family problem," he repeated ponderously. "A family problem as in, you thought your mother had called the law on you when I met you on the side of the road Sunday evening."

Clementine eyed him warily, but said nothing.

"You said she wanted you home."

She turned her face fully to him and nodded.

"Why?"

"I told you, it's a family problem."

He leaned back in his chair again and regarded her shrewdly.

"I wanted to get away," she found herself explaining. "I've never been anywhere without my mother. I love my car, but I didn't even have a say in it. It was my mother's first car and she had it restored and gave it to me as my first car. I haven't done a lot of things by myself."

Falling in love being one of those things, she thought drolly. Her mother had even had something to do with that. Reg had been handpicked for her. Her mother had introduced them with that look in her eye. That look that said, *He's the one you need, Clementine.* And Clementine had believed her, because she was so desperate to know what she needed to be happy. "I told her I was going on a vacation and that I would be back in a month. She wasn't happy. That's all I'm going to tell you, Sheriff. It's none of your business, and by that I mean your *business,*" she said, waving her hands around to indicate the whole office, trying to tell him she wasn't doing anything illegal and to please not do a little Clementine search on his computer that her mother could find out about.

"I called in this order from Cripes because I wanted to see you." He reached for the bag and opened it, peering in. Seemingly satisfied, he put the lunch aside again. "I have a proposition."

Her brows rose.

"Stay," he said. "Keep people happy for a while. In two weeks, leave as planned."

"That sounds remarkably like what I had intended to do in the first place."

"And in the meantime," he continued, "we pretend to date."

Clementine just stared at him, her mouth slightly agape.

"They'll stop forcing Doc Malone on you," he explained once he noticed that she seemed to have lost her voice. "But don't get me wrong, this is a selfish proposition. When you leave, everyone will blame me. They'll think I'm just bad marriage material given my track record. They've been on my back for a while to settle down and, frankly, it's getting on my nerves, even though I know they mean well. Hopefully, after you leave, they'll give up hope on me and concentrate on other poor bachelors in town."

"Pretend to date," she said slowly.

"Have you actually been on a date before?"

She stood, grabbing her backpack and rounding the chair before he could stop her. She was tired of looking like a fool in front of the sizzling sheriff. "I think I mentioned this before, but I'm twenty-four. I've dated, I've had sex." The silence was deafening. Oh, Lord, did she just tell him that? She'd had one fumbling encounter in college, and the whole time Winston Allen-Mcafee thought he was showing her heaven, she had been worrying about getting home too late and her mother finding out.

"Yet you've never been anywhere without your mother," he said as she walked to the door.

That stung. She turned to face him. "Until now. This counts."

"What do you say?" he asked as he stood. "Will you do it?"

"Pretend to date you."

"Yes."

"Maybe I should just leave." But she knew that was an empty threat. She didn't want to leave. She didn't want to go home.

"As I said, either way, I end up looking like the bad guy. We all get what we want this way." He started to walk around the desk, toward her. She started to back away.

On one hand, she could see the logic behind what he was saying. She didn't know how long she could put off being set up with Doc Malone. On the other hand, this was the sizzling sheriff asking her to *pretend to date him*. "Strictly pretend?" She found herself asking.

"If that's what you want."

"What?"

He just smiled. She kept backing away.

"I'm going to leave now," she said, and her back suddenly found the door. Her head knocked back against it with embarrassing force, hurting only her pride. Her hand went quickly to the doorknob. "Not town, just this office."

"How about I pick you up tonight for dinner?" He was still walking toward her. "At Cripes, so everyone will see."

"You're really serious."

"Yes." He stopped so he was standing very close

in front of her. She had to roll her head up against the door to look at him. His eyes were all over her. He finally met her eyes, smiling crookedly. "What are you afraid of? I'm trying to rescue you."

"Afraid," she tried to scoff. "Right."

He smiled some more. "Are you attracted to me? Is that it?"

She rolled her eyes. "Arrogance is such a turn-on."

"Dinner at Cripes tonight?" he said, and she hesitated, her hand trying to turn the knob. He put a hand beside her head, against the door, and leaned in, keeping the door closed. "Like it or not, Clementine, this town is smitten with you. I'm just trying to make things a little easier on you while you're here, and easier on me when you leave."

Getting out meant leaning into him to get him to move. So she did, but he didn't move at first, which meant they were body to body for a few moments. She could smell the soap he'd used that morning. She could see a little scar right under his full lower lip. Pressed against him, she had to admit, she had never felt as sexual in her life as she did in these few moments. Clementine thought she was bad at sex because of that one encounter in college and because Reg treated her so platonically, as if they had a business arrangement. But whatever Callum had must be rubbing off on her.

Rubbing off.

Now there was an image she wanted to ponder. If she moved a little, she could rub off on him, too.

She surprised herself. Blushing rapidly at her thoughts, she mumbled, "Excuse me."

He took a single, not very helpful step back.

Easier, she thought as she squeezed out the door.

This was not easier.

WHEN SHE ARRIVED back at the Gardenia Inn, she hobbled into the front office to ask Mrs. Elliott for some bandages for her blisters.

She got not only bandages, but some of Mrs. Elliott's secret stash of Hershey's miniature candy bars that she kept tucked under the front desk. Clementine thought it was a pretty fair deal, considering all her landlord wanted in return was to talk about Clementine's love life, and Clementine had been doing that all day without the chocolate reward.

"So, I heard you had a long talk with Callum, alone in his office," Mrs. Elliott said, unwrapping a Mr. Goodbar.

They were leaning in toward each other on opposite sides of the front desk. The entire motel smelled of warm apples and cinnamon spice because Mrs. Elliott had been tinkering with her apple pie recipe all day. Clementine popped a little Krackle bar into her mouth, thinking Callum had been right. Maggie had spread the word fast.

"Callum's a good man," Mrs. Elliott added.

"Mmm, hmm."

Mrs. Elliott looked her in the eye and got to the point. "Have you thought about marriage, Clementine?"

Clementine sighed. "I've been trying not to."

Mrs. Elliott shook her head. "Callum's that way, too."

"I noticed that."

Mrs. Elliott reached over and patted Clementine's hand. "I know that tightrope walker from the circus broke your heart and refused to leave life on the road for you, but you'll love again."

Clementine unwrapped a Hershey's dark chocolate.

Laughing, she said, "That's not it, either. But that's the best one yet."

Mrs. Elliott grinned. "I thought so, too." She paused then said, "You know, there's always Doc Malone."

5

IT HAD SEEMED like such a good idea until she opened the door.

He stood there with his hand raised, ready to knock again because she was taking so long. Suddenly the door swung open and it was as if someone had hit the pause button on the remote control to the universe.

He slowly lowered his hand and took a step back. His eyes traveled down her dewy neck to the swell of her breasts. The silk material of her rich red robe clung greedily to her wet body. The robe was short, but appeared even shorter because of the gathers stuck to those curvy hips.

She had one hand clutching the lapels of the robe. Her hair was up in a towel turban. She took two rather graceful and easy steps, given the situation, and disappeared behind the door. Soon her head reappeared. "What are you doing here?" she demanded.

"I'm here to pick you up for dinner."

"I thought you were Mrs. Elliott bringing me the towels I asked for."

He pushed his hair off his forehead and grinned as he said, "No. You're going to have to stay wet."

She looked as if she was biting the inside of her cheek. "I didn't think you were serious about this date business."

"Now you see that I am. Get dressed. I'll wait." He pointed to his old black Jeep Cherokee parked next to her Mercedes in front of her room. He turned and walked to the Jeep but she just stood behind the door, still peering out at him. When he reached the Jeep, he turned around. ''Well, I suppose you could go like that, but I don't think Cripes will let you in without a pair of shoes, at least.''

He leaned a hip against his Jeep. She didn't move from her post behind the door. Her towel turban was starting to slide slowly to the right and she put a hand up to stop it.

''You know, Clementine, we could talk like this all evening if you want to, fifteen feet away from each other with you in your robe, but, to tell you the truth, I'm kind of hungry.''

She stared at him a couple of moments longer, then leaned forward slightly, as if trying to see the motel's front office. She only got so far before she obviously decided that whatever she was looking for was not worth flashing Callum any more of that short, delicious robe. She pulled herself back behind the door, then surprised him by saying, ''I'll be ready in a minute.''

When the door closed, he tilted his face to the sky and exhaled as if he'd been holding his breath. He tried to think of baseball, basketball, football, paperwork, Mabel's litter box. None of it worked. Damn! He wanted this woman. No amount of distraction was going to help that.

He paced a while, aware that Mrs. Elliott was watching him from the motel office. Well, at least he was making a good show of it. Making it look real was important. The Ladies Club members were keen enough to realize when someone was trying to trick them. The problem was, he could make this look *very real*.

And what, he suddenly realized as he stopped pacing, was the matter with that? He and Clementine clearly gave off sparks. He could sense a sort of dawning awareness from her every time he got near her. Hell, it could happen. Two weeks was a perfect time frame. Long enough to get to the good stuff, short enough to avoid attachment. And Clementine would be gone before the ladies were any the wiser.

He heard the door click open and Clementine appeared in a blue silk skirt with tiny daisies printed on it and a soft yellow blouse. Her hair was still a little damp from her recent shower so she had pulled it back into a twist. God, he thought. I can't take my eyes off her.

He cleared his throat. "Your hair looks good that color. Did Vera at Tangles badger you into it?"

"No," she said, looking with noble resolve at his Jeep, like Joan of Arc facing the stake. Then she seemed to catch herself and smiled at him. "But thank you."

He opened the passenger door for her and she climbed in mutely.

"You're quiet," he said as he got behind the wheel and backed up. "I'm starting to feel like an ogre. I'm not forcing you to do anything, Clementine."

"I know. It's just that..." She hesitated. "I don't really know you."

So that was it. She was nervous. How cute. He smiled and made a sweeping motion with his hand. "Ask away."

As they passed the motel office, Mrs. Elliott waved enthusiastically. "Your mother doesn't happen to be a member of the Ladies Club, does she?" she asked, waving back.

"Both my parents are dead. My father died shortly after my sister, Maggie, was born. I was five. My mother died about ten years ago when I was living in Topeka.''

"Oh, I'm sorry." She studied his profile. "So you haven't always lived in Tried and True?"

"I was born and raised here," he answered amiably. "Then I moved to Topeka and joined the force."

"Did you like it?"

"I loved it."

"Then why did you leave?"

"Because Tried and True needed a sheriff and I owed it to everybody, especially Cobb, the former sheriff," he explained. "Old Cobb straightened me out when I was an angry, frustrated kid. Believe it or not, I was quite a wild child."

She tried not to smile. "No-oo."

He made a pained face. "Ouch."

For the first time she laughed. "Are you here to stay, then?"

"This is where I belong," he stated simply.

"You don't miss Topeka?"

He shrugged. "I miss my dog, and some of the guys I worked with, I guess."

Intrigued, she turned to him in her seat and had a minor incident with her seat belt as she did so. "Your dog? You left your dog in Topeka? Why?"

"My ex-wife, Liza, got custody of him." Before she could continue her inquisition, he stopped her by raising his hand. "Okay, it's my turn."

"Your turn to what?"

"My turn to interrogate you. I warn you, though, I'm very good at it."

He turned into a parking space in front of the restaurant.

"Well, would you look at that. We're here," she said, snapping out of her seat belt. "Good old Cripes. I guess your interrogation will have to wait."

Switching off the ignition, he gave her a mischievous look. "You're in luck. Tried and True's No Talking in Restaurants ordinance was overturned just last week. We can talk all we want now." He unsnapped his seat belt and opened his door.

"Very funny," she said as he climbed out. He walked around the Jeep to the passenger side, liking that genteel Southern part of her that waited for him to open her door.

"Could it be that you have something to hide, Clementine?" he asked, grinning as he helped her out.

"I knew it." She froze, standing in front of the door, preventing him from closing it. She pointed an accusing finger at him, touching his chest. "This has nothing to do with the Ladies Club, about getting them off your back or mine. You invited me out because you think you're the wise old protector of this town and I'm the careless child, about to do something to hurt the citizens."

He smiled at her. "I'm not that old. I'm thirty," he said. "And I've never thought of you as a child. Far from it." He hooked a hand over the top of the passenger door. "Is it my magnetism? My charm? You're having trouble keeping your hands off me." His other hand wrapped around her pointed finger and moved it away from his chest. He didn't let go.

She slid her finger out of his hand and stepped around him. "Off one particular piece of your anatomy, anyway."

"Sounds interesting," he said as he closed her door.

She gave him a mock glare. "I was referring to your neck."

When they entered Cripes, still squabbling, the whole place suddenly fell silent. Clementine stopped midstride and he came up close behind her. When his body lightly skimmed hers, he was surprised the lights didn't dim and flicker with all the electricity that surged between them. People had stopped eating. The two teenage dinner waitresses stopped with plates in their hands.

"What's going on?" Clementine asked under her breath.

"The sheriff is on a date. They're waiting for the flying pigs," he answered in her ear.

"You don't date?"

"Not if I can help it."

"Why not?"

"Because I'm never getting married again." He put his hand on the small of her back to guide her ahead. She shot forward as if he'd prodded her, and he smiled slightly.

As they took a booth seat she said, "A date doesn't mean marriage."

"In this town it does."

Eventually conversation around them resumed, though it was clear they were the subject being discussed. They ordered and Julie, their waitress, was all smiles as she brought them tall glasses of ice water with lemon, along with a basket of bread sticks.

That was when a large group of ladies rushed through the door, some obviously breathless, all of them scanning the restaurant with little jerks to their heads, making them look like a flock of pigeons. Clementine turned and smiled. She waved at the Ladies Club members who had come to see this spectacle for themselves.

"Don't call attention to yourself. Stay perfectly still and maybe they won't attack," Callum told her.

"This was your idea," Clementine pointed out, still

smiling as the ladies fanned out, taking all the available tables.

"Why did you run away from home?" he asked, not taking his eyes from her face.

She didn't turn from watching the ladies take their seats. Her smile faded a little. "I didn't run away from home," she said, finally facing him. "Where did that come from?"

"Just date conversation."

"I had to go and accept a date from the sheriff. I bet Doc Malone wouldn't interrogate me on our first date."

He decided to ignore that gibe because he didn't want her to see how much it really did rile him. "All right, let me rephrase the question." He took one of the bread sticks from the basket on the table. "What are you running from?" He crunched into the stick and smiled at her.

She folded her hands on the table. "My mother, mostly. We've been over this."

"Why?" he asked, aware that she was watching his mouth as he chewed. It was strangely provocative.

"Why what?" she asked, meeting his eyes.

"Why are you running from your mother?"

Sighing, she leaned back, seemingly resigned to answering his questions now. "Maybe it's just what she represents. Control. Too much of it."

"Control over you?" He chuckled and shook his head. "You must be kidding."

"No, I'm not. Why are you smiling?"

"For as long as I've known you, though I admit it hasn't been for very long, you've done exactly what you've wanted to." He looked at her speculatively. "Your mother must have had a time trying to control you if you're anything like you've been here these past two days."

She smiled at him, the most beautiful beaming smile, and he realized he had told her exactly what she needed to hear. His heart melted a little, just around the edges.

"What part of Georgia are you from?"

"Savannah."

"What do you do in Savannah?" He finished off the bread stick and reached for another. He offered her one but she shook her head.

"I don't do anything, really. I graduated from college last year. Now I help my mother plan lectures, symposia and fund-raising events for the Georgia Historical Society, which is based in Savannah." She made lines with her finger in the condensation on her glass. "But mostly I have tea."

"You have tea?"

"That's what the ladies in my mother's circle of friends do. Have tea and play cards."

He nodded slowly. "I figured you came from money."

She looked at him defiantly. "I've never denied it." When he didn't respond, she finally reached for a bread stick. "My mother has frozen my bank accounts in hopes that I'll come home early," she admitted, suddenly finding the bread stick she was holding very interesting.

Ah, he thought. That's why she needs money. Mommy tightened her purse strings. He didn't know how to feel about that. He did know that there were probably few socialites willing to waitress for their money, though.

"Will it work?" he asked.

"No," she said firmly. "I told her I'd be home in a month, no sooner. Look, I'm not asking you to feel sorry for me. I got myself into this. This vacation was my idea. And I'm going to complete it, on my terms.

When it comes right down to it, I don't need the money she's withholding. And you know what?" She bit into the bread stick. "I really hate tea."

He laughed.

Harlan grumpily came out of the kitchen and crossed the restaurant. He placed a bottle of red wine and two glasses on the table, then started to turn away.

"Harlan, wait," Callum called. "We didn't order wine."

"Compliments of the house," he muttered. "Or that part of the house, anyway." He pointed to his wife, Joanne, who was sitting with Vera and a couple of other ladies. "I didn't have anything to do with it, Callum. I swear."

"So they want us drunk now?" Clementine asked, grinning as Harlan stalked back to the kitchen.

"They're trying to set the mood."

"Ah."

Callum turned the bottle and read the label. "Would you like some?"

"No, thank you."

"Me, either."

"It was a nice try, though," Clementine said.

Callum picked up his water, toasted the ladies by lifting his glass to them, then took a long sip.

Soon, Julie brought over their platters of spaghetti. Clementine took one look at her plate and slapped her forehead.

Callum was really starting to like this quirky, unexpected woman. He had no idea what she was going to do next.

"What's wrong?" he asked, digging in.

"I forgot that my best friend, Suzette, told me never to eat spaghetti on the first date. She said it's hard to be sexy when you're slurping."

He raised his brows, wondering if she knew how seductive that image was. "I'll be the judge of that."

"Oh, yeah, right." She picked up her fork. "You're going to get really turned on when I have sauce on my chin and pasta in my hair."

"In your hair?"

She wagged her fork at him. "Don't underestimate me."

"Never."

After a few minutes of some serious eating, Clementine asked him, "What about Mid-May? Will you be there?"

He laughed. "*Everyone* will be there. I'll be policing the festival, along with about twenty volunteers. Kids sometimes like to pull pranks."

"I bet you have a leg up on them, though."

"Too true," he agreed. "What some kids would give for me not to be sheriff. I know all their tricks. Hell, I invented some of them." He leaned back and grabbed a bread stick. Clementine, noticing he had already finished, looked down at her own plate. She'd barely made a dent.

"Do you want some of mine?" she asked.

He lifted a brow speculatively. "I'm warning you now that I might take you up on that. If you're just trying to give me the impression your girlish appetite couldn't bear another bite even though you're still hungry, I'd retract your offer if I were you. I have the metabolism of a steam engine. I eat all the time. I do my best to never refuse the offer of food from anyone."

"I'm not trying to be coy. I don't have the metabolism of a steam engine, and I think I hate you for having one," she said, shaking her head. "I'd be glad to share this with you. I had breakfast and lunch here, you know. These hips are going to flare to the size of airplane wings.''

''Your hips are beautiful, honey.'' He paused and looked away, pushing his dark hair off his forehead with one hand. He caught Vera eyeing him from her table across the restaurant. She winked and grinned conspiratorially. He frowned at her.

Clementine pushed the plate between them and they polished it off in no time. After Julie took their empty plates, she returned shortly with two pieces of lemon meringue pie.

''We didn't order...'' he started to say, then looked at Clementine.

She smiled back. ''I'm all for anything that involves pie,'' she said.

Which, of course, had him thinking erotic thoughts about whipped cream. Spaghetti, now whipped cream. She could certainly make a meal arousing.

''Hmm,'' was all he said, and she blushed slightly as if she knew what was on his mind.

He had nearly polished off his pie when she caught him looking covetously at hers. ''No way. This one's all mine.'' And she ate slowly, enjoying each bite, apparently just to goad him.

They sat back and talked lightly, then Julie brought them their check. Clementine reached for it.

''Whoa,'' Callum said, taking the check. ''What do you think you're doing? I asked you, remember?'' He clucked his tongue and shook his head.

''Sorry. Force of—'' She stopped short. ''Never mind.''

Force of habit was what she was obviously about to say. Sure, she had money when she wasn't on the run from her mother, but surely her dates picked up the tab when she went out? Curious girl.

He left some money on the table. ''Ready to go?''

"Yes, thanks. I have to be at work early in the morning."

"Do you like working here?" he asked as they started to walk out.

She looked around the restaurant. Some ladies had already left, but some still lingered, not wanting to leave until the show was over. Clementine waved at them. "I love it," she said. "I'm having the time of my life."

The night was mild and Main was lit comfortingly by the old-fashioned lamps. Walking to the Jeep, they heard a few people yell his name. He looked down the street and saw the ritual gathering of teenagers and their trucks and cars. Callum called his greeting and waved, reminding them of the curfew, then he helped Clementine in the Jeep.

"You're a popular guy," she commented as he started the engine and headed down Main.

"What can I say? I have charisma."

She laughed. "And a badge."

Minutes later he drove into the parking lot of the Gardenia Inn and parked beside her car. There was a long silence and she made no move to get out. He had made a private bet with himself during dinner that she would be out of the Jeep and into her room before he'd come to a full stop. He turned to her and she was staring thoughtfully at him in the ambient light from the motel office farther down the parking lot. He saw, quite clearly, her eyes go to his lips. He wanted to groan as his whole body seemed to tighten with that one, probably unintentional, glance.

"So, do you still want to do this?" he asked.

She smiled. "Sure. I had fun tonight. Thank you."

"Pretend fun?"

"Pretend date," she corrected lightly. "Real fun."

There was a pause, and he leaned closer to her.

She didn't move away.

He leaned in a little more.

Their faces were very close now; he could feel her breath. Slowly he moved forward and almost, but not quite, touched his lips to hers. Both their breaths had quickened, as he angled his head. Her expectation was so sweet he could almost taste it. He watched as she closed her eyes, a surrender to him that made him feel like a better person somehow. She was still here with him, waiting for him to kiss her, and he didn't know what he'd done to deserve it.

He felt as if he was going under water, losing himself.

"Clementine..." he said softly before his lips finally met hers.

It was magic.

Suddenly she opened her eyes.

They looked at each other, their lips still touching for what seemed like a long time but could only have been seconds.

"Oh, no," she said, as if she had forgotten to put eggs in her cake batter or had scuffed her favorite pair of shoes.

And then she was gone.

SURGING OUT OF THE JEEP, she ran to her motel room door. She grappled with her keys and they fought back. She forced herself not to look at him as she entered her room.

She leaned against the bright blue door as soon as she shut it. Staring into the darkness, she listened to the sound of his Jeep as he drove away. Oh great, she thought, lightly knocking her head back against the door several times. Now, in addition to dating and having sex, he was going to put kissing on the list of things he thought she'd never done before.

But she had been kissed before.

Just not like that.

And it never should have happened.

On automatic pilot, she flicked on the light. Tossing her backpack onto the bureau, she fell back on the springy bed.

She was engaged.

She was engaged to Reg.

Oh, God, she was engaged to *Reg*.

She covered her face with her hands. All evening she was remembering strange things about him. She and Reg ate out regularly. Every Monday, Thursday and Saturday night—and Clementine always picked up the tab. She hadn't realized it until tonight. Not that she minded so much from a feminist perspective, but would it have hurt him to at least offer? She'd always assumed Reg had his own reserve. Oh, he complained of his bills and his loans from law school, but he drove a BMW, rented an expensive apartment, and had bought her a very large, mother-approved engagement ring.

It had to be Callum making her feel this way. The two naturally begged comparison. Reg had a sensitive, malleable personality, and a way of ingratiating himself to others by bestowing some compliment or another in his smarmy way. There was nothing insincere about Callum. He had a stare that could get anyone to admit to anything just to get him to stop, which probably made him a good sheriff. He was a man to be reckoned with. She thought of the way he looked tonight. Reg could never look so good in a pair of jeans. Did Reg even own a pair of jeans? Or boots? And the crisp white of Callum's shirt had contrasted with his tanned skin. Reg happened to be a firm believer in SPF.

And that kiss. She had no idea the touch of a man's

lips could do that. She had no idea the *expectation* of the touch of a man's lips could do that. Her lips tingled with satisfaction just from the briefest touch from Callum's, as if that was what her lips had wanted all along.

And that was a scary thought, that this might be what she had wanted all along. She wanted a man to make her feel that way with just one almost-kiss.

Oh, God. She rolled over and buried her face in the pillows. Two weeks on the road hadn't changed her mind. Two weeks more wasn't going to, either.

She couldn't marry Reg.

She took a deep breath and pushed herself to her knees, then sat back and crossed her legs yoga-style. She took the phone from the bedside table and placed it in front of her on the bed. Staring at it for about ten minutes, she finally dialed Reg's number, her fingers shaking slightly.

He answered on the third ring.

"Reg, this is Clementine," she said slowly.

"Clementine! Where on earth are you?"

"I'm still on vacation." No way was she going to tell him where she was. Tried and True was all hers, her secret, her sleepy paradise.

"How is the ring? Are you taking good care of it?"

She paused at the question. She pulled the yarn from under her shirt and fingered the ring. "It's fine, Reg."

"Your mother is *frantic,*" he chattered. "People are calling, wondering if there's going to be a wedding at all. Your mother and I have had to decide on the caterer and the music by ourselves."

"Reg, we need to talk."

"Your mother already put the nonrefundable deposit on the caterer, so there's nothing we can do about that if you don't like him. But maybe we can change the music if…''

"Reg…''

"Yes, dear?'' he said automatically, then continued. "Where have you been? What about the ring? I bet you get a lot of compliments on it. It wasn't my idea, you know, to cut off your credit and freeze your bank accounts. Your mother thought it would just make you come to your senses.''

"I said I'd be home in a month. Did no one believe me?'' she asked, closing her eyes. "That's not why I called. Reg, please, listen to me.''

"Of course, darling.''

"I could have waited two weeks to do this in person, but I can't let things continue as if there's going to be a wedding when there isn't. Reg, I can't marry you.'' She did it. She actually said it out loud. And it made so much sense.

Silence.

Clementine plowed ahead. "I went on this vacation to get away from all the chaos because I couldn't think straight. So many things were happening and I felt like I was caught in a hurricane. I thought that if I got away for a while, it would all make sense, that I could come to terms with it. But that hasn't happened. I don't love you, Reg, and I think you know that. My mother is a force to be reckoned with, and she wants this wedding very badly. But I can't marry you just to please her. Do you understand? It's not you, and I know that is about as clichéd as a breakup line can get. But—''

Reg suddenly laughed, as if he belatedly got the punch line. "Everything will be fine as soon as you come home, Clementine. You'll see. It's just prewedding jitters. Now, the ring—''

"It's not prewedding jitters, Reg. There's not going

to be a wedding.'' She wondered how many times she would have to say it before anyone believed her. ''I'll send you the ring by Express Mail. That will be it.''

That got him. ''No!'' he practically screamed. ''Don't send the ring by mail! It could get lost. Is it okay? Have you scratched it?''

''No,'' she said, confused by his concern. ''I'll give it back to you when I come home, then.''

''Why wait, Clementine? You've already messed up everything. Come home now and give me the ring.''

She definitely wasn't going to tell him that she couldn't afford to right now. It would just be proving her mother right, that she couldn't live without her sizable bank account. ''I'll be home later.'' Suddenly she couldn't commit to having only two more weeks to spend in Tried and True. Suddenly she wanted more time.

There was more silence before he demanded, ''Is there someone else?''

''No,'' she answered. One kiss, that was it. She was not going to make Callum her reason for breaking her engagement with Reg. One kiss did *not* have that kind of power.

''I'm not telling your mother,'' he said peevishly. ''Things are just going to go on as planned until you decide to come home.'' In other words he was still planning to marry her. He thought she was going to wimp out as she always did when it came to her mother.

''I'm going to call Mother right now.''

He obviously hadn't been expecting that, and she was painfully reminded of how spineless she'd been in the past. ''I cannot believe you're being so immature about this! What is so wrong with marrying a man your mother approves of? She *loves* me!''

"But I don't. I'm sorry, Reg. I've handled this whole thing badly from the beginning. I hope you'll forgive me.''

She hung up without saying goodbye, then put a hand to her forehead. One tether snipped, one to go.

She took a deep breath, then stared at the phone again as if to blame the cracked yellow plastic for her task ahead. She dialed her mother's private line. As she waited for her to pick up, she imagined her mother in bed in her peignoir, wearing the reading glasses she never let anyone see on her. Clementine imagined what the look on her face would be when she told her there wasn't going to be a wedding. She imagined all the things her mother was going to say, all the coercion she was going to use. All the *guilt*.

Clementine almost ended the call when her mother finally picked up and said crisply, ''Lillian Spencer speaking.''

"Mother—''

"Clementine Elizabeth Spencer, you come home this instant!'' her mother interrupted, and Clementine winced.

"Mother, I—''

"Where are you?'' she demanded.

"That doesn't—''

"Do you realize the inconvenience you've caused? What a thoughtless thing to do, taking off without telling anyone!'' In the background there was the tell-tale sound of her mother's fingernails tapping on the bedside table. A sure sign of annoyance.

Clementine willed herself to stay strong. ''I did tell—''

"You're coming home right now, Clementine.''

"I can't—''

"Don't tell me you're in trouble," her mother hissed. "Tell me where you are and I'll wire you enough money."

Clementine cradled the receiver against her shoulder and rubbed her eyes with frustration. "I don't need—"

"Then get in your car and come home. Poor Reg is beside himself. He deserves better than this, and you are embarrassing yourself. And me. I can't tell you how many people have called me asking if there's still going to be a wedding."

"I just called Reg and—"

"Then you know how distressed he is. Reg and I have worked hard to make this wedding spectacular. All you have to do is come home. You have the easiest job in all of this. All you have to do is show up. We're trying to do what is best for you, Reg and I, but you're not helping yourself or anyone. This is what you need, Clementine. We know what's best for you."

Okay. That was it. "*I'm* the only one who knows what's best for me, Mother!" Clementine said loudly. There was an ungodly silence from the other end. She took a deep breath—not too deep, she didn't want to give her mother enough time to recover—then said in a calmer voice, "Listen to me. I'm not going to marry Reg. There isn't going to be a wedding. I called Reg and told him. I don't love him. I'm sorry you went through so much trouble, and I'm sorry to hurt you, but it's final. I can't marry Reg. I can't spend the rest of my life with him just for you. *There will be no wedding.*"

"Clementine, don't be—"

For the second time in her life, Clementine hung up on someone.

She felt exhilarated. She wanted to get up and run

around the room with her fists in the air, singing the theme from *Rocky*.

So she did.

Then she called her best friend, Suzette, and told her everything.

6

CALLUM WALKED into the station the next morning, his motorcycle helmet tucked under his arm, and the first thing his sister said as she handed him his messages was, "I think she's a keeper. But I think it's awful about what her lousy ex-husband did to her, stealing her African Gray parrot then selling it to fund his gambling addiction."

Stopping on his way to his office, he turned. "Excuse me?"

"Clementine," Maggie explained. "Everyone likes her."

"You mean, the Ladies Club likes her," he said, knowing his very own sister was a Ladies Club wanna-be. She had a few more years before she was eligible, but that didn't stop her from embracing their credo: bachelors are bad. He gave her his best winning smile. "I took her to dinner. That's all. What was that about a parrot?"

Maggie laughed. "That's all? You taking a woman to dinner, in public, in front of the Ladies Club, is the Tried and True equivalent of signing a marriage contract."

He'd gotten used to the people of this town talking about him. They knew all about his childhood, his life in Topeka, his cheating ex-wife he'd left there. And he knew what they were thinking now. He smiled smugly to himself. At last, he'd finally pulled one over on the Ladies Club. A fling without marriage. Short-term satisfaction.

If only he didn't feel, after that kiss, that somehow the ladies had pulled one over on him.

One kiss was not supposed to have him thinking about Clementine all the time. One kiss was not supposed to have him wondering if she'd stay longer so he could kiss her longer. She deserved more than a two-week tryst and, damn it, he was actually starting to think that, with more time, he could court her correctly.

"Believe what you want to believe. You're going to anyway," he said as he walked over to the coffeepot and poured himself a cup. "But I'm not discussing it."

"All right." Maggie shrugged, but Callum knew he hadn't heard the last of this. Not by a long shot. "I have a surprise for you, Callum."

He took his mug and started to walk to his office, reading his messages. "I think a wedding present is a little premature."

"It's not a wedding present. Jess!" she called.

And out of Callum's office walked Jess Ray, free of his cast.

"Hey, Boss," the burly deputy said. "I'm back!"

Callum stood confused for a moment, looking to Jess, his sister, then back to Jess again.

"I got a thumbs-up from Doc Malone." Jess stuck both his thumbs up with his patented you-gotta-love-me grin. "I was bored stiff anyway." His smile faded a little as Callum continued to stare. "Jeez, Teach, I have a note from the doctor saying it's okay to come back to school." He laughed and punched Callum in the arm lightly. "Are you all right, Callum?"

Maggie walked up beside him. "He's been working too hard."

"And I'm damn sorry about that," Jess said genuinely. "But I'm back now. You can go home for the day, Callum."

"Or go see Clementine," Maggie hinted, taking his mug and messages away and nudging him toward the door.

"Who is this Clementine person anyway?" Jess asked. "I've been holed up too long."

"She's new to town," Maggie explained. "I first met her when Mac over there arrested the Ladies Club."

"You arrested the Ladies Club, Mac?" Jess asked incredulously.

"I didn't arrest anyone. It was just a big misunderstanding," he called defensively from his desk.

Callum took his coffee mug and messages from Maggie and walked to his office, slowly shaking his head.

TWO HOURS LATER, Maggie's voice came over his phone intercom.

"There's a woman on line two who says her name is Lillian Spencer and she says it's urgent, that she must talk to you personally," Maggie said.

Still staring at the computer screen, he said, "Who is Lillian Spencer?"

"A very persistent woman calling long distance."

"I'll take it." He lifted the handset and punched line two. "This is Sheriff Callum McCutcheon. How can I help you?"

"Flowers," came the crisp, measured answer. "I have ordered forty thousand dollars' worth of flowers. You want to know how you can help me? You can run my daughter out of town and back home so she can get married like she's supposed to. *That's* how you can help me."

Was it just him, or was no one making sense this morning? "Ma'am, is this a law enforcement matter you wish to discuss?"

She *tsk*ed him. There was a clicking sound in the background, like manicured fingernails drumming on polished wood. "Why else would I be calling you?"

He scrolled down the computer screen, checking the next week's schedules he'd just redone now that Jess was back on board. "And how does this involve the Truly County Sheriff's Department?"

"It involves the Truly County Sheriff's Department because I want the sheriff of Truly County to run my daughter out of town," she said, as if it made perfect sense to her. It might make sense to him, too, if he knew what in the hell she was talking about.

"Out of *this* town?" he asked patiently, wishing to God that Maggie had turned this call over to Jess.

"Are you listening to me?"

"Yes, ma'am, but so far I'm not following."

"I'll speak slowly then, so you'll have time to catch up." Callum closed his eyes with exasperation, but didn't say anything. "I have a daughter named Clementine Spencer, who is currently residing in some questionable establishment called the Gardenia Inn in your town." His eyes suddenly opened again. "She is getting married in two weeks and she needs to be home *now*. By home, I mean Savannah, Georgia, and if you don't know where that is, all you need to know is that it is east of Kansas. Head her in that direction."

Stunned, Callum leaned back in his creaky wooden office chair, rickety from years of Sheriff Cobb sitting there, and comfortable for the same reason. The open-concept office outside had been completely refurnished last year, but Callum had wanted to keep Cobb's office as it was. "Let me get this straight. You want your daughter, Clementine Spencer, home because she's getting *married?*'' he asked, incredulous.

"Yes."

Clementine was getting married? How? To whom? Why in the hell didn't she say something?

Then it struck him, *this* was Clementine's mother, the one who exerted so much control over Clementine that she'd had to run away.

"Ma'am, does your daughter know she's getting married?" Callum asked carefully, wondering if Mrs. Spencer was making this up just to get someone else to force her daughter home. Or maybe her mother was just deranged.

"What kind of question is that?" Lillian Spencer said calmly, and he realized that an outraged Southern woman didn't have to speak loudly. She only had to speak. "Of course she does. She stood for the final fitting of her dress three weeks ago."

Callum was starting to get a very bad feeling. "Then why is she not home?"

Clementine's mother sighed dramatically. She was probably fanning herself or something. "Because she said she wanted to get away for a while, that she was overwhelmed, or something like that. It's hard to remember. But how could she possibly be overwhelmed when I'm doing all the work?

"That's Clementine for you. If left to her own devices, she will just flutter around without direction because she has no idea how to do things on her own. In a town the size of yours, I imagine a wealthy socialite driving that wonderful vintage Mercedes I gave her is hard to miss. If you've met her, then you know she's scatterbrained. She's probably locked her keys in her car a dozen times already. We have the locksmith here on speed dial. She doesn't know what she's doing. But don't any of you in that country town think you can take advantage of her money. She doesn't have any at the moment. I've made sure of that.''

Callum slid his free hand up to push his hair off his forehead. Damn it all to hell. ''Does she love this man she's going to marry?'' he finally asked.

''Of course! Reginald is the best thing that's ever happened to her. Even she knows that. Why do you ask?'' she said suspiciously.

His hand dropped to his knee. ''No reason.''

''Good. Then you will run her out of town.''

''No.''

''Of course you will.''

''Mrs. Spencer, I can't help you.''

''Of course you will.''

CALLUM WALKED into Cripes carrying his helmet. He spotted Clementine right away and he felt a strange sensation somewhere in his chest, an odd mixture of an exhilarating rise in his heartbeat and a stinging hurt.

She was running away from her engagement. She had to be back in Savannah to get *married*. Clementine had kissed him last night, had reacted to him, when all the while she knew she was getting married in two weeks. He felt sorry for this poor fool Reginald. Liza had done the same thing to Callum that Clementine was doing to Reginald.

Reginald.

Clementine's mother had said the name so many times it had begun to grate on his nerves. In fact, after about twenty minutes of telling her that her daughter's impending marriage was not a matter for the sheriff's department and that he couldn't run Clementine out of town, Mrs. Spencer began to get on his nerves. He could almost understand why Clementine had wanted to get away from her persistent, overbearing mother. Lillian Spencer saw things exactly one way: her own. He had to stop her before she resorted to attempted bribery, which was exactly where the conversation was leading after the fifth time he'd told her that he had no power, authority or desire to get involved in this.

Well, desire maybe.

He just couldn't reconcile the Clementine her mother portrayed her as, and the Clementine he now watched bustle around, obviously at the end of her shift, but helping Naomi out with some lunch orders before she left. She had tied the bottom of her chambray blouse in a knot at her waist and he caught a teasing glimpse of her midriff as she bent and stretched. *God, what this woman does to me,* he thought.

He had brushed off Lillian Spencer's comments about Tried and True and the general lack of intelligence of its inhabitants, including him, knowing that city folk were always going to think of small-town people as the kindergartners of society. Her insults had no basis because she had never been to Tried and True. But she had known Clementine for twenty-four years, and nothing she said about her meshed with what he knew of her. Had he missed something? Was Clementine just a good actress? But what the hell kind of person just pretends to be competent? Something wasn't right with her mother's story, but he was too angry to figure it out. All he knew was that Clementine was getting married in two weeks and she hadn't told him before he'd kissed her.

She had just bussed a table and was on her way to the kitchen when she spotted him. She smiled. There was something different about that smile. There was nothing reserved about it anymore. She put the dishes in the kitchen and came back out.

"Word around town is that you've done an under-handed thing, Sheriff," she said, hooking her thumbs in the belt loops of her boot-cut khakis in a bad Western movie imitation. "I hear some of the ladies think you cheated Doc Malone out of a date last night."

"I'll take the doc out next week," he said, deadpan, and she laughed.

The slow pace of Tried and True was tempered only by the speed at which word traveled. People talked. And talked and talked and talked. His ex-wife, Liza, had only been to Tried and True once, right after their honeymoon, and she had vowed to never come back. They had stopped in town to stay overnight with his sister on their way back to Topeka, and Liza had actually been insulted that they'd had six separate unexpected visitors just hours after their arrival. She didn't understand that the people who had known him all his life wanted to see his new wife. That's when he'd learned that small-town America wasn't for everyone.

He wondered if Clementine was put off by the fact that being seen with him the night before had suddenly made her a public figure.

No, she'd done that all by herself already, he thought, watching her smile and say goodbye to a couple leaving the restaurant. Maybe it was a part of the little game she was playing before she went home and married *Reginald*.

"Are you here for lunch?" she asked, her thumbs still in her belt loops.

"No," he said simply. "I came to get you." He didn't want to admit that he was angrier at himself than he was at Clementine. Hell, she was the one who'd run out of the Jeep last night. She probably regretted the kiss, saw it as just temporary insanity. He was the one holding a torch, thinking long-term when he swore he never would again.

"Oh. Okay. Give me a minute. I'm going to get my things, then I'm through here." Why was she agreeing to go anywhere with him? Did she have newfound confidence in her feelings for Reginald? Was she so sure another kiss wouldn't happen? That made him even angrier. She felt something last night. He knew it.

She disappeared into the kitchen. He went to the cash register where Joanne was pretending to concentrate on her knitting, but he knew she'd heard every word. "Joanne, could you pack up a few meatloaf sandwiches for me? And two bottles of water?"

"So, you and Clementine are getting along pretty well, hmm?" she said.

He tried to look confused. "Whatever do you mean?"

"She's sweeter than you deserve, but she seems to like you. Be nice to her. I heard she lost her boyfriend in a tragic plane crash two years ago."

"You heard that, did you?"

Joanne hit him with the deadly indignant Ladies-Club-member glare. He was pretty sure they practiced it at meetings. "Be nice to her," she repeated.

Clementine appeared just as he was paying for the sandwiches. She had let her hair down and had obviously scrubbed her face, her cheeks pink from the scratchy paper towels in the rest room.

He took the bag from Joanne and held the door open for Clementine. Once out on the sidewalk, she stopped, but he walked to where he had parked his motorcycle in front of Cripes.

"You drive a motorcycle," she stated.

He straddled it. "Actually, I just like to push it around, then I sit on it when pretty ladies walk by."

She narrowed her eyes at him. "You came to get me on that?"

"Let me guess," he said. "You've never been on a motorcycle."

"It would have given my mother a heart attack."

"Your mother's not here," he said, spider-to-fly smooth.

"You're absolutely right," she agreed upon reflection. She paused, staring at the bike. He could almost read what was going through her head. She wanted to go with him, he could tell. Finally she looked back at him and studied his face for a moment before concluding, "You're hot."

He pushed his damp hair off his forehead. He'd put on the leather jacket he wore to ride into work that morning, but in the noontime heat it was too much. "You're stalling, but you're right," he said. "I've got sandwiches." He waved the bag in front of her temptingly. "And I think I know of a place you'd like to see."

She smiled and her eyes sparkled. "Where exactly might that be?"

"Someplace you've been before."

"That narrows it down." She pointed across the street to where several ladies were watching them from the beauty salon. "Tangles?"

Callum looked over his shoulder. "Are you kidding? No man has set foot in there since Vera opened it thirty years ago. Little boys press their faces against the windows, but we're forever banned from that sacred place where women keep the mysteries of perms and facials safe from mankind."

"Okay, not Tangles." She cut her eyes at him. "Not back to the Gardenia Inn, I hope."

"We'll go there together some other time," he said, hoping maybe to rattle her a little. She needed to go back to her sheltered life where her mother controlled her purse strings and her dear Reginald would take care of her. She shouldn't be going anywhere with him.

Her brows rose, but she didn't act surprised or even embarrassed by that taunt. "The grocery store? The station?"

"No."

She threw her hands in the air. "I give up."

"Let's go and I'll show you."

She hesitated only a second. "You're on."

They stuffed the bag from Cripes into her backpack, which she then shrugged into. When he handed her his extra helmet, she took it and eyed it suspiciously. He put his own helmet on, waiting for her to do the same. But after a moment of consideration, she handed the helmet back to him.

Confused at first, he then realized that she needed both her hands to pull her unruly hair back into a braid. She looked good with her lightened hair. It was as if she'd transformed herself from a harried traveler to an accomplished explorer in the time he had known her. She'd been tired and distracted when he'd met her, but she was more relaxed now. More relaxed than she was last night, even.

More at home, he realized. Which made absolutely no sense after what he'd just learned.

He watched, fascinated, as her shirt rode precariously up her midriff when she lifted her hands to braid her hair.

She took the helmet again, then slid it on. "Okay," she said, her voice muffled under the visor. "I just swing my leg over, right?"

"Right."

She stopped. "Then what do I hold on to to keep from falling off?"

"Me."

She put her hands on her hips. "But what if you fall off?"

"Trust me." He laughed because he couldn't help it. "I won't fall off."

In one try she was behind him, her hands naturally resting on his sides, grabbing fistfuls of his jacket.

"Lean in," he told her as they took off. He felt her front press tightly against his back and he wasn't prepared for the gush of desire that seared through him. It made him want to drive faster, to get more adrenaline and more blood pumping.

When they reached old Highway 108, she tugged at him and yelled, "I know where we are!"

He smiled at her excitement. Soon the old Flannery barn came into view and he slowed down. He could feel her relax, thinking he was going to stop on the side of the road, but he didn't.

"Hold on tight!" he yelled to her, then went off the road directly into the field. Man, this made him feel fifteen again.

Her arms shot around him and she held him in a death grip. He slowed over the bumpy ground, where prairie was encroaching on the unused farmland, until at last he angled them into the sprawling, abandoned barn.

He rode into the old building and stopped in its cavernous center. He cut the engine, released the kickstand, then took off his helmet. The air inside the barn smelled like cool dirt and old hay. He started to get off the bike but discovered Clementine was not about to relinquish her hold on him. He couldn't see her but he knew her eyes were squeezed shut.

"Clementine, you can let go of me now."

Slowly, ever so slowly, her arms slid off him. He dismounted in time to see her remove her helmet. She looked good even with helmet hair. She pushed some damp, curly tendrils off her face. "You could have warned me. You scared the life out of me!"

"I told you to hold on. Which you did very well, I might add. Quite a ride, wasn't it? Come on, admit it." His gaze was seductive. "You liked the adrenaline, didn't you? Isn't there something addictive about doing something wild, something you're not supposed to?"

Her eyes flicked to his lips. "It's not hard to imagine you as a wild child."

"You did like it, didn't you?" He watched her get off the bike. She had nice, long legs. He could survive for days with fantasies of those legs. "You weren't as scared as you want me to believe."

She tried not to smile. "I figured you knew where you were going."

"I used to ride over that field and through this barn when I got my first bike when I was fifteen." He pointed out the doors and she turned to wander to the open entryway. "The Flannery boys still ride out this way from time to time on their dirt bikes. They drive their father crazy," he said, struck by the beauty of her silhouette as she stood in the doorway. The sunshine blotted out all but her beautiful, curvaceous outline.

"This is wonderful. I was taking pictures of this place from the road when I locked my keys in my car." Turning around, she stepped out of the sunshine and he could see her smile. She snapped her fingers and went for her backpack. "Now that I'm here again, I have to get another picture from closer up." She pulled out a disposable camera.

"A picture?"

"Come on outside, I want a picture of you outside the barn. Don't argue." She was already heading outside. "And take off your jacket, for goodness' sake. You look like you're going to melt," she said over her shoulder.

"You sound like my sister," he complained, but did as she said anyway. "I wonder what it is about me that brings out the mothering instinct in the women of Tried and True?" His own words surprised him. Why was he already thinking of Clementine as one of the women of Tried and True? That was a scary, scary thought.

All this from one kiss.

One kiss that was not going to happen again.

So why the hell were they here?

She laughed and grabbed his hand, the touch so powerful that his heart rammed in his chest, and she pulled him outside. She was just so unassuming and easy. But she was engaged. He shouldn't be enjoying her this much.

She positioned him in front of one of the huge doors to the barn, doors that hadn't been used in his lifetime at least. "It probably has something to do with that bachelor-bad-boy stigma you have. Oh, I know you're the sheriff, but, by your own admission, you had quite the reputation when you were younger."

"I'm completely reformed."

"Completely?" she asked skeptically as she started backing up to take the picture, but he reached out and grabbed her. He turned her around and pushed her gently against the barn door. For a few moments he enjoyed the darkening of her eyes as they went to his lips again.

He let go of her abruptly and took the camera. "Almost completely," he said as he moved back a few steps to incorporate everything. He took the beautiful shot of her, confused, aroused. He stared at her for a few moments afterward. There wasn't even a breeze. He could look at her like that forever.

He wordlessly handed the camera to her, then returned to the barn. What was she doing? She wasn't acting like an engaged woman. She wasn't acting as if she had newfound confidence in her feelings for Reginald.

He took the thin blanket he always kept in the back compartment of his bike and spread it on the ground just inside the barn so that they were still inside where it was cool, but so that they also got the light from outside.

They ate in silence as she looked out toward the highway, obviously enjoying the view. He watched her and felt the same way. She finished one sandwich and he had soon polished off two.

Afterward, he leaned back and stretched his legs out, propping himself up on his elbows, wanting an explanation from her, but not wanting her to say it out loud, either. Liza had cheated. But, try as he might, he couldn't liken Clementine to Liza. So why was Clementine doing this? "Do you have any brothers or sisters?" he asked suddenly.

She was sitting cross-legged beside him, her knee almost touching his hip. "No. My father died when I was eight months old. My mother never remarried."

"A perfect scenario for a mother to concentrate all her energies onto her only child."

Clementine looked chagrined. "And that she has. I love the woman, but she can be Godzilla sometimes. And for some reason, I used to sit like Tokyo and let myself get trampled. Not anymore, though."

"Anyone special back in Savannah?"

"There was never anyone special back in Savannah," she said without hesitation.

Was she that easy a liar? Or was it the truth? Did it matter? She was going home in two weeks to get married. It was just the thought of her reacting to some other man the way she did with him. God, it felt as if someone was grinding rocks into his chest when he thought of that. He thought he had felt something awakening in her, and that he was responsible for it. He had savored the idea of being responsible for it all morning, until the call.

"So far today I've heard that your ex-husband stole your parrot and that two years ago your boyfriend died in a plane crash."

Clementine was trying not to smile. "I swear, the only thing I said was that I just left a relationship."

"And did you?"

"Yes."

He closed his eyes. It was the truth, but a half-truth.

He quickly rolled and leaned over to her, forcing her back slightly. Putting a hand on the ground on either side of her hips, he closed the space between them but didn't touch her. Her breath caught and she was obviously surprised, but she didn't move. "Why are you doing this?" he whispered.

"Doing what?" Her eyes went to his lips.

"Letting me take you out to an abandoned barn. Looking at my lips. Why? What makes a woman do this?"

"'What makes a woman do this?'" she repeated. Her beautiful, exotic, crystalline-green eyes searched his. "I guess it's the thought of wanting something so badly. I've never in my life felt as much, laughed as much, had so many people respect my thoughts, respect *me,* as much as I have here. And I want it. I want it all. That's why *I'm* doing this."

Why did she make him feel this way? Damn if he could figure it out. Damn if he wanted to.

He shifted onto his knees in front of her and cupped her face with both hands. He studied her, wordlessly telling her what he was about to do, giving her time to stop him. When he finally leaned in to kiss her, she met him halfway. Their lips met, and he was struck again by the searing tenderness he felt for her. It was magic again, but whereas last night was teasing magic, a hat trick or sleight of hand, this was full-blown magic. This was David Copperfield magic. This was I-can't-believe-this-is-happening magic.

He heard her moan softly. Slowly he leaned her back onto the blanket and covered her body with his, crushing her breasts. The soft pillow of her body welcomed him in a way that overwhelmed him with her acceptance. She wrapped her arms around him and her spread palms rubbed against his back.

Murmuring her name against her lips, he moved his hand between their bodies and undid the knot of her shirt. He wanted to see more, feel more. When there was room, his hand slid under it. He felt her arch toward his hand as it spread over her stomach. He grazed over one lace-covered breast and gently massaged, feeling its firmness, its glorious shape, how perfectly it fit his palm. He moved his hand up under the bra, eliciting a quaky gasp of breath from her as his fingers made contact with her soft skin, then, tauntingly, the rock-hard tip. Clementine had started moving under him, a restless and primal movement that had him pressing her harder against the floor.

He kissed her long and hard. Her hands were in his hair, fisting it, matching him, almost overwhelming him, with the force of her passion. The way she moved under him was a torturous paradise. He wanted to be inside her. But he also wanted her sweetness, her charm, as a part of him, as the better part of him.

Callum was so wrapped up in her, literally and figuratively, moving with her, feeling her, that he didn't realize he needed to stop until it was almost too late.

"Clementine?" It took strength he didn't know he possessed to lift his head and look down at her, when every cell was telling him to continue, to plunge toward completion.

She opened her eyes slowly, and that dark, unfocused look of passion she gave him almost did it. She moved against him.

"No," he said, smiling slightly. "Don't move. This is hard enough as it is, pardon the pun. Just wait a minute, then I'm going to move off you, okay?"

"Why?"

"Because I am as close as I have ever been to exploding with my jeans on."

She smiled sexily. "Oh."

"No. Don't even smile."

He put his face against her neck and took several deep breaths of that sweet, sexy magnolia scent. Then, moving off her, he lay on his back, looking at the cove ceiling where bats were known to hide out during the day.

What was he doing? She was engaged to be married. Liza had cheated on him, and some of the men she'd cheated with had to have known she was married. He was not going to be like that. He was not going to know and do it anyway.

"Let's go," he said. "I've got to get back to work."

"What's wrong?" she asked, watching him stand.

"Nothing," he said gruffly. "I just forgot that we were pretending."

"Oh. Yeah," she said. "I forgot that, too."

SHE HEARD his motorcycle roar off as she shut the
door to her room. He *was* a demented fairy godfather,
she thought drolly. *Look at the sexy man kiss you and
put his hand up your shirt. No, wait, I forgot, you
can't have the sexy man! Hee hee hee.* She knew it
wasn't going to be as simple as breaking up with Reg,
then everything else would fall into place. Callum
showed her that she wanted a man who would kiss
her and make her toes curl, but he didn't necessarily
have to be that man. Right?

She frowned and dropped her backpack on the bureau.

No, not right. She wanted him. But suddenly he
remembered that this is supposed to be pretend? How
could anyone think they were pretending after those
kisses?

She hadn't been in the room more than five minutes
before there was a knock at the door. She was embarrassed at how quickly she ran to answer.

"Hello, Clementine," Mrs. Elliott said when Clementine opened the door. "I saw Callum drop you off.
Did you have a nice time today?"

Clementine smiled at the older lady's barely concealed curiosity. "Yes, I did. He took me to that barn
off 108. I took pictures."

"He doesn't know it yet, but I think he's ready to
marry again—and have children this time. Callum's
great with kids. Have you seen him with his sister's
children? They adore him." When Clementine didn't
answer because she was busy imagining Callum tumbling around with his own sons and daughters, Mrs.
Elliott shook her head with a cluck of self-
admonition. "Oh, I'm sorry. I came here to give you
this." She handed Clementine a piece of neon-green
paper from a notepad. "It's a message from someone
named Suzette. She called the front office and said it

was important. She said that you already had the number at some law office.''

Suzette? She hadn't told her mother or Reg where she was, but she'd given Suzette the number to the Gardenia Inn last night when she'd called. All sorts of terrible things suddenly raced through Clementine's mind. "Thank you, Mrs. Elliott. I'll call her right away."

"I hope it isn't anything bad," Mrs. Elliott called as Clementine closed the door.

Sitting on the edge of the bed, she quickly grabbed the phone and called the law office where Suzette worked. She asked for her friend's extension and as soon as Suzette picked up, she blurted, "What's wrong? Is it Mother?"

"No, no, no," Suzette hastened to say. "Everyone is fine."

Clementine slumped against the pillows with relief. "Thank goodness." But that wasn't the end and she knew it. "All right, fess up. You wouldn't call me just to tell me everything's hunky-dory."

Suzette paused the length of a heartbeat, but to Clementine it felt like forever.

"Clementine, your mother traced your call to her last night. Now she and Reg know where you are." Suzette took a deep breath. "Your mother has been calling me every day since you left, seeing if I know anything, so this is how I found out. She told me last night. What has me worried, and this doesn't seem to concern your mother in the slightest, but I think you should know…"

"What? What is it?"

"Once Reg found out where you were, he disappeared."

7

When Maggie saw Vera Suttles march by the front window of the station, she knew exactly why she was coming to see her. Enough fooling around.

Vera charged into the station and walked directly to Maggie's desk. "I've heard some distressing reports this afternoon. It's time we get those two together once and for all," she said firmly, nodding in the direction of Callum's office, where he had holed himself that afternoon. He had taken Clementine to lunch, then come back in a foul mood. That Vera knew this already was no big surprise. She knew everything.

"I couldn't agree more," Maggie said, grinning. Her brother had fallen hard, and he didn't like it one bit. If left to his own devices, he would ruin his chance at happiness.

"We need your help. Come to our meeting tonight." With that, Vera marched back out.

And that's how Maggie came to attend her first Ladies Club meeting.

"I hereby call this meeting of the Tried and True Ladies Club to order," Vera said from the corner of the dining room in Talbert House later that evening. She beat the gavel, actually an old wooden meat tenderizing mallet, once against the old sideboard, then joined the other ladies at the long dining-room table, which sat forty.

"There are several things to discuss," Callie, the secretary, said. "What to do about Robert Talbert, for one. We just can't lose this old house." After the business was taken care of, Maggie was told that they would all adjourn to the living room and have coffee and pie. A different lady every week had the responsibility of refreshments and usually came early to prepare the things in the kitchen.

Maggie discovered that the ladies basically kept to the downstairs area. The upstairs rooms served as a communal storage area for them. Most of the members kept their household Christmas decorations stacked neatly in boxes with their names written on them in green marker. It was common knowledge that most of the lights strung up at Christmastime were found in the old Talbert home. The husbands and children of the ladies jokingly referred to the day after Thanksgiving as the time to fetch the holiday spirit because that was when they were instructed to meet at the house to bring down the lights, the plastic reindeer, the gyrating Santas and the tinsel that got all over everything.

"There are at least four of us who haven't listed what kind of pie they're donating to our pie booth at the festival," Mrs. Yardly added to the roster, looking pointedly at those four women. "The proceeds from selling our pies at Mid-May will help put a down payment on this house."

"And don't forget about the piefest Friday night," someone else piped in. "Everyone bring your pies early. We all know how hungry those men get after setting up all those booths and the stage for the festival, and we need to feed them to thank them for all their work."

Maggie was listening intently. She couldn't wait to be old enough to be a Ladies Club member. She had been born forty years too late. She *loved* this stuff. These ladies practically ran the town from this very dining room.

"Good, good. Fine, fine." Vera nodded. "These are all things we need to discuss. But I think, before anything else, we need to acknowledge our guest and talk about what is going on between our sheriff and a certain young woman from Georgia," she said, earning many nods of agreement, welcoming the change of subject. Everyone knew the ladies were always eager to discuss matchmaking, and the business of possibly losing their meeting place and Christmas-decoration storage area was apparently too depressing to think about.

"Well, as I told Vera earlier, Callum dropped Clementine off at her door at the Gardenia this afternoon and then roared off, gunning his engine like he was mad," Mrs. Elliott said. "Then Clementine had a message from Savannah. This isn't good."

"That coincides with my sighting—" Constance Beam, whose house was right across the street from Callum's. "He came home from work and practically jumped off his bike before he even stopped it. He jerked off his helmet and he had the most awful scowl on his face as he went into his house. He still hadn't come out when I left for our meeting at seven this evening."

"He was cranky all day," Maggie added, and the ladies turned to her with rapt attention. "I think they might have had a fight."

"A fight, of course," Vera said. "We can't have this. Those two have sparks enough between them to light up all of our rocking Santas."

"But what about this message from Savannah?" Mrs. Elliott fretted. "Clementine isn't thinking of leaving, is she?"

"I don't think so," answered Callie. "She promised to man our booth during the judging of the pie contest at Mid-May."

"That's three days away. We have to do something fast. She has to stay," someone added. "We can't let Callum chase her away just because of some foolish argument."

"All right, ladies," Vera said. "We need to put on our thinking caps. What we know is that those two have the makings of a lifetime commitment, which is what we want, right? We need more kids and young people in this town so we don't shrink and fade away like some ghost town. But Callum and Clementine had a fight. Now we have to bring them back together. But how?"

"I can get Clementine to come to my shop," Charlotte Lovelace, owner of Lovey's Boutique, offered. "I can spruce up her wardrobe with some pretty, eye-catching dresses. What is Callum's favorite color?"

Several ladies looked at Maggie. "Green," she said obediently.

"We need to get them together in the same place at the same time," Vera said thoughtfully.

"The piefest!" Joanne from Cripes exclaimed. "Clementine is definitely coming. I asked her this morning and she said yes. But Callum rarely comes to the piefest before the festival. We need to get him to come."

"Leave that to me," Maggie said confidently. "I've got a few tricks up my sleeve."

Several ladies murmured with approval. *I'm a shoo-in,* Maggie thought, smiling.

No one had seen Reg since the night before, which had worried Suzette enough to call Clementine, because he'd been acting strangely since Clementine had left. Reg worked at the same law firm where Suzette was a legal secretary. Clementine knew that Suzette had always disliked him and had hated how Clementine had been bulldozed by her mother into dating him in the beginning. Everything after that, of course, had been Clementine's own fault.

Leaving Tried and True, running again, would be the easy way out, and she knew it. But the new and improved Clementine Elizabeth Spencer was *not* going to run away from the same problem twice. She just wasn't in a hurry to run back to the original problem. Besides, in all probability, Reg wouldn't try to find her. He just wasn't that bold. But his disappearance made her feel a little uneasy and she had no idea why. Maybe it was the thought of Reg and Callum being in the same place at the same time. She didn't think it was physically possible. The universe was likely to explode if it happened.

One thing was sure, she never wanted anyone, especially Callum, to know how stupid and malleable she'd been in the past. She didn't want anyone knowing she'd given in to an engagement to a man she felt nothing for, that she didn't even like very much, just because she'd been afraid to say no to her mother.

And how dare her mother freeze her bank accounts, halt her credit, and then offer to wire enough money for Clementine to get home? Clementine's money was separate from her mother's. It was her inheritance from her father. Lillian Spencer had had no right, no authority, to do what she'd done. She made a mental note to call Sam Tierney, the bank president, and get things straightened out herself. The very thought made so much sense that she wondered why she hadn't done it before, why her outrage was so belated. But she knew why. She'd had to get this far from

Savannah to know who she was, and how capable she could be.

And she didn't want her old life in Savannah finding her here and messing everything up.

She was so distracted at work that she only took passing notice of the big tips she was curiously receiving. When she left work for the day, she walked down Main, unconsciously looking around for Reg's perfectly coifed head of curly blond hair. That's when Charlotte Lovelace of Lovey's Boutique suddenly appeared in front of her and literally pulled Clementine into her shop.

"I have some new dresses that just came in," Charlotte, a tiny little woman who wore a fat bun on top of her head, said. "There are two especially that I know you will look divine in!"

"I really can't afford two new dresses right now. Maybe next week?" Despite Clementine's protests, Charlotte herded her into the dressing rooms at the back of the shop.

"No, no. Don't be silly. I'm giving you these as a welcome gift, on the condition that you wear one to the piefest on Friday night and one to Mid-May on Saturday."

Charlotte handed her two dresses, gave her a little push into one of the dressing rooms, then pulled the purple privacy curtain closed with a swish. Still clutching the dresses, Clementine stared at the curtain for a moment, left with the confusing impression that the events were somehow formal, and everyone was afraid she was going to make a fool of herself by wearing something inappropriate.

The next morning at Cripes, Clementine jerked her head around every time someone entered the restaurant. She was afraid that it was going to be Reg coming to look down his nose at the town, coming to get down on his knees to beg her to let him take her away from all of this. Around ten o'clock, the bell above the door rang and Clementine swung around, dropping Randy Maddox's check on his head. That poor man. She dropped everything on him.

It was Callum's sister coming through the door. She took a seat and motioned Clementine over.

Clementine apologized to Randy and went over to her. She filled her cup with decaf, proud that she was able to do it now without getting more on the table than in the cup.

Maggie smiled and waved away Clementine's pencil and pad, saying she couldn't stay. Her eyes were green, whereas Callum's were blue. She was sweet-looking and a woman to be reckoned with at the same time. She was probably around twenty-five but her short blond ringlets made her seem very young. Little-sisterish, almost.

"Callum's been in a bad mood for two days now," Maggie said without preamble. Her eyes flashed with good humor and she grinned almost conspiratorially around her coffee cup as she took a sip. "I haven't seen him so worked up over a woman since Liza." Maggie shot her a questioning glance. "You know about Liza, don't you?"

Clementine nodded slightly, confused. All she really knew was that she had custody of Callum's dog.

"I never liked her. I like you, though." She grinned some more and wagged her eyebrows. "And so does Callum. He's trying to fight it, don't you see? It doesn't matter what your argument was about because it's just given him a good excuse to be surly."

Now this was getting really confusing. What argument? They hadn't argued. They'd just…stopped, much to her chagrin. She would take pretending any day over not seeing him at all. She missed him, a strange and curious sensation, only having known him five days. Had it really only been five days? It felt longer than that. Her connection to Callum and to this place was stronger than that.

"He's not mad at you, to be sure. He's mad at himself for falling for you."

Whoa. That one slapped her in the face. Callum had real feelings for her? But his *sister* was the one telling her? How weird was this? "Maggie, Callum and I didn't have an argu—"

"Callum has a heart that was meant to love," Maggie interrupted. "Some people are just like that. They love better than most. Callum is rough and abrupt and a cop in every sense of the word, but that will never change his heart or its desire to love someone wholly. He tried with Liza for so long, not because he loved her, but because he didn't want to not love her. But she hurt him, cheated on him, and made him think that putting that extraordinary heart of his to good use was just a waste of time. Now his heart is pulling traitor because of you.

"I know my brother better than anyone else in this world. He grew up knowing exactly what he wanted out of life, but not quite sure how to get it. Thanks to Sheriff Cobb, he didn't turn into our father, and he very well might have with his…let's say 'scandalous' youth. Our mother didn't know how to handle him. She was fragile and couldn't handle much anyway. The point is, Callum wants what we didn't have as children—a happy, loving home with a passel of happy kids."

While Clementine was still digesting this, Maggie struggled to her feet. "You're coming to the piefest tonight, aren't you?" she asked.

"Uh…yes," Clementine said. "Are you?"

"Oh, sure. My husband, Saul, helps construct the

stage for Mid-May every year and we always go to the piefest afterward. My three children will be there, too. Number four, of course, never leaves me.'' She patted her belly. ''Five more weeks. I'll see you to-night.''

''Sure, right, okay,'' she said, bewildered, as Maggie walked away.

MAGGIE WALKED BACK to the station, huffing and puffing with the extra weight she'd been carrying around for the past eight months. She swore up and down this was the last one. She loved being a mother and she loved her kids. She'd gladly have a dozen more of them—just so long as she didn't have to be the one who was pregnant. Unfortunately, Saul was no help. Neither was Callum, for that matter. He loved her kids, and he and Saul were anxiously awaiting the arrival of the next one. They were even con-spiring to name the child if it was a boy.

But it was time for Callum to have his own kids now and, come hell or high water, she and the Ladies Club were going to see that he did. Clementine was the one and everyone in town knew it. Oh, neither Callum nor Clementine knew it yet, but that didn't change anything. Maggie had truly never seen her brother so worked up before.

Now the Ladies Club needed her help and she was all for nudging Callum and Clementine in the right direction.

She tapped on Callum's office door and pushed it open, finding her brother staring at the same fax he'd been staring at when she left for Cripes. And, clearly, he hadn't yet read a word. ''Callum?''

He jerked his head up, as if surprised to find her in the doorway. ''Yes?''

She strolled casually into the office. "I was just wondering if you're going to the piefest tonight."

"The piefest?" He put the sheet of paper down and leaned back in that rickety old swivel chair, studying her. "You know I usually don't go."

"But didn't Saul tell you?" she asked innocently.

"Tell me what?"

"Isn't that just like him." She shook her head and smiled. "Apparently they're short a volunteer to help put up the stage this afternoon. He was supposed to ask you, and I assumed you had said yes. And since all the volunteers go to the church afterward for piefest, I was wondering if you were going to do the same."

"Saul needs me to help construct the stage?"

"Uh-huh." She fiddled aimlessly with the earthenware mug full of pens on his desk. "That's what he said."

He looked thoughtful. She knew him so well. She knew what was running through that mind of his. He was thinking what a great distraction it would be to do some work with his hands, to work out his frustrations, just so he wouldn't have the opportunity to think of Clementine. "Well, I guess I can give them a hand after work," he finally said.

"Great!"

Callum gave her a long look as if wondering what she was up to. Apparently not coming up with anything plausible, he shrugged it off and said, "Anything else?"

"Nope. That's about it." She wandered out of his office and went immediately to the phone. She had to call Saul and tell him not to be surprised when Callum showed up to help construct the stage and not to, under any circumstance, let him beg off the piefest.

8

THE SUN WAS LOW in the sky but the heat of the day
still lingered. Even under the shade of the cottonwood
trees, Clementine could feel a trickle of perspiration
fall between her breasts. How on earth the Ladies
Club ladies managed to look so composed as they
served pie, she had no idea. She was daydreaming of
air-conditioning.

She looked up and blew some stray curls off her
forehead, glad at least that her hair was in a loose bun
at her neck. Her eyes suddenly focused on an unexpected sight. She watched as Callum walked with an
air of annoyance toward the playground and his sister,
Maggie. She continued to watch him as he disappeared into the crowd of people gathered for the piefest.

She snapped out of her stunned daze when Charlotte Lovelace, standing beside her behind the tables,
said, "He's already noticed you. You're the first thing
he saw. He's nothing like that football player you
dated who never even knew what you were wearing.
Callum knows. Now go over there and forgive him."

She turned to Charlotte, smiling. "Football player.
I like that one."

"I can take care of the pies at this table. Vera can
help me. Go on and get him to ask you to dance. The
music's about to start."

Clementine looked at him dumbly. "Music?"

"Sure. The boys play at the piefest to warm up for their performance tomorrow at Mid-May." She pointed to where some men in matching black cowboy hats were setting up their instruments. "So, go on." The older lady shooed her away.

"All right. I'm going," Clementine said. Callum had started this, she thought. Everyone in town thought they had had a fight. It was his idea to pretend to date, and even in Imaginary Land, they had to be together to do that.

Who was she kidding? she thought as she walked toward him. She wanted to be together with him in the real world, too.

Like most of the men who had been working on Main Street to set up for the festival the next day, he was wearing a T-shirt, a light blue one that matched his eyes, and snug old jeans that were fraying at the waistband and ankles. He was talking to Randy Maddox, and she stopped a few feet away from him. She stared at him until she realized that Randy had walked away, and Callum was staring back. "I didn't know you were going to be here," she said, her voice a little quaky, and she cleared her throat.

"I hadn't intended to be, but I was hoodwinked by my sister."

She looked at him curiously. "Did we have an argument that I don't know about? Everyone seems to think we've had a fight. I'm getting sympathetic looks from the ladies. I can't say I mind the sympathy tips I'm getting at work, but I'm even being given free dresses." She turned when the music suddenly began over in the courtyard field, a lively country tune.

"It's a nice dress," he said.

She looked back at him. "I feel like a woman wearing an evening gown at a softball game. I didn't know everyone was going to be in jeans." She looked down at the deep green tea-length dress with spaghetti straps. Since she didn't want anyone to see her ring she had tied it around her waist. "I sort of promised Charlotte I would wear it."

He pushed his dark hair off his forehead and, wonder of wonders, he smiled. Have mercy. "You know what they're doing, don't you? Green is my favorite color."

She looked back toward the ladies at the pie tables. They were all making little go-on-and-do-it gestures to her. "I was sent over here to forgive you and to get you to ask me to dance," she said obediently.

He sighed. "I wanted to keep the ladies from badgering you, and I've let them do it anyway. I'm sorry." He shook his head ruefully, as if the game was over. She felt a momentary panic. It couldn't be over, it had just started.

"They weren't badgering." She paused. She knew without a doubt what she wanted, she just didn't know how to tell him. She had to say something, but what came out was so sixth-grade that she actually blushed. "I want you to ask me to dance. I mean, if you want to dance. I mean, if you'll ask me if I want to dance. With you."

"You want to pretend some more?" he asked, cocking his head slightly. Her attempt at initiating something real was obviously falling miserably short.

"No," she said simply, laughing at herself as she dropped her arms because she had been talking with her hands. "I'm through pretending. I can't promise you I'm through babbling, but I'm definitely through pretending."

He looked at her a long time, then groaned as he looked up at the sky. "I thought I could do it, but I can't. I can't stay away from you." He stepped close to her, putting his hands on her waist. He put his lips to her forehead and said, "We're going to talk about this later. We're going to talk about the truth. But, God help me, I just want to be with you."

"Maggie said you were mad at yourself," she said to his chin, and she didn't mind talking to his chin. She would talk to any of his body parts if it meant being this close to him, having him touch her.

"I probably am," he sighed, but stepped back and smiled at her. "This wasn't supposed to happen."

"I know what you mean."

The sun had finally dropped so low in the sky that the church floodlights were turned on and lit up the field. He took her hand and led her to the courtyard.

He took her in his arms and they swayed slightly to the slow rhythm of the country ballad that had begun. He held her close to him, his arm wrapped around her waist, his fingers moving sensually over the material of her dress as if it was skin he was touching. She rested her cheek on his shoulder, turning her nose to his neck where his skin was warm and moist and he smelled like soap.

He pulled her closer to him, bringing her lower body closer to his. Their legs were so intertwined she was vaguely surprised they hadn't toppled.

They swayed to the sleepy rhythm of the music as everything else around them disappeared—the other couples dancing, the people at the piefest, the trees, the town.

She wasn't a woman who didn't know what she wanted, she thought dreamily. She wasn't someone who needed someone else to direct her life. She wasn't someone who wanted or needed protecting. She wasn't a rich little girl whose mother ran her life. She was who she had always wanted to be when she was near Callum.

She opened her eyes with the sudden realization

that the new and improved Clementine was falling in love with the sheriff of Truly County, twelve hundred miles from her mother and Reg and her life as she knew it.

Suddenly, with only the slightest of pauses between tunes, the slow music stopped and a lively, randy tune began. Clementine, a little slow and addled, intoxicated by him and what he made her feel, stepped away from Callum. That's when she saw the ladies glowering at Bill Treggough, the group leader. Bill, happily playing his guitar, gestured toward some teenagers who were starting to line dance.

She looked back to Callum, who was staring at her. "You're beautiful, did you know that?" he said, and it was, quite possibly, the first time a man had ever said that to her and made her believe it. Reg certainly had never said it. He was far more likely to tell her she had a beautiful bank account. "Let's get a drink."

"I didn't realize it would get this hot," she said as he led her over to a large cooler filled with soft drinks donated by the Ladies Club. He handed her a can of Coke. "It was in the fifties in South Dakota when I left there last week."

"The weather in Kansas is as unpredictable as it comes. Drought, floods, hard winters, hot summers. It's not an easy place." He popped the top of his soda and drank, not taking his eyes off her. "But, then again, there's the smell of wind blowing across a wheat field as it brings the rain. And the sky. The mercurial flat blue sky that goes on forever. I could be anywhere in the world and still remember this sky."

"I love it here," she said. She watched the kids run around, the couples dancing and the people sitting on the grass talking and eating. Then she looked at Callum, realizing his hand was still lightly on the small of her back, and she was overwhelmed with the feeling of belonging at the piefest, in Tried and True, *to him.*

Callum's gaze, however, was now on the parking lot. She turned to see that he was watching a dark blue sedan take a slow tour of the church parking lot before heading back to the road and disappearing. It had caught his attention and she didn't know why.

They both turned from the parking lot when they heard someone call Callum's name. A little blond boy about five years old came running up to them. "Uncle Callum," he said in all seriousness, "you have to be a sucker!"

Clementine smiled and looked at Callum. "I can't wait to hear this."

Callum reached over and mussed the boy's hair affectionately. "Clementine, this is Maggie's oldest son, Elijah. Elijah, this is Clementine."

"Hi!" the little boy said. "Are you the one that's going to marry my uncle?"

"Elijah," Callum admonished, but Clementine laughed.

"Sorry," Elijah said sheepishly. "But Mom said you were going to get married soon. I just thought..."

"Tell your mother I said to stop make-believing she's in the Ladies Club."

Elijah was apparently used to Callum saying such things because he just barreled on, saying, "Uncle Callum, I was told to find you 'cause they're starting the pie toss and you have to be one of the suckers 'cause you're a town thwart."

"You mean, authority," Callum said.

"Yeah, that's right. Authwarty."

Callum groaned. "Now I remember why I try to stay away from the piefest."

"Why?" Clementine asked, watching his mouth.

She loved him so much. She wanted to kiss him every time he did that pushing-his-hair-off-his-forehead thing.

"Because every time I come, they throw pies at me." At Clementine's questioning stare he said, "What's left of the pies gets thrown at people. People pay to try to throw a leftover pie in the faces of various townspeople. Store owners, Ed from the newspaper, the mayor and a few others. But I should have remembered that law enforcement officers are uncommonly welcome targets."

"Do you have to do it?"

"No. But the money raised goes into a fund the Ladies Club sets aside to buy toys for needy families in the county at Christmas. It's not like I can refuse."

"I would pay to throw a pie at you," she said, shrugging innocently. "It's for a good cause, after all."

"I bet you would," he said.

"I have to warn you, though. I'm a pretty good aim."

Elijah ran ahead, doing his Paul Revere best as he yelled that he'd found Callum. Together Callum and Clementine walked to where people were gathered around a tall piece of plywood with a hole sawed in the middle so the sucker could poke his or her head out. Clementine noticed a man walking away, smiling as someone handed him a towel to wipe off the plethora of pie remnants that stuck to his face, some of it sticky and wet, some of it whipped-cream white.

Callum was immediately whisked away. Knowing a perfect opportunity when she saw one, Clementine took her place in the line forming for people to throw the pies at the sheriff. The line was composed of mostly kids, but some fun-loving adults, too.

Maggie came up to her and said hello and moved

with her as the line slowly inched forward. They both laughed out loud at the sight Callum made. His head poked out of the board and a few shots had come close to hitting him in the face, leaving his cheek and the left side of his nose spotted with pie filling, but most of the shots had hit just the board. A few wild throws left pies as much as twenty feet away on the ground.

Clementine handed her dollar to Vera, who gave her the remaining half of an apple pie in its pie tin. "Couldn't resist, could you?" she asked.

"I forgave him for picking that fight with me, but this will make me feel much better," Clementine said, taking aim.

Callum looked at her and grinned devilishly. "It takes two to fight. I bet you can't do it," he taunted. "Ten bucks says you can't do it."

"You lose," she said, giving the pie an expert toss and hitting Callum square in the face. Cheers went up as Callum shook off chunks of apple. She looked at him loftily and said, "M.V.P., Little League, summer 1984. Give Vera that ten dollars."

He was still laughing when Maggie pulled her away to introduce her to Elijah again, then her twin girls, and her husband, Saul. Five minutes later her back was to the pie toss, but Maggie's sudden look of surprise at something behind Clementine made her turn just in time to see Callum. He grabbed her by the waist and rubbed his cheeks against hers, smearing her face with pie.

She screeched and tried to squirm away, but Callum wasn't satisfied until her face was as sticky as his.

"There," he said, stepping back, obviously not noticing his sister's smile as she quietly walked away. "My work is done." He reached over and wiped a strawberry sliver off Clementine's chin. "You have quite an arm," he said as someone handed them towels.

She laughed and scrubbed her face. "My mother pulled me out of Little League after one season. It's really too bad. I could have gone professional." She rolled her shoulders with mock seriousness.

He smiled at her and rubbed away a smear of pie near her ear with his towel. "You're a woman of many talents."

She just raised her brows.

"Come on." He took her hand with a look that made her stomach kick.

"Where are we going?"

"I seem to recall you saying something about you being all for anything that involved pie," he said seductively, grinning as they headed toward the shady grove of cottonwoods, making a wide circle around the pie toss.

Unfortunately, not wide enough.

Clementine stepped and slid on one of the wild throws that had landed on the ground far from the board. Her feet went out from under her and she went airborne. Callum still had one of her hands in his, and as she fell, she hit his legs and pulled him down, as well.

She felt a needle-like pain sear through her wrist as her left hand hit the ground first, taking the weight of her body. Callum recovered first and was on his knees at her side before she knew what was happening.

"Are you all right?" he asked as she slowly sat up.

"Ouch," she said, cradling her wrist. "Did you see that? I didn't do anything to that pie. That was completely unprovoked."

He gingerly took her wrist and looked it over.

"I don't think it's broken," she said.

"It's swelling already. Maggie!" As soon as Maggie saw that Clementine was on the ground, she shuffled over.

"Good heavens, what happened?" she said, awkwardly dropping to her knees.

"It's terrible when good pies go bad," Clementine replied, laughing suddenly. Maggie smiled but Callum's face didn't stray one iota from its fierce concern. Clementine moved and winced.

"Stay with her," Callum ordered. "I'm getting the doctor."

"And ice!" Maggie called as he jogged away.

It felt as though the nerve endings in her wrist were on fire. Even her skin hurt. Clementine slowly rolled to her right side and used her good arm to push herself up to a standing position. Maggie had to do the same thing to get up, and they laughed at each other, making a joke about the pregnant and the maimed wallowing around on the ground at the piefest.

"Come over here and sit down." Maggie led her over to a line of chairs near the now empty pie tables. They had attracted some attention by that time and a few of the Ladies Club members began to cluck around Clementine, offering advice on how to hold her wrist and reciting recipes for home remedies.

Soon Callum weeded his way through the ladies to where Clementine was sitting, in pain but amused. He immediately crouched beside her, and she noticed he had a towel full of ice. "I brought the doc."

She looked up to see a tall, long-haired man in front of her. She knew it was Doc Malone by his ponytail, but she couldn't see his face because it was smeared with pie.

"What took you so long, Payne?" Charlotte Lovelace demanded.

"He was playing the sucker in the pie toss," Callum informed them.

Doc Malone knelt in front of her and gently took
the wrist Clementine was cradling. "Your name is
Payne?" she asked. "You're the doctor and your
name is *Payne?*"

He smiled at her. "Don't let the name fool you.
I'm practically painless. I can't see too well here. Can
you walk over to the lights?"

Callum helped her up and led her farther into the
courtyard field. Someone by that time had handed
Doc Malone a towel and he wiped the mess off his
face. He took Clementine's wrist again. Several
winces later, not all of which were Clementine's because Callum was having sympathy pains, Doc Malone finally declared, "Looks like you have a sprain.
Let me get my bag from my truck. I have a bandage.
Just keep the ice on it and I'll be back."

When Doc Malone returned, he wrapped her wrist
in a cottony gauze first, then the bandage. He was
gentle and efficient. She'd had him pegged as a kind,
conscientious man from the moment she met him.
"Rest, ice and elevation," he said, snapping shut his
old-fashioned doctor's bag. "Take some aspirin or
ibuprofen for the pain. Call me if it's still hurting in
a couple of days and we'll take some X-rays. That
probably won't be necessary, though."

"And you're not married?" Clementine asked, and
several of the ladies around her grinned.

"Believe me, it's not for lack of trying on their
part," he said.

"Come on, I'm taking you home," Callum said.

Clementine shook her head. "I can drive. I brought
my car. I didn't want to walk back in the dark."

''We can get your car tomorrow.'' He made her walk with him by putting a firm arm around her waist. ''You're not driving with that wrist.''

They said hasty good-nights to everyone because Callum was practically dragging her to the parking lot. She didn't understand his mood. He seemed almost mad.

They rode in his Jeep to the Gardenia Inn in complete silence. He pulled in front of her door, his hands gripping the wheel tightly.

''All right,'' she said, unsnapping her seat belt and turning to him. ''What gives?''

Several long seconds passed and she watched him as he worked his jaw. ''You scared me,'' he said finally.

If she had made a list of what she expected him to say, that would probably have been number six hundred and forty-three. ''I did?''

''You fell and hurt yourself and scared me.''

''It's only a sprain.''

He looked at her. ''But you're still hurt and I can't stand that I didn't prevent it or that I couldn't find the damn doctor fast enough.''

''Callum! I'll be fine. It's my own fault for not watching where I was going. And, as I recall, I knocked *you* down. Not the other way around.''

Silence. He was worried about her. He was worried about her getting hurt, and, according to his sister, he was falling hard for her.

And clearly he didn't like any of it.

She reached over and brushed some of his hair off his forehead fondly.

''I'm worked up enough as it is, Clementine,'' he said as if in warning.

She didn't say anything, just combed his thick black hair back with her fingers.

Callum groaned and leaned his head back against his seat. "You're hurt."

"I have a sprained wrist, not a sprained back. I want this. I'm not pretending. I thought I was pretty obvious in the barn, but maybe I should have said this sooner. You act like you're beating yourself up over this. Do you think you're taking advantage of me? You're not. I promise you, you're not. I don't understand."

He suddenly leaned over and kissed her hard, surprising her with the force. Grabbing her waist so she didn't lose her balance as she leaned over, he helped her straddle his lap, her legs resting on the outside of his.

"Why are you doing this?" he said as he trailed kisses down her neck. "I know why I am. I'm weak and I'm a fool and I want you so badly my teeth ache." He stopped to look her in the eye, his breathing unsteady. "But you are so sweet and sincere. Why are you doing this?"

She put her lips softly on his, settling herself more deeply in his lap. "That's the second time you've asked me that," she said breathlessly. "Is there a reason I shouldn't be doing this?"

He kissed her again, and she forgot about getting an answer. How did he become so addictive in so little time? She'd never felt for a man what she felt for Callum. She'd never reacted so physically, but she'd also never been so charmed, so wholly enamored.

She wiggled against him, eliciting a moan deep in his throat, and she could feel his erection already pushing against his soft, worn jeans. His hands went to her breasts, rubbing them through the material of her dress. Their lips never parted.

Callum's hands slid behind her back and worked

at her zipper. Before she knew it, the straps were off her arms and the top part of her dress was around her waist.

He finally broke the kiss, looking at her in the darkness as his hands forced her black strapless bra down. She gasped when his tongue found her right nipple.

Her good hand was in his hair, the other resting on his shoulder. She started moving on him again, sliding her legs wider and pressing herself fully against him.

One of his hands forced itself between them, disappearing under her skirt, then thrusting into her panties.

He slid a finger down her wet cleft and then, slowly, inside her. She stopped moving at this point, afraid of exploding too soon. But then he began to move his hand and she whimpered, realizing he wanted her to explode, without him, which wasn't fair.

"Callum…"

"Put your hands behind your neck," he said, his hand still moving against her, sliding another finger deep inside. "Both of them."

She took a shaky breath and smiled. "Am I under arrest, Sheriff?"

"Do it."

"But you need…"

"Later. I'm going to watch you. And I don't want that wrist hurt."

She did as he said, her hands trembling as she locked her fingers behind her neck. This passion was so new, so wonderful. How had she lived without knowing this? Twenty-four years seemed to have flown by, and the five days she'd known Callum had lasted forever. He kissed her breasts again, as they were lifted slightly now, and his hand set a rhythm that had her gasping. He grasped the back of her head

with his free hand and made her look at him. She bit
her lip, trying to hold back a scream, and exploded
into thousands of tiny pieces.

She rested her head against his shoulder as she
caught her breath. He wrapped his arms around her
and held her tightly to him. "What possible reason is
there not to want this?" she said softly.

The long pause that followed still didn't give her
enough time to prepare herself for what he said next.

"This is what we need to talk about, Clementine.
I know you're engaged."

Her head shot up and she tried to pull back from
him, but his hands cupped her face almost tenderly,
forcing her to look at him. "No, listen," he said.
"Your mother called me a couple of days ago, wanting me to run you out of town so you would come
home for the final weeks before your wedding."

She reached up and moved his hands away, her
languid mind and body trying to process it all. "My
mother called you? You've known... Why didn't you
tell me?"

"Why didn't you tell *me?*" he asked, not accusing,
not angry, just a simple, earnest question.

Which lit a fuse in her.

"Because I'm *not* engaged!" she said loudly. She
hastily tried to pull her bra and dress up, falling off
his lap into the passenger seat clumsily. "That's why
you've been acting so strange. You thought I was just
using you as my boy-toy before I went home to get
married." She had trouble getting her arms through
the straps of her dress and he tried to help her before
she swatted at his hands. "I broke off the engagement
the second day I was here. I went on this vacation to
try to come to terms with it, but I found that I couldn't
marry a man I didn't love, just because my mother

picked him out for me and would make my life miserable if I didn't do what she said."

"The second day you were here?" he said thoughtfully, then he hit the steering wheel lightly with the palm of his hand. "Damn it. That kiss."

She was burning mad now. "Oh, don't give yourself so much credit. I made the decision to break up with Reg on my own. Falling in love with you happened afterward." She hesitated. "I can't believe I said that," she said angrily as she flung open the door. "And I can't believe my mother called you and you didn't tell me, that you just assumed what she said was true. I thought I was different here, that people, that *you*, thought I was capable of good sense."

"Clementine, wait!"

She ran to her door and unlocked it awkwardly because of her wrist, which unfortunately gave Callum enough time to snap out of his seat belt and get out of the Jeep. She tried to slam the door behind her, not bothering with the light, just wanting to get away from him, but Callum's arm caught the door.

When she bumped into a fallen chair in the middle of the room, she stopped, looked down, then around. The room was dim, but she could still make out the fact that all her clothes were on the floor. And she hadn't left them there.

"What's wrong?" Callum asked. He flicked on the switch by the door and light flooded the room.

"Oh...my."

9

SHE STOOD, still in shock, in the middle of the room, chewing a hangnail. She'd lost control of her manicure weeks ago, somewhere in Pennsylvania. Blue lights flashed into the room through the open door. One of Callum's deputies, Luke, was talking with Mr. and Mrs. Elliott just outside.

Clementine looked around her trashed room. Clothes had been thrown from the closet and from the bureau. The drawers of the bureau had been wrenched out and the mattress had been turned upside down and was standing against the wall.

She jumped when Callum came up behind her and she felt his fingers on her back. "You're not zipped all the way," he said softly as he closed the inch or two of zipper she'd left open at the top. "Everything'll be all right. Are you sure there's nothing missing?"

"I'm positive." Someone had broken into her room, pillaged through absolutely everything, but hadn't taken a thing.

"Then whoever it was, was looking for something in particular," Callum said. "Something he didn't find."

Luke gestured to Callum from the door and he gave her shoulders a comforting squeeze before walking outside to talk. Mrs. Elliott entered the room, uneasily, stepping over some clothes to get to Clementine.

"Oh, dear," she said, giving Clementine a hug. "Oh, dear. I don't know what to say. I'm so sorry." She looked around the room worriedly. "Oh, dear."

Determined not to perpetuate the older woman's fears, Clementine smiled. "It's not your fault. I'm fine. In fact, everything is fine. Whoever it was didn't take a thing."

"Isn't that incredible?" She shook her head. "I just don't understand it. What can I do for you, dear?"

"Nothing at all." Clementine patted Mrs. Elliott's arm. "I'm just sorry that you were called away from the piefest."

"Actually, I'm glad." Mrs. Elliott gave Clementine a wry smile. "Edward was having much too good a time throwing pies at Vera."

Clementine was surprised. "Vera was a sucker?"

"Yes, believe it or not."

Clementine laughed at what a sight that must have been. Mrs. Elliott hooked her arm in Clementine's good arm, remarking, "I heard about your fall. How is your wrist?"

"I was thinking about rummaging through this mess to try to find my bottle of aspirin, to tell you the truth."

"No, no!" Mrs. Elliott said, fussing. "You come with me. I'll give you some and a nice glass of lemonade."

Clementine caught Callum's eye as she and Mrs. Elliott left the room, and she pointed toward the front office to tell him where she was going. He nodded briefly then went back to his discussion with Luke.

Mrs. Elliott escorted her through the office to the back where Clementine discovered a homey apartment, filled with more doilies and antimacassars than she had ever seen in her life. She sat on the burgundy camelback couch in the tidy living room while Mrs. Elliott went to the kitchen and returned promptly with a glass of tart lemonade and two white tablets.

Clementine thanked her and downed the aspirin, hoping they would work quickly. Her wrist really was uncomfortable.

"Oh, I haven't given you all those messages yet, have I?" Mrs. Elliott said. "With Edward hurrying me out the door this afternoon, I barely had enough time to grab my pies."

"Messages?" Clementine repeated, her thoughts suddenly foreboding.

"Yes. There are about five of them for you. I'll go get them." Mrs. Elliott shuffled out into the front office and came back with several of her neon-green notes. "Here you are. I was curious about them, to tell you the truth."

Clementine looked at the notes one by one, but could hardly make them out.

"My handwriting is horrible, I know. Here," she said, taking the notes from Clementine and picking up a pair of reading glasses from an end table, "let me read them to you. This is the first one. He called early this morning and asked to speak with the concierge. Well, I told him I didn't know who that was and that he must have the wrong number. Then he said, 'Tell Clementine Spencer that Reginald Remington Richards the Third called.'" Mrs. Elliott looked over the upper rim of her silver half-moon glasses. "He was polite at first."

Clementine's heart suddenly skipped a beat.

Mrs. Elliott thumbed through the next two notes saying they were much of the same thing. "Oh, here's where he turned rude. You see, you were out all day and he kept calling. This was late this afternoon. 'Tell

Miss Spencer that I want it back.' He said you knew what *it* was.''

She had a good idea. Her hand went immediately to her waist where she had tied the yellow string of yarn around her, the ring dangling from it resting at her navel. She didn't have it around her neck because her green dress had such a low neckline.

''Then, here's the last message. I took it as Edward was honking the car horn at me, telling me to hurry. What does this say?'' She adjusted her glasses. ''Oh! Yes, I remember. It's from that nice Suzette person who called before. She said to call her.'' She handed the messages back to Clementine.

Clementine looked at the bright green pieces of paper in her hand, trying to get a handle on things. What on earth was happening? Was Reg really here? Had he trashed her room looking for the ring? That didn't sound like him. He wasn't hot-tempered or violent. Surely there was another explanation.

If only she could think of one.

''This Reginald person, he's the one, isn't he?'' Mrs. Elliott asked gently.

Clementine looked at her blankly.

''He's the relationship you left behind.''

Clementine put a hand to her forehead. Things were going all wrong. ''He's not staying behind.''

Mrs. Elliott nodded understandingly. ''Do you love him, this Reginald?''

''No, I never did,'' Clementine answered without hesitation. ''I can't believe he called here.''

''Are you afraid of him? Are you running from him? Did he hurt you?''

''Afraid of Reg?'' Clementine laughed. ''No, no. He's the most docile person I know.''

''Boring?''

''Terribly.''

"Handsome?"

She thought of his pointed chin and the bowl of blond curls on top of his head. "He looks like a vanilla ice-cream cone."

Mrs. Elliott smiled with satisfaction. "Well, that explains so much."

"I'm going to clean up my things now," Clementine said, distracted. "Thank you for the aspirin and lemonade."

Mrs. Elliott clasped her hands anxiously in front of her. "Oh, dear," she said apologetically. "Oh, dear. We're booked because of Mid-May tomorrow. I don't have another room for you."

"That's okay. I was planning to straighten up my room and stay there tonight, anyway, so don't worry. I don't mind. Whoever broke in jimmied the lock, but there's still the dead bolt inside. I'll be fine."

"I don't think so," Callum said from the doorway into the office. She turned and faced him. He looked so sexy standing there, his legs slightly apart, his hair falling on his forehead. Her mind flashed to her sitting on his lap, in his Jeep, his hands on her. "You're coming home with me."

"I'll be fine," she repeated, even though going home with him sounded as good and comforting as a crackling fire on a snowy day. "Really."

"That's a wonderful idea," Mrs. Elliott said, clapping her hands almost joyfully. "He has extra bedrooms and you'll be safe with him. He is the sheriff, after all."

Callum walked out of the office saying, "You're staying with me, Clementine. No argument."

Arguing was, she admitted to herself, the last thing she wanted to do that night. She had so many new wrinkles to work through. Was Reg really here? And what did that mean? And why had Callum kissed her when he thought she was engaged? It had obviously frustrated him to be attracted to her, to the point of hating himself for giving in to his attraction to a supposedly engaged woman. She liked who she was around Callum, and it hurt to know that, all this time, he *didn't* like who he was around her.

When she went to her room and picked up one of her Louis Vuitton suitcases, she realized she still had the neon-green notes in her hand. She quickly stuffed them into a side pocket on the suitcase, then started picking up her things. Most of her pants and skirts had their pockets turned inside-out, as though someone was looking for something small. Something like a ring.

Callum came in when she had finished packing, and loaded her bags into his Jeep. He drove them down increasingly familiar streets, and she couldn't help but smile when she first set eyes on his house. It was a two-story white clapboard house with clematis growing up a trellis on the porch. There was an attached garage, obviously a new addition, and a Big Wheel bike and an old badminton racket in the front yard.

"What a wonderful house," she said to him as they both got out and he grabbed her luggage. She looked around and noticed that most houses on the street had lights on over their front doors and sprinklers were watering lawns throughout the neighborhood. Turning back to his house, she said, "The garage looks new."

"It is. The house needed a lot of work when I bought it. I tore down a few walls, replaced the floors, put in bigger windows downstairs. I knew there would be a lot of questions when I came back to town, so I knew people would be stopping by. They stayed and helped me with my house." He directed her up the stone path to his front porch. "Randy Mad-

dox and Bill Treggouh, they're my two best buds
from school, helped me with the garage because their
wives sent them over here to get the scoop about my
divorce. Then Vera and Vernon stopped by to give
me a welcome-back pie and ended up helping sand
the cabinets and paint the kitchen." He opened the
door and stood aside to let her enter first. "I had
people helping to pull up baseboards, move in furniture, you name it—all out of curiosity as to what I
had been up to in Topeka. And the ex-wife I left
there."

"That sounds a lot like bribery, Sheriff," she said
as she entered his house.

"Hey, I needed the help, they wanted the gossip. I
thought it was pretty fair."

She walked into the living room and stopped with
surprise. It was wonderfully, eclectically decorated.
An antique, double-wheeled coffee-grinder supported
a piece of thick square glass to serve as a low corner
table next to an overstuffed grandfather chair. There
were a couple of black book towers next to the fire-
place, and an old refinished armoire served as an entertainment center, housing his television and stereo
system. The pièce de résistance had to be the couch.
It sat against the far wall and was huge; it had to be
at least eight feet long and was solid black.

She smiled. It was wonderful.

The click of cat feet on the hardwood floor called
her attention to a fat calico wandering into the living
room to check things out. "Who is this?" she asked,
bending to pet the cat, who purred the most godawful
purr. Clementine fell in love with her right away.

"That's Mabel. She has a calorie problem. Come
on, I'll show you your room."

He led her through the living room and up a flight
of stairs. He opened a door to the right and she fol-

lowed him in, noting the fine old cast-iron bed and a few pieces of mismatched furniture. There was an empty laundry basket on the floor and, judging by the cat hair on it, an obviously little-used ironing board in the corner. Four small high side-by-side windows were uncovered.

"The guest room," he said, setting her bags down.

Mabel came in after them and started rubbing against Clementine's legs, making a noise that sounded like a faulty chainsaw.

"This is also Mabel's favorite room. I hope you don't mind."

She smiled. "Not at all."

Callum stared at her a long time. He'd tried to be easy and congenial, but everything that had happened since he'd turned on the light in her motel room two hours ago had been leading up to this. "I have to ask, Clementine," he finally said. "You know I do."

She paused. "Okay."

"I'm not ruling out the possibility of a local, but I know the kids in this town." His light blue gaze bore into her. "You know who trashed your room, don't you?"

The man had instincts coming out his ears. "I have an idea."

"Who?"

"Reg."

"Reg as in *Reginald?*"

"You know his name?" she asked, shocked. How much had her mother told him?

"Why would your fiancé be here? Why would he break into your room?"

"Ex. Ex-fiancé. I am not going to marry him. I never wanted to marry him. It just seemed to make everyone happy and...oh, forget it." If she hadn't managed to convince Callum by now of who she was, of who she was trying to be, then there was no use trying to explain how she'd managed to get into an unwanted engagement in Savannah, but do nothing about it until coming here. "I think he's after this." She took a deep breath and started to lift the hem of her dress.

"What are you doing?" he demanded, his eyes darkening.

"Don't worry. I'm not trying to distract you with sex."

"Too late."

She lifted one side of the dress above her hip and she noticed him shift slightly, his gaze hard on the strip of black satin across her hip. She found the yarn tied around her waist and worked the knot free, releasing the ring.

She let the hem fall back down and took a few steps toward him, extending the ring.

For a moment he didn't move. His eyes were hot and she felt herself grow warm under that gaze. Her mind kept flashing to that scene in the Jeep, his mouth on her breasts, his fingers driving her crazy. For a woman who'd once thought she was bad at sex, she sure was thinking about it a lot now.

"I'm sorry, Clementine," he finally said. "I underestimated you. I was going on a practiced emotion. My ex-wife cheated on me. It was what I knew, maybe all I wanted to know. I should have told you about what your mother said."

She nodded, having no earthly idea what to say. It hurt her, sure, to be underestimated again, when she had been trying so hard to get away from the old Clementine. But what hurt the most was that she was having fun while Callum was hating himself. How could she have missed that? "It's okay."

He started to say something, then seemed to decide

against it. He took the ring from her. "How valuable is it?" he asked, looking at the ring closely.

"It was appraised at a little over one-hundred thousand."

"Do you always wear it around your waist like that?"

"No, most of the time I wear it around my neck. But with this dress..." She waved her hand as the sentence faded away. Suddenly she was very tired.

"Why don't you wear it on your finger?"

"Taking it off was sort of...the first step when I left. I think I have to go back to Savannah," she said suddenly. "I mean, I know I do. Tomorrow, after the festival, I'll go. I'll take whatever problem I brought here with me." She didn't want to go. She didn't want to go so much it hurt. The thought of never seeing Callum again was as horrible as having to give up one of her senses. But she had to go. She probably had enough money to get her a few states away, if she didn't eat. Then she'd do what she'd been fighting not to do. She'd call her mother and ask her to wire some money so she could get the rest of the way home, which would be quicker than calling Sam Tierney, the bank president, on a Saturday.

His jaw worked. "You're not going anywhere. You are obviously in danger."

"You can't keep me here," she said, but it sounded more like a question than an assertion.

"I'm the sheriff," he reminded her.

"I have to go back." She rubbed her forehead and looked at him sincerely, not wanting to argue with him anymore. "He'll follow me back." She sighed and went to the edge of the bed and sat. "And he's not dangerous. Reg is...flaccid. He would never hurt me. He's barely even kissed me."

His eyes went to her lips, then traveled slowly down her body.

She wrapped her arms around herself. She couldn't believe how much she felt for him, and how much it hurt to know she was going to leave him. She remembered from the start how being near him teased her with possibilities that would never come true.

He started to take a step toward her, his eyes dark with desire, but then he hesitated. He abruptly turned to leave the room. Whether it was because he thought she was mad at him, or because he was still mad at himself, she couldn't guess. "The bathroom's right next to your room. I'll be down the hall if you need me."

I do need you. "Callum?"

He turned around and leaned against the doorjamb. "I have to leave."

"And we've both known that all along. Good night, Clementine."

As soon as he closed the door Mabel jumped up on the bed and sat beside her, purring loudly. She hadn't known it all along. In fact, it had come as a surprise to her. She had to leave.

Tomorrow, after the festival, she would head back to Savannah. If Reg *was* here, he would follow her home, and then, face-to-face, she would tell him and her mother that her life was her own. She should have done it in the first place, the moment she realized she had the courage and conviction to say it out loud, but then there had been so many reasons to stay, and so few reasons to go back.

CALLUM LAY IN BED with his hands tucked behind his head, staring at the ceiling, listening to the occasional sounds of the house settling.

He'd been upset when she hurt her wrist, but he

was damn near berserk over this. What if the ladies hadn't made her go to the piefest? What would have happened then, if she was in her room when the mysterious Reg showed up? This was a lot more serious than Clementine thought it was. He had to keep to her here. He had to keep her safe, near him, where he could...

His mind kept going back to the feel of her pressing against him in the Jeep, the taste of her skin. She was so tight, so sweet.

He'd known she was going to be trouble the moment he'd set eyes on her, but he hadn't realized what kind of trouble she was going to be. She threatened his smugness, his righteousness, his cynicism. He'd made a fool of himself, and possibly one of the biggest mistakes of his life, by letting what happened with Liza affect his relationship with Clementine. He didn't want her to leave. He was thinking about marriage and babies and having her in his bed every night for the rest of their lives.

But he'd spent so much time fighting it, fighting himself, that now there wasn't sufficient reason or incentive enough for her to stay, even when it was too dangerous for her to go. Hell, he'd put her in jail before he let her go when there was a man following her who could do what he did to her motel room. But that wasn't the same as her staying because she wanted to. Would she still leave when the threat to her was eliminated? And he *would* eliminate it.

He groaned and sat up. Reaching for his jeans, he pulled them on. He silently left his room and walked down the hall, noticing that her light was out. Resisting the urge to check on her, he went downstairs and grabbed a bag of cookies on his way to the living room. He slouched on the couch, not bothering to turn on the lights.

Another fool burying his sorrows in Oreos.

As he sat there, pulling Oreos apart and eating the filling first, going over and over the scene in the Jeep and thinking about how nice his house felt with Clementine in it, he slowly became aware of the fact that there seemed to be much more traffic on the street than usual. He waited a few minutes longer, scraping off the white filling of an Oreo with his teeth. He watched the beam of headlights shine over the top of the curtains and cross the wall. He listened, and it began to dawn on him that it was the same car passing back and forth with marked regularity.

He set the bag of cookies aside and got up from the couch. Standing with his back against the wall by the window, he lifted the curtain slightly. A dark sedan went down the street. It was a car strikingly similar to the one he had noticed in the church parking lot earlier that day. It was too far away and too dark to see the plates. A minute passed. The car went back up the street. Its brake lights shone just as it passed Callum's house, then it continued up the street.

When the car passed again, Callum dropped the curtain and went to the phone. He called Luke, who immediately patrolled the area, but by that time the car was gone. Luke pulled into the driveway and Callum met him outside.

"Don't get all dressed up on my account," Luke said, walking up the porch steps and grinning at Callum's lack of shirt and shoes. "So what's with the suspicious car?"

"I don't know. It could have something to do with Clementine." He gestured vaguely toward the house.

Luke chuckled. "She's staying here? You son of a gun."

"She's in the guest room. Your mind's in the gutter," he chided. "I can only hope the Ladies Club sets you up soon." He shook his head sagely.

Luke shifted uncomfortably. "Haven't you noticed I've been eating at Cripes a lot more often these days? I'm always being invited to lunch by one or more members of the Ladies Club."

Now Callum grinned. "Is that so?"

"Yeah. It's Naomi they want to set me up with. She works the lunch crowd."

Callum's brows rose. "Well, you and Nome were once an item."

"That was ten years ago. And Naomi has made it more than clear she wants nothing more to do with me. I just wish those ladies would stop inviting me out to eat."

He smiled smugly. "You *are* looking pretty well-fed lately."

"At least they haven't managed to get to me like they have with you," Luke returned. "You don't see Naomi staying with me, do you?"

"She's in the *guest room*," Callum repeated. "Listen, that break-in wasn't local, and you and I both know it. Clementine is wearing quite a rock on a necklace and she seems to think it might be the source of the trouble."

"You think she knows something?"

"Yes," he said. "She knows. Do me a favor and take Jess over to the church parking lot to get Clementine's car. If whoever broke into her room discovers her car, he might look there next. We don't have the manpower to stake it out and wait. Besides, if we're lucky, I'm completely off base."

Luke regarded him seriously. "Sure, I'll do it. I'll keep a lookout for the car and patrol this area as often as I can tonight."

"Here are the keys." He withdrew Clementine's

key ring from his pocket. Just looking at it reminded him of her, as if it was some small piece of her, warm in his hand. He'd had the keys all along, ever since she opened her motel door earlier that evening. He'd picked them up when she dropped them on the floor after seeing her room.

Saying good-night, he went back in the house and clicked on a lamp on the end table next to the couch. Restlessly, he walked over to the bookshelf towers and scanned the titles. He finally grabbed a Travis McGee novel by John D. MacDonald and went back to the couch to read. That's when he realized the irony. This was all he needed, he thought, looking down at the paperback. To read something about a man lucky at solving all mysteries except the one involving love.

10

By the time Saturday morning dawned, bright and warm, Callum had had about two hours of sleep, and he'd had to force himself to get that. At 8:00 a.m., he was back on his living room couch, without the Oreos this time, talking on the phone to Luke.

"How much of the county were you able to canvass last night?" He heard a creak on the steps. The fourth step from the top always creaked. "Yeah, I understand that. Yeah, I know." He heard the swish of bare feet. "With so much traffic rolling into the county today it would be a wasted effort, so I'm glad you got done what you did last night."

Clementine suddenly walked around the corner. Her hair was in glorious disarray and her bare feet made sleepy shuffling sounds against the hardwood floor. When she saw him there, she stopped short, then turned to leave.

He reached out and grabbed her hand, which curiously held several pieces of garishly bright green notepad paper. She turned and he held her eyes as he said, "Right. I'll find you there. We'll be leaving soon." He hung up. "Morning," he said, still holding her hand. She was wearing that clingy red robe he'd seen before, but what intrigued him more was the wisp of lace that peeked out from the V neckline. He found himself wondering how short and how sheer that lace was.

"I didn't mean to interrupt your phone call."

"You didn't. What are those?" He indicated the green notes.

"Messages." She transferred the notes to the hand he wasn't holding, not letting him see them. "Mrs. Elliott gave them to me last night. I was going to call my friend Suzette. Collect, of course," she said, as if that was important for him to understand. "I wasn't going to charge it to your phone bill."

"I wouldn't have cared. I want you to make yourself at home."

"I—I couldn't," she stammered, as if it hadn't occurred to her that he welcomed her there. "I mean, this is your home. I'm not going to take advantage."

"Your Southern manners are charming, but stop being so formal. So why did Suzette call you?"

"I, uh, don't know exactly. The message just said to call her." She tucked the messages into the front pocket of her robe.

"Could it be about Reginald...what's his last name?"

Clementine looked chagrined. "Reginald Remington Richards."

Callum's brows rose.

"The Third."

"Are you going to call?"

She shrugged. "I guess not. It won't change anything. And she probably won't be up, anyway. She might not even be home yet. She likes Friday nights. She's...social."

He was still holding her hand, but she was standing an arm's length away from him. He pulled her forward as he said, "But you've never been...social?"

She shuffled over to him and he looked up at her, loving the feel of her sleepy warmth. He wanted to bury his face in her stomach. "No. I met Suzette just a couple of years ago. She's a legal secretary at the law firm of my mother's personal attorney. It's where Reg works, too.''

"So she could have information on him."

"It won't make a difference."

"Call."

She used the back of her bandaged hand to push her hair out of her face and sighed. "I'll try."

He scooted over and she took his place on the couch. Her robe rode high on her thighs as she sat and his body's reaction was instantaneous. He let go of her hand so she could reach for the phone and he had to resist the urge to move his hand up her leg. He hoped to God Suzette would say that Reg was still in Savannah so Clementine wouldn't feel she had to leave because of him. She lifted the handset to her ear and dialed. She let it ring fourteen times before she hung up. "She's not home."

Damn it. "She doesn't have an answering machine?" What kind of person doesn't have an answering machine?

"She has Caller ID, but your number probably came up as out of area."

"You shouldn't leave until you know what she wanted."

"Stop it. Reg is not dangerous. I will handle this."

That's when Mabel came sauntering in, purring loud enough to be heard next door. She rubbed up against their legs.

"She's hungry," Callum translated.

Clementine smiled at the fat cat. "I'm not surprised."

They both stood and Mabel waddled quickly into the kitchen ahead of them. She jumped on the countertop and waited for Callum to give her breakfast.

He retrieved a can from the cabinet and opened it for her. She contentedly hunkered down to eat.

"Coffee?" he asked Clementine.

"I'd love some," she said, looking around the airy, modern kitchen.

He busied himself by measuring the grounds and pouring the water into the coffeemaker. While the coffee was brewing, he turned to her. "Did you sleep well?" he asked, leaning against the counter and staring at her as if he couldn't get enough. She was beautiful this morning. She hadn't bothered tying her hair back and it fell wildly over her shoulders, curl tangled in curl. Her eyes were sleepy, erotic.

"Pretty well." She crossed her arms over her chest and he realized his gaze had unintentionally traveled lower. "How about you?"

He cursed himself for being so obvious. "Fine. I slept fine. How is your wrist?"

"Better this morning." She brought it out and moved it back and forth as if testing it. "It wasn't awkward to sleep on at all. I thought it would be torture."

The gurgling of the coffeemaker was the perfect excuse to get off the entirely too arousing subject of Clementine and her bedroom behaviors.

He brought down two mugs, which were part of a set his mother had given him when he'd moved to Topeka a year before she'd died. The third one had a broken handle and was now his penholder in his office. He poured Clementine a cup and handed it to her. "Milk or sugar?"

"Sugar."

He handed her the sugar bowl and she spooned in a couple of helpings and stirred. Sipping her coffee, she lifted herself onto one of the kitchen stools at the island counter, carefully folding her robe over her legs, withholding the identity of the lacy garment she wore underneath.

Her eyes lingered for a moment on the serenity of the beautiful windowed breakfast nook overlooking his backyard. She sighed as if in regret as she shifted her gaze, then lifted her cup to her lips. "Will you take me to get my car?" she said softly.

He shrugged in the direction of the driveway. "It's outside. Luke and Jess got it for you last night. The keys are on the table in the entranceway." He moved beside her. "Can I ask you a favor?"

She looked up at him leerily. But the heat was still there. "Okay."

"Will you let me take you to the festival?" He pushed some hair off her shoulder and he felt an infinitesimal shudder run through her. "You're going to love Mid-May. It goes out with a bang."

She seemed to smile despite herself. "Is that a well-known fact or a personal promise?"

His whole body ached and pulled. He'd never felt anything like it. "Both," he said roughly.

He wasn't going to tell her about the suspicious car last night. He suspected that one of the reasons she wanted to leave so soon was because she didn't like the fact that she had brought something so disturbing to Tried and True, a place she clearly loved. He wasn't going to give her another reason to leave. He'd given her too many already.

Now he had to give her reasons to stay.

Because he couldn't help it, he started by kissing her senseless, right there in the kitchen, against the island counter. He released her abruptly and told her to go get ready for Mid-May.

WHEN SHE FINISHED showering and struggling fruitlessly with her hair, she came back downstairs. After that completely unexpected kiss in the kitchen, she pretty much expected his rapt attention, but she was reasonably sure Callum didn't notice the red-and-white-checked gingham dress she was wearing as he ushered her out the door. It was the second dress from Lovey's Boutique she'd promised to wear. With its shirtwaist, long skirt and quaint patch pockets, it could have been campy, but it wasn't. The dress was strapless and exposed her shoulders and showed enough of her chest to be as provocative as it was cute.

He confirmed her suspicion when he insisted on taking his bike. She wasn't all that experienced with motorcycles, but common sense told her bikes and dresses just didn't mix. And she was right.

It was a relatively short ride from Callum's house to Main Street but, even at a residential speed, her skirt flew up, exposing her legs all the way to the thigh. That, she thought, was when he finally had to notice. With her bare legs pressing against his, it was hard to ignore.

He parked his bike along Wild Rose because Main was closed to traffic. There were many cars parked along the side streets and she caught sight of crowds of people as Callum swung his leg off the bike and offered his hand to her. She showed even more leg as she got off.

"Sorry about the bike. I had to get us out of that house fast, before I was tempted to make us late," he said, keeping her hand in his as they walked toward Main. "You look beautiful, Clementine."

"Thank you," she said softly, missing him already.

She knew she'd kept saying she would leave in two weeks, but she'd never had any clear vision in her head of how she was going to do it. She had arrived in Tried and True almost a week ago, and known almost immediately that she wanted to stay.

Callum was wearing his sunglasses, the reflective kind. She couldn't see his eyes, but got the impression he was patrolling the crowd as they walked onto Main. He had mentioned something earlier about stopping by the station to pick up a walkie-talkie because he was going to be on duty during the festival.

She was immediately enchanted with Mid-May. Booths were set up and were just now opening all along the sidewalks on either side of the street. It seemed the entire populace of Tried and True and busloads of tourists who were wearing bright fanny packs and colored plastic sun visors, milled around.

She saw one booth belonging to Cripes, which served food from an outside grill, and had added funnel cake for good measure. Cripes restaurant was closed that day because of the festival, but it was Saturday anyway, Clementine's first day off. She would always claim her five days of employ at Cripes as an accomplishment. She could envision herself working there longer, not because she needed the money, but because it was meaningful to her and she served a purpose. But it was her own fault that she had to leave Tried and True.

Charlotte Lovelace had set up a booth showcasing some of her handmade bead jewelry, Sandy's Soda Shop booth served ice cream and shaved ice and drinks, and the Ladies Club had a particularly large booth to showcase the pies they sold by the piece or by the pie. There were dozens more booths, but she didn't recognize the vendors.

"They come in from out of town," Callum explained when she asked. "Mid-May has grown in the past few years and has attracted a lot of day tourists.

And these vendors come specifically to rent sidewalk space and sell their wares.''

Clementine saw that one woman offered palm readings, another man drew caricatures, someone was selling hats and sunglasses and another sold carved figurines and pottery.

"This is wonderful," she leaned into Callum to say. They walked toward the end of Main Street where the road looped around like a cul-de-sac in front of the sheriff's department and the courthouse. In the loop, right in front of the two county buildings, a stage had been constructed, the back facing the sheriff's department. There was a sectioned-off area in front where people could dance. As they approached, the noise level escalated.

"There's Luke," Callum said, spying the deputy over near the stage. "I need to talk to him."

"You go ahead. I want to look around a bit." She tried to wiggle her hand out of his.

"It will only take a second," he insisted.

She blew some tendrils of hair off her forehead. With her sprained wrist, it was impossible to do anything with her hair but to let it fall free in all its curly glory. "What could possibly happen here, Callum?"

"I'm the sheriff," he said evenly. "It's my job to make sure nothing threatens the safety of the people in this town."

"I would never intentionally do anything to threaten the people in this town!" she exclaimed. What was the matter with him? "That's why I'm leaving."

"I meant *your* safety. You *are* a person in this town." He scowled at her. "And you're not leaving yet."

"Don't you think you're carrying this thing just a little too far? Oh, don't give me that look," she said when he continued to scowl at her. "I'll be over at the Ladies Club booth, all right?" She pointed to the booth.

He seemed to debate over that. Finally he said, "All right. But stay there. This won't take long."

Clementine stalked over to the Ladies Club booth where Vera reminded her that at eleven o'clock she would need to man the booth while the pie judging was held over on the nearby stage. It was only a quarter to ten, so she promised the ladies she'd be back on time, then walked out into the swarm of people.

SHE'D DISAPPEARED, and he wondered why he was so surprised. He'd been gone all of three minutes as he went over to Luke to ask for an update on the dark sedan. Luke had finished his night shift and was doing some extra patrolling for the festival. Mac and Jess were also on duty, along with some volunteers. Luke hadn't been able to tell him anything new, but complained that the Ladies Club members were trying to get him to ask Naomi to dance when the music competition started.

Smiling with sympathy, he told Luke to keep an eye out. But when he turned around, Clementine had vanished. Vera pointed him in the direction she had headed, but he knew how difficult it was going to be to find a self-proclaimed meanderer in the midst of all these people. But he needed to have her near him. He had a distinct, prickly sensation that told him trouble was brewing around her. He couldn't explain it, but his need to watch over her was strong.

After twenty grueling minutes, he finally caught sight of her. Her golden curls stood out, making her beautifully noticeable. She was standing at one of the booths, laughing and making chitchat with the vendor, then she moved on to peruse another booth. Cal-

lum astutely took in her actions and, ever aware of
everyone around, immediately noticed a man imitat-
ing her actions, following her from booth to booth.

He wasn't local. Definitely a city boy. He was
about five-ten and looked to be in his late-twenties,
his hair absurdly fluffy and light blond. He was wearing dark slacks and a matching jacket over a white
band-collar button-down shirt. There were creases in
the clothes he wore, as if he'd been wearing them too
long, and there was a suspicious bulge under the back
of his jacket. He was jittery, maybe from lack of sleep
or too much caffeine. Callum recognized the posture
of desperation, and all that desperation was focused
on Clementine.

From a close but unobtrusive distance Callum began to follow the man as he followed Clementine.
Callum wished he could contact Luke or Jess or Mac,
but, whereas they had their walkie-talkies, Callum
hadn't been to the station yet to pick his up. And he'd
be damned if he was going to leave Clementine now.

She was totally oblivious to the attention she attracted. She didn't know how beautiful she was. The
way she moved was graceful and her dress played up
her innocence, but the gentle curve of her exposed
shoulders, the extravagant flare of her hips, and those
legs that went on forever, made a man forget about
innocence and think carnal thoughts instead. All night
he could smell her on him.

His desire to protect her was rooted a lot deeper
than just an ordinary sense of duty and he knew it.
He was in love with her. Madly, truly in love with a
woman he was determined not to lose.

She stopped by the Cripes booth. The man stopped.
And so did Callum. He suddenly felt a raw chill run
down his spine. This man was looking at her like
Callum was, taking in her fine features, but with much

less emotion. Coveting her without respecting her. Was this Reg? Was he the one who'd trashed her motel room? Was he after the ring? Or was he after more than that? His anger suddenly took a different turn and he wanted to tackle the man for what he was obviously thinking.

Clementine sat down to eat something she'd bought at the Cripes booth and the man stood at a distance and watched her. Callum started to approach him with his I'm-the-sheriff-are-you-behaving-yourself speech, when he noticed Clementine, always in his peripheral vision, leaving to head back up the street. A crowd of teenagers passed by at that moment and the stranger didn't see her.

Cursing under his breath, Callum reluctantly followed her instead of approaching the man. As long as he was near her, she was safe. He didn't want to take the chance of going after the man, losing him, then having him find Clementine first.

By THE TIME CLEMENTINE had reached the other end of the street, she had realized she was growing a little hungry, so she stopped by the Cripes booth to get a funnel cake. When Harlan handed her the paper plate with the warm, powdered-sugar funnel cake on it, then waved away her attempt to pay him, tears formed in her eyes and all she could manage was, "Thank you." There wasn't time to tell him how his giving her a job had made all the difference, how it had given her confidence in herself, how it had played a part in changing her life.

She sat next to some giggling local children on the sidewalk edge, trying to get a hold of herself.

Taking a deep breath, she started in on her funnel cake. She lazily scanned the crowds and suddenly had the odd feeling she was being watched. She tried to ignore it for a while, munching unassumingly. It was Callum making her act this way, making her leery. But he'd been overreacting. Nothing bad could happen at Mid-May. She knew she was just being paranoid, playing to Callum's suspicions, but she decided to throw away her paper plate and go back to the Ladies Club booth anyway.

As she headed back up the street, she couldn't help but look over her shoulder to see if she was being followed, smiling at her own foolishness even as she did so. What was the matter with her?

But then, as she approached the Ladies Club booth, she saw him.

Just for a moment, she spotted his profile as a group of fanny-packers brushed past her. She moved her head, to look around them as they passed, but he was gone. Then she saw Mrs. Elliott jogging past her in that direction, calling, "Yoo-hoo! Yoo-hoo! Sir!"

It had been Reg, no doubt about it.

The most unexpected emotion passed through her. She was happy. She was happy Reg was at Mid-May. He wanted the ring, and she could give it to him now, today. Maybe they could even have a cup of coffee and talk about things. They could have a civilized conversation and shake hands amicably before he left. And she could stay in Tried and True then! With the way she'd been acting, she understood that he was worried she might not ever come back to Savannah with his ring. Reg was smarmy, but ultimately a reasonable man. She knew he felt as little sexually for her as she did for him. They'd only ever shared brief kisses. He'd never made any advances. Surely, now that some time had passed, he understood why she couldn't go through with the wedding. He had come here to discuss the end of the relationship and to take his expensive ring back. The more she thought about it, the more sense it made. Of course. The whole trashing of her room still confused her, but she knew he really didn't mean any harm.

"Clementine?"

She spun around at the voice and was so happy to see Callum that she spontaneously hugged him. He immediately hugged her back with a force and emotion that surprised her.

She looked back over her shoulder to where she had last seen Reg. With any luck, she'd keep Reg and Callum apart, and explain the whole thing to Callum later. Much later. "I have to find someone right now, but I'll see you in a little while, okay?"

He held his hands on her waist and prompted her to turn to face him again. She did and realized he had taken off his sunglasses and put them in the front pocket of his denim shirt. His smoky, light blue eyes looked stressed. "You want to explain Mr. Fluffy Hair to me?" He asked.

She gaped at him. "You've seen him? How did you know?"

"I've been following him as he's followed you."

"Reg has been following me?"

"I thought it was the infamous Reginald," Callum said gruffly, steering her away. "I don't think your ex-fiancé has taken kindly to being dumped."

11

"COME WITH ME," Callum said, leading her past the Ladies Club booth and toward the stage, or, more accurately, to the buildings behind the stage.

"Where are we going?"

"To the station."

She felt the first prickle of concern. "Why are we going there?"

"Because I know you'll be safe there."

"Stop it, Callum," she said vehemently. "This is Reg. You don't know him, he's not dangerous. I don't know what my mother said to you, but don't believe a word. I am capable of taking care of myself."

"I know you are," Callum said, still relentlessly pulling her with him.

"I can't go to the station." She dug in her heels. "Callum, stop. I have to man the Ladies Club booth during the judging of the pie contest." She pointed to the stage where the pie contest was about to start. Callum seemed to hesitate, so she added, "Do you really want them to know it was you who prevented one of them from participating in it?"

He huffed out an irritated breath, then led her over to the booth, the threat of retribution from the Ladies Club apparently an ingrained fear in the local inhabitants. Callum opened the hip-high side door to the booth. Vera scurried out, saying, "It's good to see you two together. Now make yourselves at home. I left a note on how much is what and the money box is on the lower shelf. Wish me luck!''

Immediately, a couple with children came by and Clementine busied herself by serving them their requested pie slices while Callum made change for them. When the kids left, he nudged her away from the opening, as if not wanting anyone, Reg in particular, to see her. He stood at the counter, so she took a seat in one of the several folding chairs in the large booth, which was hot and smelled sugary, like a pastry kitchen. There were shelves all lined with pies covered with clear plastic domed covers.

"I kept telling everyone that I wanted to get away, that I was overwhelmed, but they didn't believe me," she said, wanting to tell him the truth, so he'd stop hating himself, or resenting her, or whatever in the world he was feeling that was making him act this way. He turned to look at her. "There were all these wedding plans, and I didn't know how to stop them. I'd been engaged to Reg for four months, and had dated him for six, but I felt as if I hadn't been asked if I wanted any of it. I never even said yes to Reg at the engagement party. He asked me in front of two hundred people, put the ring on my finger and everyone clapped. That was it. Then my mother started with all the plans. And I kept quiet and let it all happen because it seemed to make everyone happy."

Callum looked skeptical, and Clementine understood his disbelief. Intelligent people didn't let these kinds of things happen to themselves. "It's true, all of it. You've talked to my mother. She's not an easy woman to say no to."

He almost smiled. "You're right, she's not."

"I told you that my mother cut off my bank accounts and credit cards, trying to get me to come home. As you know now, that's because the wedding

couldn't exactly happen without the runaway bride.
But when I got here..." She paused, almost saying
and kissed you, but didn't. "I suddenly knew what I
had to do. So I called my mother and Reg. I told them
that there wasn't going to be a wedding. Neither one
of them was very happy, but I was going to clean up
the mess when I had enough money to get home. Or
that had been the plan. I know Reg wants his ring
back, which is understandable. I'm going to give it
back to him. I offered to send it back by mail, but he
got hysterical over that. He obviously wants to know
that it's all right. He wouldn't hurt me. All this worry
is needless. I can take care of myself. For the first
time in my life, I know I can."

Callum didn't say anything.

"I'm not asking you to let me handle it myself,"
she said, seeing the need to clarify. "I'm telling you
I'm going to handle it myself."

"And then what?" he asked quietly. His back was
to the opening and the light behind him caught blue-
black highlights in his hair.

"What do you mean?"

"Are you still going back?"

She opened her mouth to say no, then pressed her
lips together. Did he want her to stay? She decided
to get Reg out of the way before she tackled Callum.
She almost smiled at that image. Tackling him. In a
bedroom, maybe. She was going to stay, but was he
ready to hear it?

They were suddenly interrupted by a steady stream
of eager pie-eaters. Then the disgruntled Ladies Club
members who had been eliminated in the first round
of the pie contest started heading back to the booth,
some of them grumbling that it was a new judge who
had made them lose.

"Come on." Callum took her by the hand and led her out of the booth.

They had gone about three steps when Clementine stopped in her tracks. She had looked up at the stage to see which of the ladies had made it to the final round, and saw Reg.

Reg was one of the judges in the pie contest.

"What in the…"

Callum followed her gaze. He immediately turned her around and headed to a nearby booth. Tossing some bills at the vendor, he grabbed a wide-brimmed straw hat.

He put it on Clementine's head and said, "Push your hair up under it."

"I don't understand why you're doing this. This is Reg. He signed a petition to have 'Monday Night Football' banned from local television. He's never been in a fight. He thinks a right hook is a character in *Peter Pan*," she said as he skimmed the dance area, trying to ease around the stage without Reg seeing them. "He's a judge in a pie contest, for heaven's sake."

"And the winner is…Vera Suttles with her strawberry-rhubarb pie!" the head judge said into the microphone.

There was a flurry of activity on the stage. Reg started to dart off to the side and down the steps, but he was called back in order to return his black cardboard top hat that said Judge on it. All six judges wore the hats, making them look like a group of Abe Lincolns in a school play. The pie contest dated back to the founding of the town, so everyone thought it was appropriate that the judges looked like founding fathers. The tables were being removed quickly and Vera pranced around with the blue ribbon on her chest, waving to the crowds, as Bill and his band set up their instruments. Vera had to leave the stage when they started playing, but she did so reluctantly. Reg relinquished his top hat, his curly blond hair springing up as he did so, and he immediately headed for the steps again, almost knocking Vera over. She called to him, but he ignored her.

Callum, having watched all this, too, knew that they were going to run headlong into Reg at the side of the stage, so he grabbed Clementine and pulled her onto the dance floor in front of the stage. He pushed the straw hat low on her forehead and held her close. She could feel the ring against her belly as Callum squeezed against her.

Over his shoulder Clementine saw Callum's deputy, Luke, dancing with Naomi from Cripes. They seemed like an odd pair because it didn't look as if they wanted to be dancing with each other in the first place. Luke said something to Naomi and she pushed herself away from him. Glaring at him with what seemed like tears in her eyes, she stalked away from him. Luke shook his head and ran a hand agitatedly through his hair.

"It looks like Naomi and Luke had a fight," Clementine said absently.

"What?"

"Luke and Naomi," she repeated. "They were dancing but then she ran away from him."

"Luke is here? Where?" He spun her around so he could see where she was looking.

"Right over there."

"He's not there anymore. Damn it. I need him." Callum spun her around again.

"Why would they be fighting?" Clementine asked.

"Who?"

"Luke and Naomi."

He made a distracted sound. "The Ladies Club has been trying to get them back together."

"*Back* together?"

"They were sweethearts in high school before she moved away for a couple of years."

"Why did she move away?"

"Clementine, please!" Callum reprimanded. "Reg is right at the edge of the dance area, looking around. The Ladies Club ladies keep pestering him. They're surrounding him. Damn it, what are they doing?"

Clementine tried to pull away to get a look at Reg and whatever the Ladies Club members were doing to him, but Callum held her head in place. She was still convinced that there wasn't any real danger and that Callum was grossly overreacting. "I'm getting tired of this, Callum," she said evenly. "I don't want you to protect me. This is my problem. I ran away from it once and I'm not doing it again. He wants this ring and I want to give it to him. I can see where he's coming from. The ring is worth a lot of money, of course he wants it back…"

"Stop…defending…him…to…me," Callum said slowly, crisply.

"I'm not," she said, surprised. "I mean, he's not a threat. I'll just give him the ring back, okay? It is as simple as that. Stop trying to take over. This has nothing to do with you." She tried to move again, but he wouldn't let go. "I never wanted to involve you in this."

"Too late. Move with me across the dance area. Slowly, so he won't see you."

She tried to laugh. "He's not…"

"Just do it, Clementine. You need to trust me." His voice was rough and low, and for the first time she felt genuine worry. "Damn," he muttered under his breath. He was tense, his grip on her so tight she could feel his fingers dig into her waist.

"What?"

"He's circling the dance area. And the ladies are clucking behind him. They know who he is, don't they? I bet they were the ones who made him a judge, trying to keep him away from you. We can't walk away without him seeing us. I wish I had a damn walkie-talkie so I could tell Luke to get the ladies away from that man."

"I mentioned that he looked like a vanilla ice-cream cone, so they could've recognized him," Clementine admitted. "But listen, Callum, this wouldn't be a problem if you'd just let me give him the ring. Reg is not a totally unreasonable man."

"Then you never knew him." She felt tension in his shoulders. "I'm going to lead you to the left-hand side of this dancing area. As soon as we reach the edge, I'm going to take your hand and run behind the stage and into the station. Be prepared. Ready? Now!" With that he took off and she had no choice but to follow.

Clementine nearly tripped over the curb as Callum dragged her into the station. She immediately jerked her hand out of his, slightly out of breath from the mad dash.

Mac was in the station and got up from his desk, surprised, as they burst in. "Where is Jess?" Callum barked.

"Patrolling the parking areas in his car."

"Call him in, now."

Mac didn't question him and did it right away. Clementine finally caught her breath and glared at Callum.

"All right, that's *it!*" she snapped. "I will not allow this to go any further. I ran away from people trying to dictate my life and my actions and I didn't travel halfway across the country to let it happen all over again. *Stop* trying to tell me what to do. I did the wrong thing. I admit it. I ran away from something I should have stood up to. I should have stopped the engagement before it ever happened.'' She pulled up the side of her skirt and Mac's mouth fell open as she briefly flashed lace. Callum easily stepped in front of her to block his view. She all but tore the yarn off. ''He wants this,'' she said, holding up the ring. ''I'm going to give it back to him. God, I've made such a mess of things. Don't try to stop me because this has absolutely nothing—I repeat, *nothing* to do with you.'' She started to turn to go outside, but Callum wrapped his fingers around her bare upper arm.

''You made it have something to do with me the moment you entered this county. Now,'' he said calmly, ''Mac, here, is going to escort you back to the holding cells where you can sit under lock and key and stew all you want while I deal with this man you're nobly but irrationally trying to protect.''

Clementine looked to Mac, who looked as surprised as she was. Still, he grabbed a set of keys from his desk drawer and started to walk over to her.

''Jail?'' she said loudly, the day taking a turn she didn't expect. ''You're going to put me in jail? Why?'' She looked at him incredulously. The hurt was welling up inside her, slowly moving to all ends of her body, making her tingle with it and, even though she knew she was saying things she would regret, she couldn't seem to help it. ''This isn't doing your job. This is letting your anger at yourself, or your anger at me, take over. This has nothing to do with you.''

''I want you safe,'' he said simply. ''Lock her up, Mac.''

"Safe. Sure. That's a laugh," she joked. "Safe from a man who cried during *Titanic*. Why won't you listen to me? What possible reason is there not to believe me?"

"Mac," Callum said, and Mac took her arm to lead her to the back of the station.

She jerked Mac to a stop and turned to glare at Callum. "You can't throw me in jail. If you do, my mother will have to bail me out. Don't you see? This is going to make her think she's been right all along. That I can't take care of myself. Let me do this."

Callum squeezed his eyes shut for a moment and pushed his hair off his forehead. The man looked haggard with worry, and it was all for nothing. "I'm not throwing you in jail and your mother won't have to bail you out. I promise." He sighed. "Mac, as soon as she's secure, come back out. I'll need backup. And I need a damn walkie-talkie."

Callum stepped inside his office and Clementine let an apologetic Mac take her through a small hallway to the holding cells.

This was ridiculous. She had to get out of the station and return the damn ring to Reg. She gave Mac a sideways look. She waited until he had opened the door to the holding cell and had stepped back for her to enter, then she let the ring she was holding drop to the floor in front of her.

"Oh, no," she cried softly, not beyond using her Southern wiles at a time such as this. They were like her superpowers that she'd sworn to use for good, not evil. But desperate times called for desperate measures. If she'd had a hankie, she'd have put it to her mouth. "Not my ring! Is it scratched? Is it broken? It's an *heir*loom. Oh, I'm *devastated!*" Her own words took her aback. She sounded like her mother.

"It's all right," he said, kneeling to pick up the ring. "If it is, I'm sure it can be fixed."

Saying a silent but sincere apology to Mac, she gave the deputy a good push and he went sprawling into the cell. She immediately shut the door, snatched the ring and the keys he'd dropped, then threw the keys out of reach.

"Hey!" Mac yelled. "Stop! You can't do this!"

But she was already running out.

She realized that Mac's shouts could be heard out in the office area as soon as she reached it. Knowing she had very little time before Callum came out of his office to investigate, she ran full-speed across the room toward the door.

She passed right by his office and glanced in as she ran by. He looked up from where he was standing behind his desk, opening a drawer with a key.

"Clementine, come back here!" she heard him thunder as she reached the door and pushed it open.

12

CLEMENTINE HIT THE STREET running. Her first priority was to lose Callum. Then she would find Reg.

She heard Callum yell after her as she darted past the stage and drowned herself in the sea of people. Soon she couldn't hear him shouting at all.

Her heart was pounding thickly in her chest, not so much with the exertion but with anxiety. When it came right down to it, she had just run away from the sheriff. He had flexed his muscle and used his authority to try to put her in jail so now, as absurd as it seemed, she was running from the law.

Her mother was going to love this.

Not knowing where to begin, she zigzagged down the street, darting here and there so Callum wouldn't be able to find her easily. At first it seemed that the street was saturated with so many people that she didn't have a prayer of finding one specific person. Then she suddenly recognized someone—Luke, who was very evidently searching for someone, namely her. Damn those walkie-talkies, she thought irritably.

She silently cursed Callum for getting things organized so quickly. He must really think she was incompetent. But she had to do this. She *wasn't* trying to protect Reg. As tempted as she was to blame this all on Reg, or her mother, she really was the one responsible.

She darted to the other side of the street, away from Luke.

Clementine skulked around the booths, trying to avoid anyone with a walkie-talkie. Callum forming a posse didn't make things any easier on her. What was with him? Give him a tiny problem and he snowballs it into a national disaster. This was Reg. She'd known him almost a year. She'd been engaged to him for four months. She *knew* he wasn't dangerous.

Oh, who was she trying to kid? Being angry with Callum just eased the ache in her heart. She'd run out of chances with him the moment she locked Mac in the cell and taken off. If she had a hundred years, she would not understand that man. What was so wrong with wanting to do this herself? Was there something about her that made people want to take over her life?

She anxiously twisted the ring she now wore on her finger, just so she wouldn't lose it. She suddenly froze when she saw Mac at a nearby booth, then slowly backed away, turning as she did so. At least the poor guy had been set free. She looked around anxiously. Things were getting tight and she had to work fast. Where was Reg?

Then she remembered what Callum said about the Ladies Club pestering Reg when he was looking around for her.

Clementine headed to the pie booth.

She went right to the side door and entered, only to find it extremely crowded inside. And there, in the middle of the booth, sat Reg.

"I don't *want* another piece of pie!" Reg whined. "I am trying to be nice about this, but if you don't stop pushing food in my face, I'm going to get very angry. I don't even *like* pie."

The ladies gasped at the blasphemy.

"Reg, what are you doing in here?" Clementine

asked. He turned at the sound of her voice and she
got a good look at his face. Reg had a very angry
black eye. "Good Lord, what *happened* to you?"

Reg jumped out of his chair, knocking the plate
with Callie's lemon meringue pie aside and it fell with
a splat to the floor. He didn't say excuse me, and Reg
always said excuse me. "Finally!" he said, pushing
some ladies out of the way to get to Clementine. He
was trying to smile, but there was something precar-
ious about him. "Let's go."

"I'm not going anywhere, Reg."

"She's in love with the sheriff," Vera told him.

Clementine suddenly looked around at the dozen
or so ladies who were elbow to elbow in the booth,
making a circle around them and watching with great
interest. "Um, hi, everybody. This, I guess you already know, is my ex-fiancé," she said awkwardly.
"Reg, this is the Tried and True Ladies Club."

Reg looked at her, his pale blue eyes glittering and
ghostly compared to the dark shiner around his left
eye. "Ex-nothing. Stop this nonsense now. We're going back to Savannah," he said firmly, as if that
would be enough to convince her. Maybe it would
have been. Once.

"No, Reg. Your coming here has just made things
easier. Here is your ring." She pulled the ring off her
finger and forced it into his hand. "You go back to
Savannah. I'm staying here."

"She's in love with the sheriff," Callie repeated.

Reg rolled his eyes and ran both hands through his
hair, making his blond curls fluff out like cotton. "I
cannot believe the trouble you've caused. Everything
was so perfect. To think, at one time I thought you
were sweet. A little gullible maybe, but sweet. But
then you go and leave me high and dry."

That stung—and stunned her. She never thought

she'd hear harsh words come out of Reg's mouth. "I'm sorry I let it go this far. I really am," she said sincerely. "Take the ring and leave, Reg. I'm not going to marry you."

"For almost an entire year, you're nice and catatonic." Once he started, he couldn't seem to stop. "I work your mother nicely, knowing you would be the easy part to all of this because you would do exactly what she told you to. But then suddenly you wake up and leave. You never even thought about me, did you? You never thought about what this would do to me. I'm in trouble now and it's all because you couldn't stay catatonic for just one month longer. One month, Clementine!"

Clementine looked at him oddly. "Trouble? Why are you in trouble? What's wrong?"

"I need your money, Clementine."

"Reg, will you listen to yourself?" she implored, seeing things take an alarming turn. Something wasn't right. "Why do you need my money? You have your own."

Reg laughed. "What money? I have no money. I've never had money. I am up to my ears in debt."

She knew. Suddenly she understood, and it made so much sense. How could she have been so stupid? "I'm not leaving." Clementine looked Reg in the eye and said, "I'm in love with the sheriff."

"We're going back to Savannah to get married," Reg said, as if talking to a child. "It's what I want and it's what your mother wants. You know this has to be done. I don't care that you're in love with the sheriff as long as you don't care I'm only marrying you for your money. I should probably even thank the man for what he's done for you. You look better than you ever have."

"Clementine, could I have a word with you outside?'' Clementine spun and the ladies cleared away so she could see Callum standing at the counter. She winced at the look on his face. He was livid, his fingers curling tightly around the outside edges of the booth's opening as if trying to keep it from collapsing.

''Callum, it's okay. Just give me a minute,'' she said, determined to handle this on her own before he hauled her off to jail again.

''So this is the sheriff, is it?'' Reg commented like a fool.

''And you must be Reg,'' Callum answered in the same tone of voice. ''Clementine, come out here *now*. Ladies, you need to follow her. There are regulations and you're over the capacity of people allowed in your booth at one time.''

''We're taking care of this, Callum,'' Vera said.

Callum bored holes into Vera with his stare, obviously trying to communicate something to her. ''Vera, don't argue with me,'' he said slowly in a voice that anyone but a member of the Ladies Club would blanch at.

Vera waved her hand dismissively. ''I know he has a gun, Callum. We've been trying to get it away from him for the past hour.''

''A gun?'' Clementine said, appalled, taking a step back from Reg, and she heard Callum curse. *Reg had a gun?* She didn't think Reg even knew what one looked like. Who was this person? she thought, staring at him. She realized now that she never really knew him. All this time, and she never knew he was broke, that he was only marrying her for her money, that he would come after her armed in order to haul her back to Savannah. She flushed with the thought of actually having accused Callum of interfering because he was angry, instead of trying to protect her because she was in danger.

Reg started to reach around to his back, an unpracticed move that made him look awkward. "That's right, Clementine, and if you don't come with me..."

There were some shuffling sounds and Clementine looked up. All the ladies were holding pies now, one in each hand, and they looked as if they weren't afraid to use them. "Don't you dare!" Callum yelled to the ladies as he hurtled into the booth, Clementine ducked, and pies started to fly.

After it was all over with, Reg was facedown in pie muck in the booth with his hands cuffed behind his back, and Vera was holding a blueberry filling-covered pistol.

"I told you we were taking care of it," Vera said, handing the gun over to Callum.

He glared at Vera. The back of his shirt had taken the brunt of the attack and it was covered with pie. He fairly shouted, "You're right, Vera. Why on earth does this county even have a sheriff's department when we have the Ladies Club to fight crime!" He hoisted Reg up and escorted him out of the booth without a word or even a glance at Clementine. Mac and Luke, whom she hadn't noticed until then, followed him.

"He's mad," Clementine said, feeling shaky and bereft, wondering if she could ever make things right with him now. There had been an armed man at Mid-May, and Clementine had brought him there. Not only that, she had tried to convince everyone that he was harmless.

"He'll get over it," Vera said.

The ladies were all looking at her expectantly, standing ankle-deep in the pies they'd labored over. They had come up with a boyfriend who ran away with his masseuse, an ex-husband who stole her parrot, a circus performer who refused to leave life on the road for her, and a football player who ignored her. Clementine didn't realize until that moment that the truth was even stranger than fiction. And she owed the ladies this tale.

So she told them the whole story, from running away from her overbearing mother and a lavish wedding she almost went through with just to please her, even though she didn't even like Reg and, it turned out, he was only going to marry her for her money. She told them about being rich, but when she went on this vacation her mother had cut her money off in order to get her daughter to come home. She told them about agreeing to pretend to date Callum because she was only going to stay two weeks at first and she didn't want to hurt any feelings, and she told them about to falling in love with Callum.

When she finally finished, she looked up and the booth was full of more ladies, and she could barely see daylight because of the Ladies Club members who were gathered around the outside of the booth to hear her story.

There was silence at first, then Mrs. Elliott said, "Well, we've never had a socialite in Tried and True. Wouldn't a cotillion be nice? Clementine, you're going to have to show us how to have a cotillion."

DAYLIGHT eventually turned into a clear pink dusk. When the vendors started closing up shop, people began bringing lawn chairs, folding chairs and pillows out into the street. They were settling themselves into misshapen rows all along Main as if to watch some show. Clementine was surprised to see this as she walked out of the Ladies Club booth, where she had spent the rest of the afternoon helping them clean up.

The last band of the day was packing up on the stage, so whatever entertainment the people in the street were waiting for wasn't going to come from there. She had pulled her hair back into a ponytail, and the hat Callum had given her fell down her back, hanging by the chin strap around her neck. As she walked down Main, dodging children and legs stretched out from lawn chairs, a warm breeze teased her bare shoulders, which were still a little sticky with pie.

She was looking for Callum because she had a lot to apologize for, and she wanted to tell him she was staying. She was expecting one of two reactions from him when she told him this: either he would be happy, or he would call out the National Guard.

She spotted Mac talking to a vendor who was closing up. First thing's first, she thought. Taking a deep breath, knowing she had to eat crow, Clementine walked over to him and tapped him on the shoulder. "Hi, Mac."

The young deputy gave a slight nod, as if any sudden movement might set her off.

"I'm sorry," she said sincerely. "I'm sorry I tricked you and locked you in the cell."

He tried to act nonchalant, shaking one shoulder stiffly. "'S'okay."

"No, it's not. Come by Cripes next week. I'll give you breakfast on me."

He looked a little leery.

"For a month."

He finally smiled a little. "Okay. I might."

She hesitated. On the one hand, she really wanted to know about Reg. On the other, she was eager to make him a part of her past and to forget him. But she had to ask. "What happened with Reg?"

Mac looked faintly surprised. "You mean, Callum hasn't told you?"

"I haven't seen him."

He looked confused. "But he knew you were in the Ladies Club booth all day. He told me where you were and to keep an eye on you. He wanted to make sure you were safe."

"Oh." But he didn't come by, or tell her what had happened. He was mad. She had to think of a way to set things right with him. She couldn't stand the thought of living in Tried and True with Callum thinking ill of her. Somehow, she didn't think free breakfast for a month was going to work with him. "I think I'm the last person Callum wants to see right now." She reached out and touched Mac's arm imploringly. "Please tell me what happened."

Mac shifted uncomfortably from one foot to the other. "I don't know if I'm supposed to tell you."

When he hesitated, she said, "Please."

Mac hooked his thumbs in his belt and rocked back on his heels. "Well," he said. "I guess you know it started with Callum being worried about your room being vandalized, and then there was the car. There was a dark blue sedan that had toured the church parking lot while you were at the piefest, according to Callum, then it passed by his house several times late last night while you were there."

Clementine's brows shot up. "A car following me?" And he didn't tell her? "It was Reg in the car?"

"Yup. Then today, Callum saw someone following you around the festival. Since this guy was focused solely on you, Callum wanted to put you in a safe place before we went after him, but then the Ladies Club got involved."

Clementine was shaking her head slowly. She

wouldn't have made such a fool of herself if she had known Reg had been stalking her. This would have been useful information. "Callum didn't tell me any of this. So where is Reg now? Is he in the jail?"

"He was arrested in Noosely, Nebraska, about three hours ago," Mac said. "The car he was driving was stolen. So was the ring he had given you."

Reg had given her a *stolen* ring? She'd been traveling around the country with stolen property? This was so far from what she expected to hear. "I don't understand. Why did you let him go?"

"Callum wanted him as far away from you as he could get him, and we all agreed. After taking his gun, Callum had Luke escort him to the car, then follow him out of Truly County, which borders Nebraska. A few calls, and the cops out there had him. It now has nothing to do with you, or this county."

"I see," she said with more calm than she felt. "And where is Callum now?"

"He's at the station."

"Thank you, Mac," she said, then she turned and headed to the station, as mad as a hornet.

13

SHE STRODE THROUGH the door and went right to his office. He was sitting, punching keys on the computer. He'd obviously heard the clang of the front door as she'd opened it because he looked up when she appeared. He had cleaned up and changed into a khaki-colored uniform shirt with snap buttons. She'd managed to wash up as best she could, but her dress still bore the signs of the pie fight in the Ladies Club booth.

"You knew he'd been following me," she said from the doorway, her hands on her hips. "You knew he'd been following me and didn't say anything. What part of that did you think I wouldn't find dangerous? You had me make a fool of myself by declaring to anyone who would listen that I was an emancipated adult who was, come hell or high water, going to take care of her own business, when all along you knew why I shouldn't go near Reg."

"I know and I'm sorry," he said. He shook his head and pivoted his chair away from the computer. "When I saw the two of you there in that booth, I...can't explain it." He rubbed his forehead, then pushed his hair away. He sat back and closed his tired blue eyes. "For as long as I live, I'll regret that. I wanted to talk to you, to explain everything, but I knew you'd be angry, so I decided to just sit here and wait for the fallout I clearly deserve."

Clementine stood in the doorway, awkwardly letting her arms drop to her sides. "Oh," she said.

Callum opened his eyes but didn't move. "You expected me to argue with you?" he asked, surprised.

She shook her head and threw her hands in the air, unable to believe herself, or Callum, or even her life up to this point. "You know," she said, "I was never this ornery and difficult in Savannah. Now I jump at the chance to be as confrontational as I can possibly be. I don't know what's gotten into me." She stopped suddenly and pointed at him seriously. "This is not to be confused with being irrational. For the record, I never would have gone near Reg if I'd known he'd had a gun."

"I know. You would have left sooner if you'd known. You would have left, thinking he was going to follow you out of town where he wouldn't be a danger to anyone but you, and you would somehow fix it all when you got back to Savannah."

She looked away from him. The truth didn't settle too well. "Maybe."

He finally leaned forward. "That's why I didn't tell you. It was all selfish. I didn't want you to go, and I was sure I could protect you. But in the end, it was a bunch of ladies with pie who saved you."

Clementine stilled, her eyes meeting his. "You didn't want me to go?"

"No. I love you, Clementine."

She was pretty sure a person shouldn't go through this many emotions in so short a time. She wanted to fly now, whereas before she was angrily stomping the ground. She put the fingers of her good hand in her hair. "Stop it," she said. "I want to be mad at you."

He stood and walked around the desk. He stopped at the opposite side and leaned back against it, getting closer, but giving her time. She noticed the knees of his jeans were still stained with pie from when he'd knelt to cuff Reg. "I've given you enough reason to be. I'm sorry about thinking you were engaged and acting like a damn martyr because I couldn't keep my hands off you."

She shook her head. "I was having such a good time here, with you," she said. "I can't stand that you were torturing yourself the whole time, and I didn't even know, just like the flighty, oblivious socialite I don't want to be. That's why I wanted to confront Reg. Because the old Clementine wouldn't have."

He crossed his arms over his chest and smiled at her. "Clementine, every moment I've spent with you—hell, every moment I've spent *near* you, has been the best. You make me feel wonderful. I was making myself feel bad."

"Really?"

"Yes." He pierced her with that light blue gaze. "So what are you going to do, Clementine?"

She smiled. She loved this man who loved her. "It seems to be changing as I go along," she said airily, but her heart was pounding. "First I thought it was going to take some sexy dresses and a lot of takeout delivery to get you to forgive me."

"I could go for that."

"Then it was going to be moving into Vera's basement apartment and trading my car in for a four-wheel drive to prove to you that I am not a twit and that I'm capable of taking care of myself."

"You don't have to move anywhere. All your stuff's where it should be. And Mabel likes you."

She was almost trembling. "Next I was going to storm in here and argue with you, then avoid you for weeks because I was so mad."

"And now?" he prompted in a low voice that oozed with sexuality.

Her breath was quick. How could he do this to her from across the room? "Now I was thinking of closing and locking this door, and walking over there to you to see what ideas you have."

"I like that one the best." She could see his light eyes darken. "But I'm warning you, if you close and lock that door, you're mine. You're not leaving. You're going to stay in Tried and True."

She smiled. "I'm staying."

He straightened and her heart flipped, but then he rounded his desk again, taking the seat he had vacated. "Close and lock the door."

He sat back in his chair slowly, and raked his eyes down her body. It startled her how much she wanted him, how, even with just a look, he could turn her liquid.

"That dress," he said.

She made a show of looking down at it, then back at him innocently.

"I've been wondering how it stays up. There aren't any straps."

She shrugged with one shoulder. "I've got enough to give it leverage," she said huskily.

"Come here."

She made her feet move. She entered the office, closing and locking the door behind her. As she made her way around the desk, he turned to face her.

"I still don't understand it," he said softly.

"What?"

"That dress."

She turned around and showed him the back, feeling warm and jittery. She wanted him so much. "It's zippered."

She felt him skim her body as he stood. He lifted

the hat off her head, dropping it to the floor. Her breath was stuttered as his hands lifted to cup her breasts through the material of the dress.

"They're definitely enough to give *me* leverage."

Her laugh was breathy. Reaching behind her, she placed her hand on the back of his head and moved slightly against him. He buried his face in her neck and continued to massage her breasts. Groaning, he dropped his hands to her zipper and pulled it down. The dress fell to her feet, and her strapless bra soon followed. She turned around and he looked at her, then collapsed into the chair behind him.

"You're beautiful. I knew you would be." He took her waist, nudging her forward so she straddled his jeans-clad legs and sat. They were face-to-face for a few long seconds, their breathing ragged, as if they'd run through half the county to get to where they were. She looked into his beautiful eyes and fell in love all over again.

They leaned in at the same time, as if it was choreographed, and their lips met. They kissed for a long time, gentle nips at first, then the heat grew and the frenzy started.

With her good hand, she worked at the snap buttons of his shirt and almost ripped it off his shoulders, pinning his arms. He grunted as her hands splayed across his chest, her fingers running through the fine dark hair, her lips still pressed against his. She'd never been this bold, this sexual, with any man before. Callum no longer overwhelmed her with possibilities of things that wouldn't come true, but with things about to come true.

He finally broke the kiss and made her stand. He threw his shirt off, then leaned forward and pushed the papers and to-do trays off his desk to the floor where they clattered and fluttered in all directions.

Lifting her, he settled her on the desk beside the computer. Undoing his buckle and unzipping his jeans, he moved between her legs and kissed her again. His thumbs hooked her lace panties and she lifted her bottom as he peeled them off. She thought he said something like, "I've wanted to hold on to these hips since I met you," but he kissed her again before she could say anything.

"After we damn near set that barn on fire," he said in between kisses, "I was determined not to be caught unprepared again."

"That's very responsible of you," she said as her hands went to the waistband of his open jeans.

"Greedy. It's greedy of me."

She impatiently pushed down his jeans. He closed his eyes when her hand found him, the unexpectedly smooth texture, the moist tip. "Wow," she said, which made her blush with the innocence and inadequacy of the word. But her single, simple word brought a smile to his lips.

He withdrew some packets from the pocket of his jeans on the floor. Tearing one open, she watched with hot, achy fascination as he sheathed himself.

As he moved between her legs again, she lay back on the desk. "Relax," he said. "Just let me in."

She tried to look indignant, not an easy thing to do in the position she was in. "I've had sex before." She laughed at her words, her nervousness.

"Not like this you haven't, I promise. Just once before, right?"

She smiled slightly, her heart racing. "How did you know?"

He entered her slowly, stretching her until he was fully inside. "I spend a lot of time thinking about you," he whispered. "Look at me, Clementine."

She hadn't realized she had closed her eyes. The

moment her lids opened and she focused on him, he thrust.

Her breath caught and she arched.

Slowly, he built a rhythm that had her wrapping her legs around his hips as she writhed under him. She lifted her hands above her head and grasped the edge of the mammoth desk as his thrusts became harder and she felt a coil of pleasure tighten in her womb. It was so much, so frenzied, that all she could do was hold on and let the whole exquisite thing happen.

She cried out as the explosion came. Callum thrust once, twice, more and shuddered above her, then covered her body with his.

After a few moments he whispered into her ear. *"Wow."*

"THERE'S SOMETHING I WANT to show you," he said, holding her hand and leading her out of his office, which he hadn't bothered to straighten. Anyone who looked in there could tell that something had just happened on that desktop. Something like tap dancing. Or sex.

"There's more?" she asked cheekily, using her other hand to push back her wild curls. Callum had freed her hair from the ponytail at some point. Their clothes were back on, although somewhat disheveled.

"Oh, that was just the tip of the iceberg, honey," he laughed. "But that's not what I meant." He led her back to the holding cells.

She looked at him strangely. "Are you going to put me in jail again?"

"I would have to have backup to do that," he said as he led her past the cells to a door at the end of the hallway. "I got a call from your friend Suzette."

"She called you? What did she say?"

"When you didn't call her back, then she couldn't get an answer at the Gardenia Inn today because everyone was at the festival, she was concerned enough to call the local authorities." He retrieved a key ring from his pocket and unlocked the door.

"I need to call her."

"She wants you to. She told me a few things about Reg that I think you should hear, though."

Clementine knew she needed to hear whatever he was going to tell her, but she didn't want to hear it. She followed him into the storage room. "Is this what you wanted to show me? Very nice."

"No," he said as he led her through the storage room to a door at the other end. "Did Mac tell you your engagement ring was stolen?"

"Yes."

"There's more to it, according to Suzette. Apparently Reg bought the stolen ring with money he borrowed from a very touchy, very illegal, source."

"Reg borrowed money from the mob?" she asked, shaking her head at his desperation, but no longer surprised by what he was capable of. Callum opened the door to yet another room, and she said, "Is this what you wanted to show me?"

"You're so impatient." At the end of this room he opened a door to a flight of dusty steps. "When you went on vacation, Suzette said rumors were flying that there wasn't going to be a wedding. Apparently his *friends* starting putting pressure on Reg to either marry you quickly for the security of your bank account, or to give them the ring that was bought with their money. Suzette said that was how he got the black eye. She also said he'd been fired for reporting hours he didn't work, and that his BMW had been repossessed, which is why he stole a car." He unlocked the door at the top of the steps, then stopped.

"According to Suzette, Savannah society is reeling. Your mother is eating up the limelight, saying she never knew what you saw in Reg. Suzette said she didn't think it even occurred to your mother that Reg might try to come after you."

"It wouldn't. Suzette is a good friend. I want her to come visit soon." It was disappointing and hurtful, but it was over. They would never have to talk about Reg again. She leaned against him and made a show of looking around. "Nice staircase."

"Patience is a virtue."

"I'm not feeling very virtuous."

"Okay, I can tell you don't want to talk about Reg anymore. Neither do I. You just needed to know that. Case closed. *This* is what I wanted you to see," he said, opening the door, and she stepped out onto the rooftop.

She walked with him over to the edge, which was surrounded by a chest-high wall of smooth gray tile. She looked out and smiled. Below them she could see the entire length of Main Street and just how many people were at the festival, all of them still mysteriously sitting on folding chairs, lawn chairs and pillows, facing away from the sheriff's department.

The sky was a dark twilight purple, fading to black. But she could still see, off to the sides, some of the houses over the tops of the buildings on Main. Tried and True lay in front of her in all its peaceful, lovely glory.

"This is beautiful," she said reverently.

"Sheriff Cobb first showed me this place," he said. "I used to love to come up here when I was a teenager. A lot of people used to think I was walking into the sheriff's department so often because I was in trouble, but it was actually because I liked to come up here in the evening and look at everything. It gave me a sense of belonging, to know that Cobb would let me up here by myself, that everything I saw from up here, I knew by heart.''

She looked over at him and studied his profile, his long, straight nose, the strong chin. ''Sheriff Cobb must have been a special man.''

''He changed my life,'' he said. ''I give him the credit for any good I do as a law enforcement officer. When you grow up a wild child, you discover that there are very few people who make you want to be a better person. Cobb was one of those people. He made me want to be better. You're one of those people, too, Clementine.'' He reached over to touch her cheek. ''You make me a better person by loving me. I don't know what I did to deserve it, but I'm going to try my damnedest to live up to your love.''

She smiled tremulously. ''Thank you for showing me this place.''

''This isn't all I wanted to show you.''

''No?''

''Uh-uh.''

She looked around, confused. ''What then?''

''Wait.'' He moved behind her and wrapped his arms around her.

She smiled and leaned back against him, her hands folded on the wall in front of her. ''What are we looking for? Stars? There aren't many out tonight.''

''Shh. No. Not stars,'' he said. ''Wait. You'll see.''

Seconds later she heard a whizzing sound and there was a bright red explosion directly above them. She leaned her head back against Callum's shoulder and looked up as the red was followed by blue followed by green followed by white. She laughed. ''They're so close!'' she yelled over the hiss, roar and pop. ''So this is what you meant by Mid-May going out with a bang!''

They stayed on the roof, arms wrapped around each other, until the fireworks show was over. They were still up there when everyone went home, sitting side by side with their backs against the gray tile wall, looking up at the thick dark blue canopy of the sky. Callum's arm was around her and she had her head on his shoulder. The tangy smoke from the fireworks was finally fading off in the breeze and the night was quiet. Clementine could feel her body hum with the satisfaction of knowing everything was finally right. She understood what Callum meant by being up here and feeling a sense of belonging, of knowing everything by heart.

Callum nuzzled her hair, his breath warm on her scalp. "So, when are you going to tell your mother?" he asked softly.

She lifted her head to look at him, and his expression was so tender that she wanted to cry. She loved this man, this man who didn't care if she had money, this man who knew she could take care of herself but wanted to protect her anyway, this man who, for some miraculous reason, thought she made him a better person. "Tell her what?" she asked.

Callum lowered his lips to hers, smiling. "That you're getting married."

Epilogue

THAT SEPTEMBER the Ladies Club coerced Ed Harlow into running the wedding as front page news in the weekly *Examiner*. Ed thought it was ridiculous because practically the whole town had been at the wedding, but the Ladies Club prevailed, as they usually did. There was a big photograph of Callum and Clementine, hand in hand as they walked down the steps of the church. There was another photograph of the mother of the bride, who looked bored and uncomfortable, as if someone had told her to just stand there and smile and not touch anything. There were also two smaller photographs of the wedding cake and of the wedding party. In the wedding party photograph there were Callum and Clementine, of course, but then there was Suzette paired with Doc Malone and Naomi paired with Luke. The latter two couples looked as if they were trying just a little too hard to act casual.

The accompanying article listed the attendance number, the food that was served at the reception, including who made what kind of pie, and that the honorary wedding baby was Callum's new nephew Calvin. The article also mentioned that the newlyweds were honeymooning in New England and that Callum was looking forward to the car trip with his new wife because, "She's experienced at this sort of thing."

Ed Harlow was forced, again, to mention how grateful the Ladies Club members were to Clementine for buying the old Talbert home and giving it to them. He was convinced that they wouldn't have made such a fuss over this wedding being front-page news had it not been for Clementine's generosity.

Or maybe not. Something was up. The Ladies Club said to reserve the *Examiner* the week before Christmas for big news, because they were going to make sure there was going to be another wedding by then.

That was why Ed Harlow decided to end the article with this:

And so, all you bachelors out there, beware! One down. You could be next. The Tried and True Ladies Club is on a roll.

HARLEQUIN®
Duets™

TWO ROMANTIC COMEDIES IN ONE FUN VOLUME!

Don't miss double the laughs in

Once Smitten
and
Twice Shy

From acclaimed Duets author

Darlene Gardner

Once Smitten—that's Zoe O'Neill and Jack Carter, all right! It's a case of "the one who got away" and Zoe's out to make amends!

In *Twice Shy,* Zoe's two best friends, Amy Donatelli and Matt Burke, are alone together for the first time and each realizes they're "the one who never left!"

Any way you slice it, these two tales serve up a big dish of romance, with lots of humor on the side!

Volume #101
Coming in June 2003

Available at your favorite retail outlet.

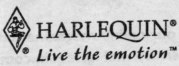

HARLEQUIN®
Live the emotion™

Visit us at www.eHarlequin.com

HDDD99DG

eHARLEQUIN.com

Sit back, relax and enhance your romance
with our great magazine reading!

- **Sex and Romance!** Like your romance
  hot? Then you'll *love* the sensual reading
  in this area.

- **Quizzes!** Curious about your lovestyle?
  His commitment to you? Get the
  answers here!

- **Romantic Guides and Features!**
  Unravel the mysteries of love with
  informative articles and advice!

- **Fun Games!** Play to your heart's content....

**Plus...romantic recipes,
top ten lists,
Lovescopes...and more!**

**Enjoy our online magazine today—
visit www.eHarlequin.com!**

The world's bestselling romance series.

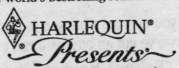

Seduction and Passion Guaranteed!

Every book is part of a miniseries in 2003.
These are just some of the exciting themes you can expect...

Your dream ticket to the vacation of a lifetime!

Tall, dark—and ready to marry!

They're guaranteed to raise your pulse!

They're the men who have everything—except a bride....

Marriage is their mission....

Legally wed, but he's never said, "I love you..."

They speak the language of passion

Passion™

Sophisticated spicy stories— seduction and passion guaranteed

Pick up a Harlequin Presents® novel and you will enter a world of spine-tingling passion and provocative, tantalizing romance!

Available wherever Harlequin books are sold.

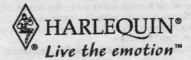

Live the emotion™

Visit us at www.eHarlequin.com

HPMINP03

If you enjoyed what you just read,
then we've got an offer you can't resist!

Take 2 bestselling
love stories FREE!
Plus get a FREE surprise gift!

Three brothers, one tuxedo…and one destiny!

Date With Destiny

A brand-new anthology from
USA TODAY bestselling author

KRISTINE ROLOFSON
MURIEL JENSEN
KRISTIN GABRIEL

The package said "R. Perez" and inside was a tuxedo. But which Perez brother—Rick, Rafe or Rob—was it addressed to? This tuxedo is on a mission…to lead each of these men to the altar!

DATE WITH DESTINY will introduce you to the characters of *Forrester Square…* an exciting new continuity starting in August 2003.

Forrester Square

LEGACIES . LIES . LOVE .

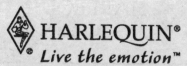

HARLEQUIN®
Live the emotion™

Visit us at www.eHarlequin.com

PHDWD

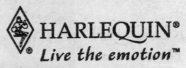